For my beloved father, Michael Alan Smith (1957-2020).
His absence is a jagged rift in the sky, but the power
of his memory keeps the monsters at bay.
Thank you for believing in me, Dad, even when --
especially when -- I didn't believe in myself.
~ Jennifer

Life can reward us with something better
in the midst of a wrong choice.
~ Sana

Oh, friend: Don't hold back your grief.
Mourning is the door to healing,
and healing is your strength.
~ Marjorie

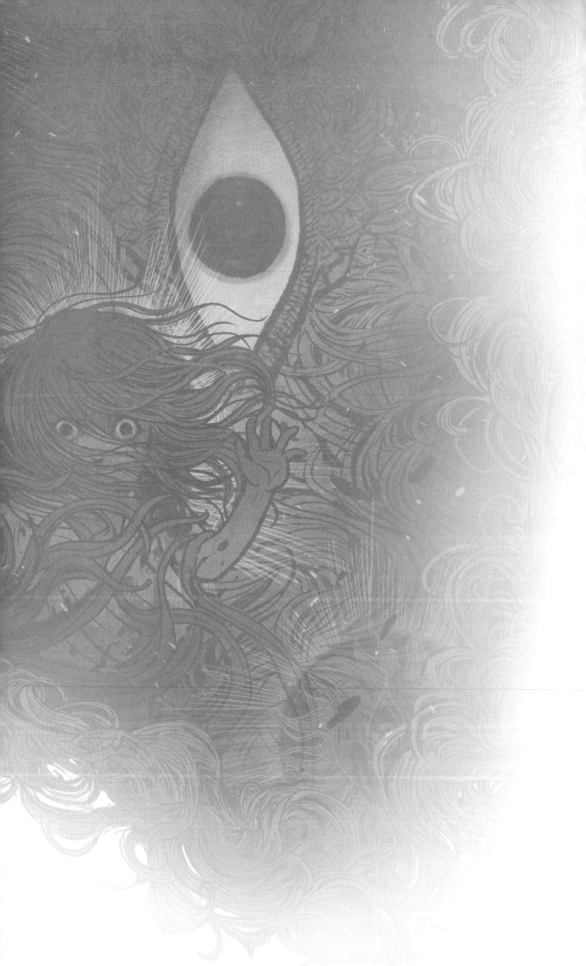

MONSTRESS™

VOLUME FIVE
WARCHILD

Collecting
MONSTRESS
Issues 25–30

MARJORIE LIU
WRITER

SANA TAKEDA
ARTIST

RUS WOOTON
LETTERING & DESIGN

JENNIFER M. SMITH
EDITOR

ERIKA SCHNATZ
PRODUCTION ARTIST

CERI RILEY
EDITORIAL ASSISTANT

MONSTRESS
created by
MARJORIE LIU &
SANA TAKEDA

CHAPTER TWENTY-FIVE

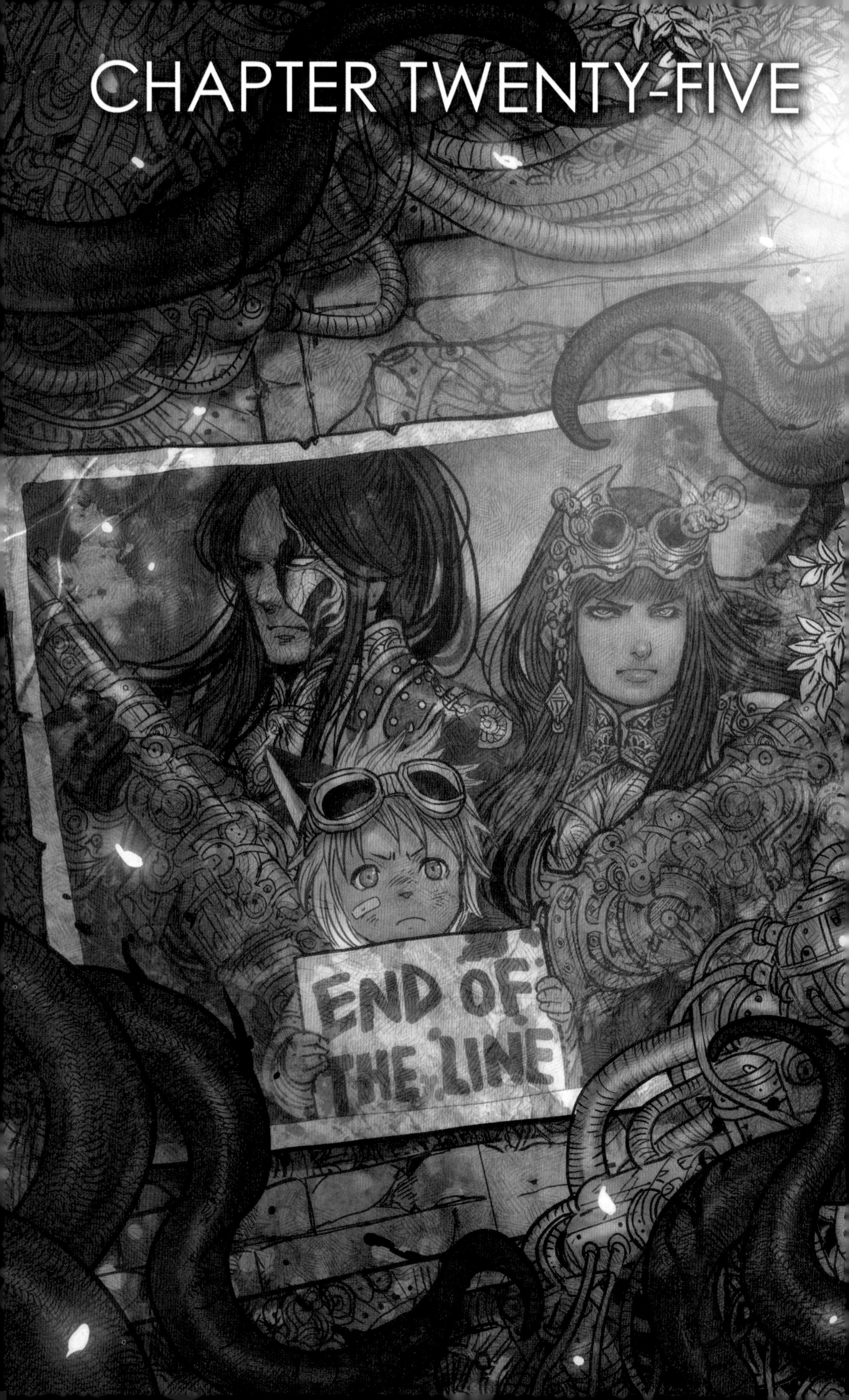
END OF THE LINE

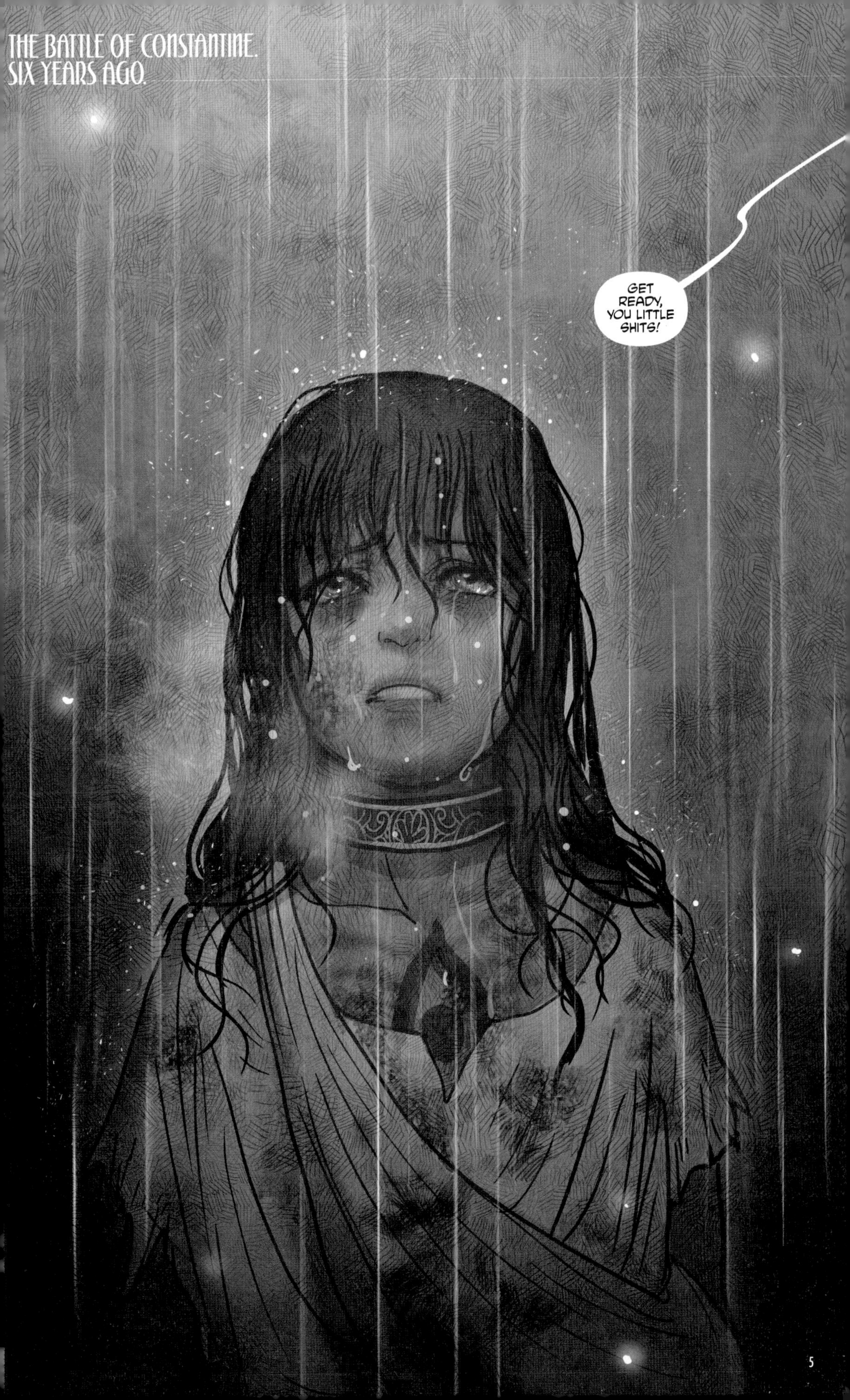
THE BATTLE OF CONSTANTINE.
SIX YEARS AGO.
GET READY, YOU LITTLE SHITS!

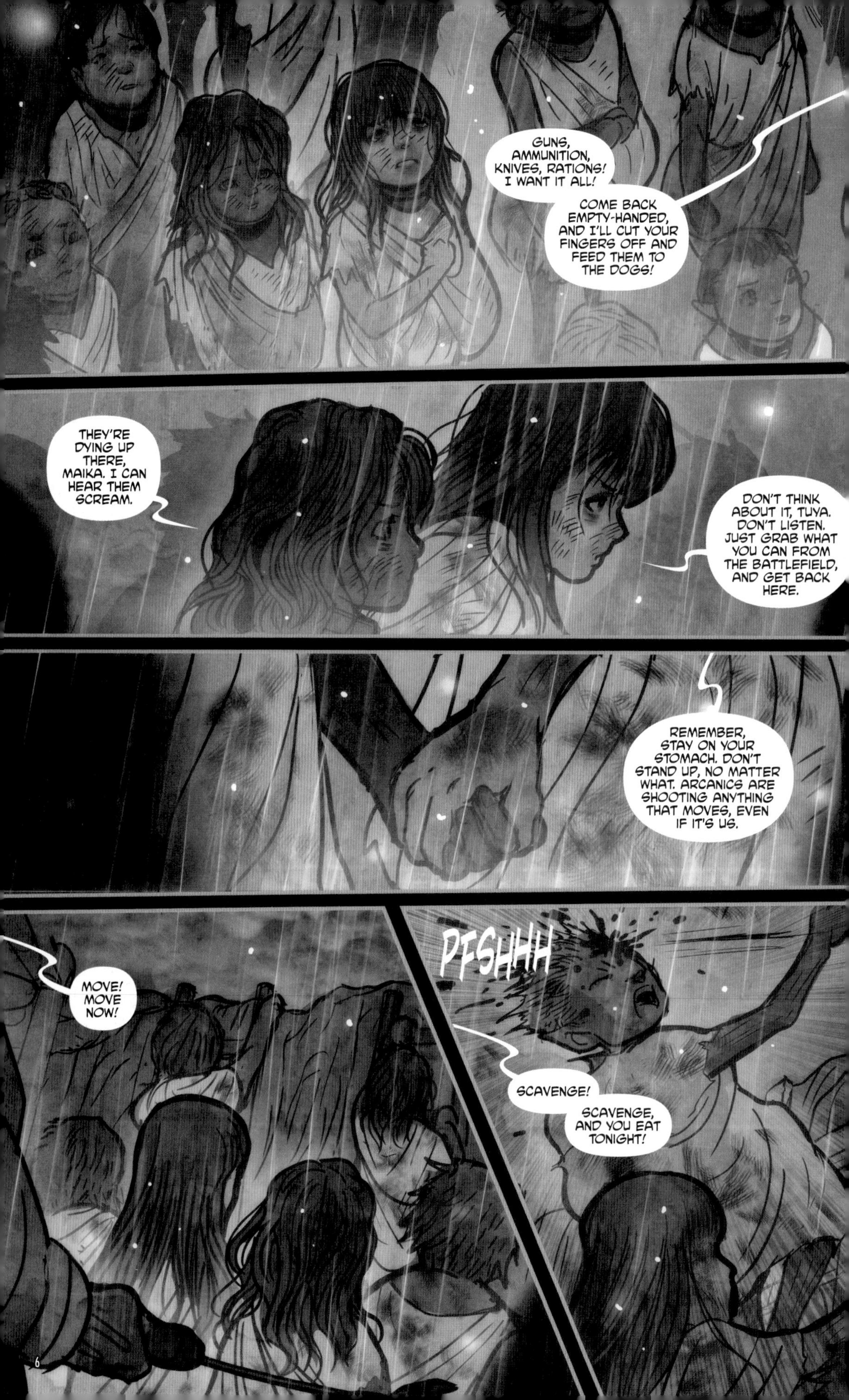
GUNS, AMMUNITION, KNIVES, RATIONS! I WANT IT ALL!
COME BACK EMPTY-HANDED, AND I'LL CUT YOUR FINGERS OFF AND FEED THEM TO THE DOGS!
THEY'RE DYING UP THERE, MAIKA. I CAN HEAR THEM SCREAM.
DON'T THINK ABOUT IT, TUYA. DON'T LISTEN. JUST GRAB WHAT YOU CAN FROM THE BATTLEFIELD, AND GET BACK HERE.
REMEMBER, STAY ON YOUR STOMACH. DON'T STAND UP, NO MATTER WHAT. ARCANICS ARE SHOOTING ANYTHING THAT MOVES, EVEN IF IT'S US.
MOVE! MOVE NOW!
PFSHHH
SCAVENGE!
SCAVENGE, AND YOU EAT TONIGHT!

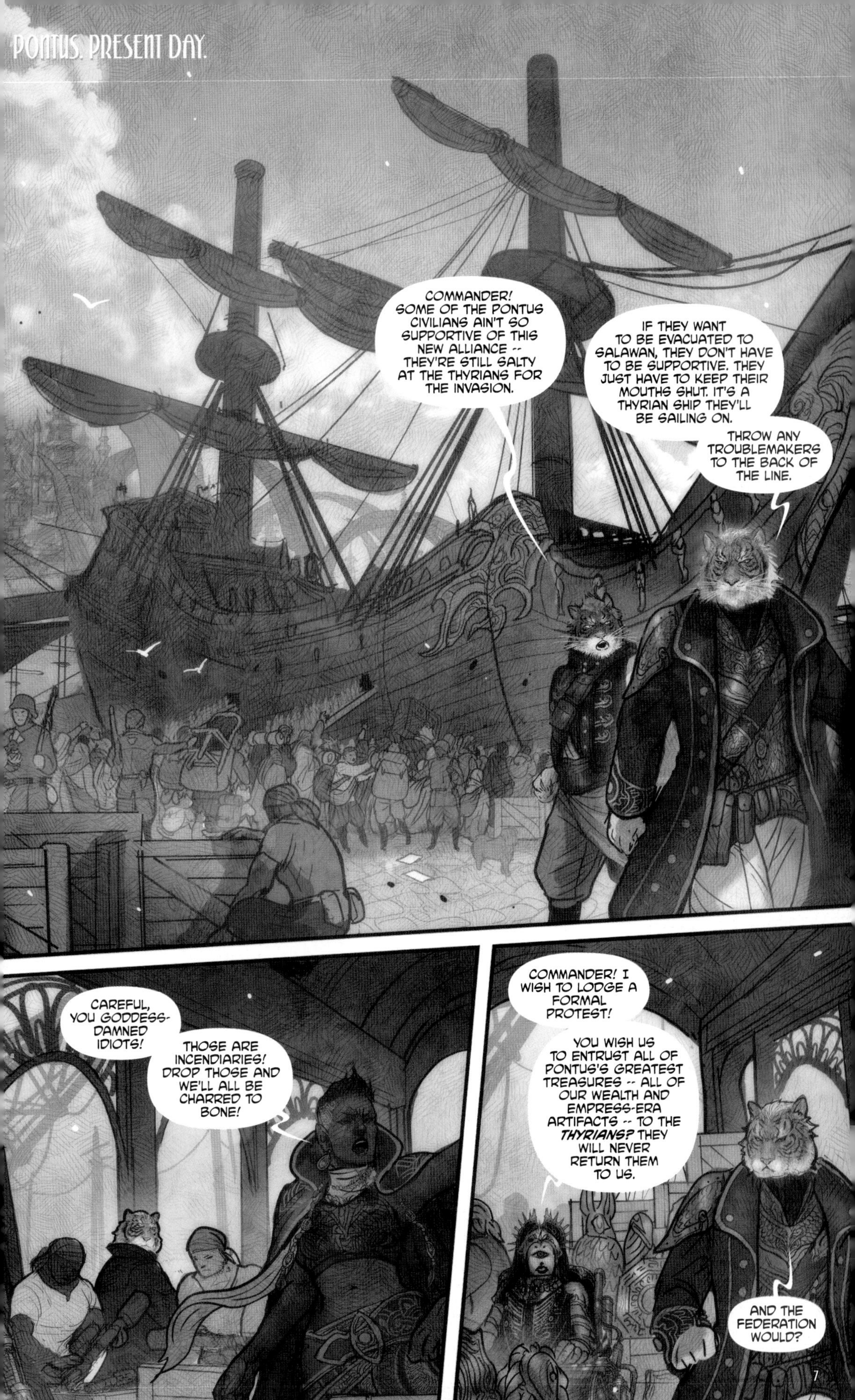
PONTUS. PRESENT DAY.
COMMANDER! SOME OF THE PONTUS CIVILIANS AIN'T SO SUPPORTIVE OF THIS NEW ALLIANCE -- THEY'RE STILL SALTY AT THE THYRIANS FOR THE INVASION.
IF THEY WANT TO BE EVACUATED TO SALAWAN, THEY DON'T HAVE TO BE SUPPORTIVE. THEY JUST HAVE TO KEEP THEIR MOUTHS SHUT. IT'S A THYRIAN SHIP THEY'LL BE SAILING ON.
THROW ANY TROUBLEMAKERS TO THE BACK OF THE LINE.
CAREFUL, YOU GODDESS-DAMNED IDIOTS!
THOSE ARE INCENDIARIES! DROP THOSE AND WE'LL ALL BE CHARRED TO BONE!
COMMANDER! I WISH TO LODGE A FORMAL PROTEST!
YOU WISH US TO ENTRUST ALL OF PONTUS'S GREATEST TREASURES -- ALL OF OUR WEALTH AND EMPRESS-ERA ARTIFACTS -- TO THE *THYRIANS?* THEY WILL NEVER RETURN THEM TO US.
AND THE FEDERATION WOULD?

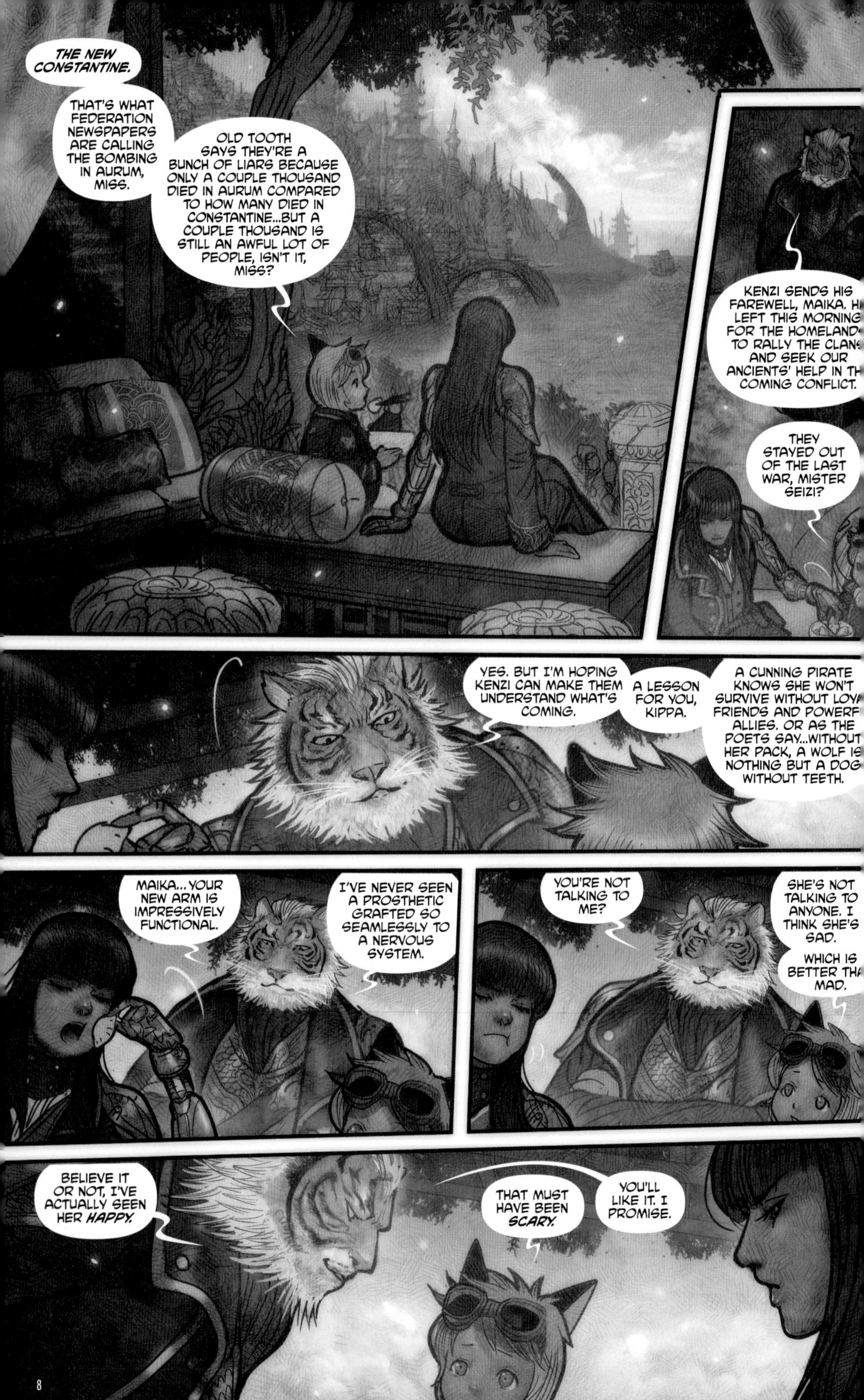
THE NEW CONSTANTINE.
THAT'S WHAT FEDERATION NEWSPAPERS ARE CALLING THE BOMBING IN AURUM, MISS.
OLD TOOTH SAYS THEY'RE A BUNCH OF LIARS BECAUSE ONLY A COUPLE THOUSAND DIED IN AURUM COMPARED TO HOW MANY DIED IN CONSTANTINE...BUT A COUPLE THOUSAND IS STILL AN AWFUL LOT OF PEOPLE, ISN'T IT, MISS?
KENZI SENDS HIS FAREWELL, MAIKA. H LEFT THIS MORNING FOR THE HOMELAND TO RALLY THE CLAN AND SEEK OUR ANCIENTS' HELP IN TH COMING CONFLICT.
THEY STAYED OUT OF THE LAST WAR, MISTER SEIZI?
YES. BUT I'M HOPING KENZI CAN MAKE THEM UNDERSTAND WHAT'S COMING.
A LESSON FOR YOU, KIPPA.
A CUNNING PIRATE KNOWS SHE WON'T SURVIVE WITHOUT LOY FRIENDS AND POWERF ALLIES. OR AS THE POETS SAY...WITHOUT HER PACK, A WOLF IS NOTHING BUT A DOG WITHOUT TEETH.
MAIKA... YOUR NEW ARM IS IMPRESSIVELY FUNCTIONAL.
I'VE NEVER SEEN A PROSTHETIC GRAFTED SO SEAMLESSLY TO A NERVOUS SYSTEM.
YOU'RE NOT TALKING TO ME?
SHE'S NOT TALKING TO ANYONE. I THINK SHE'S SAD.
WHICH IS BETTER TH MAD.
BELIEVE IT OR NOT, I'VE ACTUALLY SEEN HER *HAPPY.*
THAT MUST HAVE BEEN *SCARY.*
YOU'LL LIKE IT. I PROMISE.

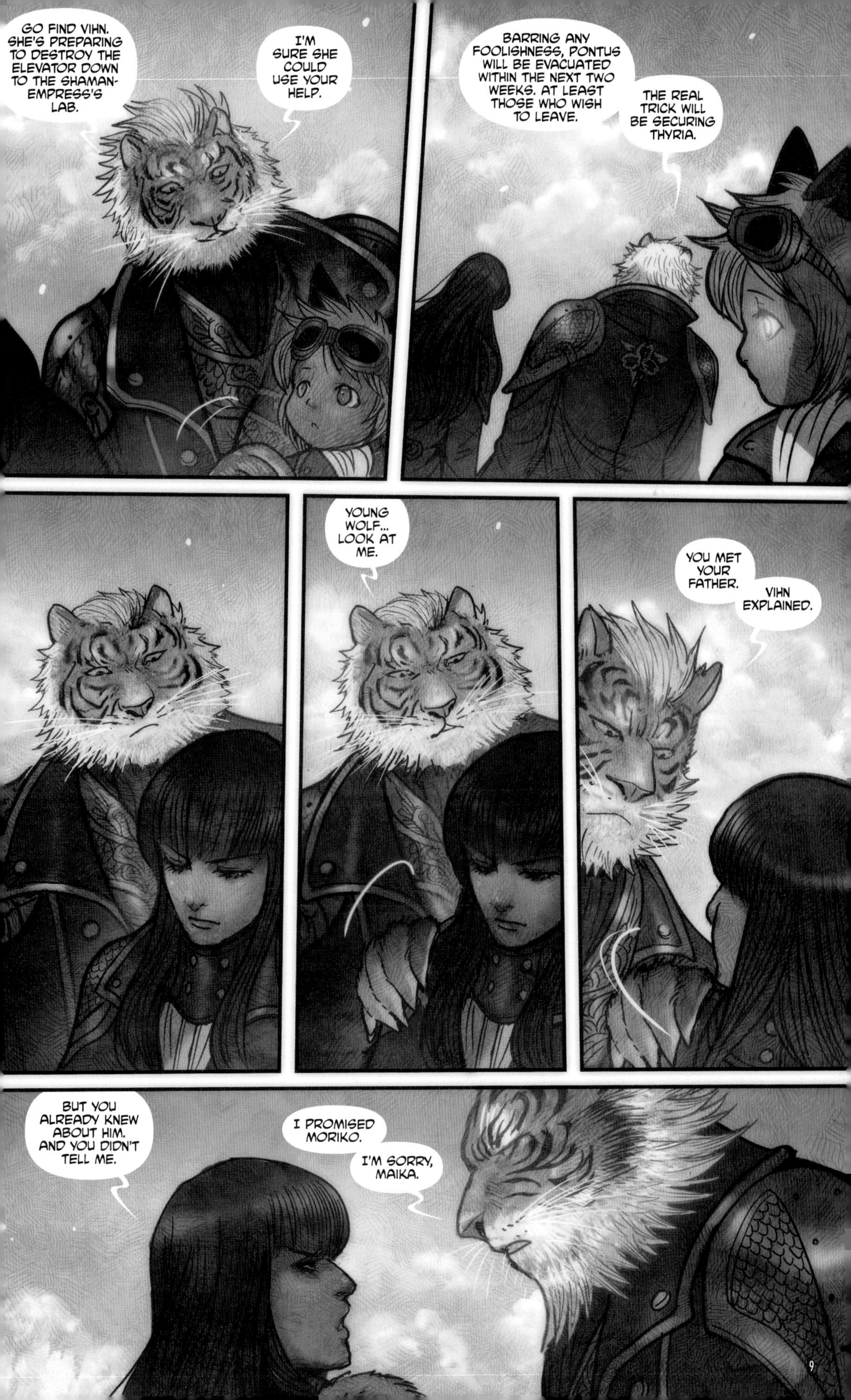
GO FIND VIHN. SHE'S PREPARING TO DESTROY THE ELEVATOR DOWN TO THE SHAMAN-EMPRESS'S LAB.
I'M SURE SHE COULD USE YOUR HELP.
BARRING ANY FOOLISHNESS, PONTUS WILL BE EVACUATED WITHIN THE NEXT TWO WEEKS. AT LEAST THOSE WHO WISH TO LEAVE.
THE REAL TRICK WILL BE SECURING THYRIA.
YOUNG WOLF... LOOK AT ME.
YOU MET YOUR FATHER.
VIHN EXPLAINED.
BUT YOU ALREADY KNEW ABOUT HIM. AND YOU DIDN'T TELL ME.
I PROMISED MORIKO.
I'M SORRY, MAIKA.

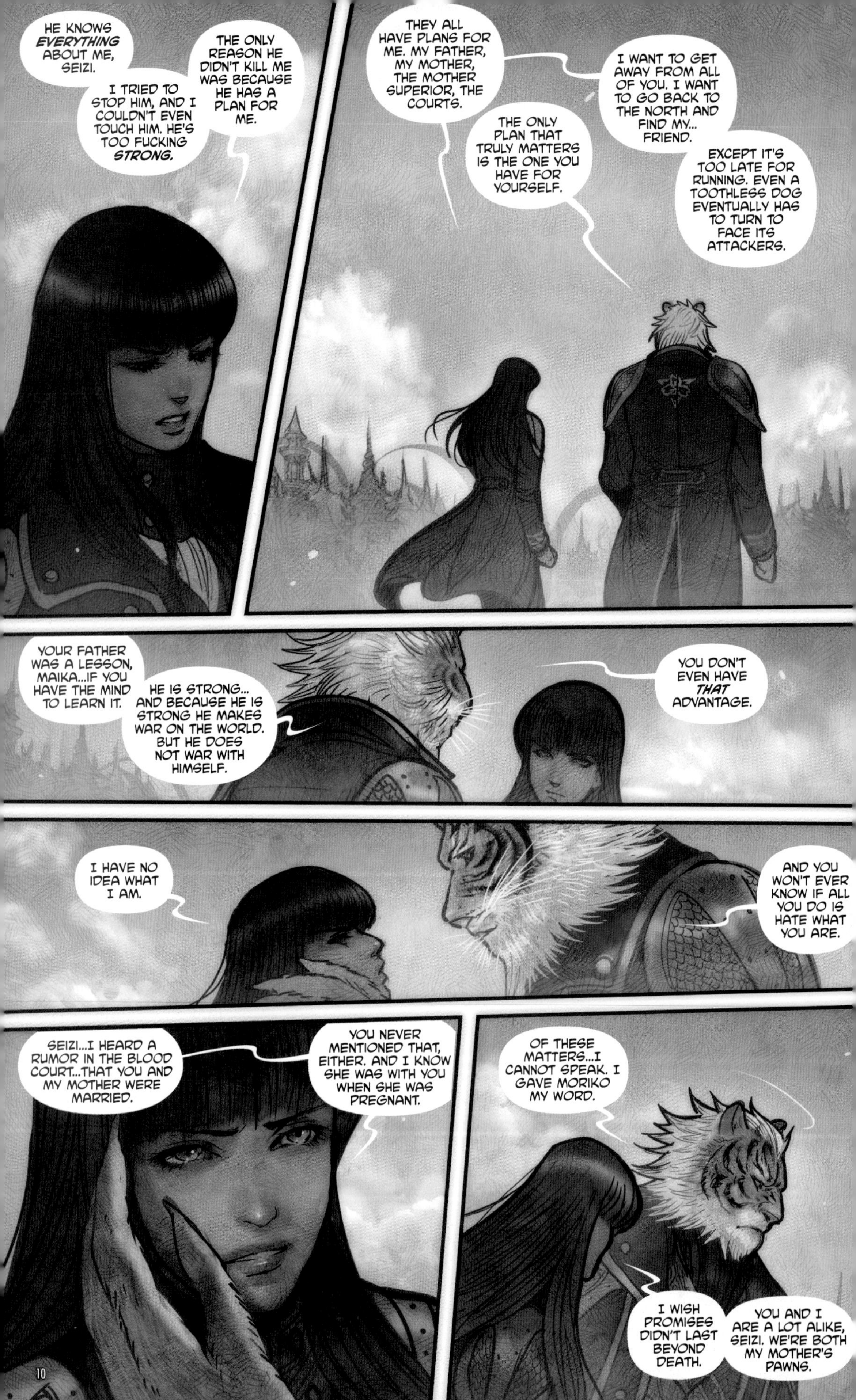
HE KNOWS EVERYTHING ABOUT ME, SEIZI.
I TRIED TO STOP HIM, AND I COULDN'T EVEN TOUCH HIM. HE'S TOO FUCKING STRONG.
THE ONLY REASON HE DIDN'T KILL ME WAS BECAUSE HE HAS A PLAN FOR ME.
THEY ALL HAVE PLANS FOR ME. MY FATHER, MY MOTHER, THE MOTHER SUPERIOR, THE COURTS.
I WANT TO GET AWAY FROM ALL OF YOU. I WANT TO GO BACK TO THE NORTH AND FIND MY... FRIEND.
THE ONLY PLAN THAT TRULY MATTERS IS THE ONE YOU HAVE FOR YOURSELF.
EXCEPT IT'S TOO LATE FOR RUNNING. EVEN A TOOTHLESS DOG EVENTUALLY HAS TO TURN TO FACE ITS ATTACKERS.
YOUR FATHER WAS A LESSON, MAIKA...IF YOU HAVE THE MIND TO LEARN IT.
HE IS STRONG... AND BECAUSE HE IS STRONG HE MAKES WAR ON THE WORLD. BUT HE DOES NOT WAR WITH HIMSELF.
YOU DON'T EVEN HAVE THAT ADVANTAGE.
I HAVE NO IDEA WHAT I AM.
AND YOU WON'T EVER KNOW IF ALL YOU DO IS HATE WHAT YOU ARE.
SEIZI...I HEARD A RUMOR IN THE BLOOD COURT...THAT YOU AND MY MOTHER WERE MARRIED.
YOU NEVER MENTIONED THAT, EITHER. AND I KNOW SHE WAS WITH YOU WHEN SHE WAS PREGNANT.
OF THESE MATTERS...I CANNOT SPEAK. I GAVE MORIKO MY WORD.
I WISH PROMISES DIDN'T LAST BEYOND DEATH.
YOU AND I ARE A LOT ALIKE, SEIZI. WE'RE BOTH MY MOTHER'S PAWNS.

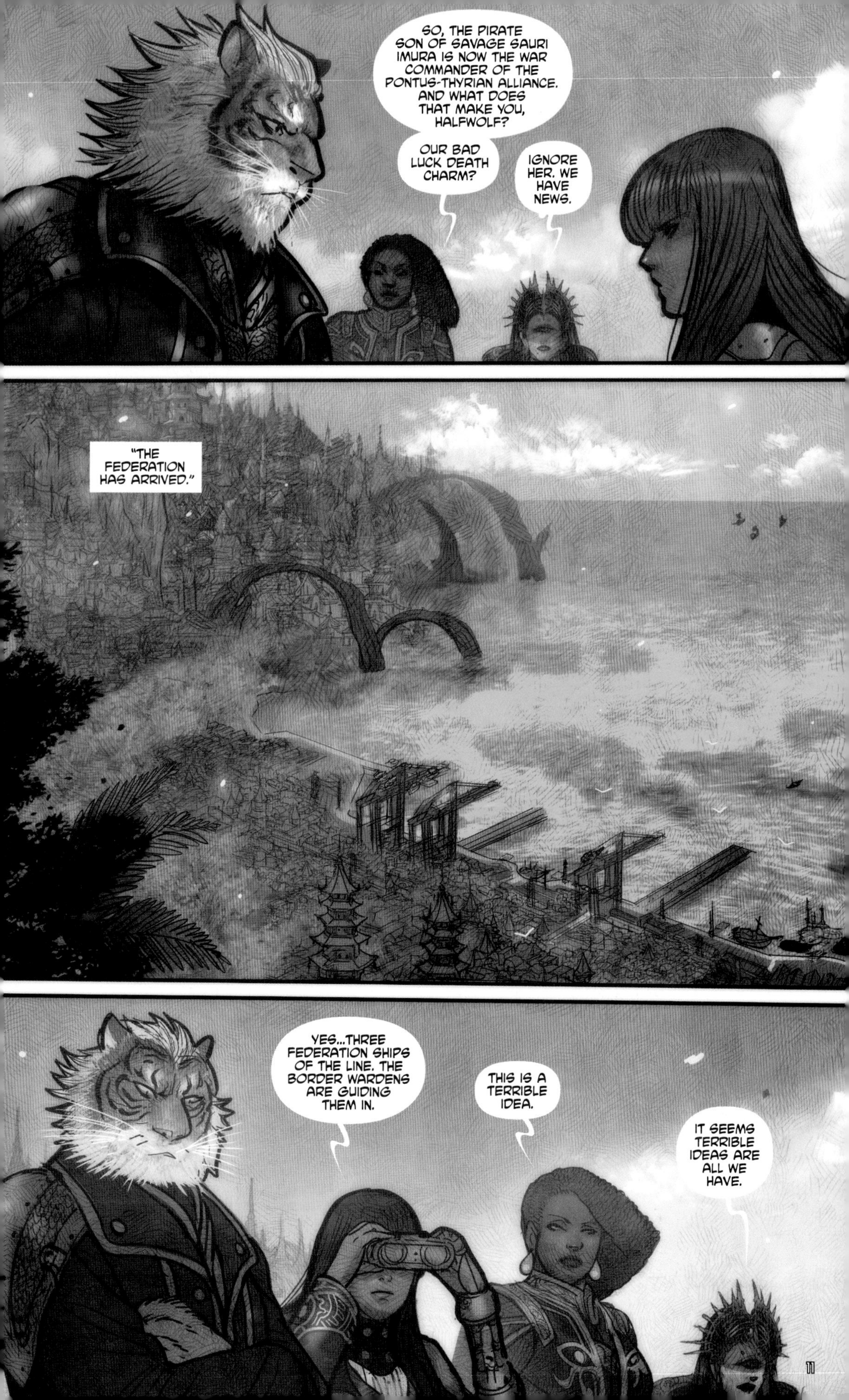
SO, THE PIRATE SON OF SAVAGE SAURI IMURA IS NOW THE WAR COMMANDER OF THE PONTUS-THYRIAN ALLIANCE. AND WHAT DOES THAT MAKE YOU, HALFWOLF?
OUR BAD LUCK DEATH CHARM?
IGNORE HER. WE HAVE NEWS.
"THE FEDERATION HAS ARRIVED."
YES...THREE FEDERATION SHIPS OF THE LINE. THE BORDER WARDENS ARE GUIDING THEM IN.
THIS IS A TERRIBLE IDEA.
IT SEEMS TERRIBLE IDEAS ARE ALL WE HAVE.

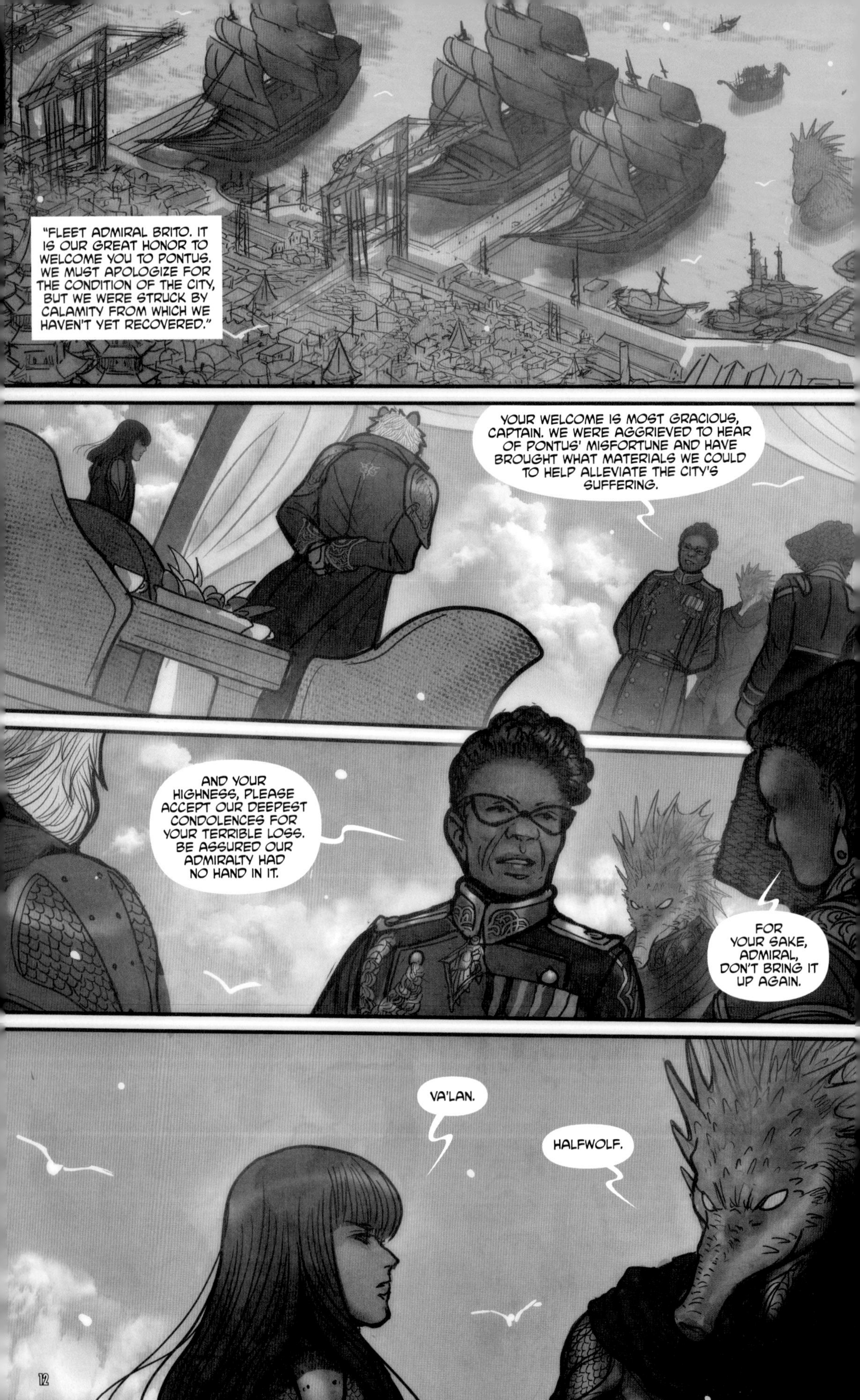
"FLEET ADMIRAL BRITO. IT IS OUR GREAT HONOR TO WELCOME YOU TO PONTUS. WE MUST APOLOGIZE FOR THE CONDITION OF THE CITY, BUT WE WERE STRUCK BY CALAMITY FROM WHICH WE HAVEN'T YET RECOVERED."
YOUR WELCOME IS MOST GRACIOUS, CAPTAIN. WE WERE AGGRIEVED TO HEAR OF PONTUS' MISFORTUNE AND HAVE BROUGHT WHAT MATERIALS WE COULD TO HELP ALLEVIATE THE CITY'S SUFFERING.
AND YOUR HIGHNESS, PLEASE ACCEPT OUR DEEPEST CONDOLENCES FOR YOUR TERRIBLE LOSS. BE ASSURED OUR ADMIRALTY HAD NO HAND IN IT.
FOR YOUR SAKE, ADMIRAL, DON'T BRING IT UP AGAIN.
VA'LAN.
HALFWOLF.

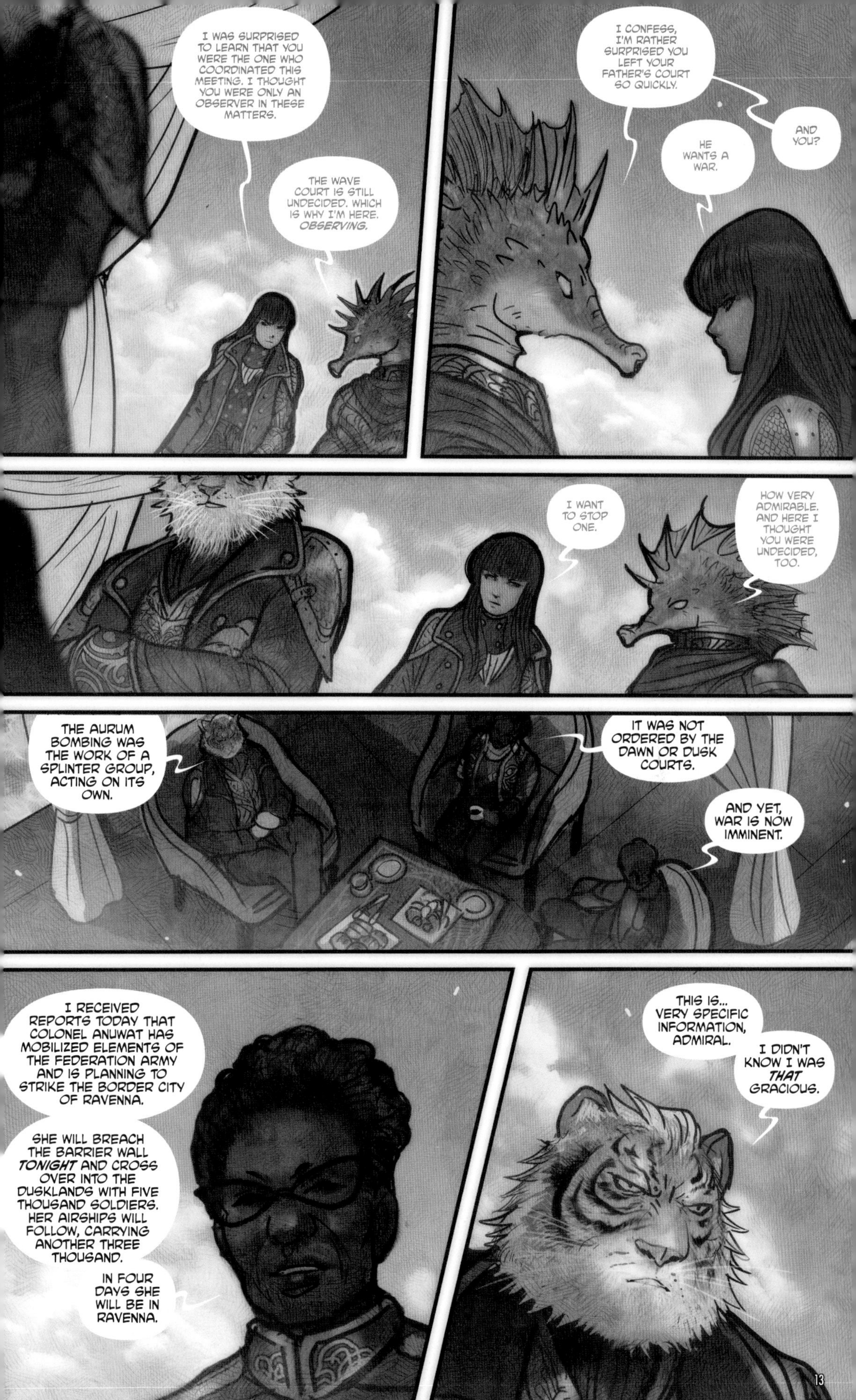
I WAS SURPRISED TO LEARN THAT YOU WERE THE ONE WHO COORDINATED THIS MEETING. I THOUGHT YOU WERE ONLY AN OBSERVER IN THESE MATTERS.
THE WAVE COURT IS STILL UNDECIDED. WHICH IS WHY I'M HERE. *OBSERVING.*
I CONFESS, I'M RATHER SURPRISED YOU LEFT YOUR FATHER'S COURT SO QUICKLY.
AND YOU?
HE WANTS A WAR.
I WANT TO STOP ONE.
HOW VERY ADMIRABLE. AND HERE I THOUGHT YOU WERE UNDECIDED, TOO.
THE AURUM BOMBING WAS THE WORK OF A SPLINTER GROUP, ACTING ON ITS OWN.
IT WAS NOT ORDERED BY THE DAWN OR DUSK COURTS.
AND YET, WAR IS NOW IMMINENT.
I RECEIVED REPORTS TODAY THAT COLONEL ANUWAT HAS MOBILIZED ELEMENTS OF THE FEDERATION ARMY AND IS PLANNING TO STRIKE THE BORDER CITY OF RAVENNA.
SHE WILL BREACH THE BARRIER WALL *TONIGHT* AND CROSS OVER INTO THE DUSKLANDS WITH FIVE THOUSAND SOLDIERS. HER AIRSHIPS WILL FOLLOW, CARRYING ANOTHER THREE THOUSAND.
IN FOUR DAYS SHE WILL BE IN RAVENNA.
THIS IS... VERY SPECIFIC INFORMATION, ADMIRAL.
I DIDN'T KNOW I WAS *THAT* GRACIOUS.

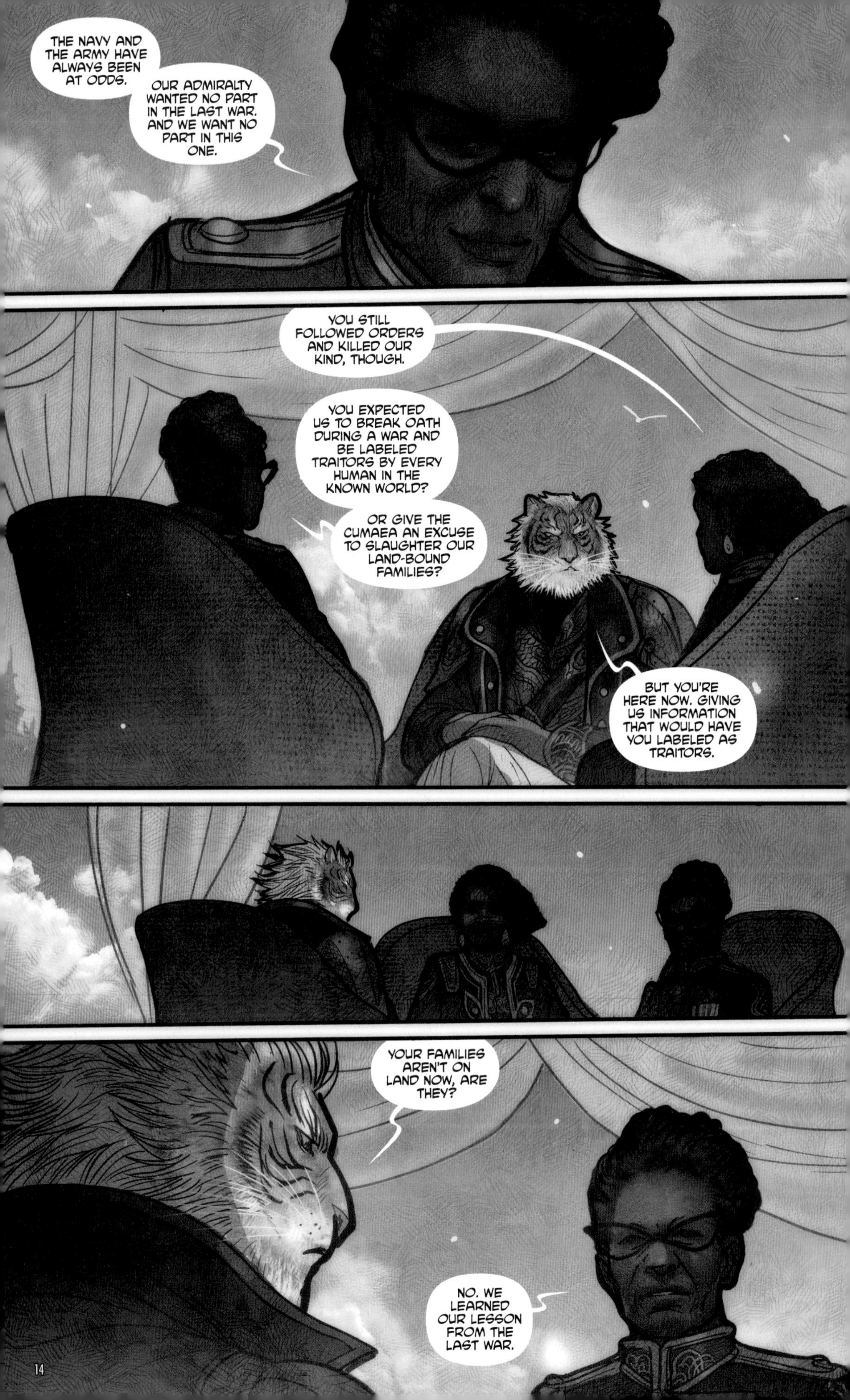

THE NAVY AND THE ARMY HAVE ALWAYS BEEN AT ODDS.
OUR ADMIRALTY WANTED NO PART IN THE LAST WAR. AND WE WANT NO PART IN THIS ONE.
YOU STILL FOLLOWED ORDERS AND KILLED OUR KIND, THOUGH.
YOU EXPECTED US TO BREAK OATH DURING A WAR AND BE LABELED TRAITORS BY EVERY HUMAN IN THE KNOWN WORLD?
OR GIVE THE CUMAEA AN EXCUSE TO SLAUGHTER OUR LAND-BOUND FAMILIES?
BUT YOU'RE HERE NOW. GIVING US INFORMATION THAT WOULD HAVE YOU LABELED AS TRAITORS.
YOUR FAMILIES AREN'T ON LAND NOW, ARE THEY?
NO. WE LEARNED OUR LESSON FROM THE LAST WAR.

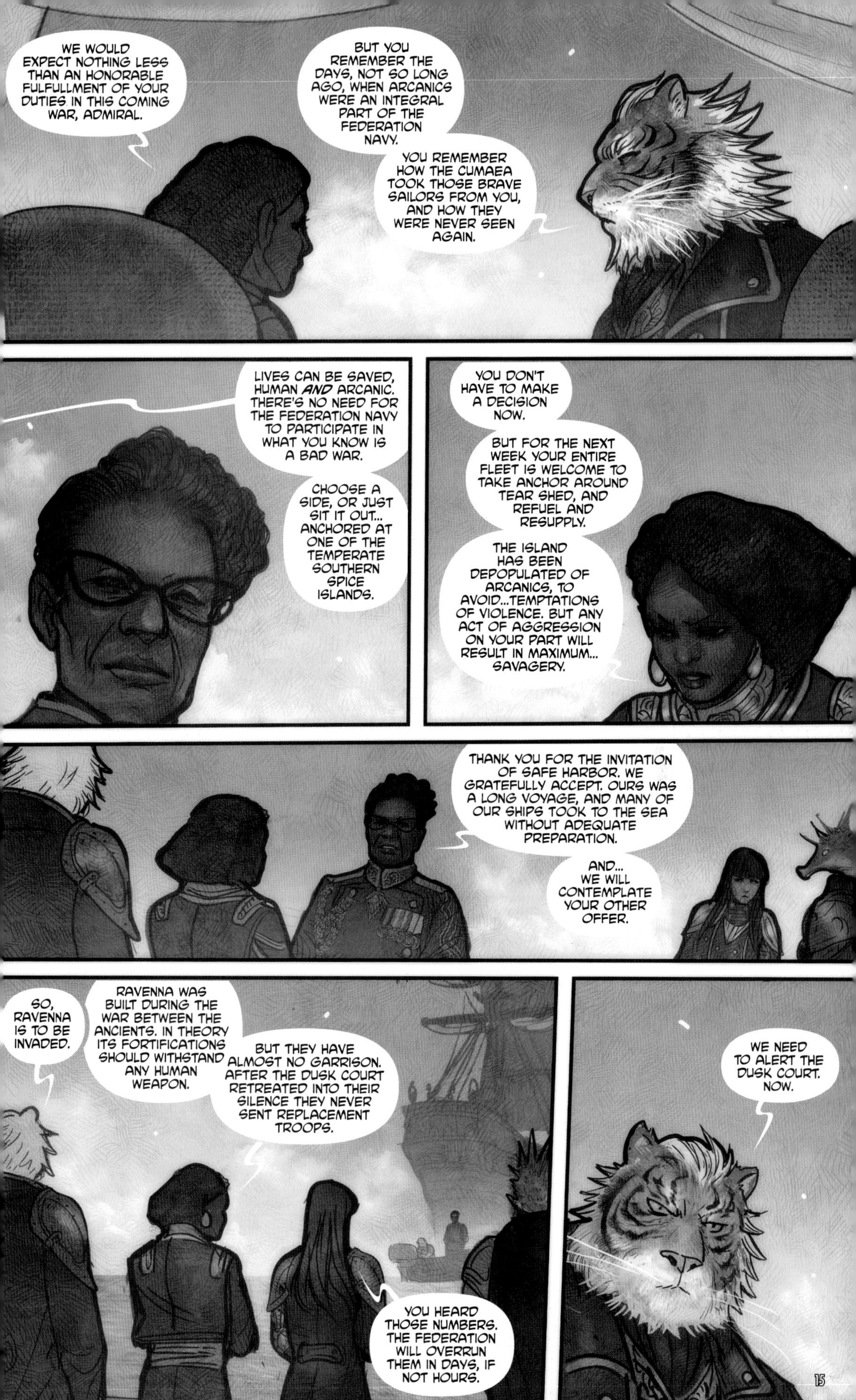
WE WOULD EXPECT NOTHING LESS THAN AN HONORABLE FULFULLMENT OF YOUR DUTIES IN THIS COMING WAR, ADMIRAL.
BUT YOU REMEMBER THE DAYS, NOT SO LONG AGO, WHEN ARCANICS WERE AN INTEGRAL PART OF THE FEDERATION NAVY.
YOU REMEMBER HOW THE CUMAEA TOOK THOSE BRAVE SAILORS FROM YOU, AND HOW THEY WERE NEVER SEEN AGAIN.
LIVES CAN BE SAVED, HUMAN *AND* ARCANIC. THERE'S NO NEED FOR THE FEDERATION NAVY TO PARTICIPATE IN WHAT YOU KNOW IS A BAD WAR.
CHOOSE A SIDE, OR JUST SIT IT OUT... ANCHORED AT ONE OF THE TEMPERATE SOUTHERN SPICE ISLANDS.
YOU DON'T HAVE TO MAKE A DECISION NOW.
BUT FOR THE NEXT WEEK YOUR ENTIRE FLEET IS WELCOME TO TAKE ANCHOR AROUND TEAR SHED, AND REFUEL AND RESUPPLY.
THE ISLAND HAS BEEN DEPOPULATED OF ARCANICS, TO AVOID...TEMPTATIONS OF VIOLENCE. BUT ANY ACT OF AGGRESSION ON YOUR PART WILL RESULT IN MAXIMUM... SAVAGERY.
THANK YOU FOR THE INVITATION OF SAFE HARBOR. WE GRATEFULLY ACCEPT. OURS WAS A LONG VOYAGE, AND MANY OF OUR SHIPS TOOK TO THE SEA WITHOUT ADEQUATE PREPARATION.
AND... WE WILL CONTEMPLATE YOUR OTHER OFFER.
SO, RAVENNA IS TO BE INVADED.
RAVENNA WAS BUILT DURING THE WAR BETWEEN THE ANCIENTS. IN THEORY ITS FORTIFICATIONS SHOULD WITHSTAND ANY HUMAN WEAPON.
BUT THEY HAVE ALMOST NO GARRISON. AFTER THE DUSK COURT RETREATED INTO THEIR SILENCE THEY NEVER SENT REPLACEMENT TROOPS.
YOU HEARD THOSE NUMBERS. THE FEDERATION WILL OVERRUN THEM IN DAYS, IF NOT HOURS.
WE NEED TO ALERT THE DUSK COURT. NOW.

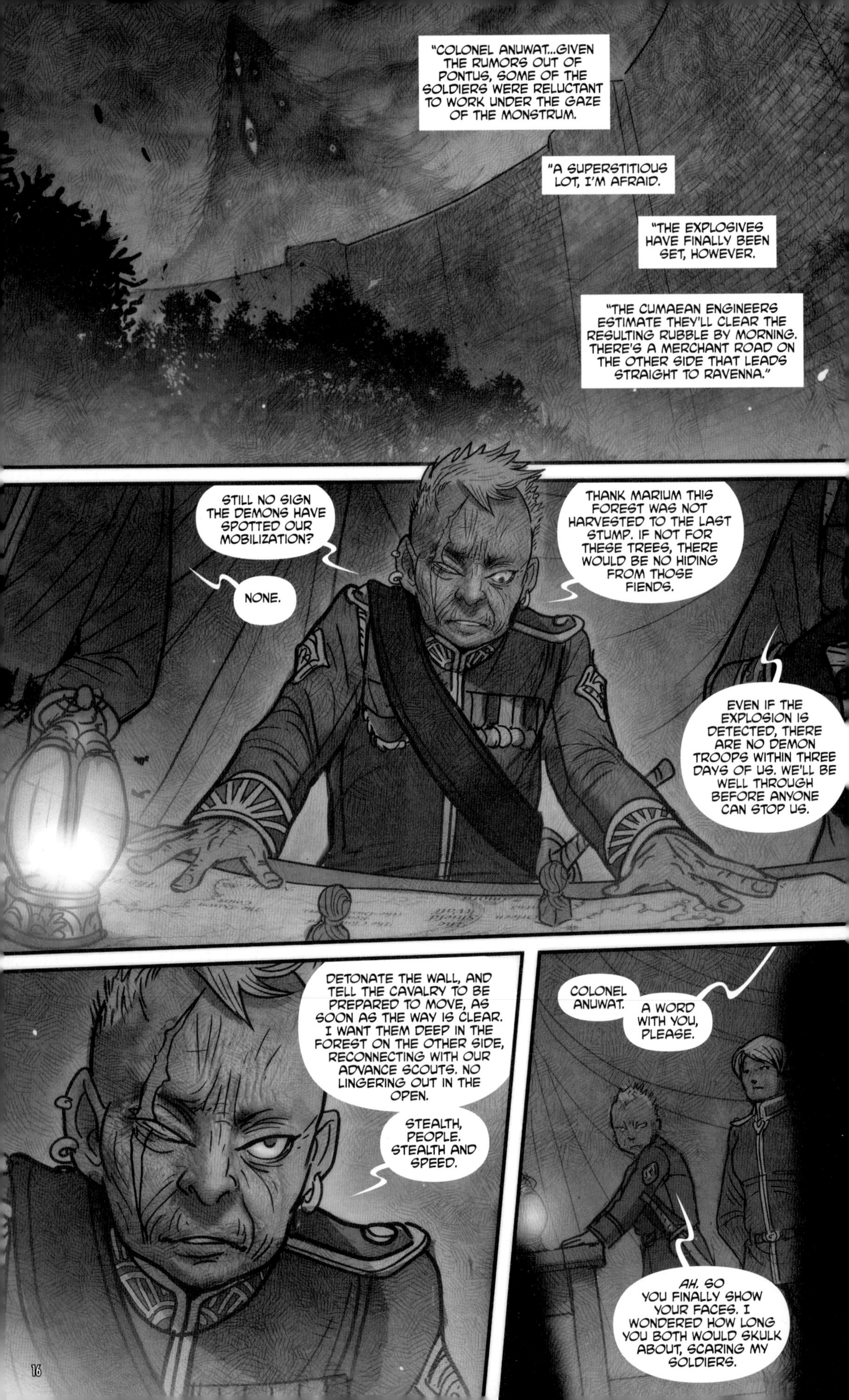
"COLONEL ANUWAT...GIVEN THE RUMORS OUT OF PONTUS, SOME OF THE SOLDIERS WERE RELUCTANT TO WORK UNDER THE GAZE OF THE MONSTRUM.
"A SUPERSTITIOUS LOT, I'M AFRAID.
"THE EXPLOSIVES HAVE FINALLY BEEN SET, HOWEVER.
"THE CUMAEAN ENGINEERS ESTIMATE THEY'LL CLEAR THE RESULTING RUBBLE BY MORNING. THERE'S A MERCHANT ROAD ON THE OTHER SIDE THAT LEADS STRAIGHT TO RAVENNA."
STILL NO SIGN THE DEMONS HAVE SPOTTED OUR MOBILIZATION?
NONE.
THANK MARIUM THIS FOREST WAS NOT HARVESTED TO THE LAST STUMP. IF NOT FOR THESE TREES, THERE WOULD BE NO HIDING FROM THOSE FIENDS.
EVEN IF THE EXPLOSION IS DETECTED, THERE ARE NO DEMON TROOPS WITHIN THREE DAYS OF US. WE'LL BE WELL THROUGH BEFORE ANYONE CAN STOP US.
DETONATE THE WALL, AND TELL THE CAVALRY TO BE PREPARED TO MOVE, AS SOON AS THE WAY IS CLEAR. I WANT THEM DEEP IN THE FOREST ON THE OTHER SIDE, RECONNECTING WITH OUR ADVANCE SCOUTS. NO LINGERING OUT IN THE OPEN.
STEALTH, PEOPLE. STEALTH AND SPEED.
COLONEL ANUWAT.
A WORD WITH YOU, PLEASE.
AH. SO YOU FINALLY SHOW YOUR FACES. I WONDERED HOW LONG YOU BOTH WOULD SKULK ABOUT, SCARING MY SOLDIERS.

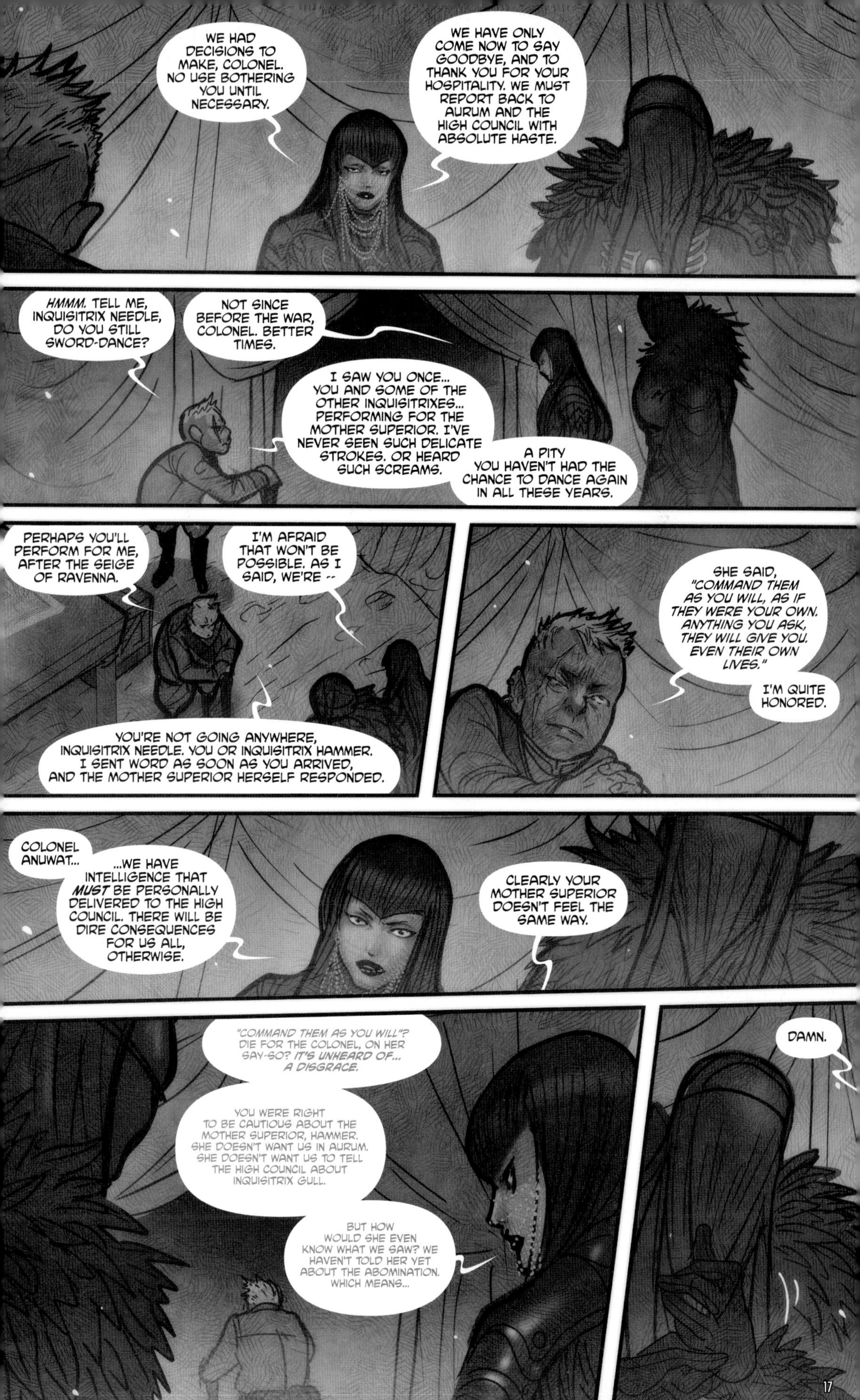
WE HAD DECISIONS TO MAKE, COLONEL. NO USE BOTHERING YOU UNTIL NECESSARY.
WE HAVE ONLY COME NOW TO SAY GOODBYE, AND TO THANK YOU FOR YOUR HOSPITALITY. WE MUST REPORT BACK TO AURUM AND THE HIGH COUNCIL WITH ABSOLUTE HASTE.
HMMM. TELL ME, INQUISITRIX NEEDLE, DO YOU STILL SWORD-DANCE?
NOT SINCE BEFORE THE WAR, COLONEL. BETTER TIMES.
I SAW YOU ONCE... YOU AND SOME OF THE OTHER INQUISITRIXES... PERFORMING FOR THE MOTHER SUPERIOR. I'VE NEVER SEEN SUCH DELICATE STROKES. OR HEARD SUCH SCREAMS.
A PITY YOU HAVEN'T HAD THE CHANCE TO DANCE AGAIN IN ALL THESE YEARS.
PERHAPS YOU'LL PERFORM FOR ME, AFTER THE SEIGE OF RAVENNA.
I'M AFRAID THAT WON'T BE POSSIBLE. AS I SAID, WE'RE --
YOU'RE NOT GOING ANYWHERE, INQUISITRIX NEEDLE. YOU OR INQUISITRIX HAMMER. I SENT WORD AS SOON AS YOU ARRIVED, AND THE MOTHER SUPERIOR HERSELF RESPONDED.
SHE SAID, *"COMMAND THEM AS YOU WILL, AS IF THEY WERE YOUR OWN. ANYTHING YOU ASK, THEY WILL GIVE YOU. EVEN THEIR OWN LIVES."*
I'M QUITE HONORED.
COLONEL ANUWAT...
...WE HAVE INTELLIGENCE THAT *MUST* BE PERSONALLY DELIVERED TO THE HIGH COUNCIL. THERE WILL BE DIRE CONSEQUENCES FOR US ALL, OTHERWISE.
CLEARLY YOUR MOTHER SUPERIOR DOESN'T FEEL THE SAME WAY.
"COMMAND THEM AS YOU WILL"? DIE FOR THE COLONEL, ON HER SAY-SO? *IT'S UNHEARD OF... A DISGRACE.*
YOU WERE RIGHT TO BE CAUTIOUS ABOUT THE MOTHER SUPERIOR, HAMMER. SHE DOESN'T WANT US IN AURUM. SHE DOESN'T WANT US TO TELL THE HIGH COUNCIL ABOUT INQUISITRIX GULL.
BUT HOW WOULD SHE EVEN KNOW WHAT WE SAW? WE HAVEN'T TOLD HER YET ABOUT THE ABOMINATION. WHICH MEANS...
DAMN.

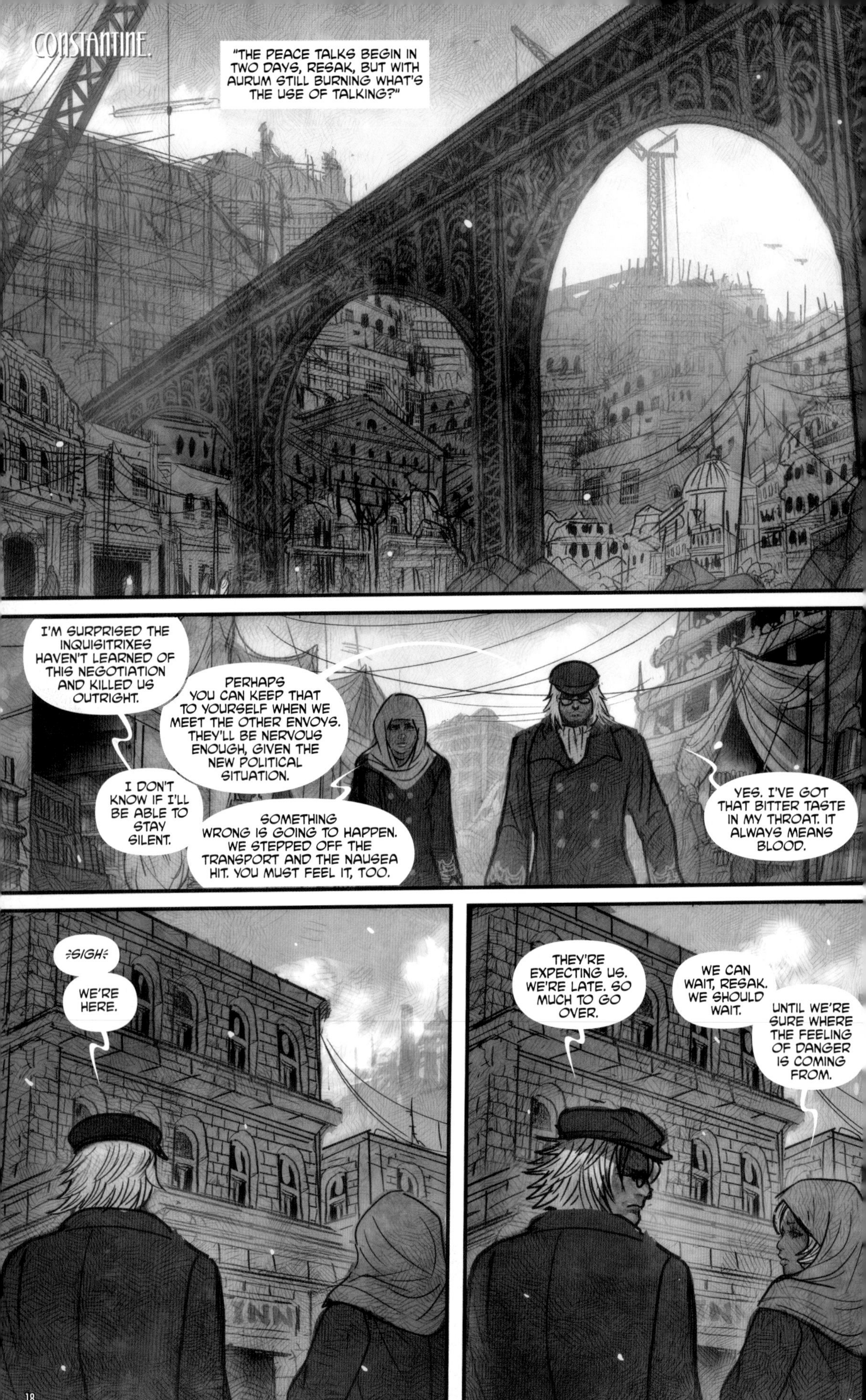
"THE PEACE TALKS BEGIN IN TWO DAYS, RESAK, BUT WITH AURUM STILL BURNING WHAT'S THE USE OF TALKING?"
I'M SURPRISED THE INQUISITRIXES HAVEN'T LEARNED OF THIS NEGOTIATION AND KILLED US OUTRIGHT.
PERHAPS YOU CAN KEEP THAT TO YOURSELF WHEN WE MEET THE OTHER ENVOYS. THEY'LL BE NERVOUS ENOUGH, GIVEN THE NEW POLITICAL SITUATION.
I DON'T KNOW IF I'LL BE ABLE TO STAY SILENT.
SOMETHING WRONG IS GOING TO HAPPEN. WE STEPPED OFF THE TRANSPORT AND THE NAUSEA HIT. YOU MUST FEEL IT, TOO.
YES. I'VE GOT THAT BITTER TASTE IN MY THROAT. IT ALWAYS MEANS BLOOD.
SIGH
WE'RE HERE.
INN
THEY'RE EXPECTING US. WE'RE LATE. SO MUCH TO GO OVER.
WE CAN WAIT, RESAK. WE SHOULD WAIT.
UNTIL WE'RE SURE WHERE THE FEELING OF DANGER IS COMING FROM.

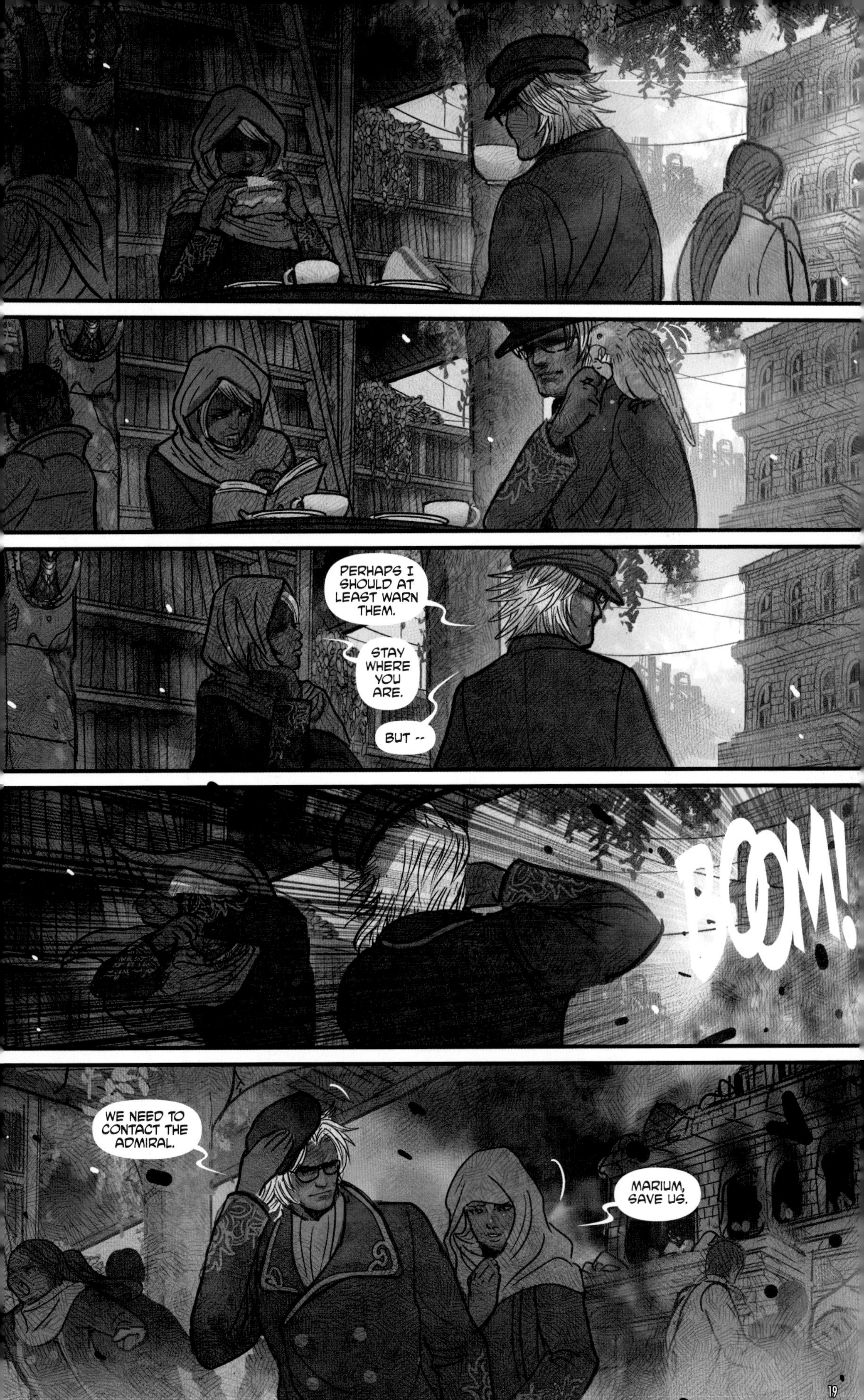
PERHAPS I SHOULD AT LEAST WARN THEM.
STAY WHERE YOU ARE.
BUT --
BOOM!
WE NEED TO CONTACT THE ADMIRAL.
MARIUM, SAVE US.

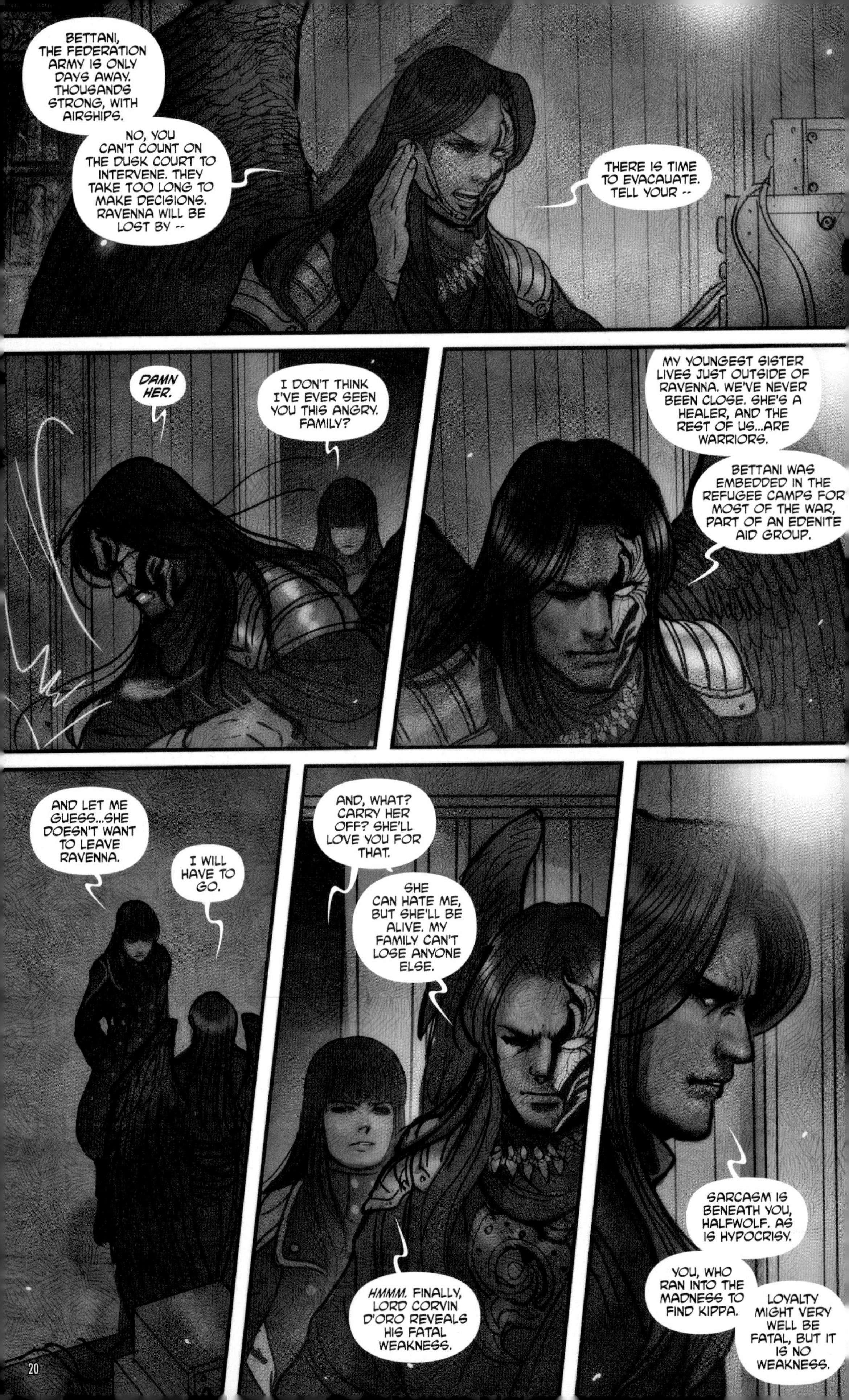
BETTANI, THE FEDERATION ARMY IS ONLY DAYS AWAY. THOUSANDS STRONG, WITH AIRSHIPS.
NO, YOU CAN'T COUNT ON THE DUSK COURT TO INTERVENE. THEY TAKE TOO LONG TO MAKE DECISIONS. RAVENNA WILL BE LOST BY --
THERE IS TIME TO EVACUATE. TELL YOUR --
DAMN HER.
I DON'T THINK I'VE EVER SEEN YOU THIS ANGRY. FAMILY?
MY YOUNGEST SISTER LIVES JUST OUTSIDE OF RAVENNA. WE'VE NEVER BEEN CLOSE. SHE'S A HEALER, AND THE REST OF US...ARE WARRIORS.
BETTANI WAS EMBEDDED IN THE REFUGEE CAMPS FOR MOST OF THE WAR, PART OF AN EDENITE AID GROUP.
AND LET ME GUESS...SHE DOESN'T WANT TO LEAVE RAVENNA.
I WILL HAVE TO GO.
AND, WHAT? CARRY HER OFF? SHE'LL LOVE YOU FOR THAT.
SHE CAN HATE ME, BUT SHE'LL BE ALIVE. MY FAMILY CAN'T LOSE ANYONE ELSE.
HMMM. FINALLY, LORD CORVIN D'ORO REVEALS HIS FATAL WEAKNESS.
SARCASM IS BENEATH YOU, HALFWOLF. AS IS HYPOCRISY.
YOU, WHO RAN INTO THE MADNESS TO FIND KIPPA.
LOYALTY MIGHT VERY WELL BE FATAL, BUT IT IS NO WEAKNESS.

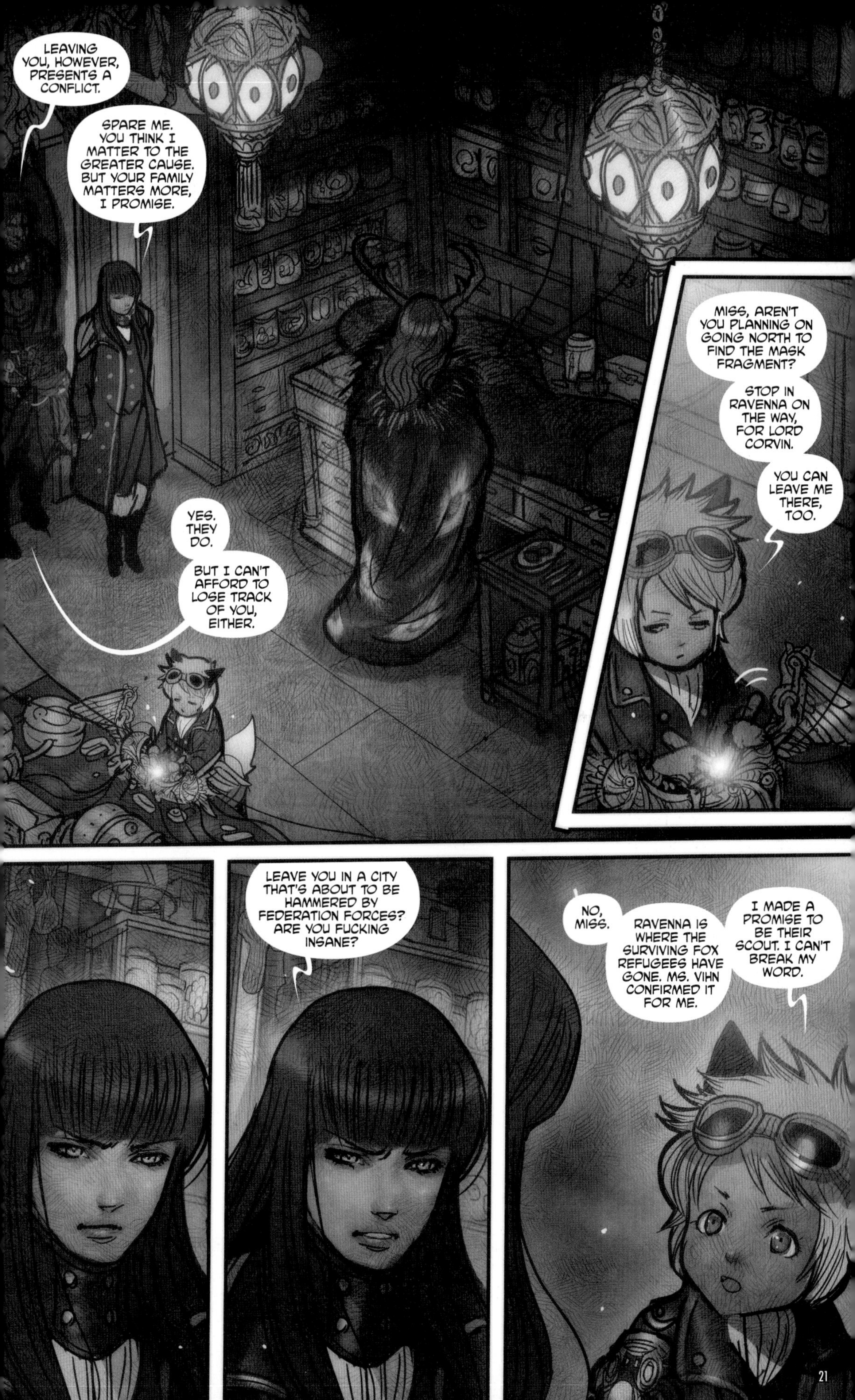
LEAVING YOU, HOWEVER, PRESENTS A CONFLICT.
SPARE ME. YOU THINK I MATTER TO THE GREATER CAUSE. BUT YOUR FAMILY MATTERS MORE, I PROMISE.
YES. THEY DO.
BUT I CAN'T AFFORD TO LOSE TRACK OF YOU, EITHER.
MISS, AREN'T YOU PLANNING ON GOING NORTH TO FIND THE MASK FRAGMENT?
STOP IN RAVENNA ON THE WAY, FOR LORD CORVIN.
YOU CAN LEAVE ME THERE, TOO.
LEAVE YOU IN A CITY THAT'S ABOUT TO BE HAMMERED BY FEDERATION FORCES? ARE YOU FUCKING INSANE?
NO, MISS.
RAVENNA IS WHERE THE SURVIVING FOX REFUGEES HAVE GONE. MS. VIHN CONFIRMED IT FOR ME.
I MADE A PROMISE TO BE THEIR SCOUT. I CAN'T BREAK MY WORD.

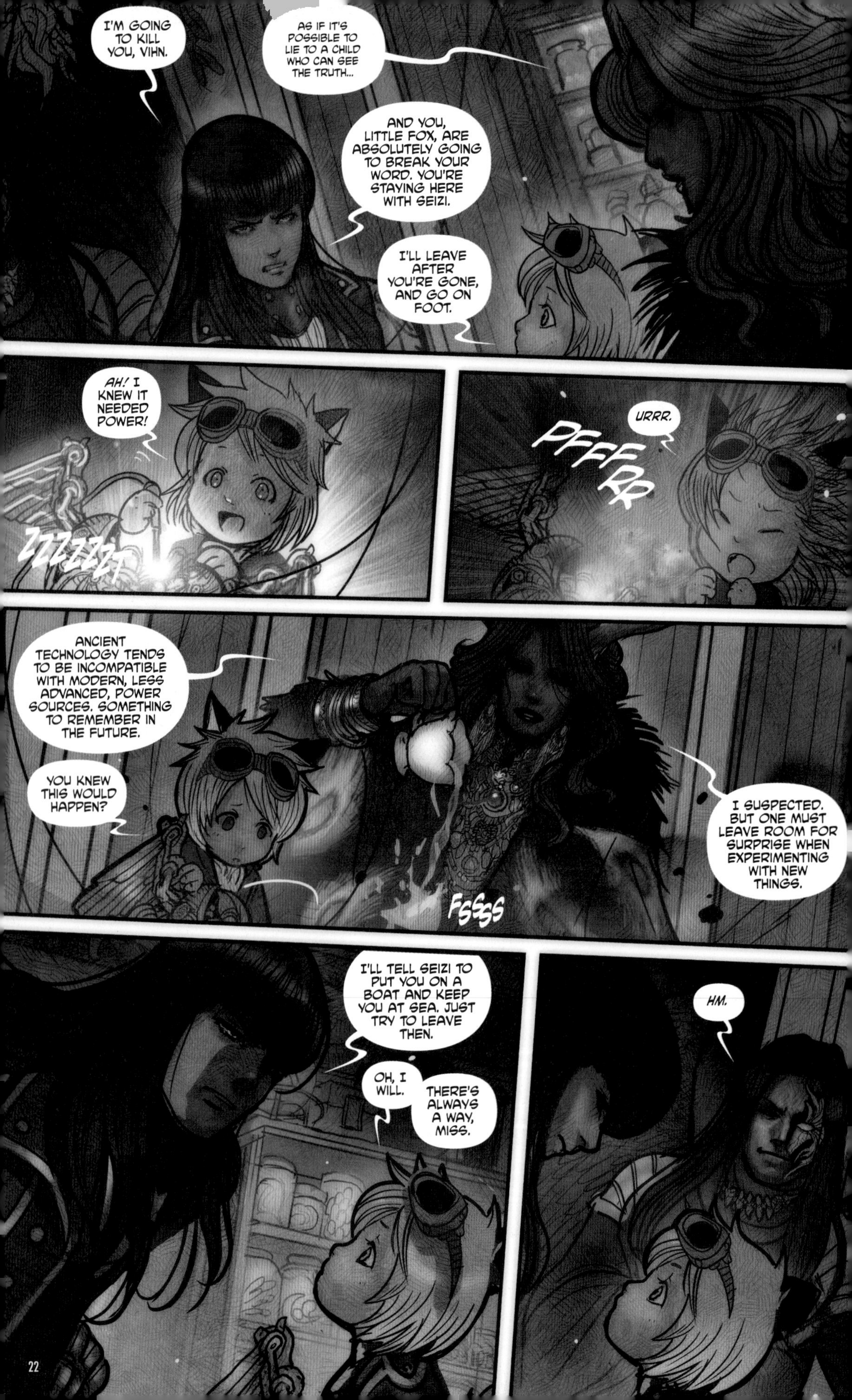
I'M GOING TO KILL YOU, VIHN.
AS IF IT'S POSSIBLE TO LIE TO A CHILD WHO CAN SEE THE TRUTH...
AND YOU, LITTLE FOX, ARE ABSOLUTELY GOING TO BREAK YOUR WORD. YOU'RE STAYING HERE WITH SEIZI.
I'LL LEAVE AFTER YOU'RE GONE, AND GO ON FOOT.
AH! I KNEW IT NEEDED POWER!
ZZZZZZZT
URRR.
PFFFRR
ANCIENT TECHNOLOGY TENDS TO BE INCOMPATIBLE WITH MODERN, LESS ADVANCED, POWER SOURCES. SOMETHING TO REMEMBER IN THE FUTURE.
YOU KNEW THIS WOULD HAPPEN?
I SUSPECTED. BUT ONE MUST LEAVE ROOM FOR SURPRISE WHEN EXPERIMENTING WITH NEW THINGS.
FSSSS
I'LL TELL SEIZI TO PUT YOU ON A BOAT AND KEEP YOU AT SEA. JUST TRY TO LEAVE THEN.
OH, I WILL.
THERE'S ALWAYS A WAY, MISS.
HM.

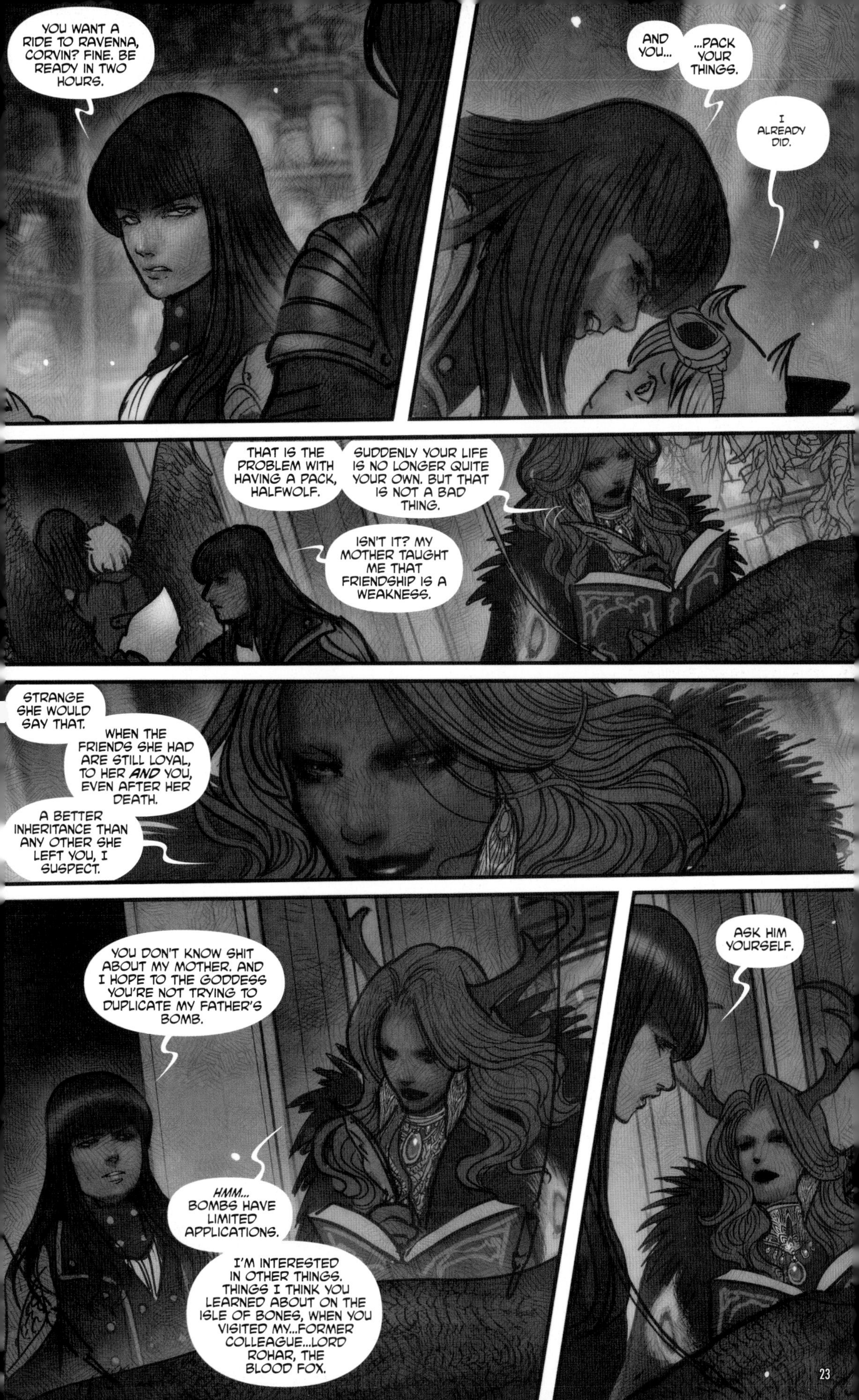
YOU WANT A RIDE TO RAVENNA, CORVIN? FINE. BE READY IN TWO HOURS.
AND YOU...
...PACK YOUR THINGS.
I ALREADY DID.
THAT IS THE PROBLEM WITH HAVING A PACK, HALFWOLF.
SUDDENLY YOUR LIFE IS NO LONGER QUITE YOUR OWN. BUT THAT IS NOT A BAD THING.
ISN'T IT? MY MOTHER TAUGHT ME THAT FRIENDSHIP IS A WEAKNESS.
STRANGE SHE WOULD SAY THAT.
WHEN THE FRIENDS SHE HAD ARE STILL LOYAL, TO HER *AND* YOU, EVEN AFTER HER DEATH.
A BETTER INHERITANCE THAN ANY OTHER SHE LEFT YOU, I SUSPECT.
YOU DON'T KNOW SHIT ABOUT MY MOTHER. AND I HOPE TO THE GODDESS YOU'RE NOT TRYING TO DUPLICATE MY FATHER'S BOMB.
HMM... BOMBS HAVE LIMITED APPLICATIONS.
I'M INTERESTED IN OTHER THINGS. THINGS I THINK YOU LEARNED ABOUT ON THE ISLE OF BONES, WHEN YOU VISITED MY...FORMER COLLEAGUE...LORD ROHAR, THE BLOOD FOX.
ASK HIM YOURSELF.

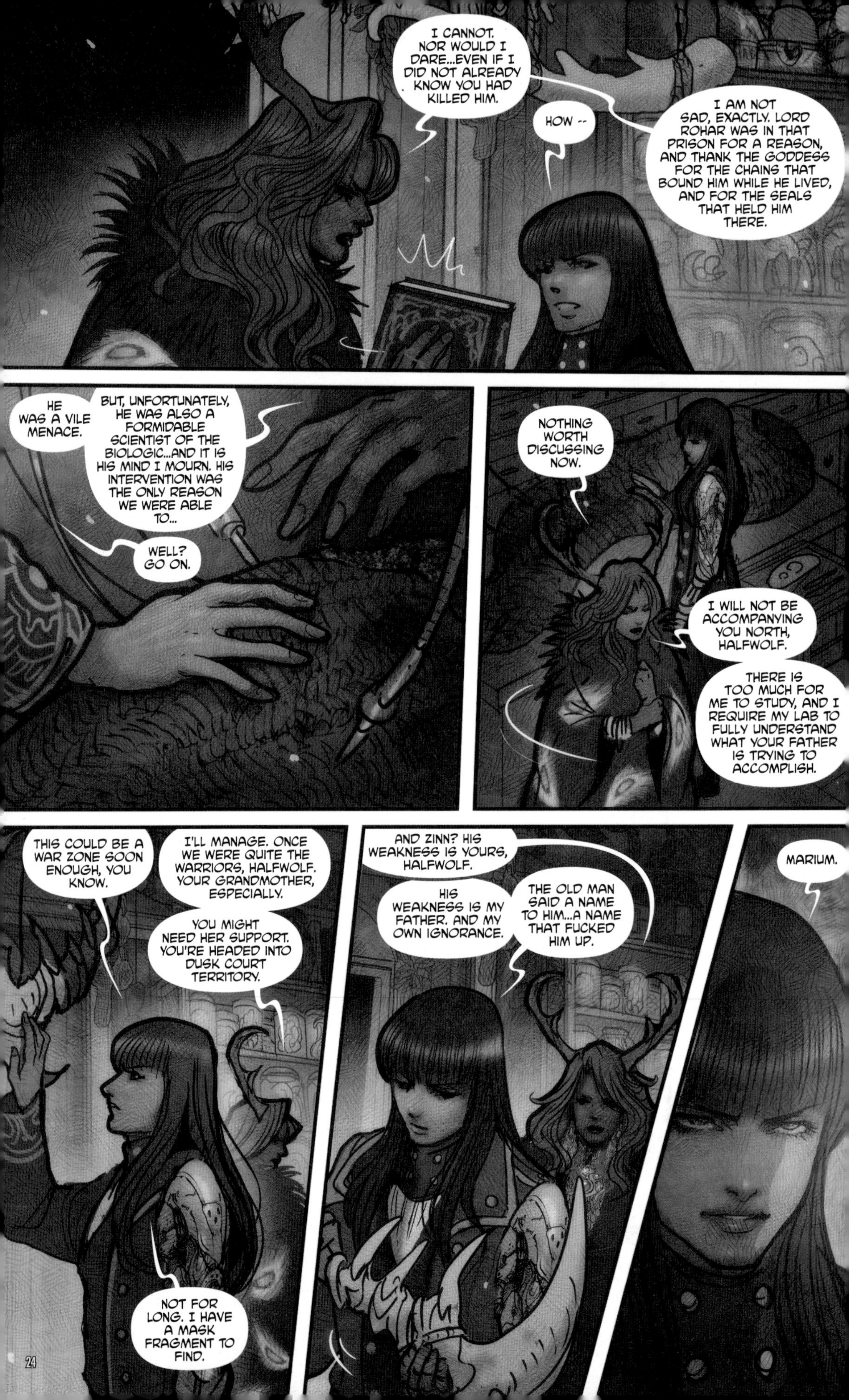
I CANNOT. NOR WOULD I DARE...EVEN IF I DID NOT ALREADY KNOW YOU HAD KILLED HIM.
HOW --
I AM NOT SAD, EXACTLY. LORD ROHAR WAS IN THAT PRISON FOR A REASON, AND THANK THE GODDESS FOR THE CHAINS THAT BOUND HIM WHILE HE LIVED, AND FOR THE SEALS THAT HELD HIM THERE.
HE WAS A VILE MENACE.
BUT, UNFORTUNATELY, HE WAS ALSO A FORMIDABLE SCIENTIST OF THE BIOLOGIC...AND IT IS HIS MIND I MOURN. HIS INTERVENTION WAS THE ONLY REASON WE WERE ABLE TO...
WELL? GO ON.
NOTHING WORTH DISCUSSING NOW.
I WILL NOT BE ACCOMPANYING YOU NORTH, HALFWOLF.
THERE IS TOO MUCH FOR ME TO STUDY, AND I REQUIRE MY LAB TO FULLY UNDERSTAND WHAT YOUR FATHER IS TRYING TO ACCOMPLISH.
THIS COULD BE A WAR ZONE SOON ENOUGH, YOU KNOW.
I'LL MANAGE. ONCE WE WERE QUITE THE WARRIORS, HALFWOLF. YOUR GRANDMOTHER, ESPECIALLY.
YOU MIGHT NEED HER SUPPORT. YOU'RE HEADED INTO DUSK COURT TERRITORY.
NOT FOR LONG. I HAVE A MASK FRAGMENT TO FIND.
AND ZINN? HIS WEAKNESS IS YOURS, HALFWOLF.
HIS WEAKNESS IS MY FATHER. AND MY OWN IGNORANCE.
THE OLD MAN SAID A NAME TO HIM...A NAME THAT FUCKED HIM UP.
MARIUM.

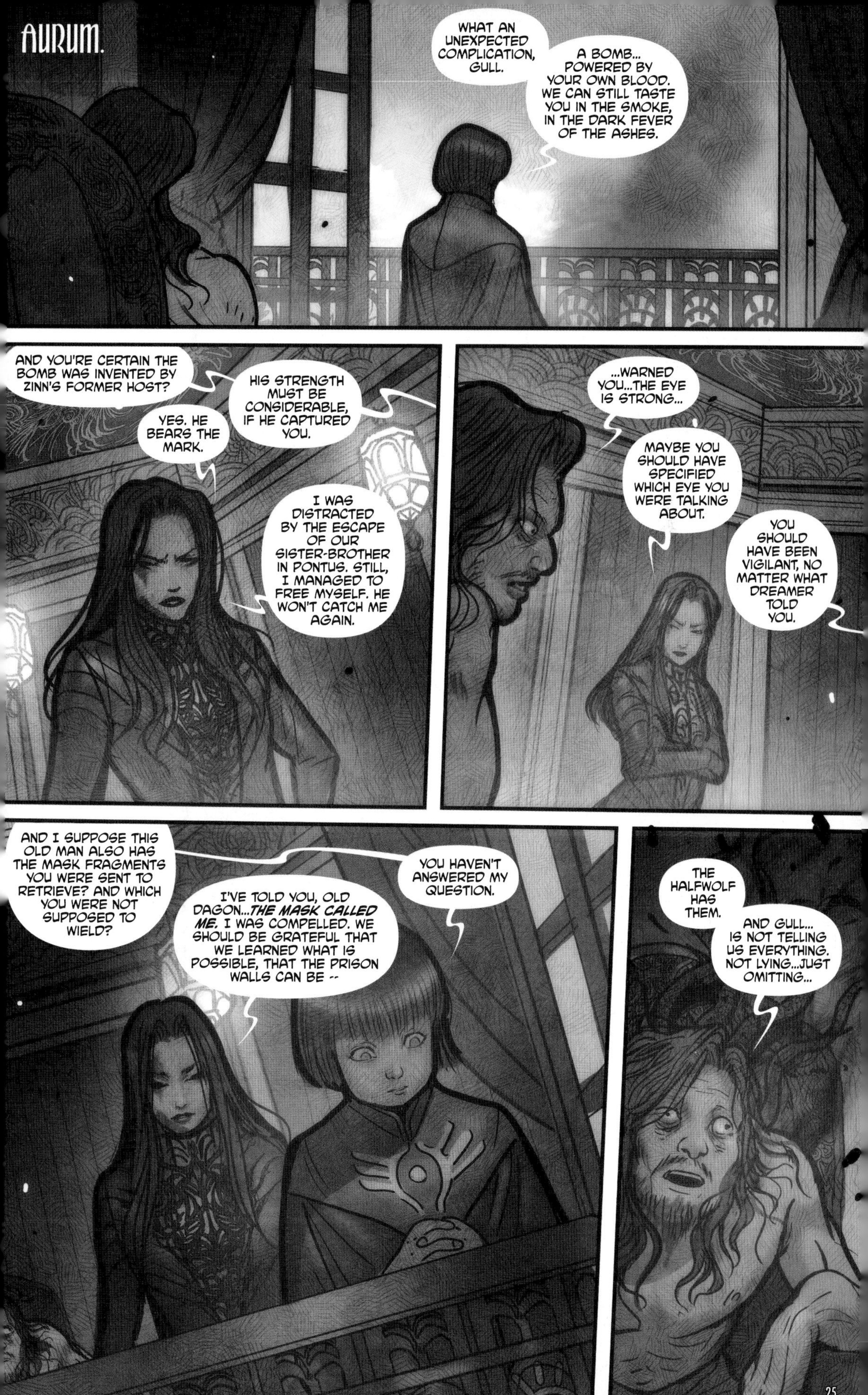
WHAT AN UNEXPECTED COMPLICATION, GULL.
A BOMB... POWERED BY YOUR OWN BLOOD. WE CAN STILL TASTE YOU IN THE SMOKE, IN THE DARK FEVER OF THE ASHES.
AND YOU'RE CERTAIN THE BOMB WAS INVENTED BY ZINN'S FORMER HOST?
YES. HE BEARS THE MARK.
HIS STRENGTH MUST BE CONSIDERABLE, IF HE CAPTURED YOU.
I WAS DISTRACTED BY THE ESCAPE OF OUR SISTER-BROTHER IN PONTUS. STILL, I MANAGED TO FREE MYSELF. HE WON'T CATCH ME AGAIN.
...WARNED YOU...THE EYE IS STRONG...
MAYBE YOU SHOULD HAVE SPECIFIED WHICH EYE YOU WERE TALKING ABOUT.
YOU SHOULD HAVE BEEN VIGILANT, NO MATTER WHAT DREAMER TOLD YOU.
AND I SUPPOSE THIS OLD MAN ALSO HAS THE MASK FRAGMENTS YOU WERE SENT TO RETRIEVE? AND WHICH YOU WERE NOT SUPPOSED TO WIELD?
I'VE TOLD YOU, OLD DAGON...*THE MASK CALLED ME.* I WAS COMPELLED. WE SHOULD BE GRATEFUL THAT WE LEARNED WHAT IS POSSIBLE, THAT THE PRISON WALLS CAN BE --
YOU HAVEN'T ANSWERED MY QUESTION.
THE HALFWOLF HAS THEM.
AND GULL... IS NOT TELLING US EVERYTHING. NOT LYING...JUST OMITTING...

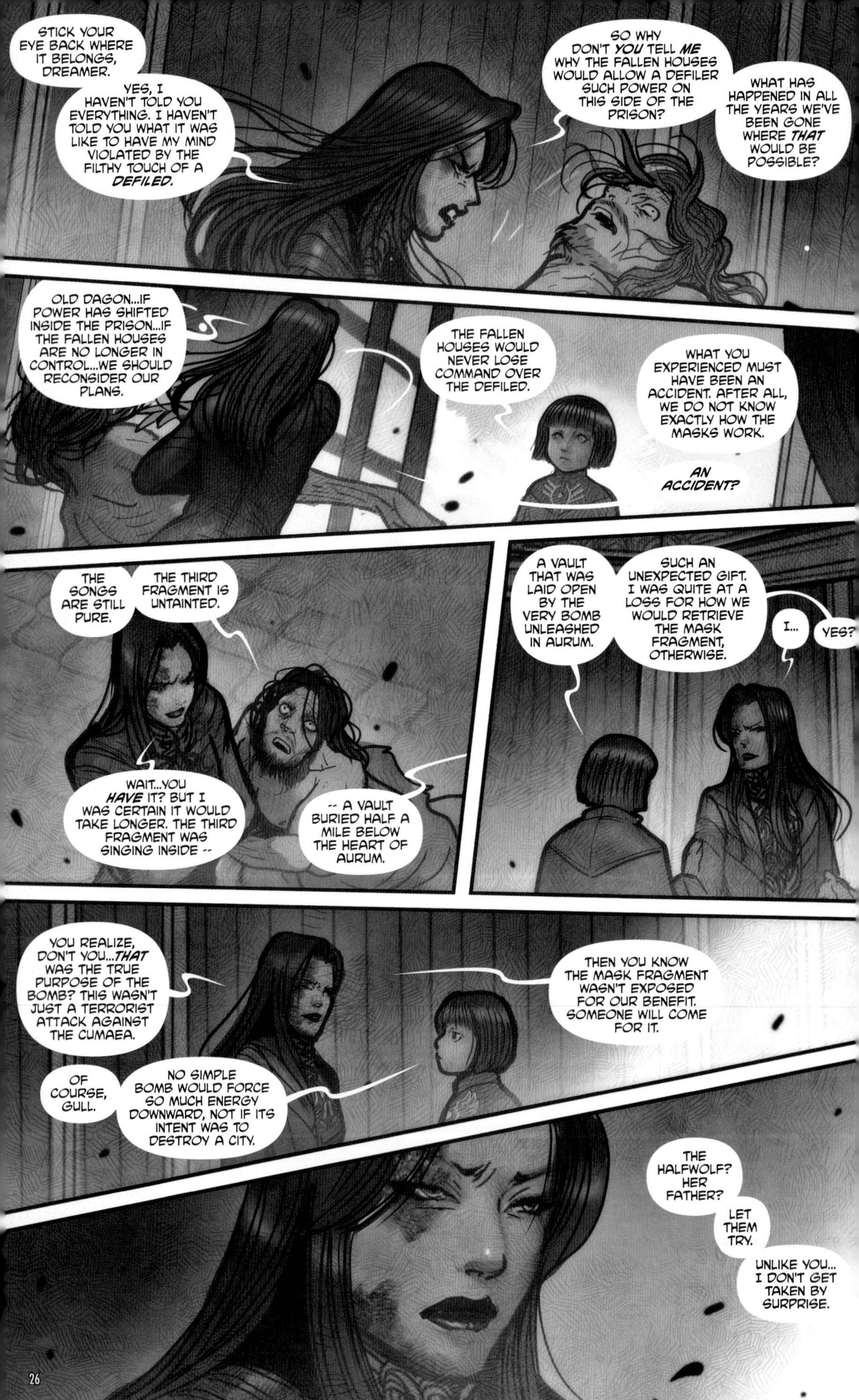

STICK YOUR EYE BACK WHERE IT BELONGS, DREAMER.
YES, I HAVEN'T TOLD YOU EVERYTHING. I HAVEN'T TOLD YOU WHAT IT WAS LIKE TO HAVE MY MIND VIOLATED BY THE FILTHY TOUCH OF A *DEFILED.*
SO WHY DON'T *YOU* TELL *ME* WHY THE FALLEN HOUSES WOULD ALLOW A DEFILER SUCH POWER ON THIS SIDE OF THE PRISON?
WHAT HAS HAPPENED IN ALL THE YEARS WE'VE BEEN GONE WHERE *THAT* WOULD BE POSSIBLE?
OLD DAGON...IF POWER HAS SHIFTED INSIDE THE PRISON...IF THE FALLEN HOUSES ARE NO LONGER IN CONTROL...WE SHOULD RECONSIDER OUR PLANS.
THE FALLEN HOUSES WOULD NEVER LOSE COMMAND OVER THE DEFILED.
WHAT YOU EXPERIENCED MUST HAVE BEEN AN ACCIDENT. AFTER ALL, WE DO NOT KNOW EXACTLY HOW THE MASKS WORK.
AN ACCIDENT?
THE SONGS ARE STILL PURE.
THE THIRD FRAGMENT IS UNTAINTED.
WAIT...YOU *HAVE* IT? BUT I WAS CERTAIN IT WOULD TAKE LONGER. THE THIRD FRAGMENT WAS SINGING INSIDE --
-- A VAULT BURIED HALF A MILE BELOW THE HEART OF AURUM.
A VAULT THAT WAS LAID OPEN BY THE VERY BOMB UNLEASHED IN AURUM.
SUCH AN UNEXPECTED GIFT. I WAS QUITE AT A LOSS FOR HOW WE WOULD RETRIEVE THE MASK FRAGMENT, OTHERWISE.
I...
YES?
YOU REALIZE, DON'T YOU...*THAT* WAS THE TRUE PURPOSE OF THE BOMB? THIS WASN'T JUST A TERRORIST ATTACK AGAINST THE CUMAEA.
THEN YOU KNOW THE MASK FRAGMENT WASN'T EXPOSED FOR OUR BENEFIT. SOMEONE WILL COME FOR IT.
OF COURSE, GULL.
NO SIMPLE BOMB WOULD FORCE SO MUCH ENERGY DOWNWARD, NOT IF ITS INTENT WAS TO DESTROY A CITY.
THE HALFWOLF? HER FATHER?
LET THEM TRY.
UNLIKE YOU... I DON'T GET TAKEN BY SURPRISE.

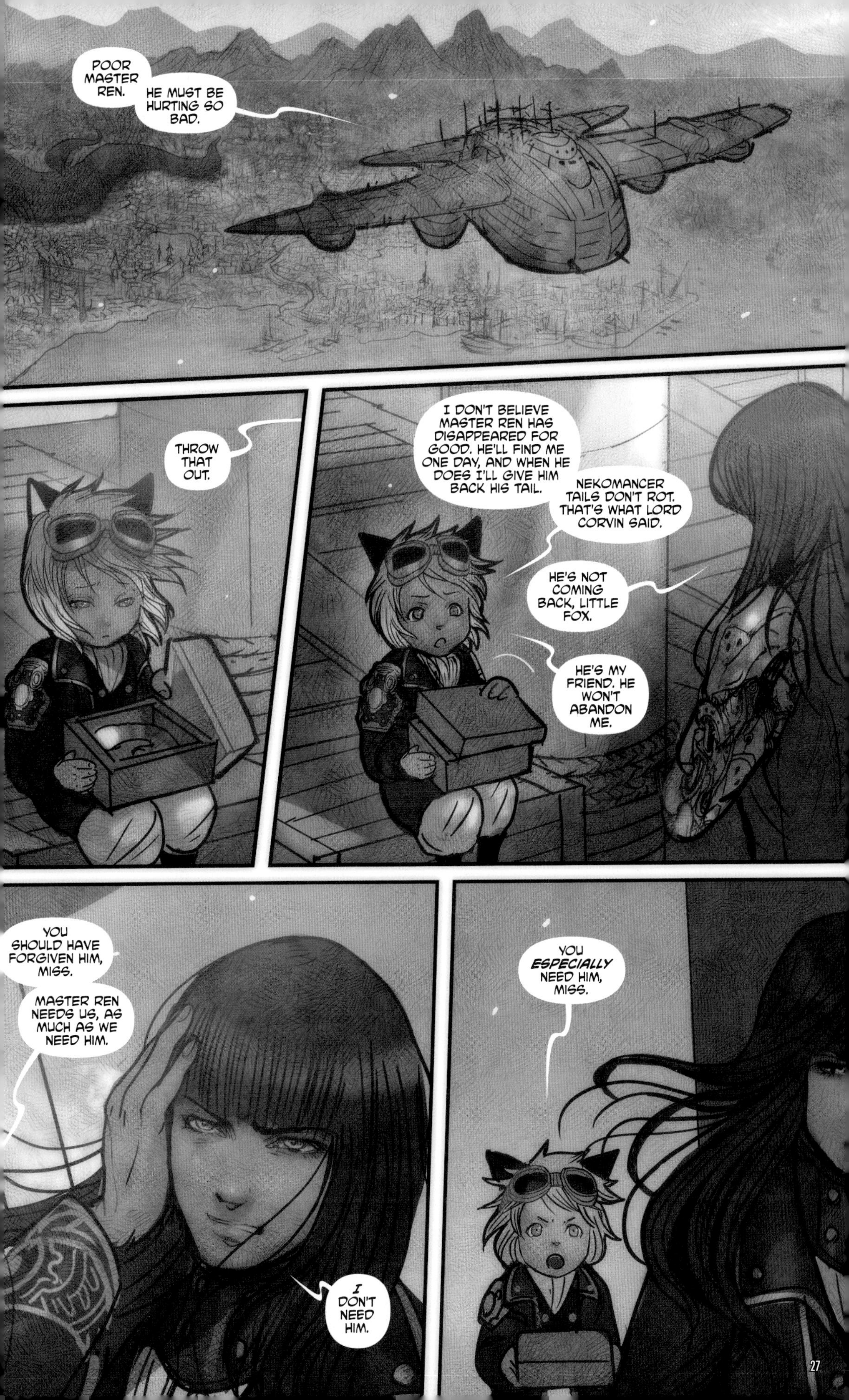

POOR MASTER REN.
HE MUST BE HURTING SO BAD.
THROW THAT OUT.
I DON'T BELIEVE MASTER REN HAS DISAPPEARED FOR GOOD. HE'LL FIND ME ONE DAY, AND WHEN HE DOES I'LL GIVE HIM BACK HIS TAIL.
NEKOMANCER TAILS DON'T ROT. THAT'S WHAT LORD CORVIN SAID.
HE'S NOT COMING BACK, LITTLE FOX.
HE'S MY FRIEND. HE WON'T ABANDON ME.
YOU SHOULD HAVE FORGIVEN HIM, MISS.
MASTER REN NEEDS US, AS MUCH AS WE NEED HIM.
I DON'T NEED HIM.
YOU ESPECIALLY NEED HIM, MISS.

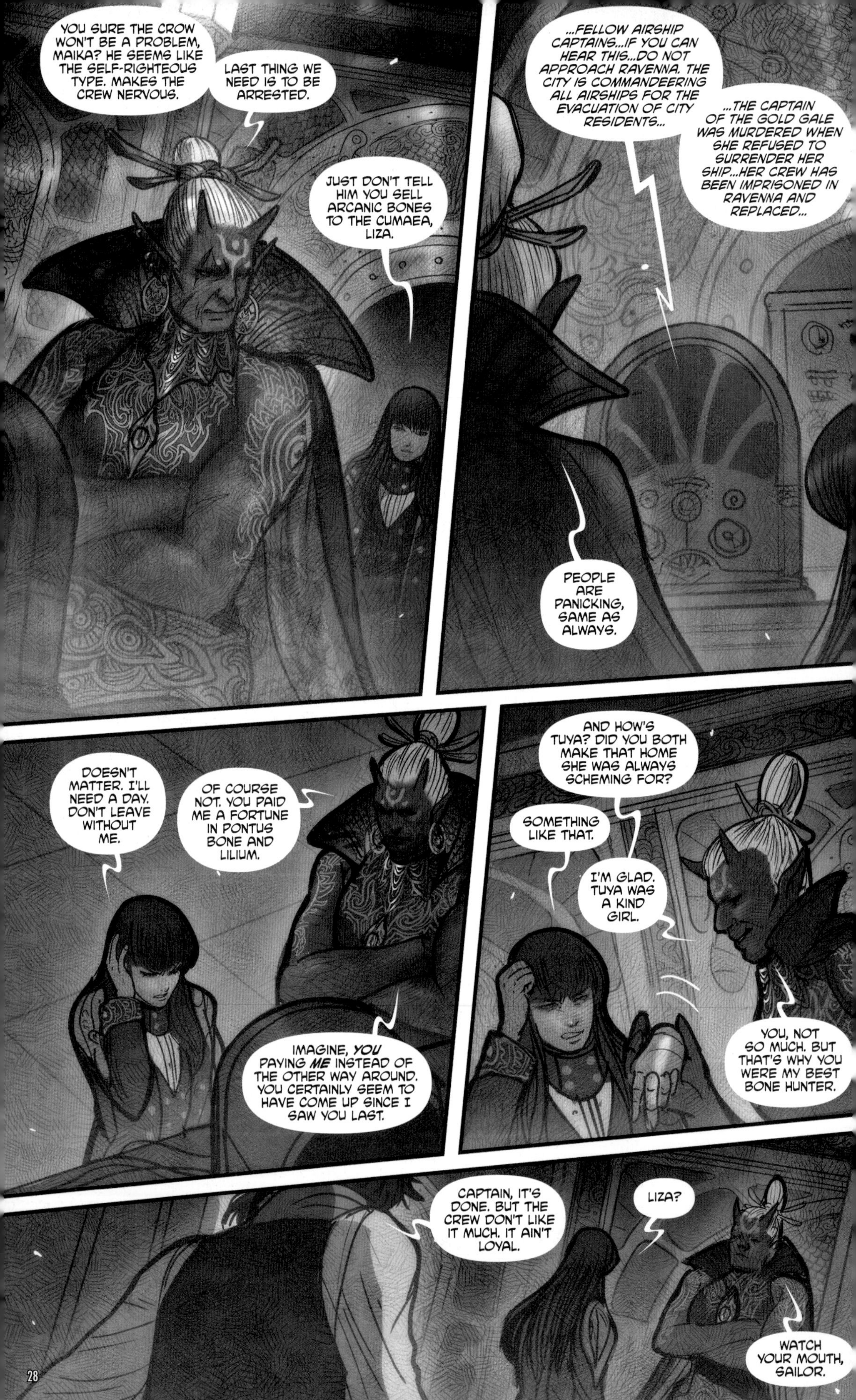
YOU SURE THE CROW WON'T BE A PROBLEM, MAIKA? HE SEEMS LIKE THE SELF-RIGHTEOUS TYPE. MAKES THE CREW NERVOUS.
LAST THING WE NEED IS TO BE ARRESTED.
JUST DON'T TELL HIM YOU SELL ARCANIC BONES TO THE CUMAEA, LIZA.
...FELLOW AIRSHIP CAPTAINS...IF YOU CAN HEAR THIS...DO NOT APPROACH RAVENNA. THE CITY IS COMMANDEERING ALL AIRSHIPS FOR THE EVACUATION OF CITY RESIDENTS...
...THE CAPTAIN OF THE GOLD GALE WAS MURDERED WHEN SHE REFUSED TO SURRENDER HER SHIP...HER CREW HAS BEEN IMPRISONED IN RAVENNA AND REPLACED...
PEOPLE ARE PANICKING, SAME AS ALWAYS.
DOESN'T MATTER. I'LL NEED A DAY. DON'T LEAVE WITHOUT ME.
OF COURSE NOT. YOU PAID ME A FORTUNE IN PONTUS BONE AND LILIUM.
IMAGINE, *YOU* PAYING *ME* INSTEAD OF THE OTHER WAY AROUND. YOU CERTAINLY SEEM TO HAVE COME UP SINCE I SAW YOU LAST.
AND HOW'S TUYA? DID YOU BOTH MAKE THAT HOME SHE WAS ALWAYS SCHEMING FOR?
SOMETHING LIKE THAT.
I'M GLAD. TUYA WAS A KIND GIRL.
YOU, NOT SO MUCH. BUT THAT'S WHY YOU WERE MY BEST BONE HUNTER.
CAPTAIN, IT'S DONE. BUT THE CREW DON'T LIKE IT MUCH. IT AIN'T LOYAL.
LIZA?
WATCH YOUR MOUTH, SAILOR.

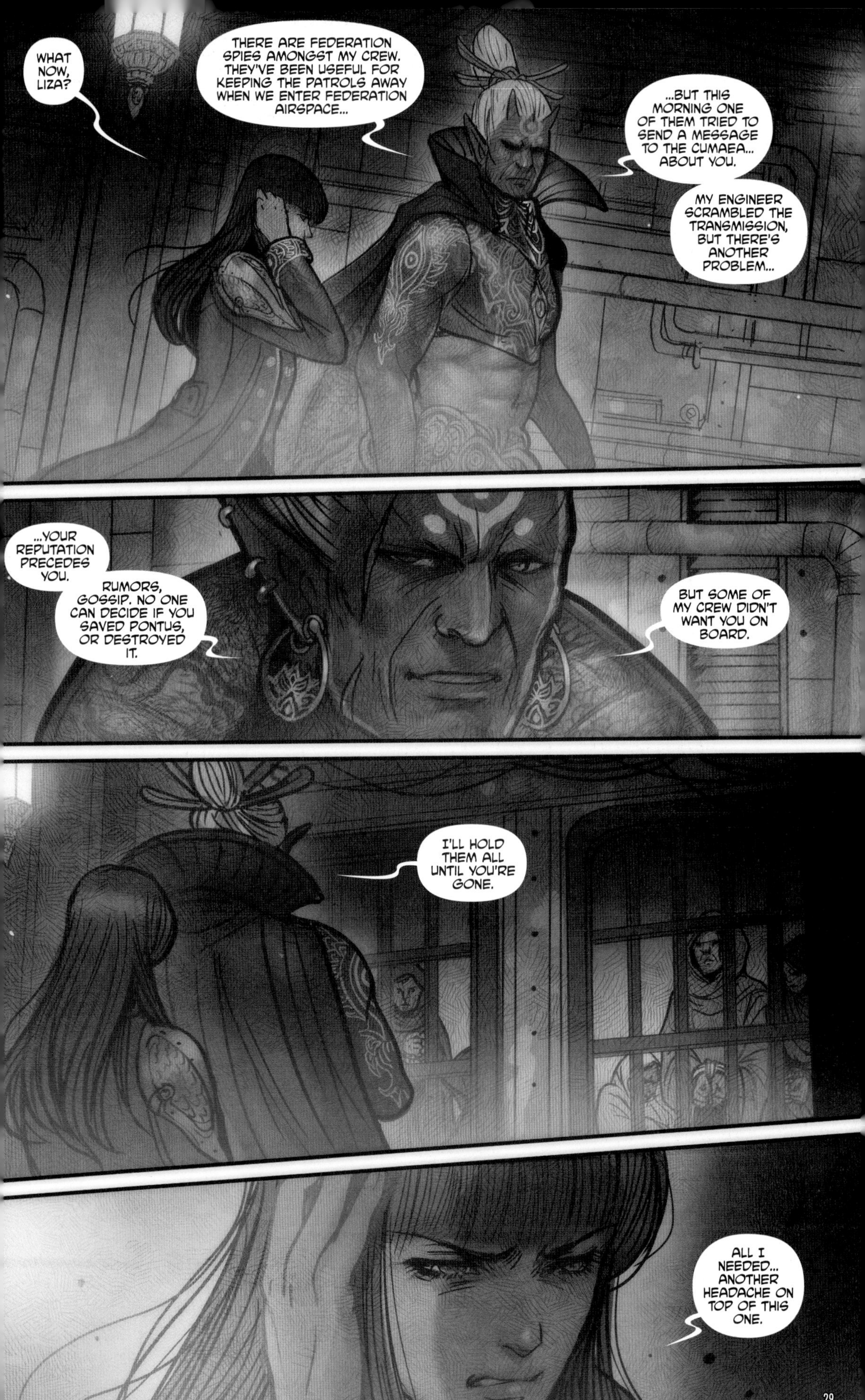
WHAT NOW, LIZA?
THERE ARE FEDERATION SPIES AMONGST MY CREW. THEY'VE BEEN USEFUL FOR KEEPING THE PATROLS AWAY WHEN WE ENTER FEDERATION AIRSPACE...
...BUT THIS MORNING ONE OF THEM TRIED TO SEND A MESSAGE TO THE CUMAEA... ABOUT YOU.
MY ENGINEER SCRAMBLED THE TRANSMISSION, BUT THERE'S ANOTHER PROBLEM...
...YOUR REPUTATION PRECEDES YOU.
RUMORS, GOSSIP. NO ONE CAN DECIDE IF YOU SAVED PONTUS, OR DESTROYED IT.
BUT SOME OF MY CREW DIDN'T WANT YOU ON BOARD.
I'LL HOLD THEM ALL UNTIL YOU'RE GONE.
ALL I NEEDED... ANOTHER HEADACHE ON TOP OF THIS ONE.

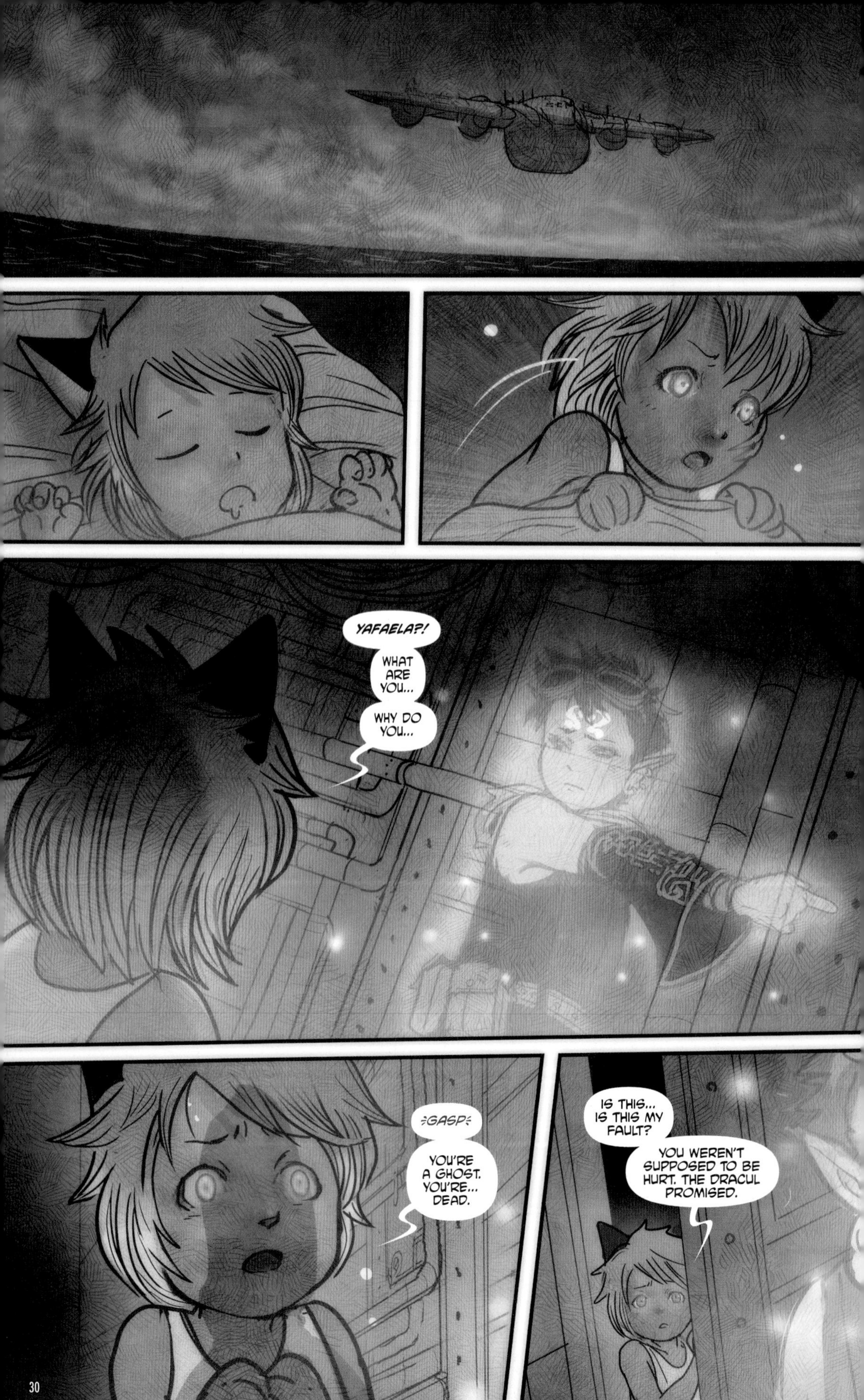
YAFAELA?!
WHAT ARE YOU...
WHY DO YOU...
GASP
YOU'RE A GHOST. YOU'RE... DEAD.
IS THIS... IS THIS MY FAULT?
YOU WEREN'T SUPPOSED TO BE HURT. THE DRACUL PROMISED.

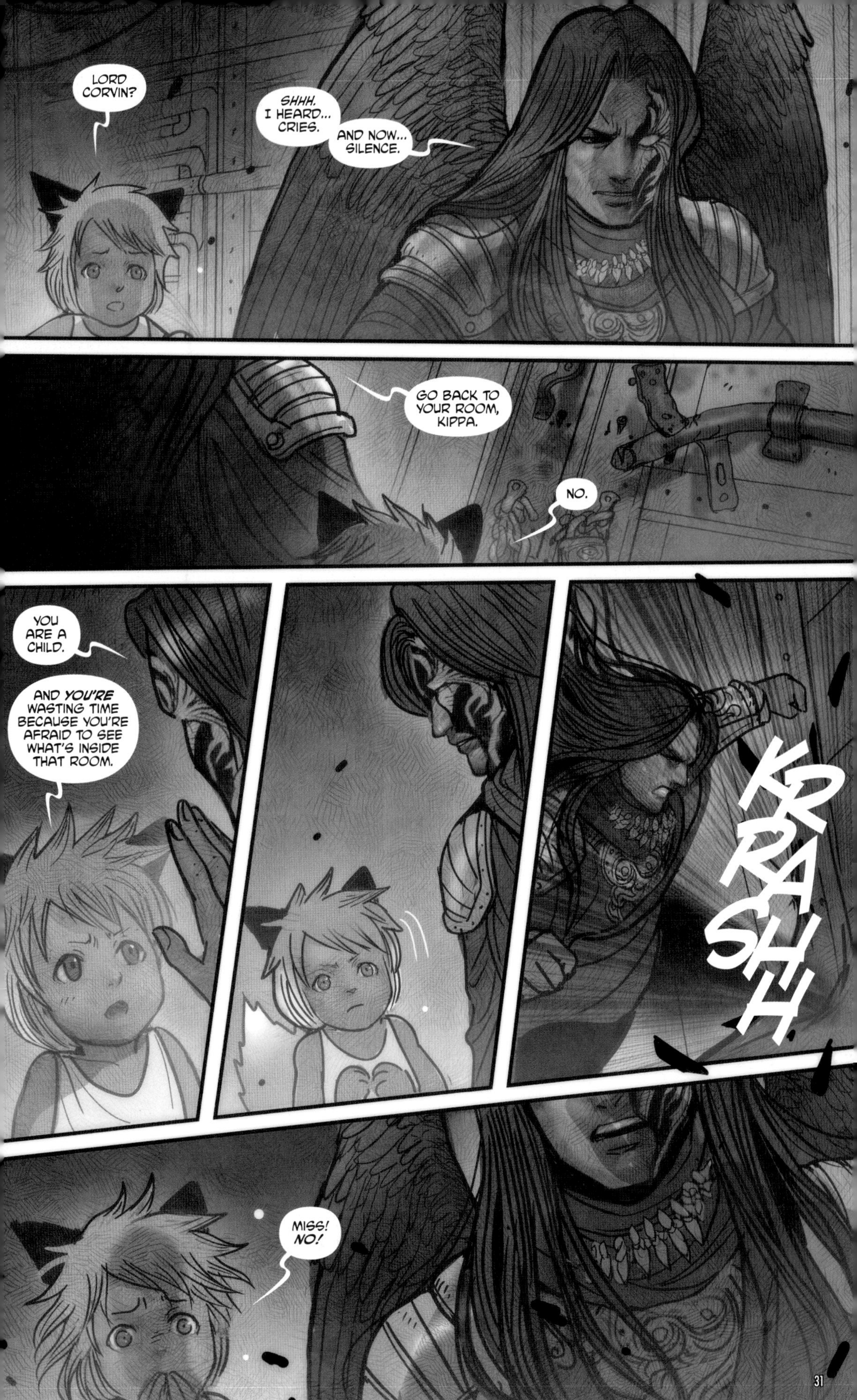
LORD CORVIN?
SHHH. I HEARD... CRIES.
AND NOW... SILENCE.
GO BACK TO YOUR ROOM, KIPPA.
NO.
YOU ARE A CHILD.
AND YOU'RE WASTING TIME BECAUSE YOU'RE AFRAID TO SEE WHAT'S INSIDE THAT ROOM.
KRASHH.
MISS! NO!

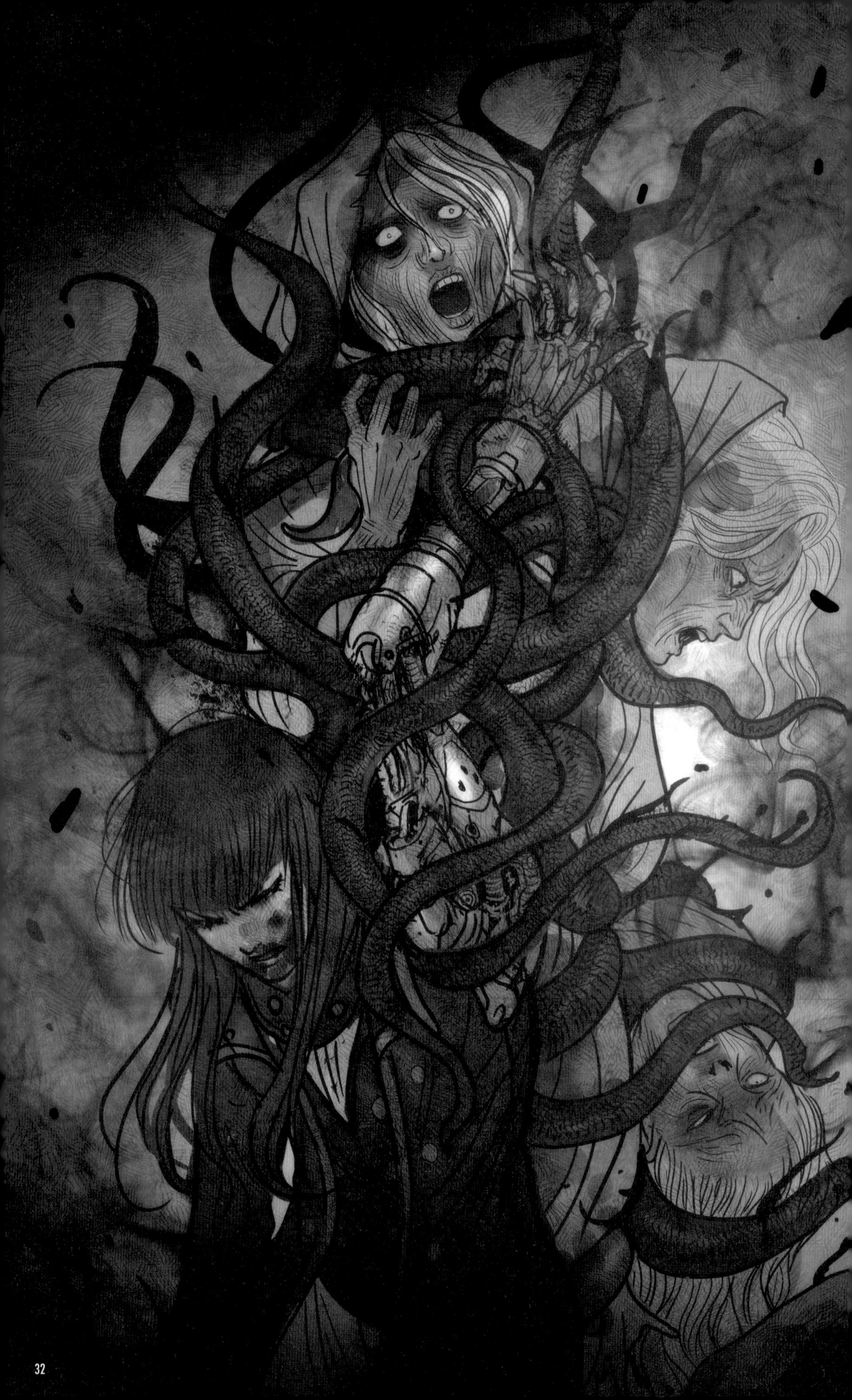

CHAPTER TWENTY-SIX

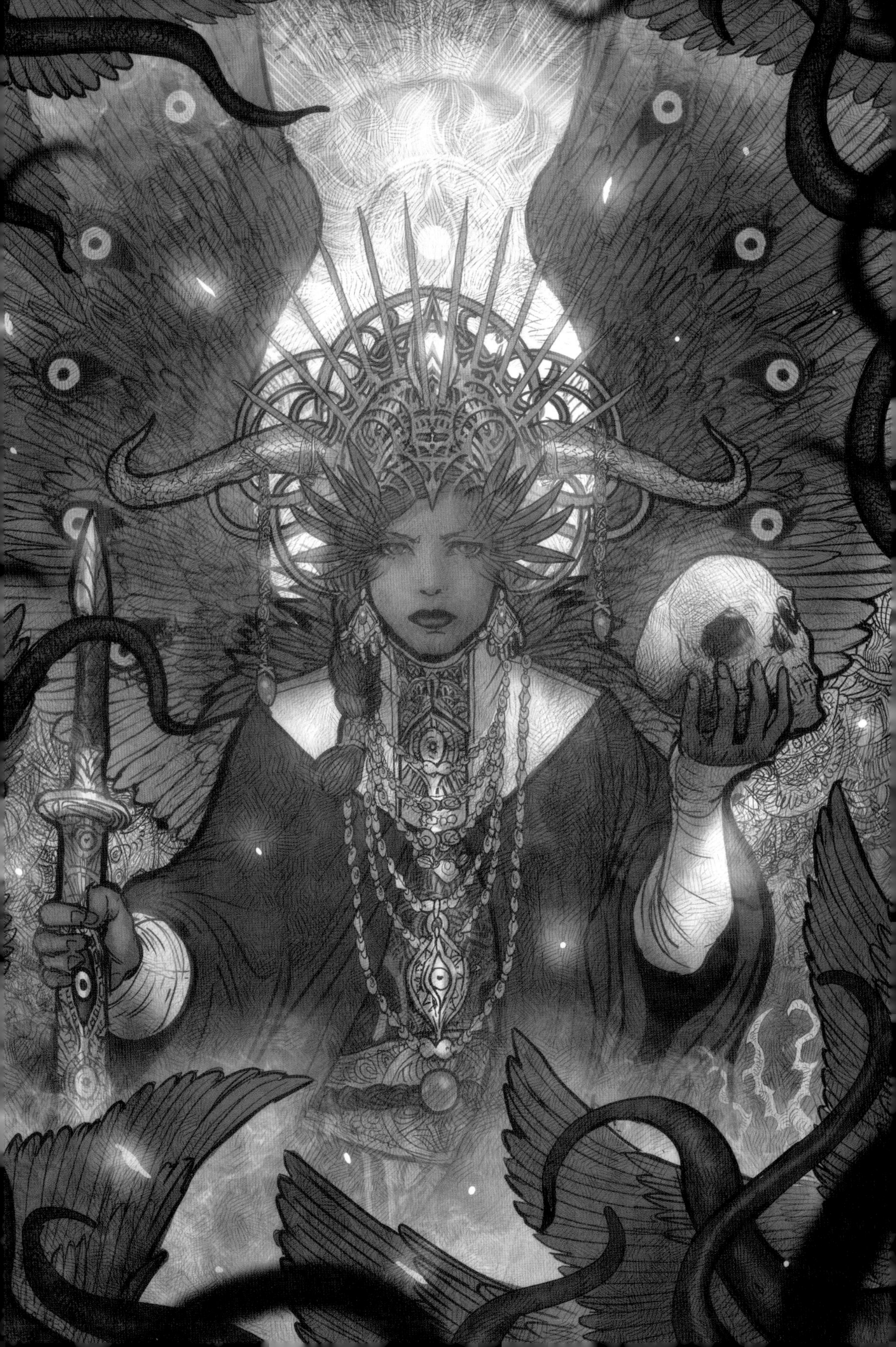

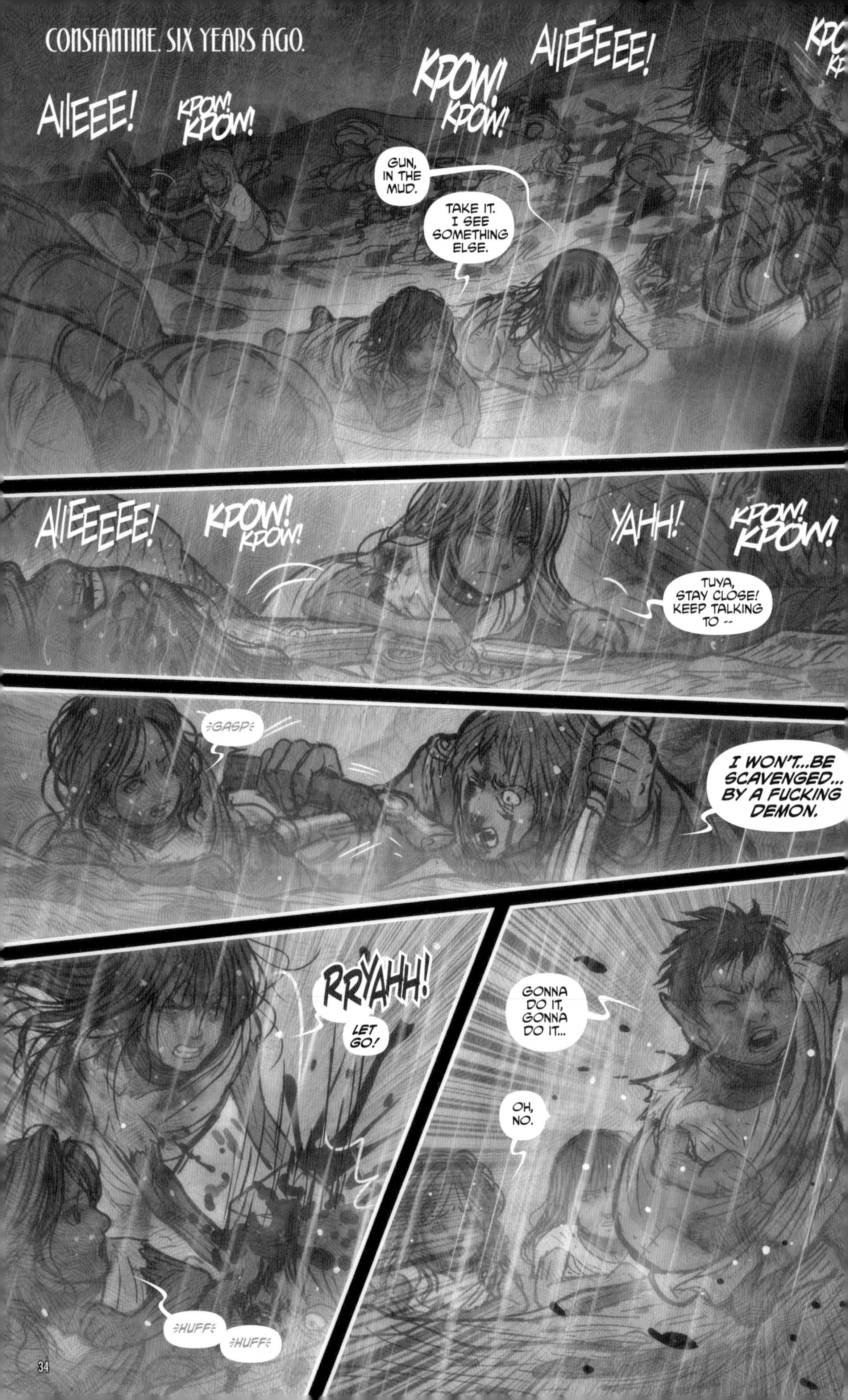
CONSTANTINE. SIX YEARS AGO.
AIIEEE!
KPOW! KPOW!
KPOW! KPOW!
AIIEEEEE!
GUN, IN THE MUD.
TAKE IT. I SEE SOMETHING ELSE.
AIIEEEEE!
KPOW! KPOW!
YAHH!
KPOW! KPOW!
TUYA, STAY CLOSE! KEEP TALKING TO --
GASP
I WON'T...BE SCAVENGED... BY A FUCKING DEMON.
RRYAHH!
LET GO!
HUFF
HUFF
GONNA DO IT, GONNA DO IT...
OH, NO.

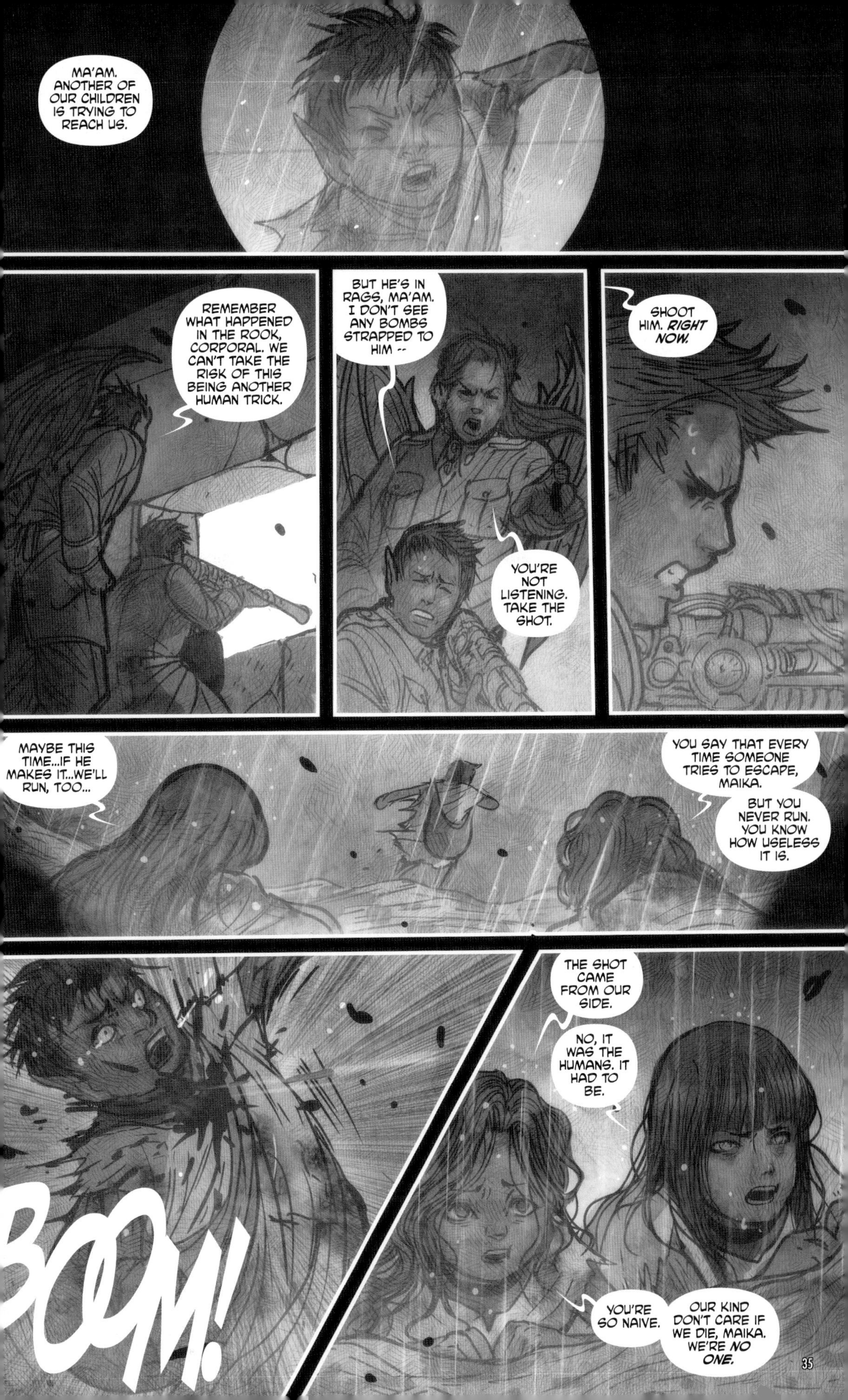
MA'AM. ANOTHER OF OUR CHILDREN IS TRYING TO REACH US.
REMEMBER WHAT HAPPENED IN THE ROOK, CORPORAL. WE CAN'T TAKE THE RISK OF THIS BEING ANOTHER HUMAN TRICK.
BUT HE'S IN RAGS, MA'AM. I DON'T SEE ANY BOMBS STRAPPED TO HIM --
YOU'RE NOT LISTENING. TAKE THE SHOT.
SHOOT HIM. *RIGHT NOW.*
MAYBE THIS TIME...IF HE MAKES IT...WE'LL RUN, TOO...
YOU SAY THAT EVERY TIME SOMEONE TRIES TO ESCAPE, MAIKA.
BUT YOU NEVER RUN. YOU KNOW HOW USELESS IT IS.
BOOM!
THE SHOT CAME FROM OUR SIDE.
NO, IT WAS THE HUMANS. IT HAD TO BE.
YOU'RE SO NAIVE.
OUR KIND DON'T CARE IF WE DIE, MAIKA. WE'RE *NO ONE.*

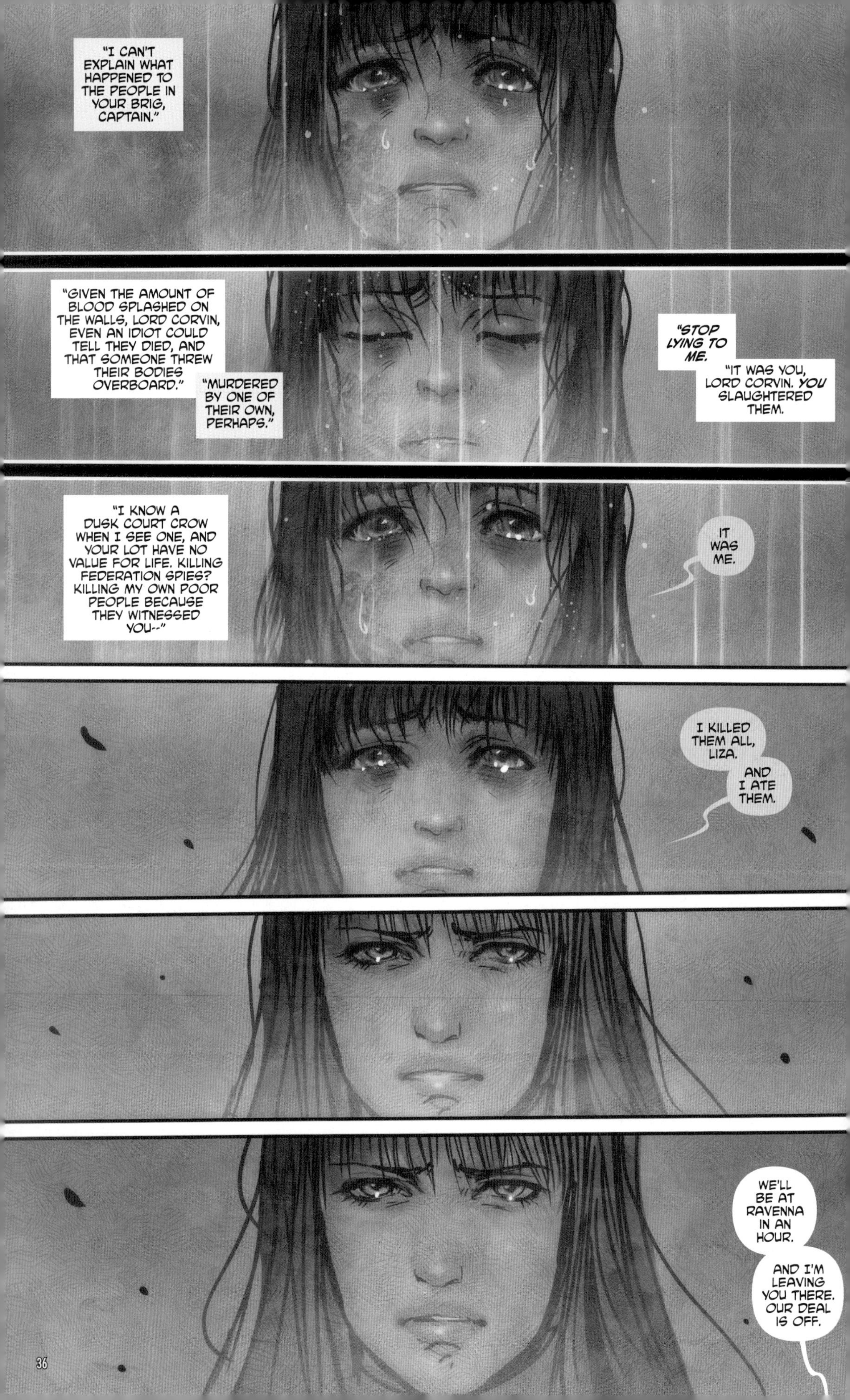
"I CAN'T EXPLAIN WHAT HAPPENED TO THE PEOPLE IN YOUR BRIG, CAPTAIN."
"GIVEN THE AMOUNT OF BLOOD SPLASHED ON THE WALLS, LORD CORVIN, EVEN AN IDIOT COULD TELL THEY DIED, AND THAT SOMEONE THREW THEIR BODIES OVERBOARD."
"MURDERED BY ONE OF THEIR OWN, PERHAPS."
"STOP LYING TO ME.
"IT WAS YOU, LORD CORVIN. YOU SLAUGHTERED THEM.
"I KNOW A DUSK COURT CROW WHEN I SEE ONE, AND YOUR LOT HAVE NO VALUE FOR LIFE. KILLING FEDERATION SPIES? KILLING MY OWN POOR PEOPLE BECAUSE THEY WITNESSED YOU--"
IT WAS ME.
I KILLED THEM ALL, LIZA.
AND I ATE THEM.
WE'LL BE AT RAVENNA IN AN HOUR.
AND I'M LEAVING YOU THERE. OUR DEAL IS OFF.

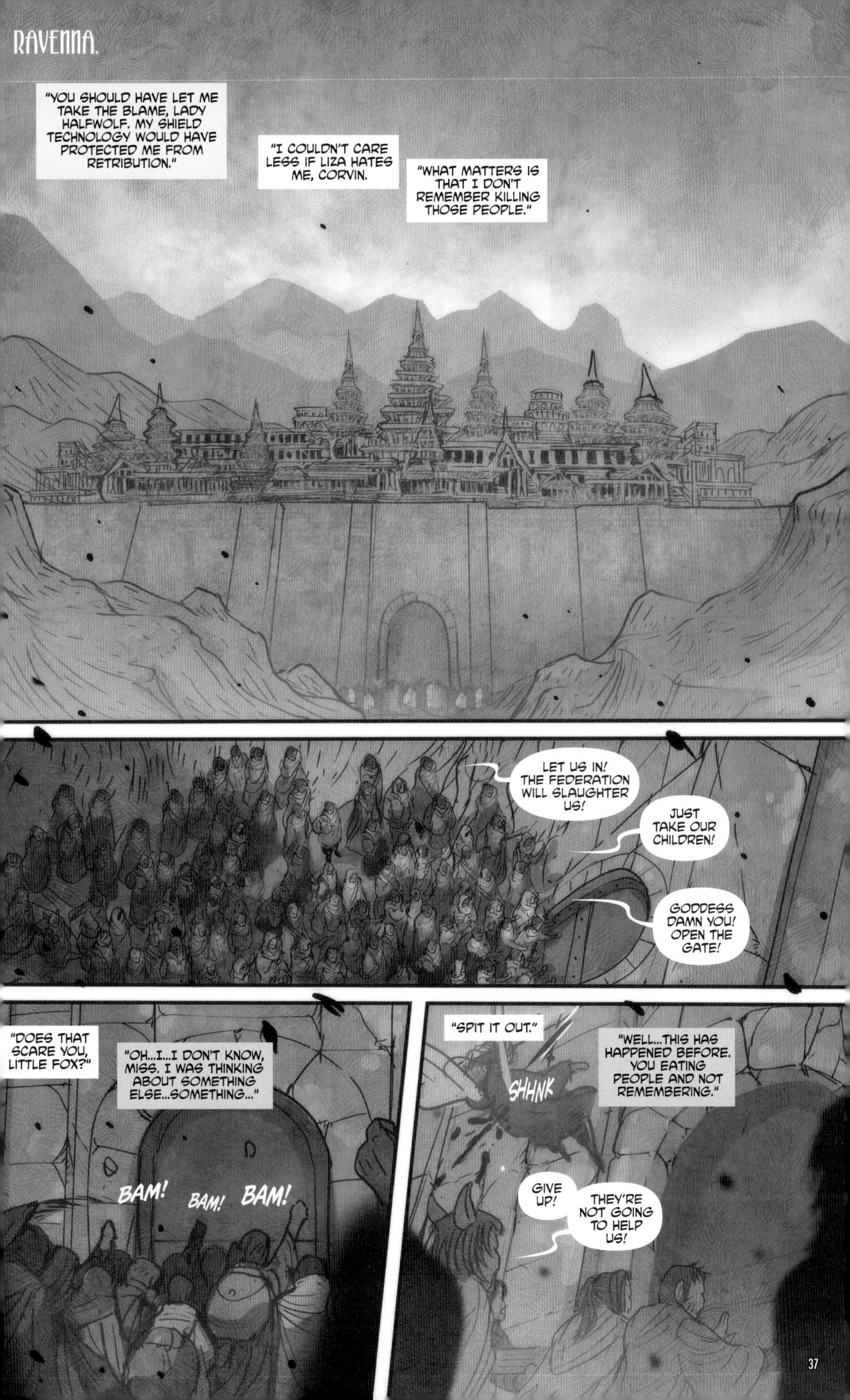
RAVENNA.
"YOU SHOULD HAVE LET ME TAKE THE BLAME, LADY HALFWOLF. MY SHIELD TECHNOLOGY WOULD HAVE PROTECTED ME FROM RETRIBUTION."
"I COULDN'T CARE LESS IF LIZA HATES ME, CORVIN.
"WHAT MATTERS IS THAT I DON'T REMEMBER KILLING THOSE PEOPLE."
LET US IN! THE FEDERATION WILL SLAUGHTER US!
JUST TAKE OUR CHILDREN!
GODDESS DAMN YOU! OPEN THE GATE!
"DOES THAT SCARE YOU, LITTLE FOX?"
"OH...I...I DON'T KNOW, MISS. I WAS THINKING ABOUT SOMETHING ELSE...SOMETHING..."
BAM! BAM! BAM!
"SPIT IT OUT."
SHHNK
"WELL...THIS HAS HAPPENED BEFORE. YOU EATING PEOPLE AND NOT REMEMBERING."
GIVE UP!
THEY'RE NOT GOING TO HELP US!

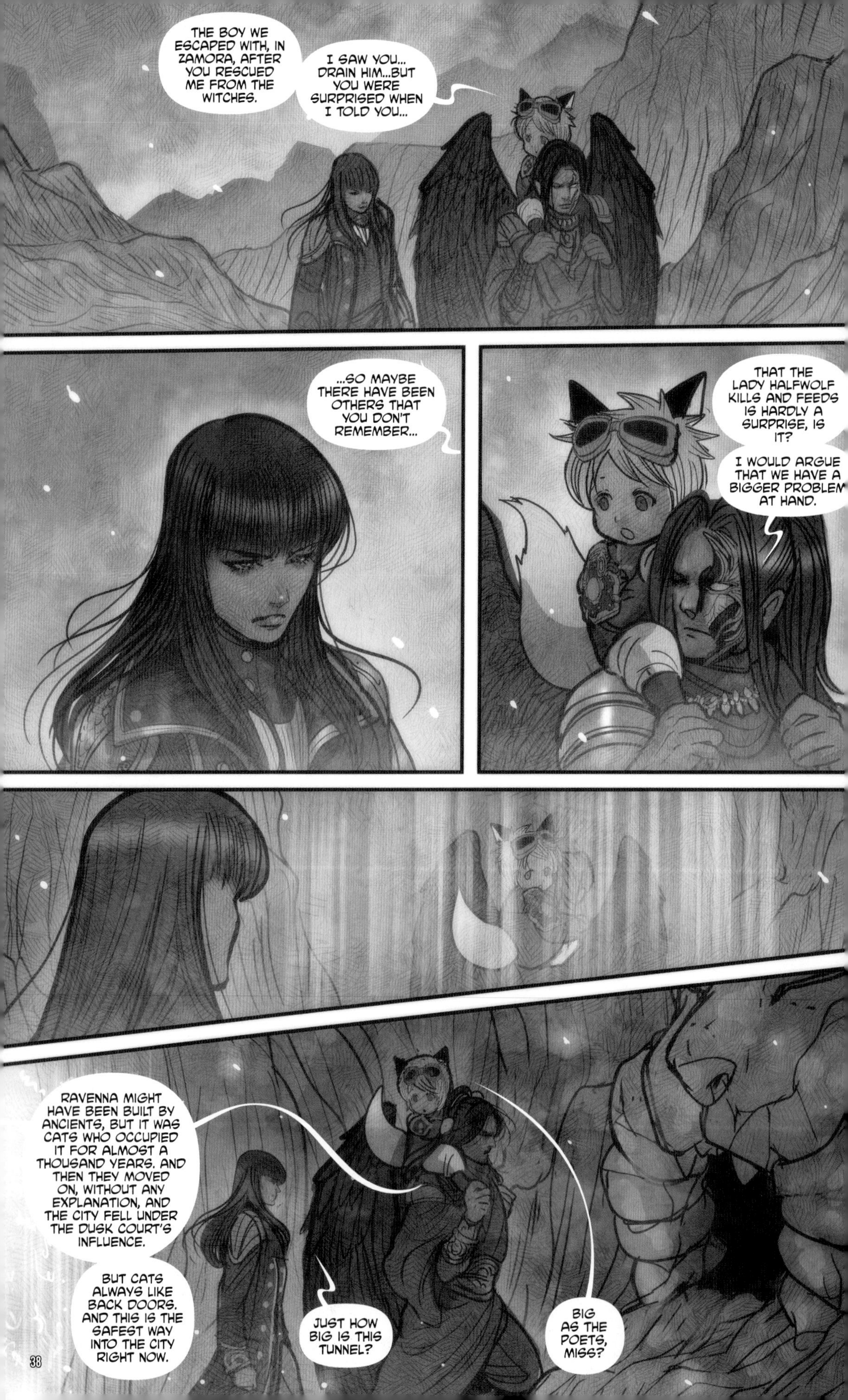
THE BOY WE ESCAPED WITH, IN ZAMORA, AFTER YOU RESCUED ME FROM THE WITCHES.
I SAW YOU... DRAIN HIM...BUT YOU WERE SURPRISED WHEN I TOLD YOU...
...SO MAYBE THERE HAVE BEEN OTHERS THAT YOU DON'T REMEMBER...
THAT THE LADY HALFWOLF KILLS AND FEEDS IS HARDLY A SURPRISE, IS IT?
I WOULD ARGUE THAT WE HAVE A BIGGER PROBLEM AT HAND.
RAVENNA MIGHT HAVE BEEN BUILT BY ANCIENTS, BUT IT WAS CATS WHO OCCUPIED IT FOR ALMOST A THOUSAND YEARS. AND THEN THEY MOVED ON, WITHOUT ANY EXPLANATION, AND THE CITY FELL UNDER THE DUSK COURT'S INFLUENCE.
BUT CATS ALWAYS LIKE BACK DOORS. AND THIS IS THE SAFEST WAY INTO THE CITY RIGHT NOW.
JUST HOW BIG IS THIS TUNNEL?
BIG AS THE POETS, MISS?

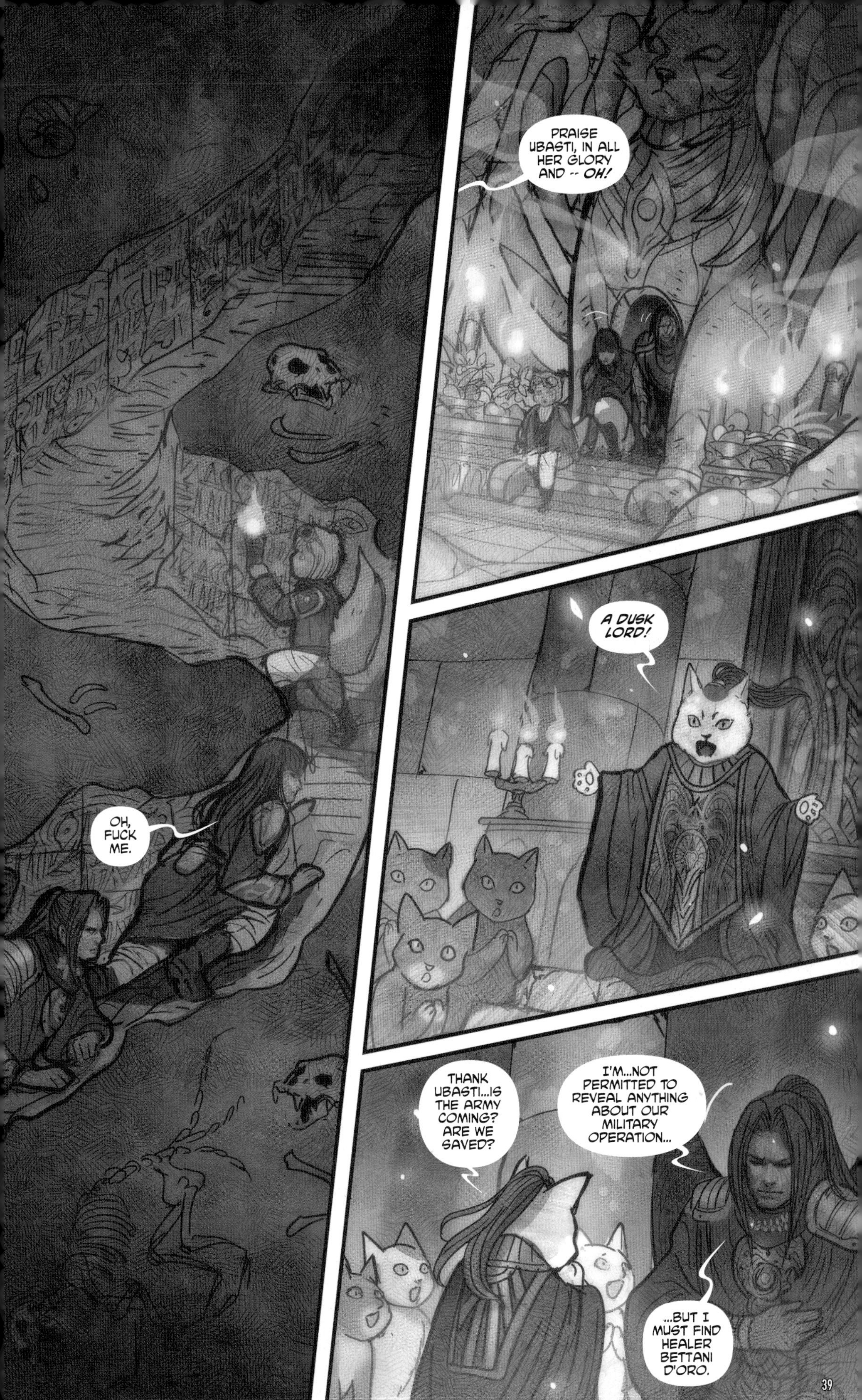
OH, FUCK ME.
PRAISE UBASTI, IN ALL HER GLORY AND -- *OH!*
A DUSK LORD!
THANK UBASTI...IS THE ARMY COMING? ARE WE SAVED?
I'M...NOT PERMITTED TO REVEAL ANYTHING ABOUT OUR MILITARY OPERATION...
...BUT I MUST FIND HEALER BETTANI D'ORO.

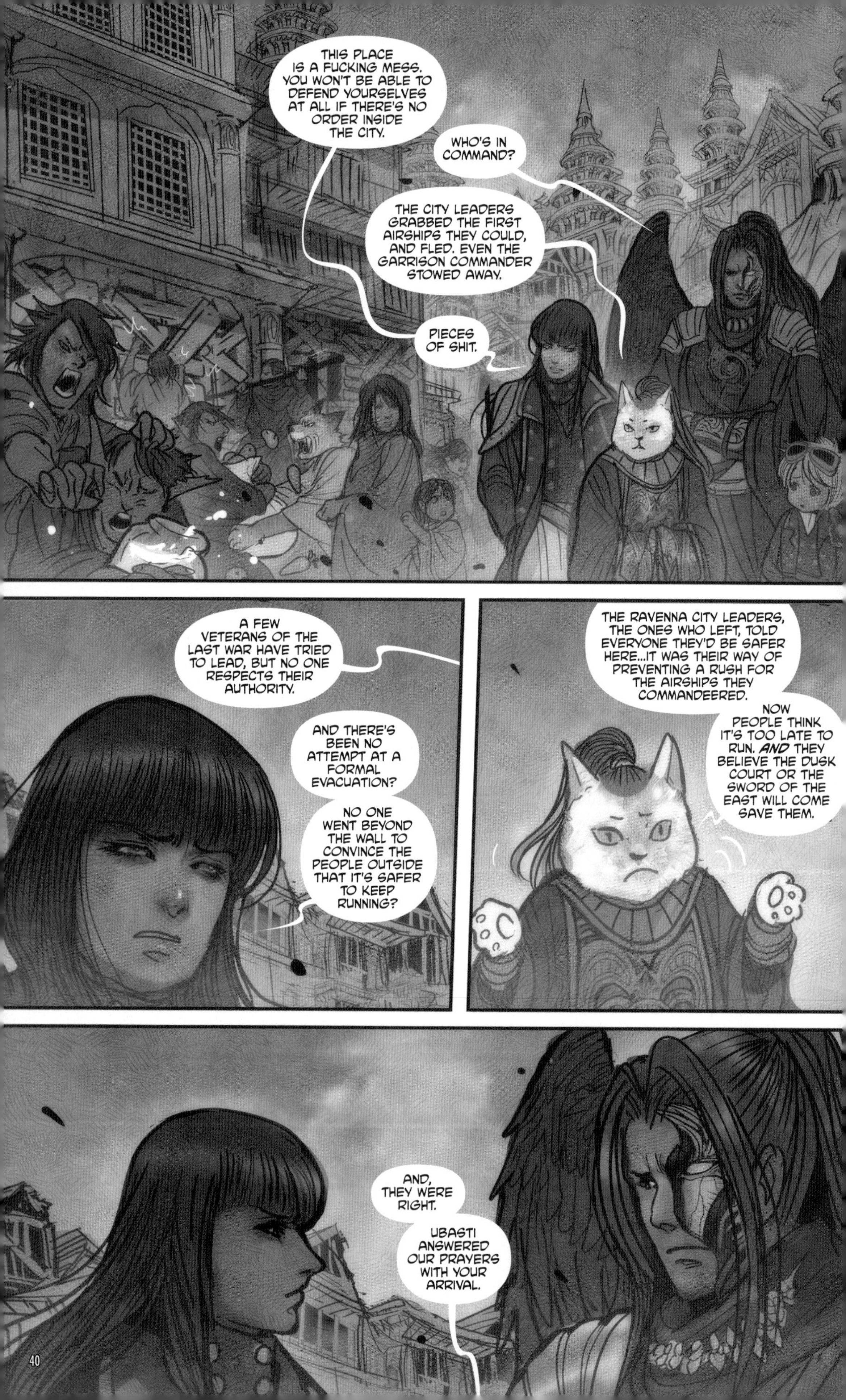

THIS PLACE IS A FUCKING MESS. YOU WON'T BE ABLE TO DEFEND YOURSELVES AT ALL IF THERE'S NO ORDER INSIDE THE CITY.
WHO'S IN COMMAND?
THE CITY LEADERS GRABBED THE FIRST AIRSHIPS THEY COULD, AND FLED. EVEN THE GARRISON COMMANDER STOWED AWAY.
PIECES OF SHIT.
A FEW VETERANS OF THE LAST WAR HAVE TRIED TO LEAD, BUT NO ONE RESPECTS THEIR AUTHORITY.
AND THERE'S BEEN NO ATTEMPT AT A FORMAL EVACUATION?
NO ONE WENT BEYOND THE WALL TO CONVINCE THE PEOPLE OUTSIDE THAT IT'S SAFER TO KEEP RUNNING?
THE RAVENNA CITY LEADERS, THE ONES WHO LEFT, TOLD EVERYONE THEY'D BE SAFER HERE...IT WAS THEIR WAY OF PREVENTING A RUSH FOR THE AIRSHIPS THEY COMMANDEERED.
NOW PEOPLE THINK IT'S TOO LATE TO RUN. *AND* THEY BELIEVE THE DUSK COURT OR THE SWORD OF THE EAST WILL COME SAVE THEM.
AND, THEY WERE RIGHT.
UBASTI ANSWERED OUR PRAYERS WITH YOUR ARRIVAL.

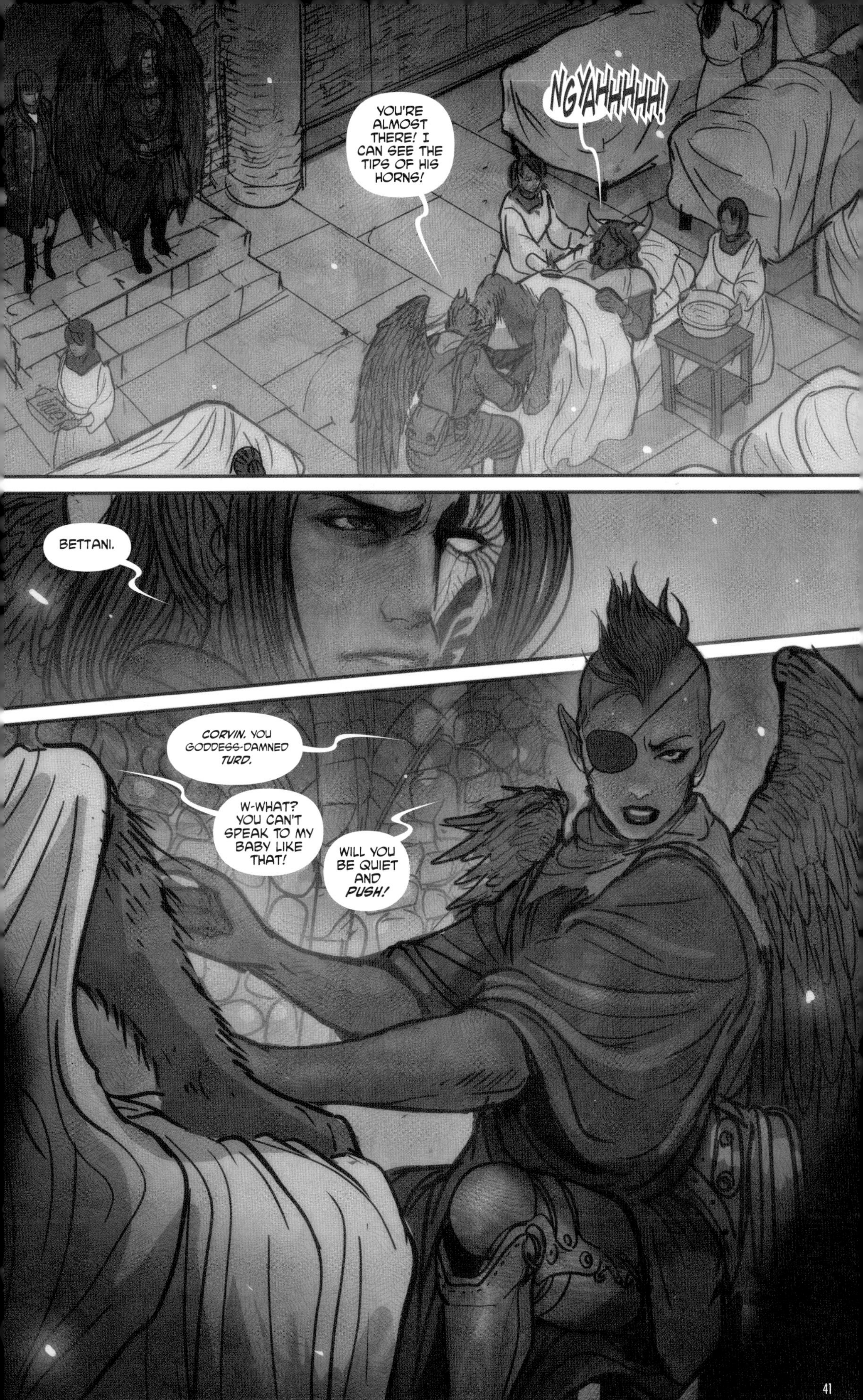

YOU'RE ALMOST THERE! I CAN SEE THE TIPS OF HIS HORNS!
NGYAHHHHH!
BETTANI.
CORVIN, YOU GODDESS-DAMNED *TURD*.
W-WHAT? YOU CAN'T SPEAK TO MY BABY LIKE THAT!
WILL YOU BE QUIET AND *PUSH!*

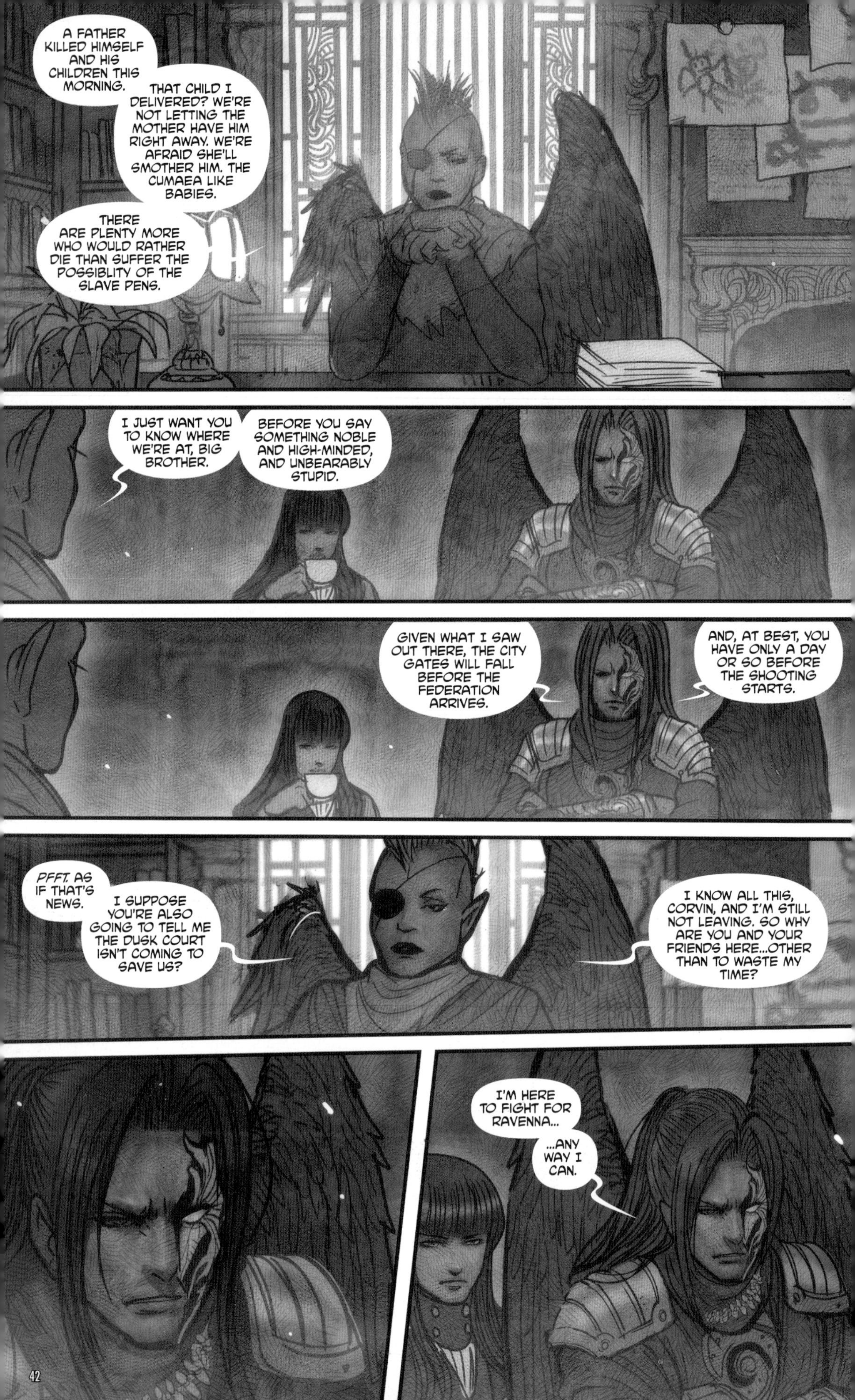
A FATHER KILLED HIMSELF AND HIS CHILDREN THIS MORNING.
THAT CHILD I DELIVERED? WE'RE NOT LETTING THE MOTHER HAVE HIM RIGHT AWAY. WE'RE AFRAID SHE'LL SMOTHER HIM. THE CUMAEA LIKE BABIES.
THERE ARE PLENTY MORE WHO WOULD RATHER DIE THAN SUFFER THE POSSIBLITY OF THE SLAVE PENS.
I JUST WANT YOU TO KNOW WHERE WE'RE AT, BIG BROTHER.
BEFORE YOU SAY SOMETHING NOBLE AND HIGH-MINDED, AND UNBEARABLY STUPID.
GIVEN WHAT I SAW OUT THERE, THE CITY GATES WILL FALL BEFORE THE FEDERATION ARRIVES.
AND, AT BEST, YOU HAVE ONLY A DAY OR SO BEFORE THE SHOOTING STARTS.
PFFT. AS IF THAT'S NEWS.
I SUPPOSE YOU'RE ALSO GOING TO TELL ME THE DUSK COURT ISN'T COMING TO SAVE US?
I KNOW ALL THIS, CORVIN, AND I'M STILL NOT LEAVING. SO WHY ARE YOU AND YOUR FRIENDS HERE...OTHER THAN TO WASTE MY TIME?
I'M HERE TO FIGHT FOR RAVENNA...
...ANY WAY I CAN.

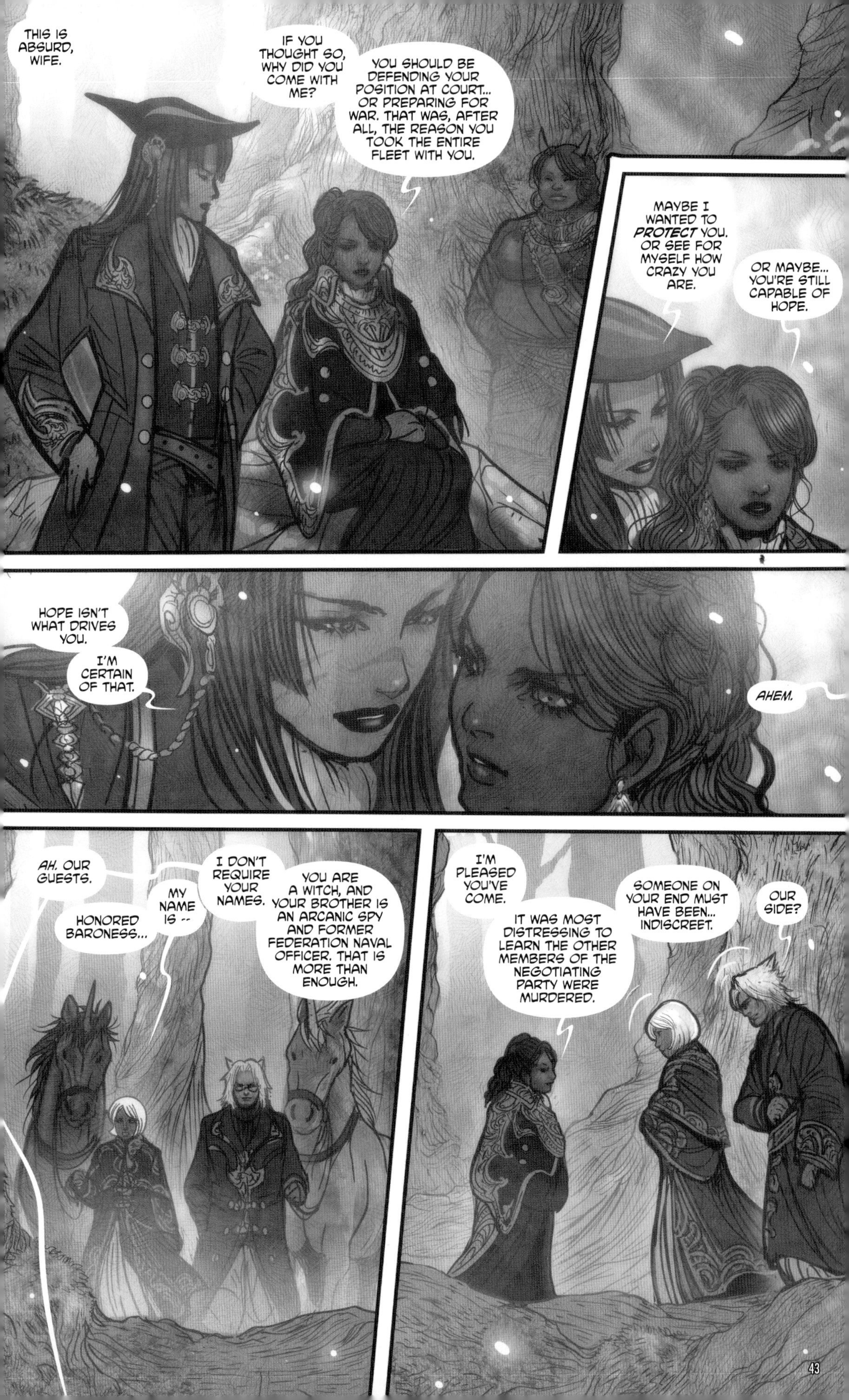

THIS IS ABSURD, WIFE.
IF YOU THOUGHT SO, WHY DID YOU COME WITH ME?
YOU SHOULD BE DEFENDING YOUR POSITION AT COURT... OR PREPARING FOR WAR. THAT WAS, AFTER ALL, THE REASON YOU TOOK THE ENTIRE FLEET WITH YOU.
MAYBE I WANTED TO *PROTECT* YOU. OR SEE FOR MYSELF HOW CRAZY YOU ARE.
OR MAYBE... YOU'RE STILL CAPABLE OF HOPE.
HOPE ISN'T WHAT DRIVES YOU.
I'M CERTAIN OF THAT.
AHEM.
AH. OUR GUESTS.
HONORED BARONESS...
MY NAME IS --
I DON'T REQUIRE YOUR NAMES.
YOU ARE A WITCH, AND YOUR BROTHER IS AN ARCANIC SPY AND FORMER FEDERATION NAVAL OFFICER. THAT IS MORE THAN ENOUGH.
I'M PLEASED YOU'VE COME.
IT WAS MOST DISTRESSING TO LEARN THE OTHER MEMBERS OF THE NEGOTIATING PARTY WERE MURDERED.
SOMEONE ON YOUR END MUST HAVE BEEN... INDISCREET.
OUR SIDE?

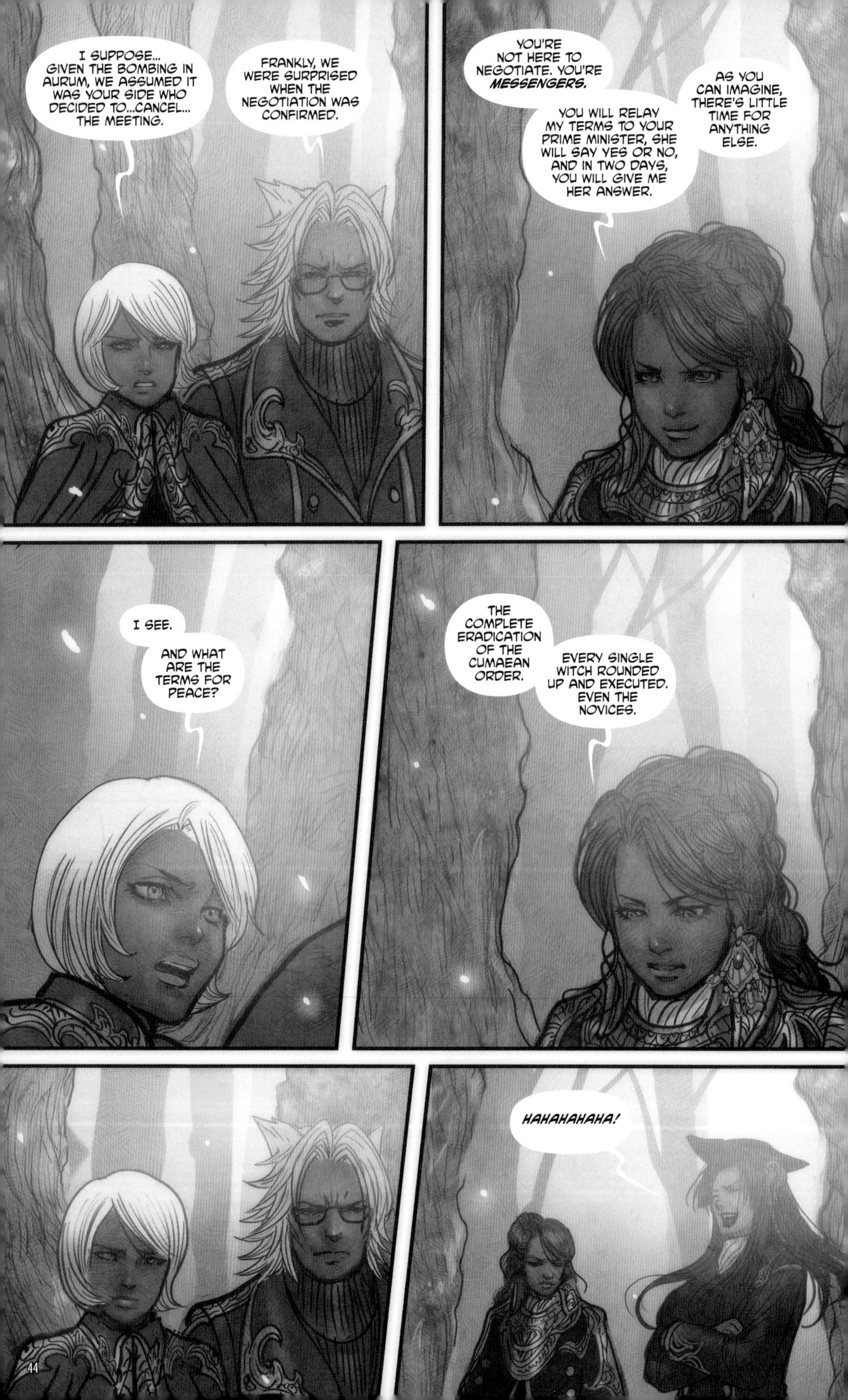
I SUPPOSE... GIVEN THE BOMBING IN AURUM, WE ASSUMED IT WAS YOUR SIDE WHO DECIDED TO...CANCEL... THE MEETING.
FRANKLY, WE WERE SURPRISED WHEN THE NEGOTIATION WAS CONFIRMED.
YOU'RE NOT HERE TO NEGOTIATE. YOU'RE *MESSENGERS.*
YOU WILL RELAY MY TERMS TO YOUR PRIME MINISTER, SHE WILL SAY YES OR NO, AND IN TWO DAYS, YOU WILL GIVE ME HER ANSWER.
AS YOU CAN IMAGINE, THERE'S LITTLE TIME FOR ANYTHING ELSE.
I SEE.
AND WHAT ARE THE TERMS FOR PEACE?
THE COMPLETE ERADICATION OF THE CUMAEAN ORDER.
EVERY SINGLE WITCH ROUNDED UP AND EXECUTED. EVEN THE NOVICES.
HAHAHAHAHA!

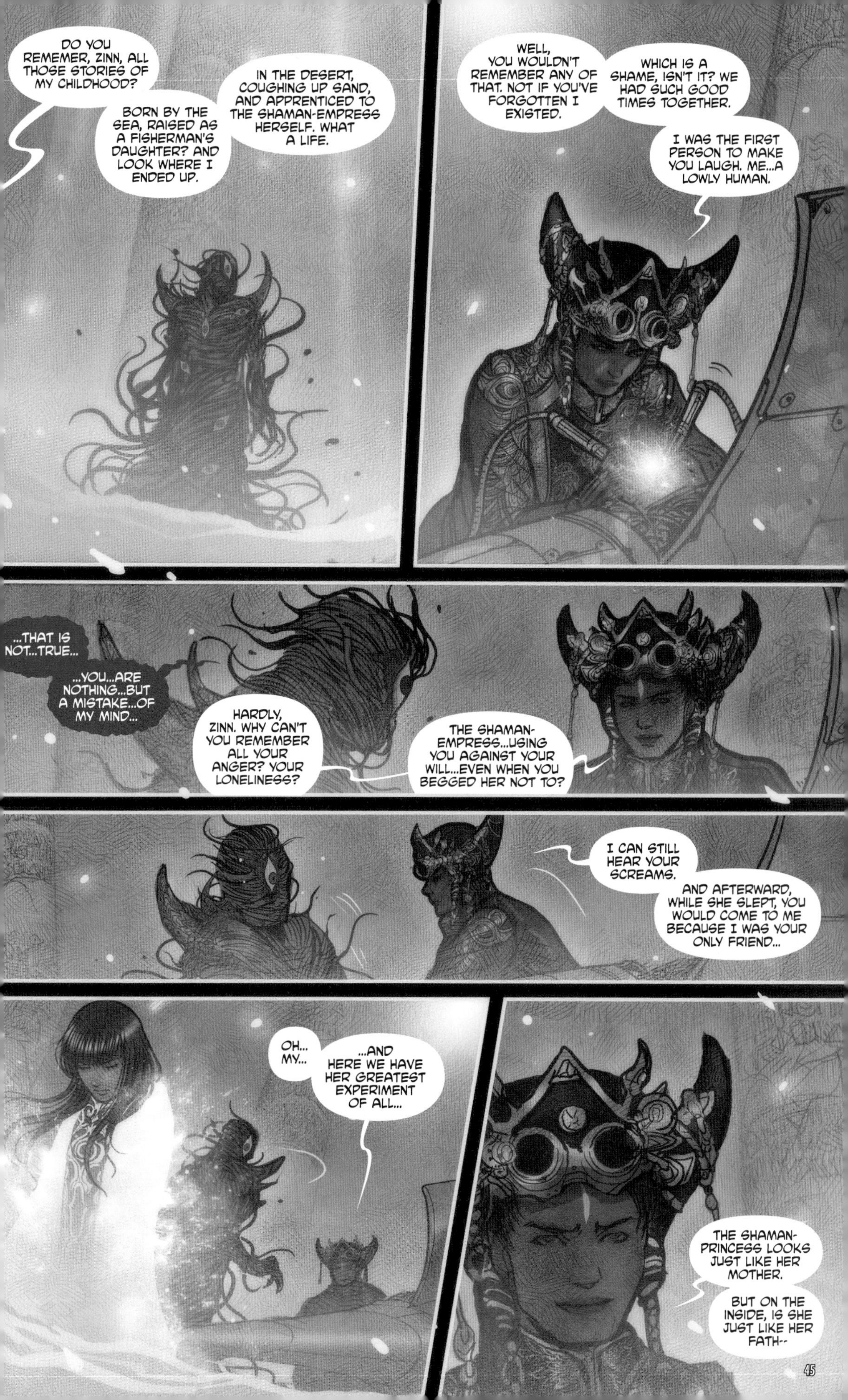
DO YOU REMEMER, ZINN, ALL THOSE STORIES OF MY CHILDHOOD?
BORN BY THE SEA, RAISED AS A FISHERMAN'S DAUGHTER? AND LOOK WHERE I ENDED UP.
IN THE DESERT, COUGHING UP SAND, AND APPRENTICED TO THE SHAMAN-EMPRESS HERSELF. WHAT A LIFE.
WELL, YOU WOULDN'T REMEMBER ANY OF THAT. NOT IF YOU'VE FORGOTTEN I EXISTED.
WHICH IS A SHAME, ISN'T IT? WE HAD SUCH GOOD TIMES TOGETHER.
I WAS THE FIRST PERSON TO MAKE YOU LAUGH. ME...A LOWLY HUMAN.
...THAT IS NOT...TRUE...
...YOU...ARE NOTHING...BUT A MISTAKE...OF MY MIND...
HARDLY, ZINN. WHY CAN'T YOU REMEMBER ALL YOUR ANGER? YOUR LONELINESS?
THE SHAMAN-EMPRESS...USING YOU AGAINST YOUR WILL...EVEN WHEN YOU BEGGED HER NOT TO?
I CAN STILL HEAR YOUR SCREAMS.
AND AFTERWARD, WHILE SHE SLEPT, YOU WOULD COME TO ME BECAUSE I WAS YOUR ONLY FRIEND...
OH... MY...
...AND HERE WE HAVE HER GREATEST EXPERIMENT OF ALL...
THE SHAMAN-PRINCESS LOOKS JUST LIKE HER MOTHER.
BUT ON THE INSIDE, IS SHE JUST LIKE HER FATH--

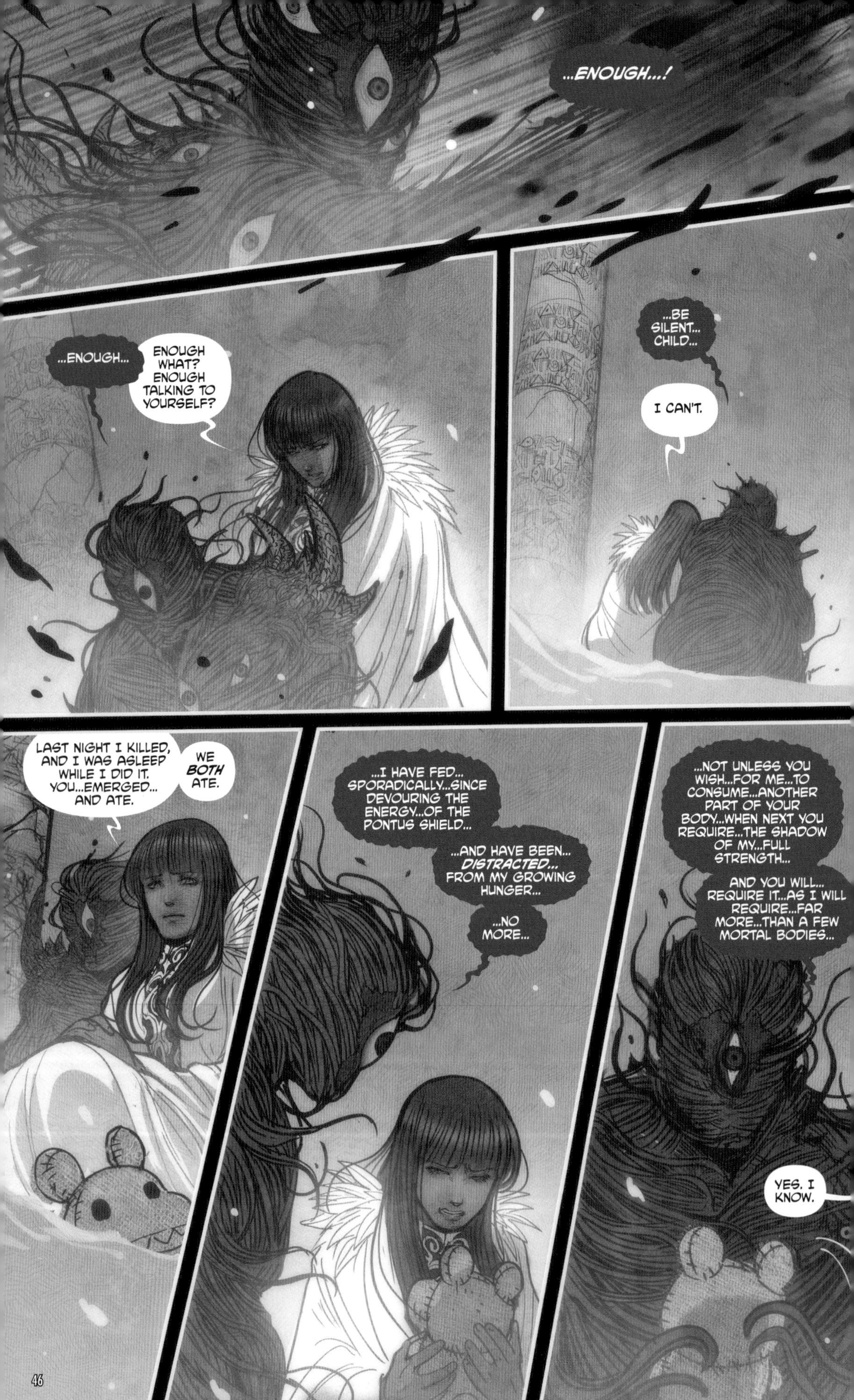
...ENOUGH...!
...ENOUGH...
ENOUGH WHAT? ENOUGH TALKING TO YOURSELF?
...BE SILENT... CHILD...
I CAN'T.
LAST NIGHT I KILLED, AND I WAS ASLEEP WHILE I DID IT. YOU...EMERGED... AND ATE.
WE BOTH ATE.
...I HAVE FED... SPORADICALLY...SINCE DEVOURING THE ENERGY...OF THE PONTUS SHIELD...
...AND HAVE BEEN... DISTRACTED... FROM MY GROWING HUNGER...
...NO MORE...
...NOT UNLESS YOU WISH...FOR ME...TO CONSUME...ANOTHER PART OF YOUR BODY...WHEN NEXT YOU REQUIRE...THE SHADOW OF MY...FULL STRENGTH...
AND YOU WILL... REQUIRE IT...AS I WILL REQUIRE...FAR MORE...THAN A FEW MORTAL BODIES...
YES. I KNOW.

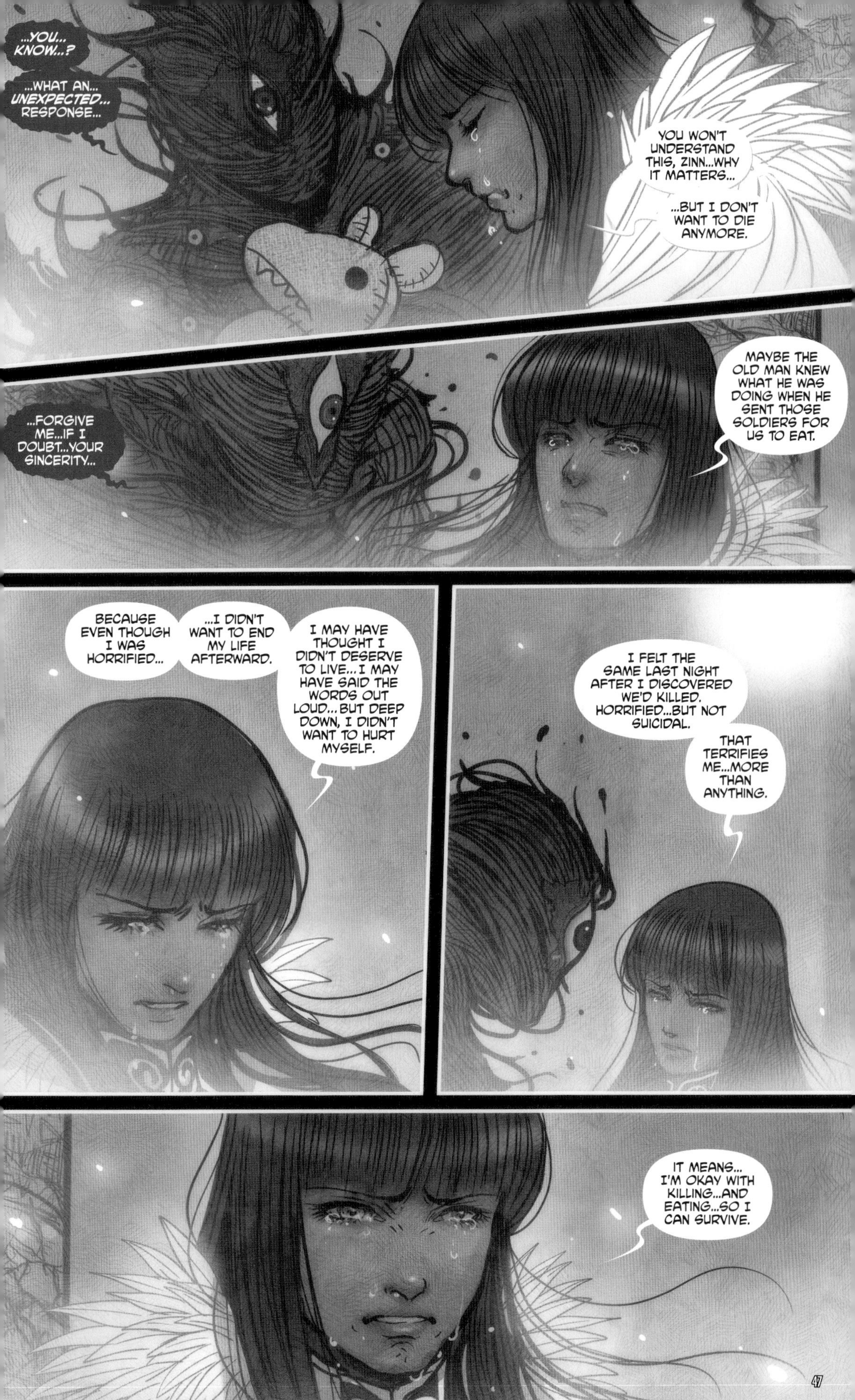
...YOU... KNOW...?
...WHAT AN... UNEXPECTED... RESPONSE...
YOU WON'T UNDERSTAND THIS, ZINN...WHY IT MATTERS...
...BUT I DON'T WANT TO DIE ANYMORE.
...FORGIVE ME...IF I DOUBT...YOUR SINCERITY...
MAYBE THE OLD MAN KNEW WHAT HE WAS DOING WHEN HE SENT THOSE SOLDIERS FOR US TO EAT.
BECAUSE EVEN THOUGH I WAS HORRIFIED...
...I DIDN'T WANT TO END MY LIFE AFTERWARD.
I MAY HAVE THOUGHT I DIDN'T DESERVE TO LIVE...I MAY HAVE SAID THE WORDS OUT LOUD...BUT DEEP DOWN, I DIDN'T WANT TO HURT MYSELF.
I FELT THE SAME LAST NIGHT AFTER I DISCOVERED WE'D KILLED. HORRIFIED...BUT NOT SUICIDAL.
THAT TERRIFIES ME...MORE THAN ANYTHING.
IT MEANS... I'M OKAY WITH KILLING...AND EATING...SO I CAN SURVIVE.

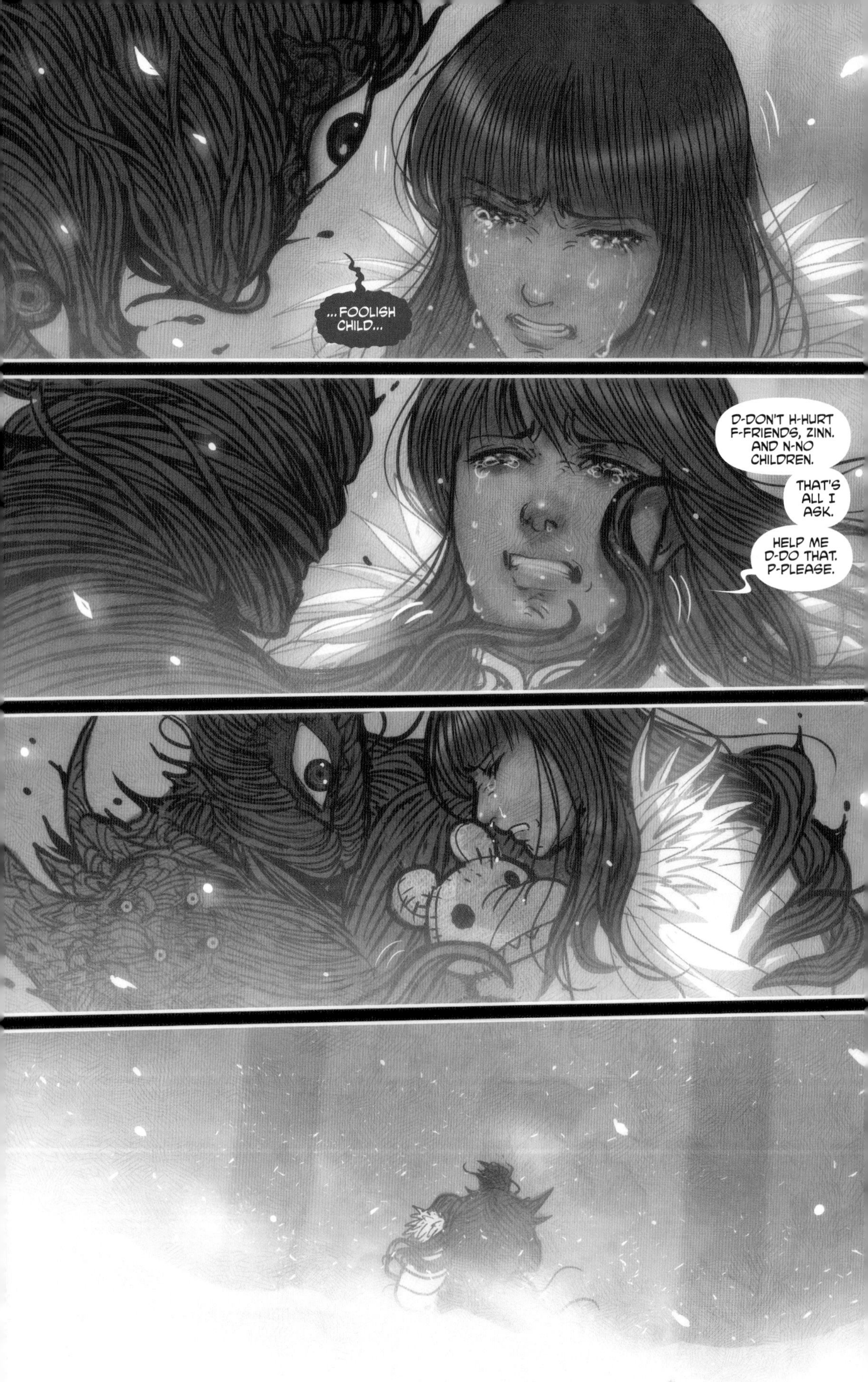
...FOOLISH CHILD...
D-DON'T H-HURT F-FRIENDS, ZINN. AND N-NO CHILDREN.
THAT'S ALL I ASK.
HELP ME D-DO THAT. P-PLEASE.

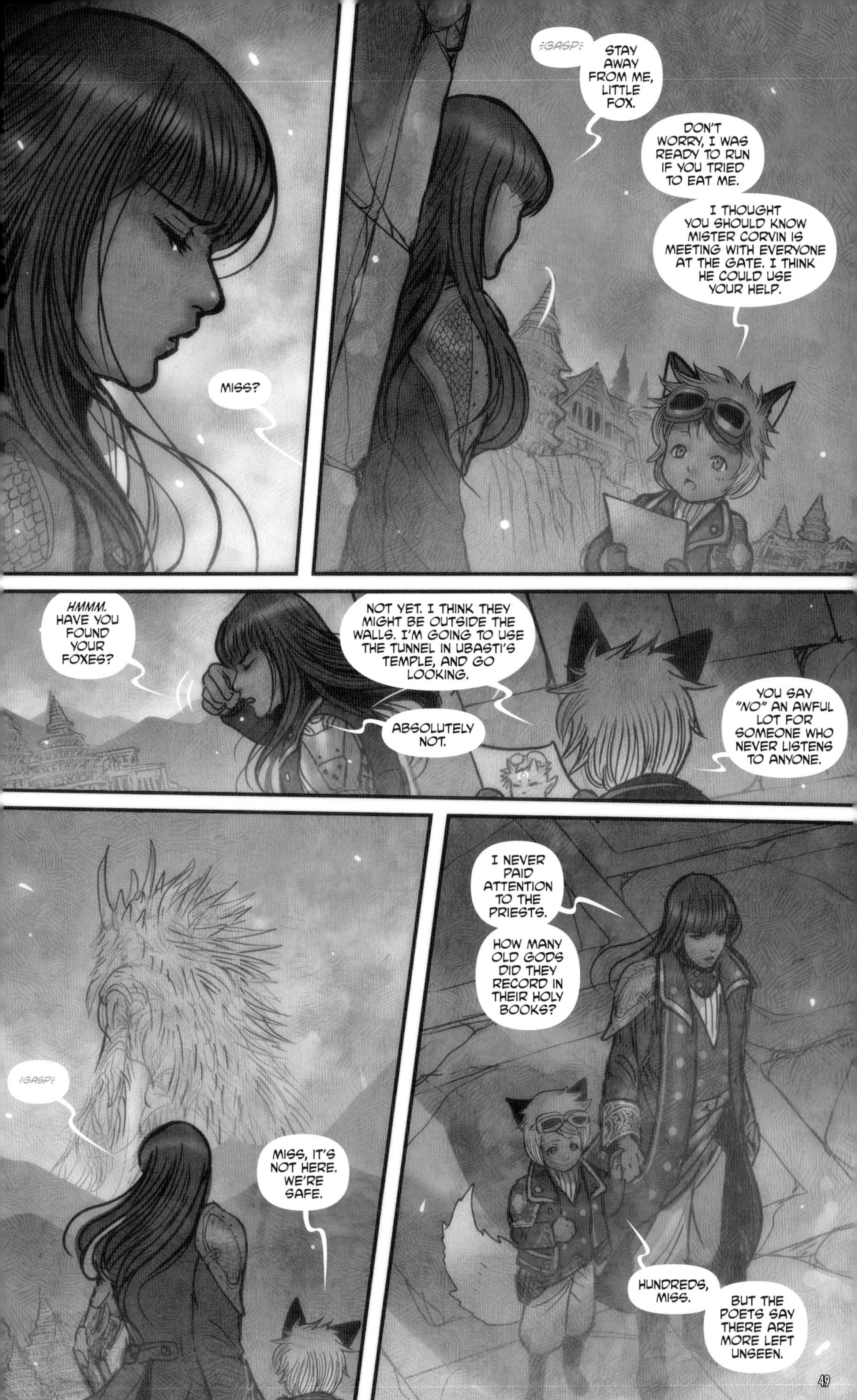
MISS?
GASP
STAY AWAY FROM ME, LITTLE FOX.
DON'T WORRY, I WAS READY TO RUN IF YOU TRIED TO EAT ME.
I THOUGHT YOU SHOULD KNOW MISTER CORVIN IS MEETING WITH EVERYONE AT THE GATE. I THINK HE COULD USE YOUR HELP.
HMMM. HAVE YOU FOUND YOUR FOXES?
NOT YET. I THINK THEY MIGHT BE OUTSIDE THE WALLS. I'M GOING TO USE THE TUNNEL IN UBASTI'S TEMPLE, AND GO LOOKING.
ABSOLUTELY NOT.
YOU SAY "NO" AN AWFUL LOT FOR SOMEONE WHO NEVER LISTENS TO ANYONE.
GASP
MISS, IT'S NOT HERE. WE'RE SAFE.
I NEVER PAID ATTENTION TO THE PRIESTS.
HOW MANY OLD GODS DID THEY RECORD IN THEIR HOLY BOOKS?
HUNDREDS, MISS.
BUT THE POETS SAY THERE ARE MORE LEFT UNSEEN.

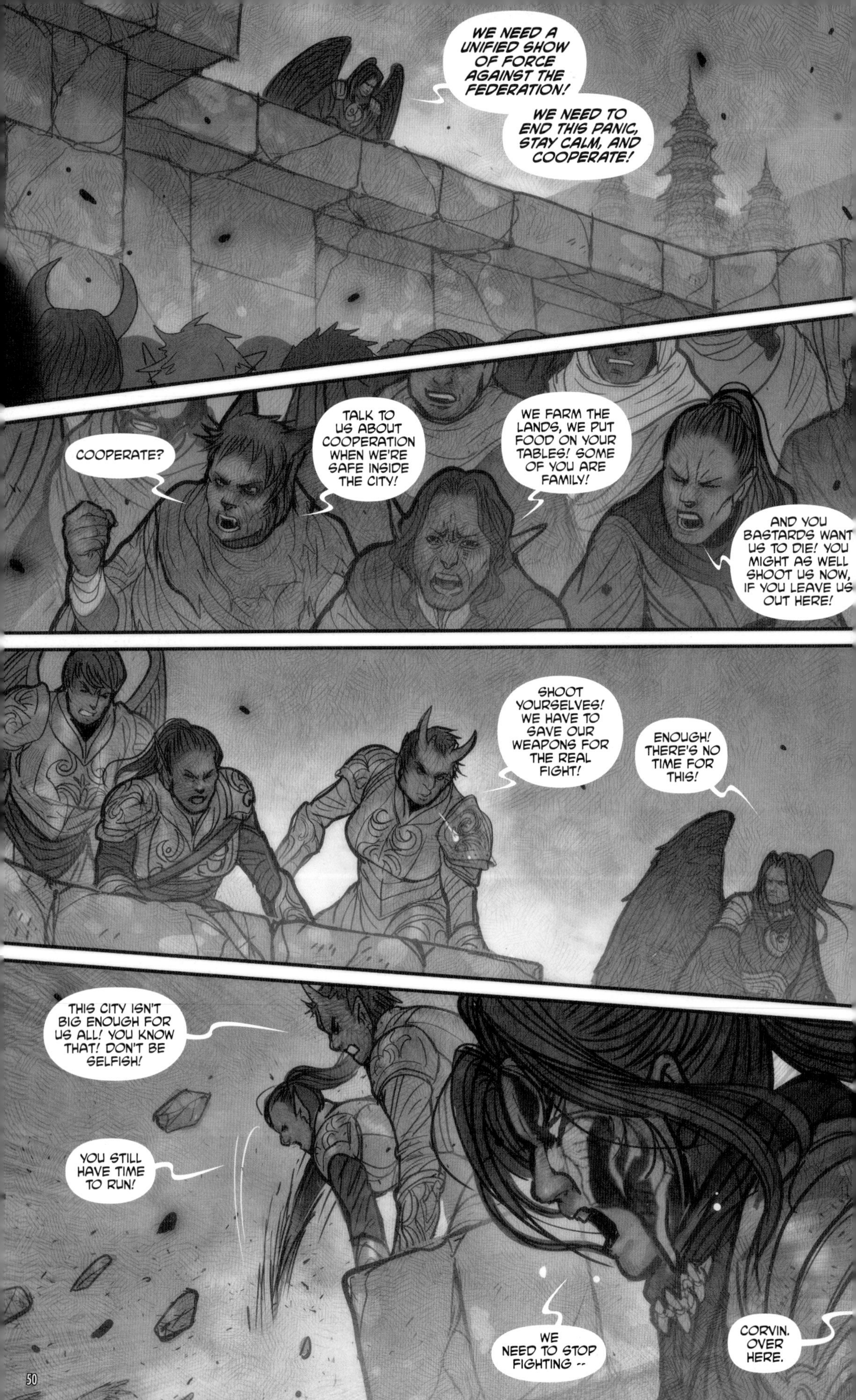
WE NEED A UNIFIED SHOW OF FORCE AGAINST THE FEDERATION!
WE NEED TO END THIS PANIC, STAY CALM, AND COOPERATE!
COOPERATE?
TALK TO US ABOUT COOPERATION WHEN WE'RE SAFE INSIDE THE CITY!
WE FARM THE LANDS, WE PUT FOOD ON YOUR TABLES! SOME OF YOU ARE FAMILY!
AND YOU BASTARDS WANT US TO DIE! YOU MIGHT AS WELL SHOOT US NOW, IF YOU LEAVE US OUT HERE!
SHOOT YOURSELVES! WE HAVE TO SAVE OUR WEAPONS FOR THE REAL FIGHT!
ENOUGH! THERE'S NO TIME FOR THIS!
THIS CITY ISN'T BIG ENOUGH FOR US ALL! YOU KNOW THAT! DON'T BE SELFISH!
YOU STILL HAVE TIME TO RUN!
WE NEED TO STOP FIGHTING --
CORVIN. OVER HERE.

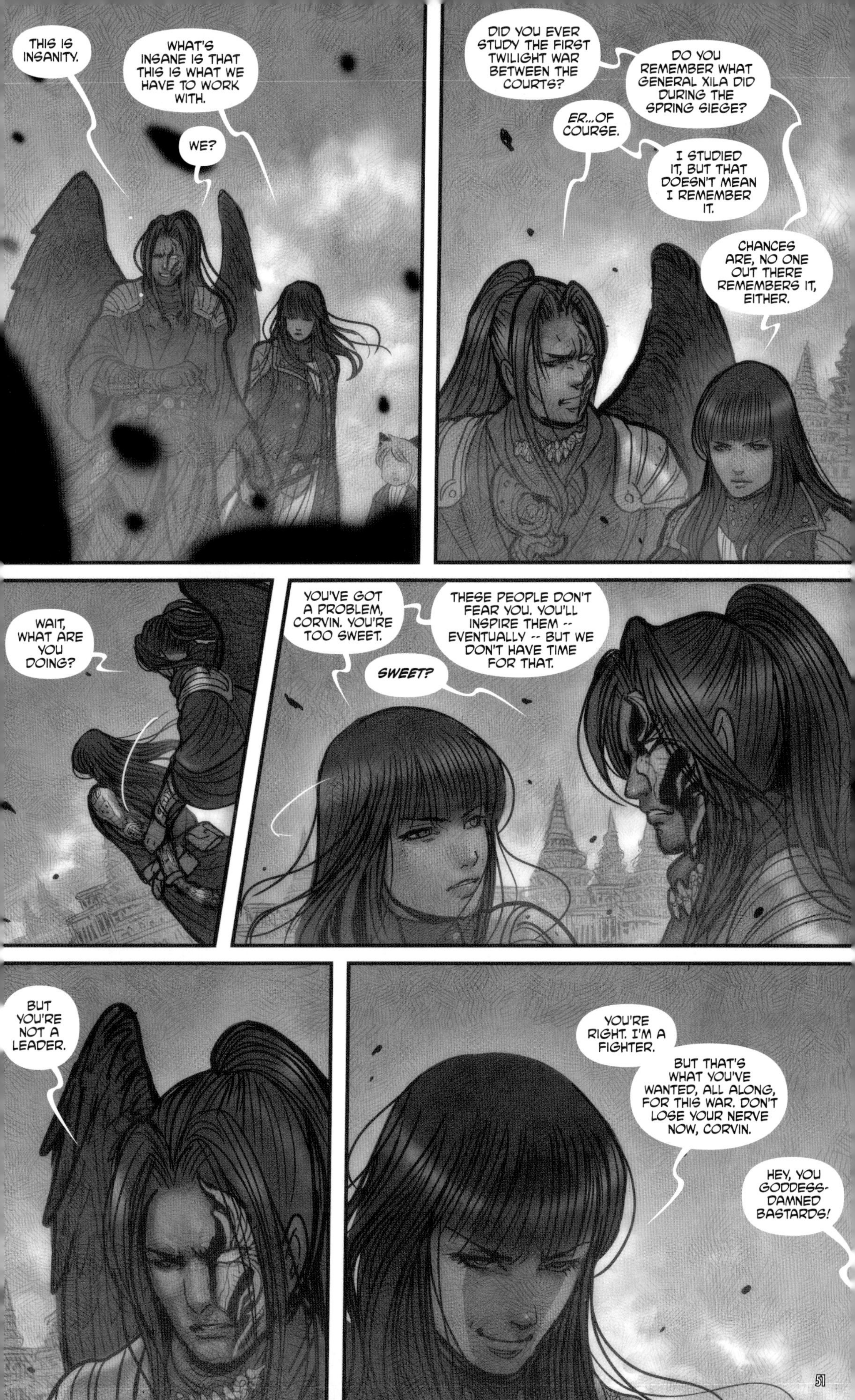
THIS IS INSANITY.
WHAT'S INSANE IS THAT THIS IS WHAT WE HAVE TO WORK WITH.
WE?
DID YOU EVER STUDY THE FIRST TWILIGHT WAR BETWEEN THE COURTS?
DO YOU REMEMBER WHAT GENERAL XILA DID DURING THE SPRING SIEGE?
ER...OF COURSE.
I STUDIED IT, BUT THAT DOESN'T MEAN I REMEMBER IT.
CHANCES ARE, NO ONE OUT THERE REMEMBERS IT, EITHER.
WAIT, WHAT ARE YOU DOING?
YOU'VE GOT A PROBLEM, CORVIN. YOU'RE TOO SWEET.
THESE PEOPLE DON'T FEAR YOU. YOU'LL INSPIRE THEM -- EVENTUALLY -- BUT WE DON'T HAVE TIME FOR THAT.
SWEET?
BUT YOU'RE NOT A LEADER.
YOU'RE RIGHT. I'M A FIGHTER.
BUT THAT'S WHAT YOU'VE WANTED, ALL ALONG, FOR THIS WAR. DON'T LOSE YOUR NERVE NOW, CORVIN.
HEY, YOU GODDESS-DAMNED BASTARDS!

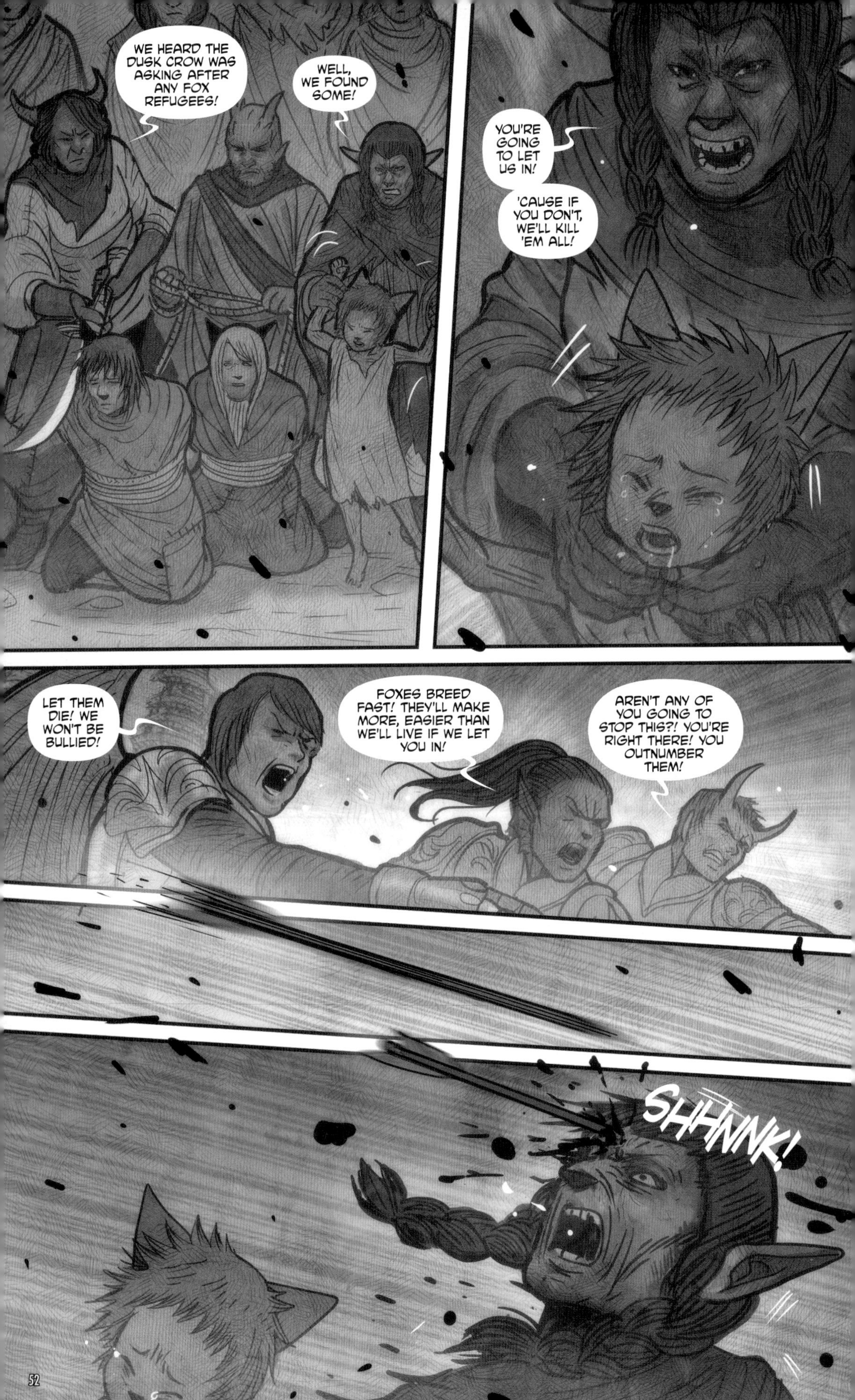
WE HEARD THE DUSK CROW WAS ASKING AFTER ANY FOX REFUGEES!
WELL, WE FOUND SOME!
YOU'RE GOING TO LET US IN!
'CAUSE IF YOU DON'T, WE'LL KILL 'EM ALL!
LET THEM DIE! WE WON'T BE BULLIED!
FOXES BREED FAST! THEY'LL MAKE MORE, EASIER THAN WE'LL LIVE IF WE LET YOU IN!
AREN'T ANY OF YOU GOING TO STOP THIS?! YOU'RE RIGHT THERE! YOU OUTNUMBER THEM!
SHHNNK!

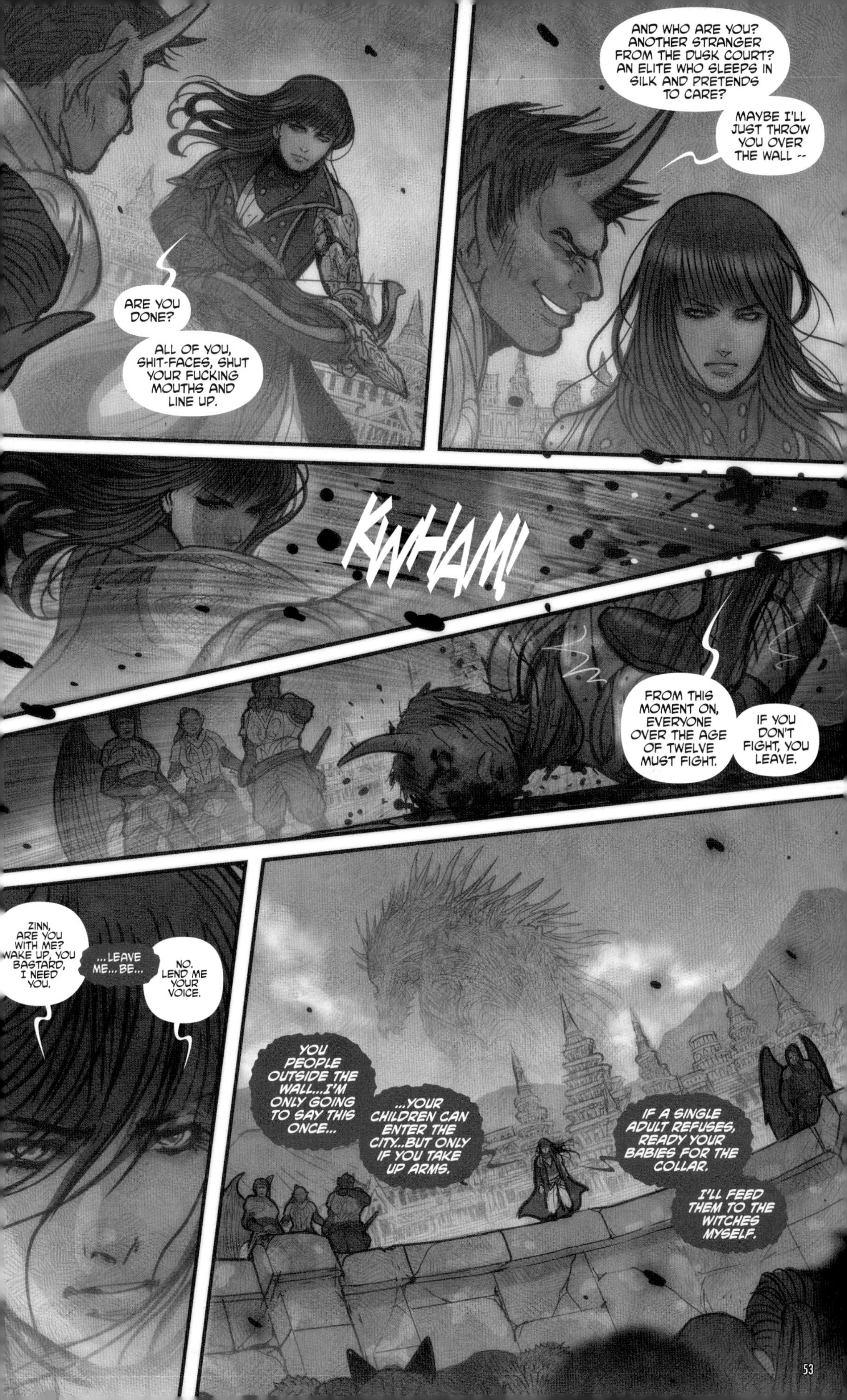
ARE YOU DONE?
ALL OF YOU, SHIT-FACES, SHUT YOUR FUCKING MOUTHS AND LINE UP.
AND WHO ARE YOU? ANOTHER STRANGER FROM THE DUSK COURT? AN ELITE WHO SLEEPS IN SILK AND PRETENDS TO CARE?
MAYBE I'LL JUST THROW YOU OVER THE WALL --
KWHAM!
FROM THIS MOMENT ON, EVERYONE OVER THE AGE OF TWELVE MUST FIGHT.
IF YOU DON'T FIGHT, YOU LEAVE.
ZINN, ARE YOU WITH ME? WAKE UP, YOU BASTARD, I NEED YOU.
...LEAVE ME... BE...
NO. LEND ME YOUR VOICE.
YOU PEOPLE OUTSIDE THE WALL...I'M ONLY GOING TO SAY THIS ONCE...
...YOUR CHILDREN CAN ENTER THE CITY...BUT ONLY IF YOU TAKE UP ARMS.
IF A SINGLE ADULT REFUSES, READY YOUR BABIES FOR THE COLLAR.
I'LL FEED THEM TO THE WITCHES MYSELF.

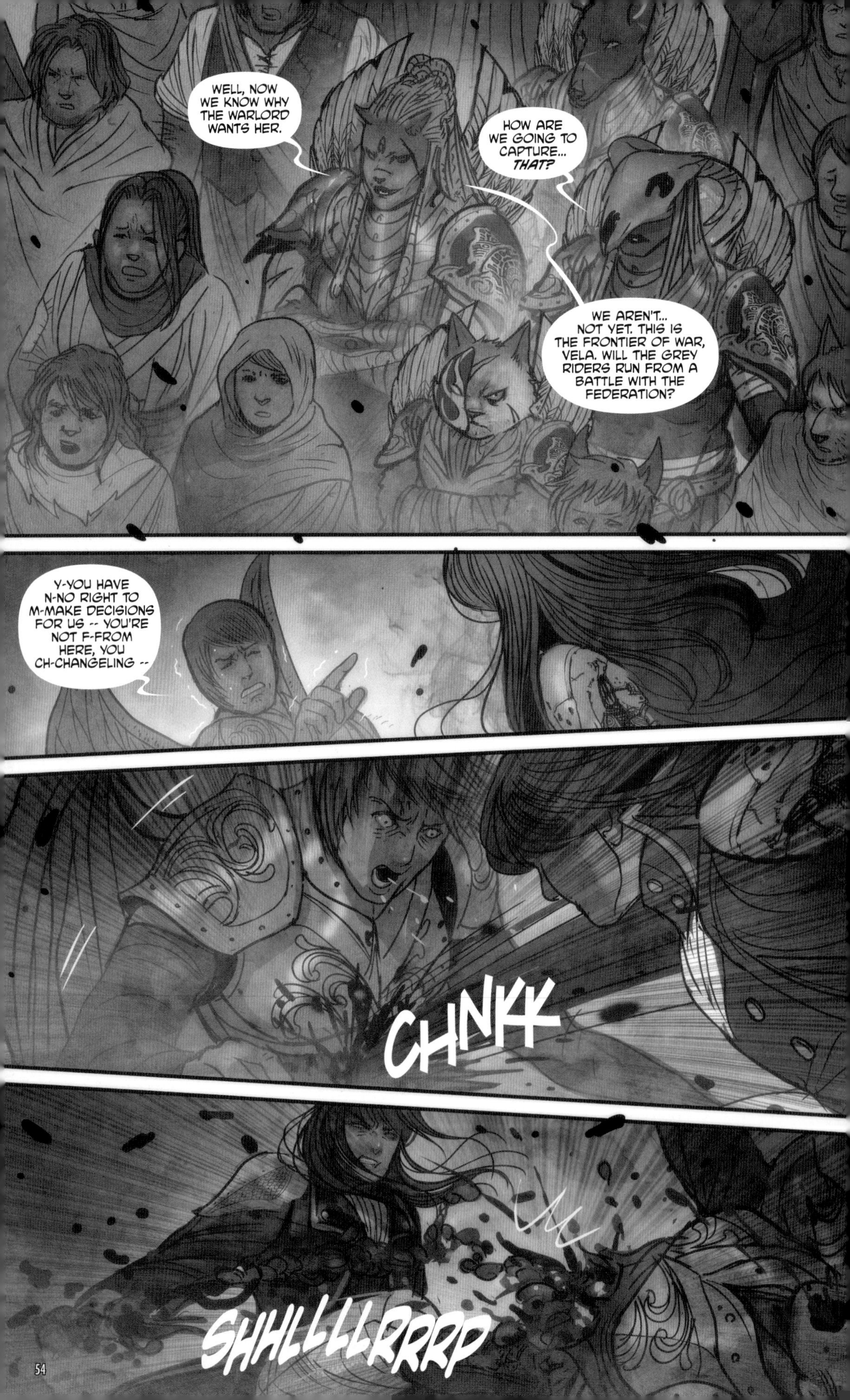
WELL, NOW WE KNOW WHY THE WARLORD WANTS HER.
HOW ARE WE GOING TO CAPTURE... *THAT?*
WE AREN'T... NOT YET. THIS IS THE FRONTIER OF WAR, VELA. WILL THE GREY RIDERS RUN FROM A BATTLE WITH THE FEDERATION?
Y-YOU HAVE N-NO RIGHT TO M-MAKE DECISIONS FOR US -- YOU'RE NOT F-FROM HERE, YOU CH-CHANGELING --
CHNKK
SHHLLLLRRRP

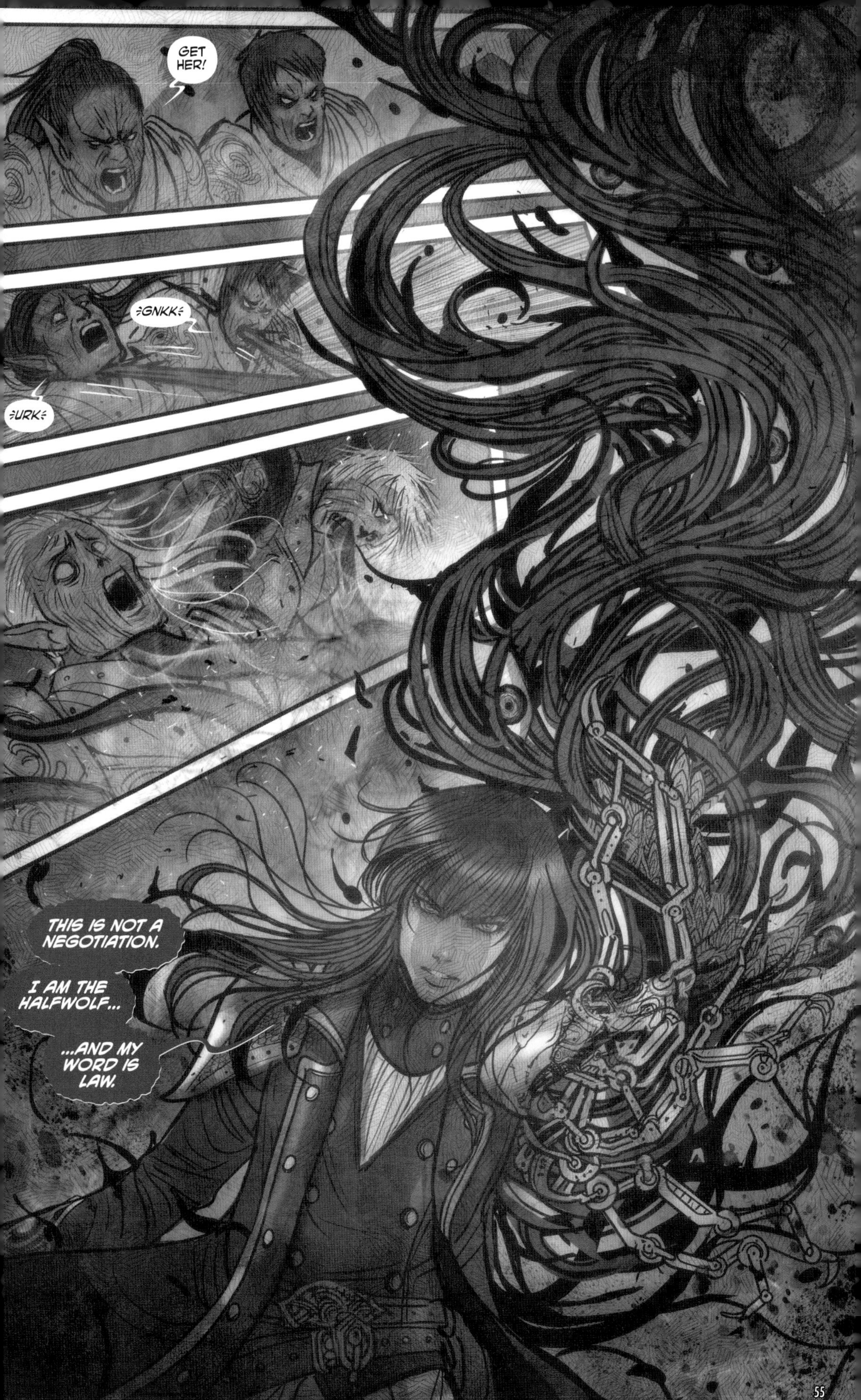
GET HER!
GNKK
URK
THIS IS NOT A NEGOTIATION.
I AM THE HALFWOLF...
...AND MY WORD IS LAW.

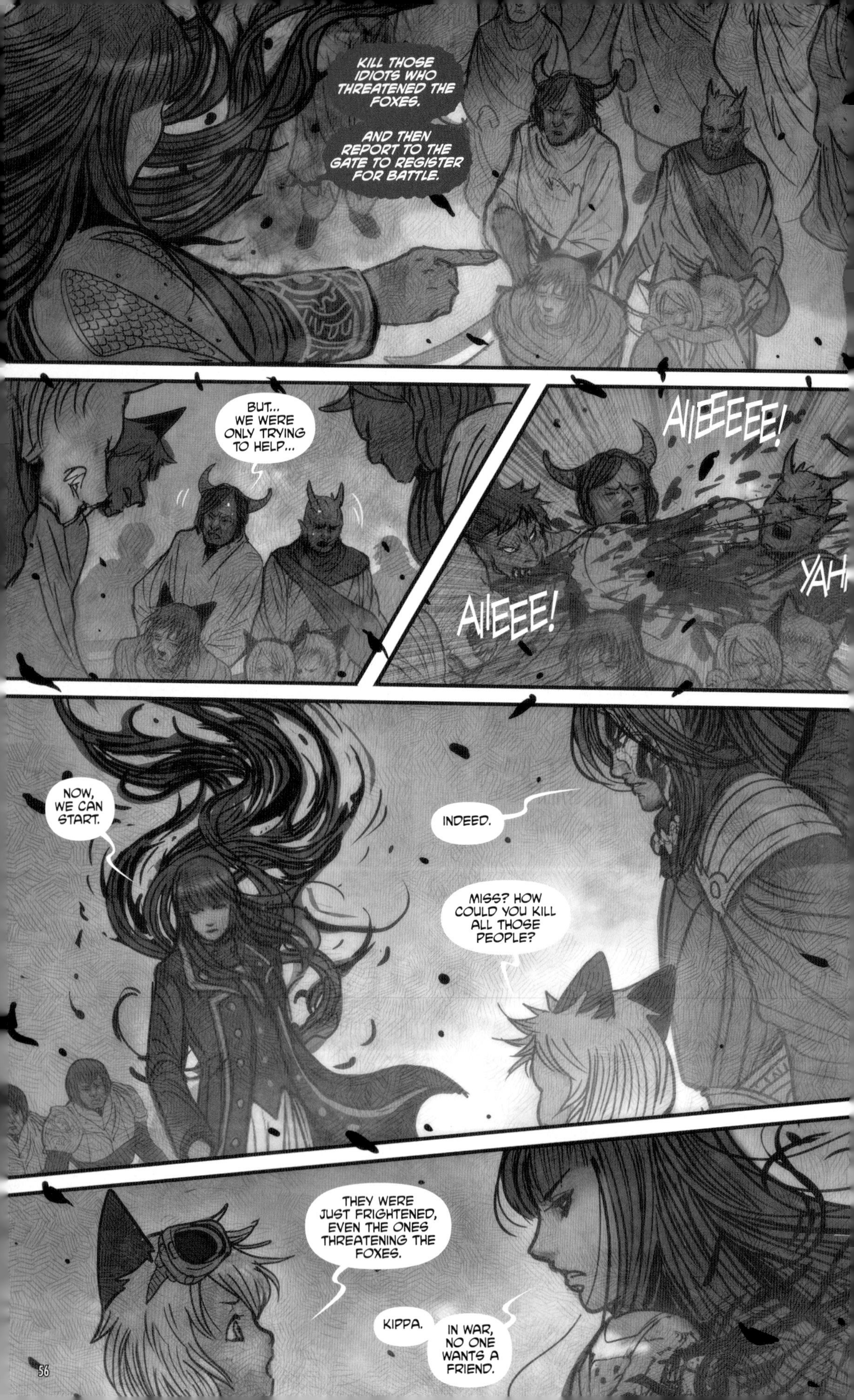
KILL THOSE IDIOTS WHO THREATENED THE FOXES.
AND THEN REPORT TO THE GATE TO REGISTER FOR BATTLE.
BUT... WE WERE ONLY TRYING TO HELP...
AIIEEEEEE!
AIIEEE!
YAH
NOW, WE CAN START.
INDEED.
MISS? HOW COULD YOU KILL ALL THOSE PEOPLE?
THEY WERE JUST FRIGHTENED, EVEN THE ONES THREATENING THE FOXES.
KIPPA.
IN WAR, NO ONE WANTS A FRIEND.

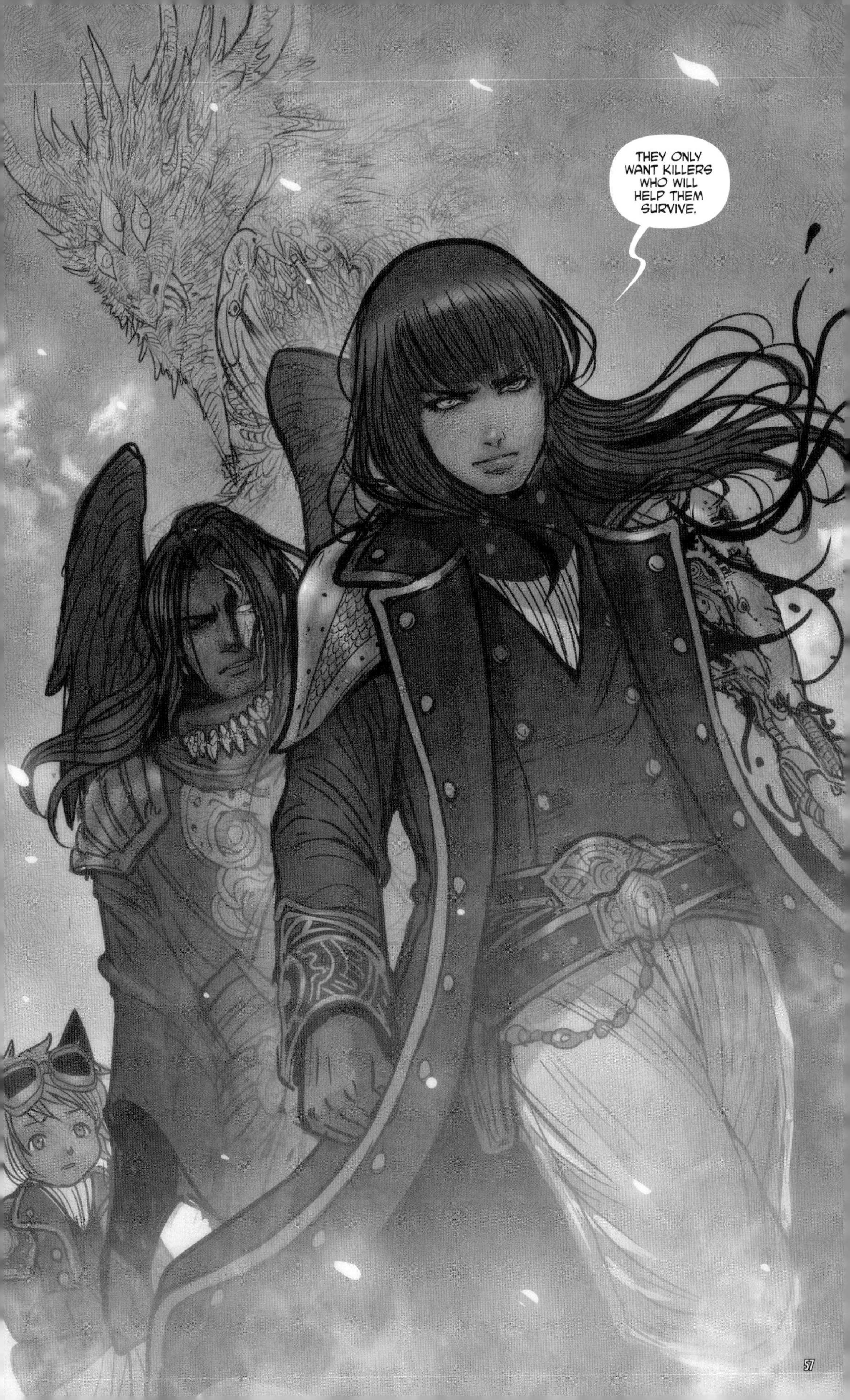
THEY ONLY WANT KILLERS WHO WILL HELP THEM SURVIVE.

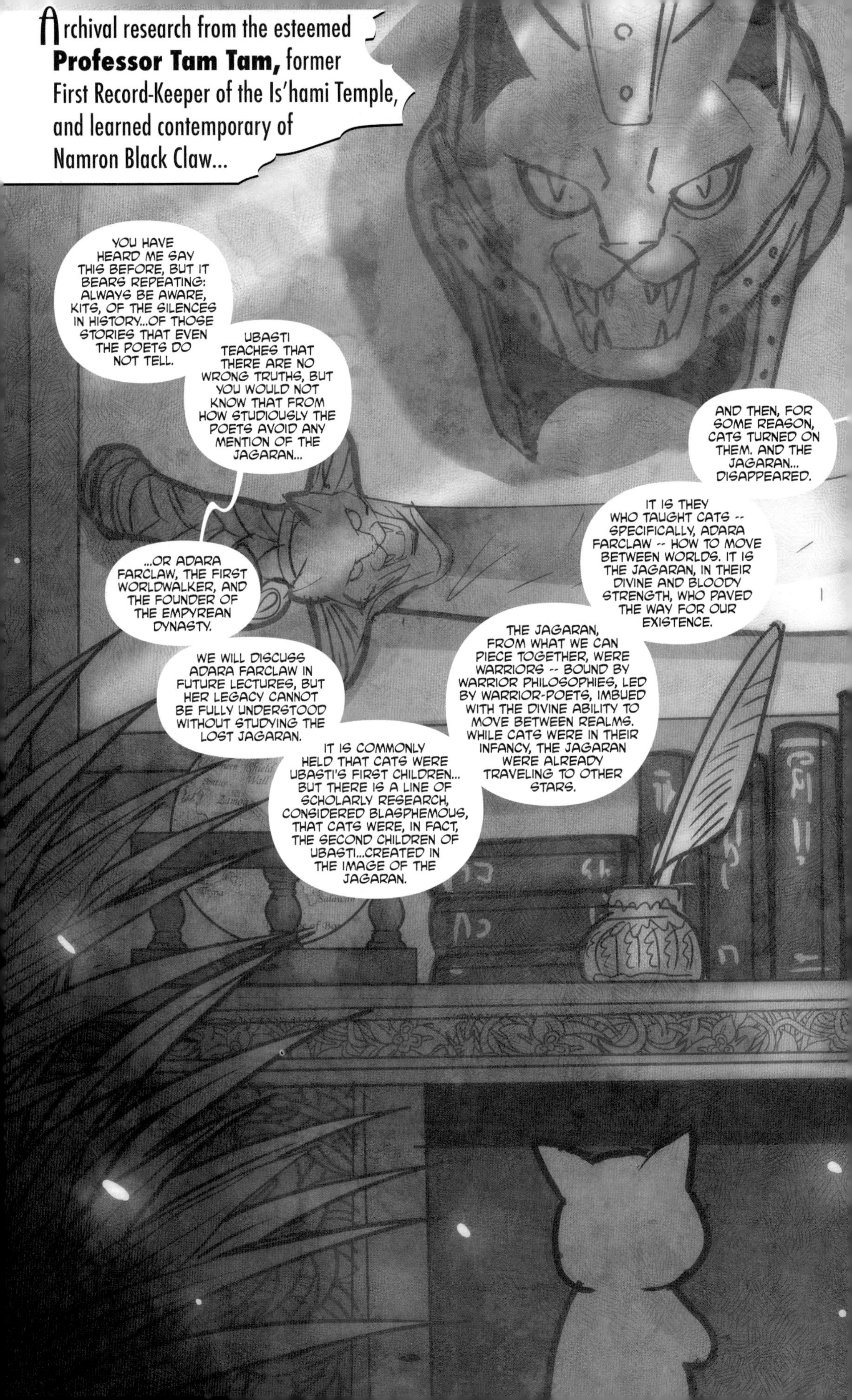
Archival research from the esteemed **Professor Tam Tam,** former First Record-Keeper of the Is'hami Temple, and learned contemporary of Namron Black Claw...
YOU HAVE HEARD ME SAY THIS BEFORE, BUT IT BEARS REPEATING: ALWAYS BE AWARE, KITS, OF THE SILENCES IN HISTORY...OF THOSE STORIES THAT EVEN THE POETS DO NOT TELL.
UBASTI TEACHES THAT THERE ARE NO WRONG TRUTHS, BUT YOU WOULD NOT KNOW THAT FROM HOW STUDIOUSLY THE POETS AVOID ANY MENTION OF THE JAGARAN...
...OR ADARA FARCLAW, THE FIRST WORLDWALKER, AND THE FOUNDER OF THE EMPYREAN DYNASTY.
WE WILL DISCUSS ADARA FARCLAW IN FUTURE LECTURES, BUT HER LEGACY CANNOT BE FULLY UNDERSTOOD WITHOUT STUDYING THE LOST JAGARAN.
IT IS COMMONLY HELD THAT CATS WERE UBASTI'S FIRST CHILDREN... BUT THERE IS A LINE OF SCHOLARLY RESEARCH, CONSIDERED BLASPHEMOUS, THAT CATS WERE, IN FACT, THE SECOND CHILDREN OF UBASTI...CREATED IN THE IMAGE OF THE JAGARAN.
THE JAGARAN, FROM WHAT WE CAN PIECE TOGETHER, WERE WARRIORS -- BOUND BY WARRIOR PHILOSOPHIES, LED BY WARRIOR-POETS, IMBUED WITH THE DIVINE ABILITY TO MOVE BETWEEN REALMS. WHILE CATS WERE IN THEIR INFANCY, THE JAGARAN WERE ALREADY TRAVELING TO OTHER STARS.
IT IS THEY WHO TAUGHT CATS -- SPECIFICALLY, ADARA FARCLAW -- HOW TO MOVE BETWEEN WORLDS. IT IS THE JAGARAN, IN THEIR DIVINE AND BLOODY STRENGTH, WHO PAVED THE WAY FOR OUR EXISTENCE.
AND THEN, FOR SOME REASON, CATS TURNED ON THEM. AND THE JAGARAN... DISAPPEARED.

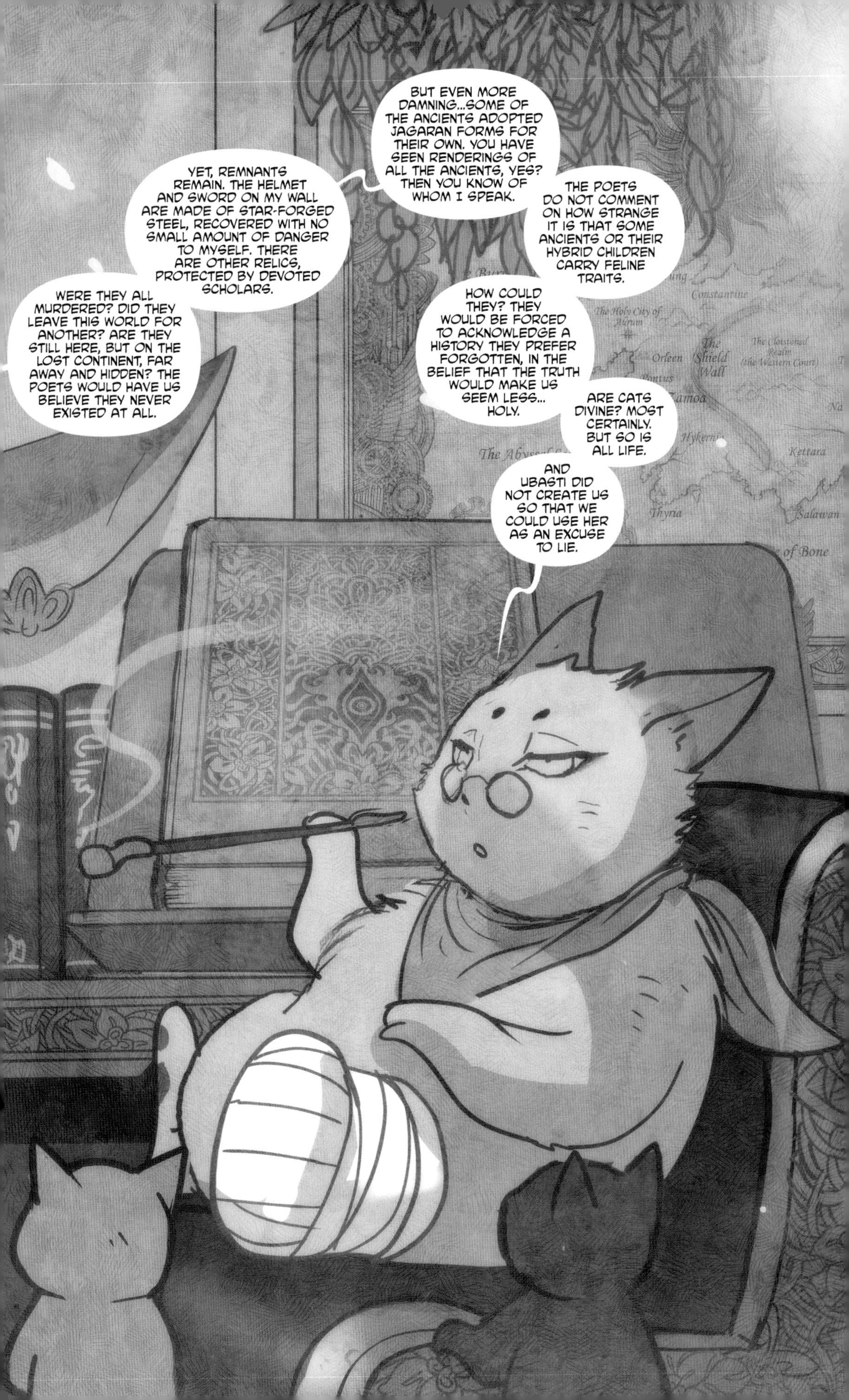

WERE THEY ALL MURDERED? DID THEY LEAVE THIS WORLD FOR ANOTHER? ARE THEY STILL HERE, BUT ON THE LOST CONTINENT, FAR AWAY AND HIDDEN? THE POETS WOULD HAVE US BELIEVE THEY NEVER EXISTED AT ALL.
YET, REMNANTS REMAIN. THE HELMET AND SWORD ON MY WALL ARE MADE OF STAR-FORGED STEEL, RECOVERED WITH NO SMALL AMOUNT OF DANGER TO MYSELF. THERE ARE OTHER RELICS, PROTECTED BY DEVOTED SCHOLARS.
BUT EVEN MORE DAMNING...SOME OF THE ANCIENTS ADOPTED JAGARAN FORMS FOR THEIR OWN. YOU HAVE SEEN RENDERINGS OF ALL THE ANCIENTS, YES? THEN YOU KNOW OF WHOM I SPEAK.
THE POETS DO NOT COMMENT ON HOW STRANGE IT IS THAT SOME ANCIENTS OR THEIR HYBRID CHILDREN CARRY FELINE TRAITS.
HOW COULD THEY? THEY WOULD BE FORCED TO ACKNOWLEDGE A HISTORY THEY PREFER FORGOTTEN, IN THE BELIEF THAT THE TRUTH WOULD MAKE US SEEM LESS... HOLY.
ARE CATS DIVINE? MOST CERTAINLY. BUT SO IS ALL LIFE.
AND UBASTI DID NOT CREATE US SO THAT WE COULD USE HER AS AN EXCUSE TO LIE.
Constantine
Orleen
The Shield Wall
Kettara
Thyria
Salawan

CHAPTER TWENTY-SEVEN

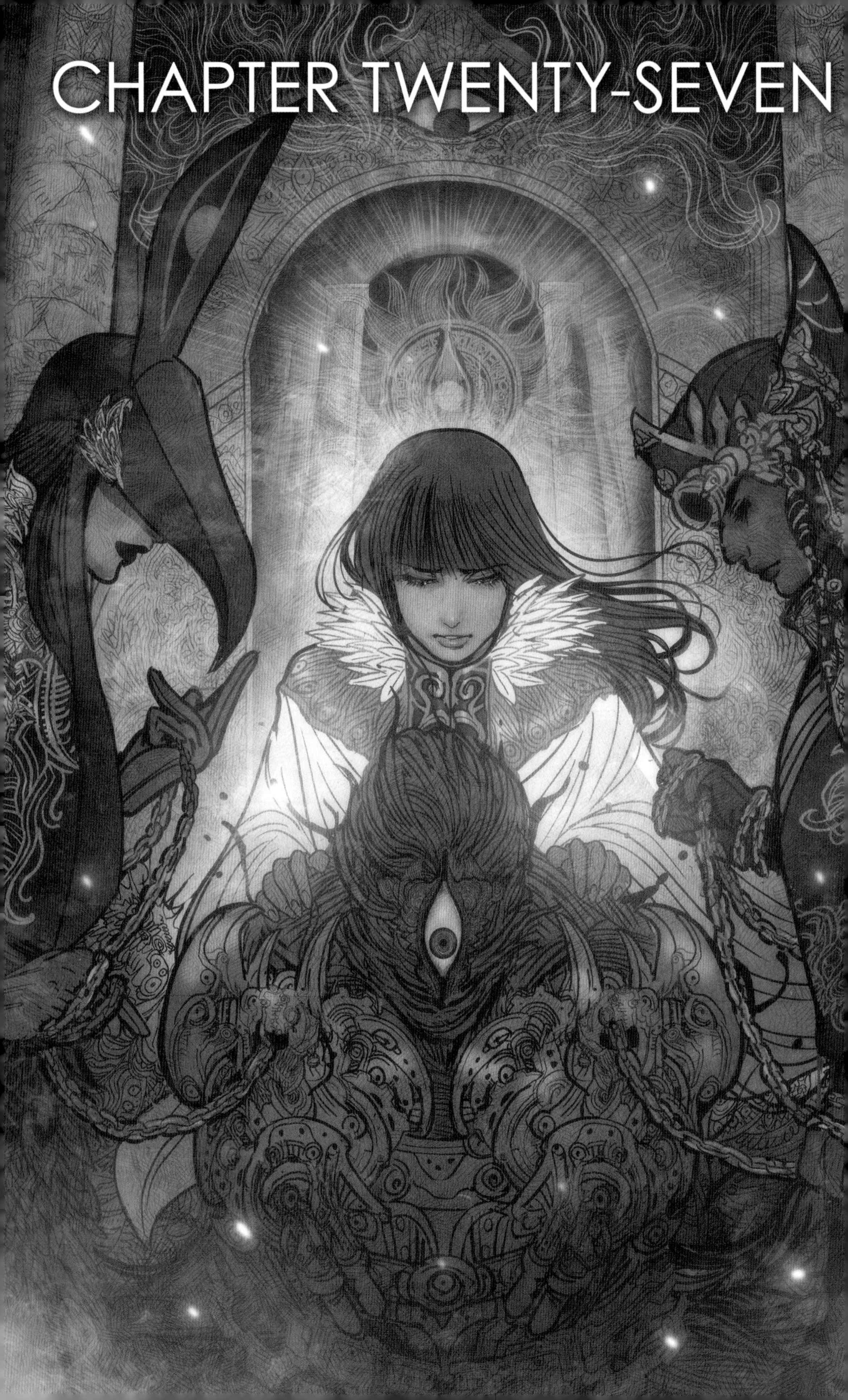

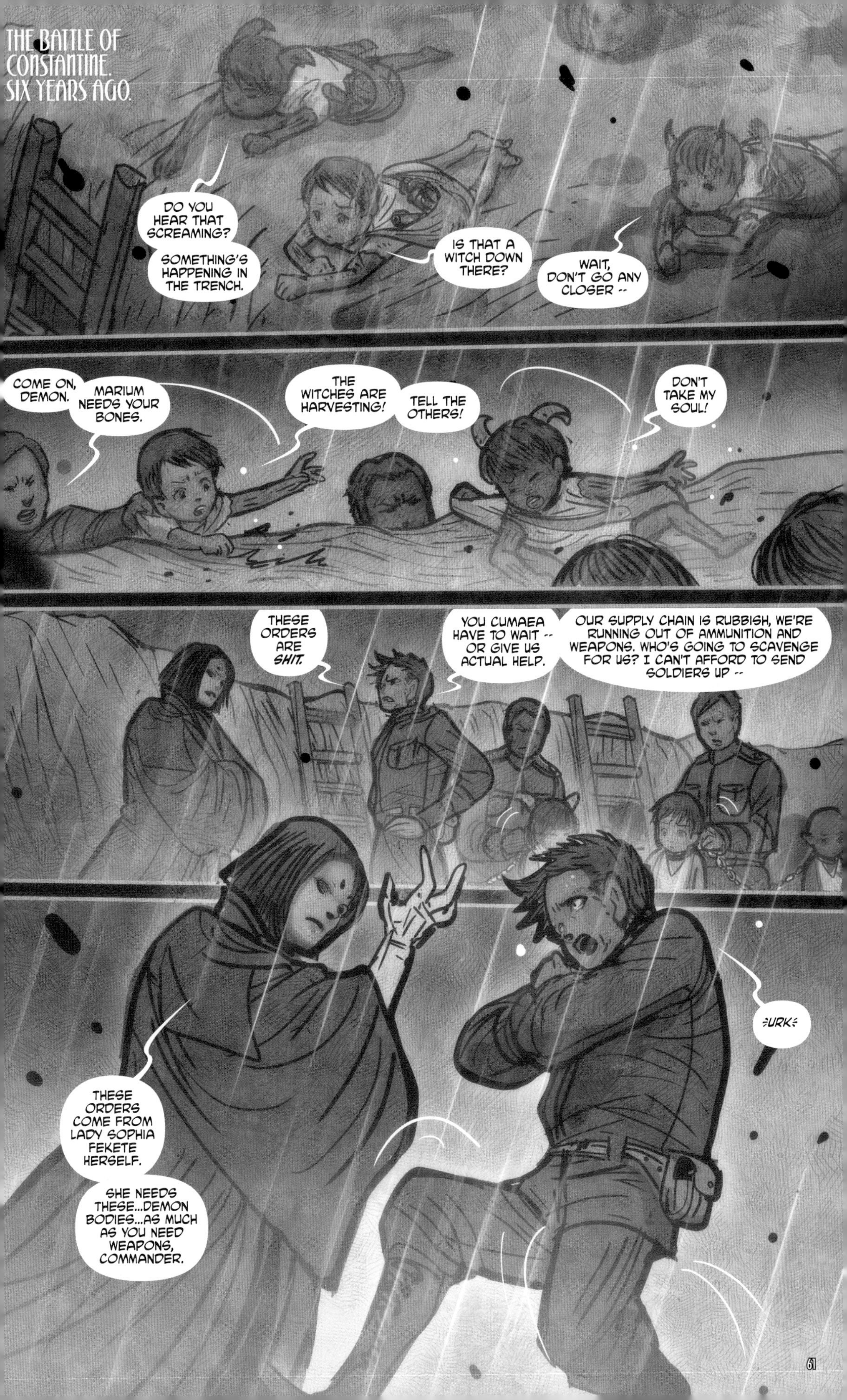
THE BATTLE OF CONSTANTINE. SIX YEARS AGO.
DO YOU HEAR THAT SCREAMING?
SOMETHING'S HAPPENING IN THE TRENCH.
IS THAT A WITCH DOWN THERE?
WAIT, DON'T GO ANY CLOSER --
COME ON, DEMON.
MARIUM NEEDS YOUR BONES.
THE WITCHES ARE HARVESTING!
TELL THE OTHERS!
DON'T TAKE MY SOUL!
THESE ORDERS ARE SHIT.
YOU CUMAEA HAVE TO WAIT -- OR GIVE US ACTUAL HELP.
OUR SUPPLY CHAIN IS RUBBISH, WE'RE RUNNING OUT OF AMMUNITION AND WEAPONS. WHO'S GOING TO SCAVENGE FOR US? I CAN'T AFFORD TO SEND SOLDIERS UP --
URK
THESE ORDERS COME FROM LADY SOPHIA FEKETE HERSELF.
SHE NEEDS THESE...DEMON BODIES...AS MUCH AS YOU NEED WEAPONS, COMMANDER.

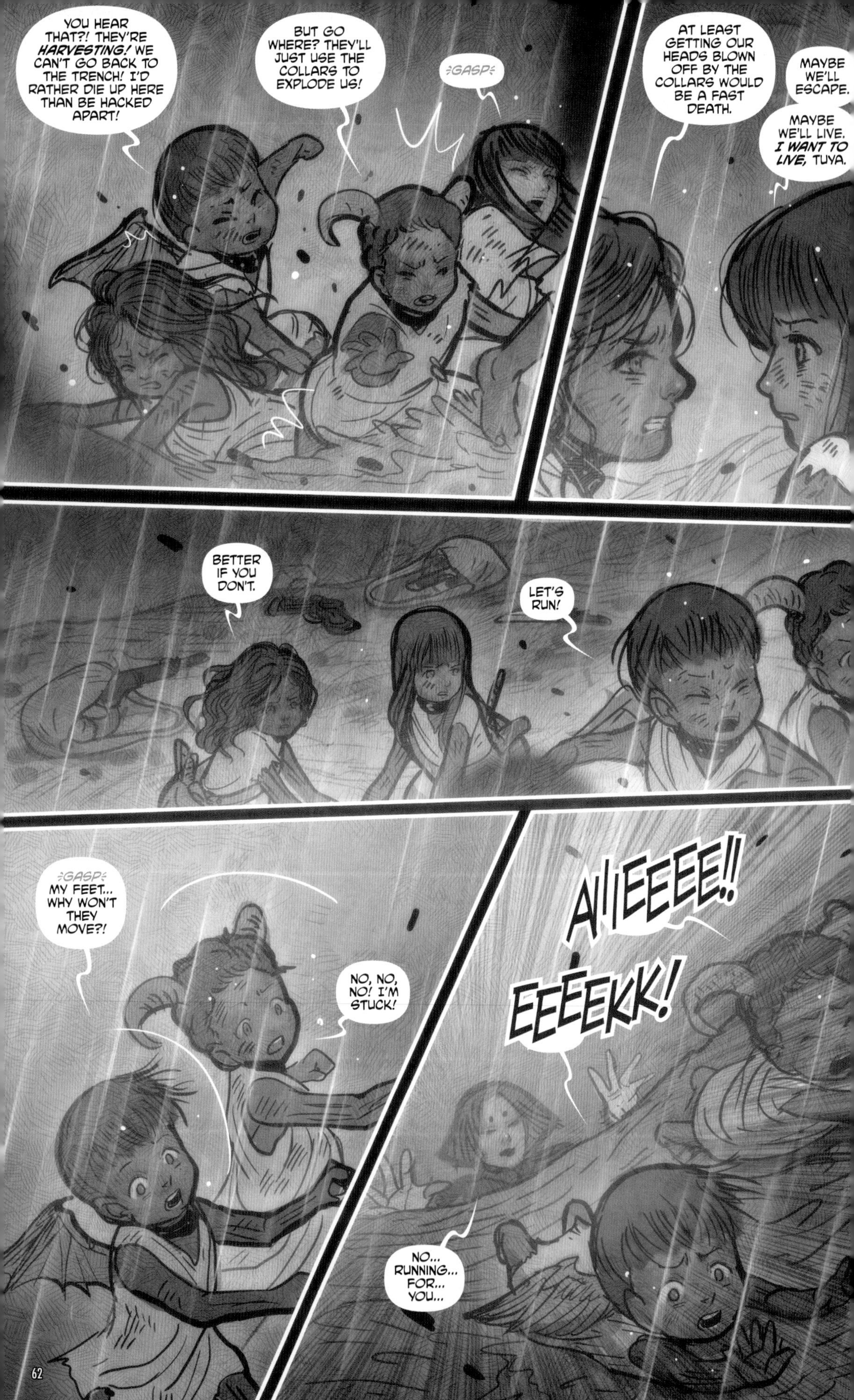
YOU HEAR THAT?! THEY'RE HARVESTING! WE CAN'T GO BACK TO THE TRENCH! I'D RATHER DIE UP HERE THAN BE HACKED APART!
BUT GO WHERE? THEY'LL JUST USE THE COLLARS TO EXPLODE US!
GASP
AT LEAST GETTING OUR HEADS BLOWN OFF BY THE COLLARS WOULD BE A FAST DEATH.
MAYBE WE'LL ESCAPE.
MAYBE WE'LL LIVE. I WANT TO LIVE, TUYA.
BETTER IF YOU DON'T.
LET'S RUN!
GASP
MY FEET... WHY WON'T THEY MOVE?!
NO, NO, NO! I'M STUCK!
AIIEEEE!!
EEEEKK!
NO... RUNNING... FOR... YOU...

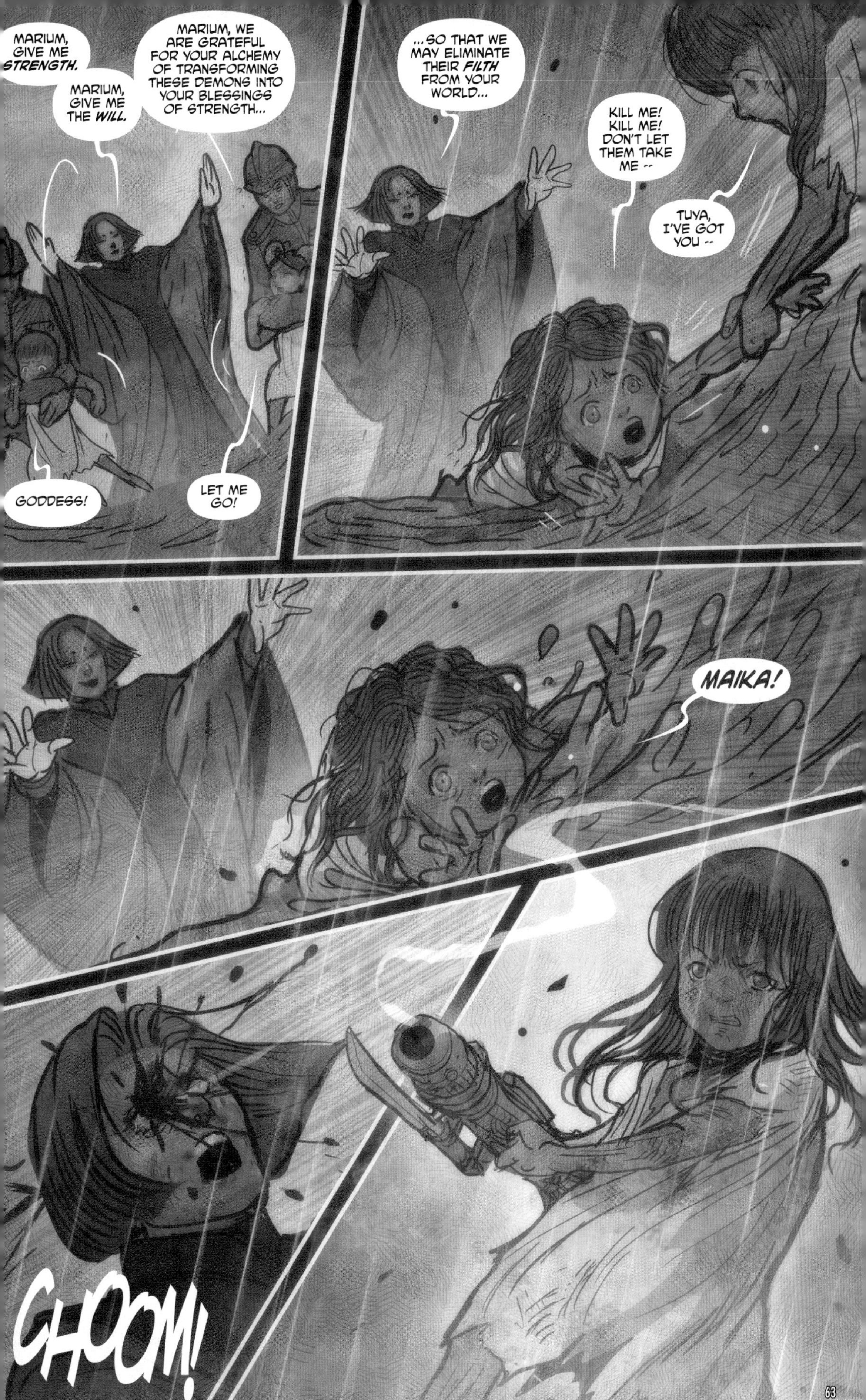
MARIUM, GIVE ME STRENGTH.
MARIUM, GIVE ME THE WILL.
MARIUM, WE ARE GRATEFUL FOR YOUR ALCHEMY OF TRANSFORMING THESE DEMONS INTO YOUR BLESSINGS OF STRENGTH...
GODDESS!
LET ME GO!
...SO THAT WE MAY ELIMINATE THEIR FILTH FROM YOUR WORLD...
KILL ME! KILL ME! DON'T LET THEM TAKE ME --
TUYA, I'VE GOT YOU --
MAIKA!
CHOOM!

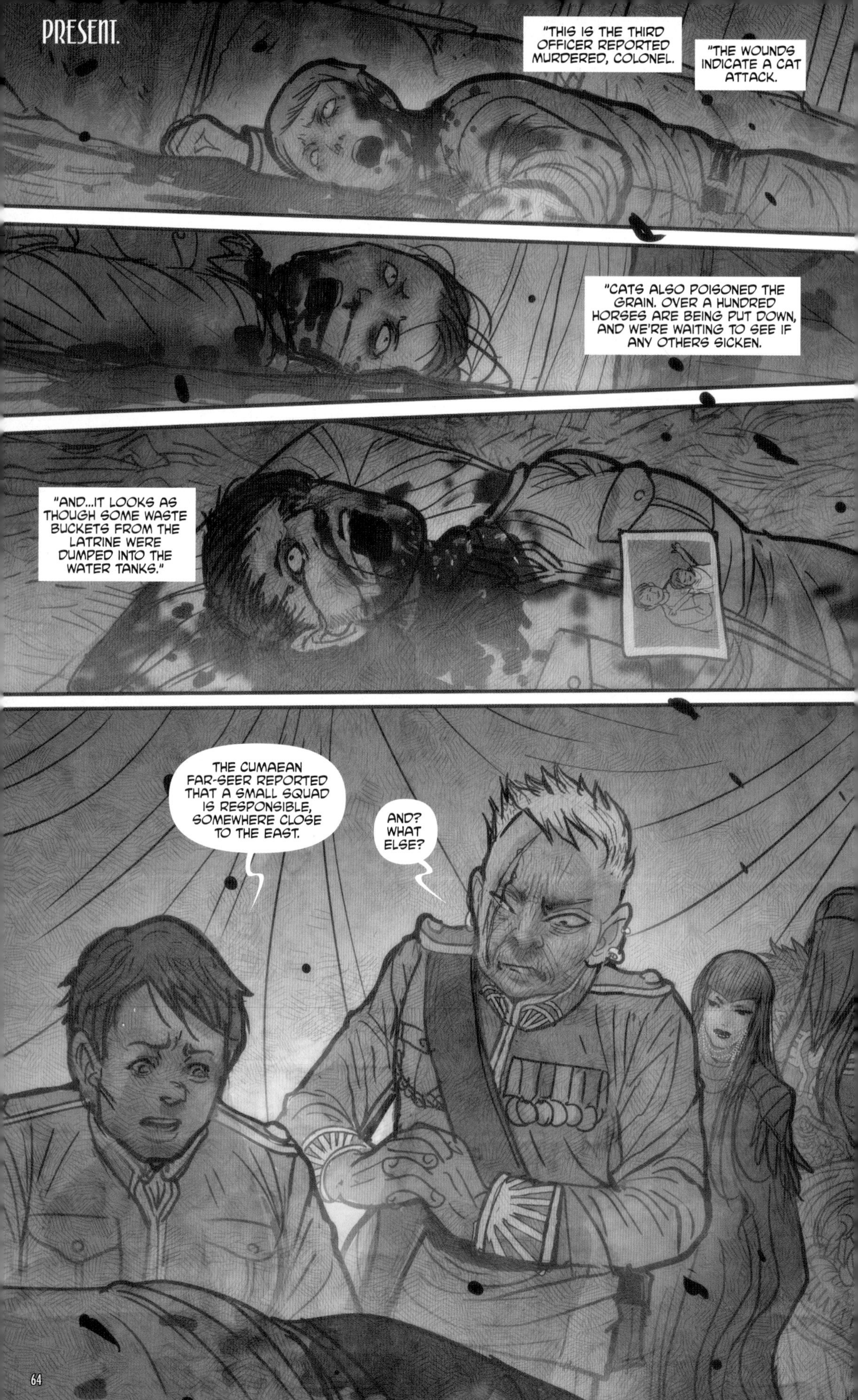
PRESENT.
"THIS IS THE THIRD OFFICER REPORTED MURDERED, COLONEL.
"THE WOUNDS INDICATE A CAT ATTACK.
"CATS ALSO POISONED THE GRAIN. OVER A HUNDRED HORSES ARE BEING PUT DOWN, AND WE'RE WAITING TO SEE IF ANY OTHERS SICKEN.
"AND...IT LOOKS AS THOUGH SOME WASTE BUCKETS FROM THE LATRINE WERE DUMPED INTO THE WATER TANKS."
THE CUMAEAN FAR-SEER REPORTED THAT A SMALL SQUAD IS RESPONSIBLE, SOMEWHERE CLOSE TO THE EAST.
AND? WHAT ELSE?

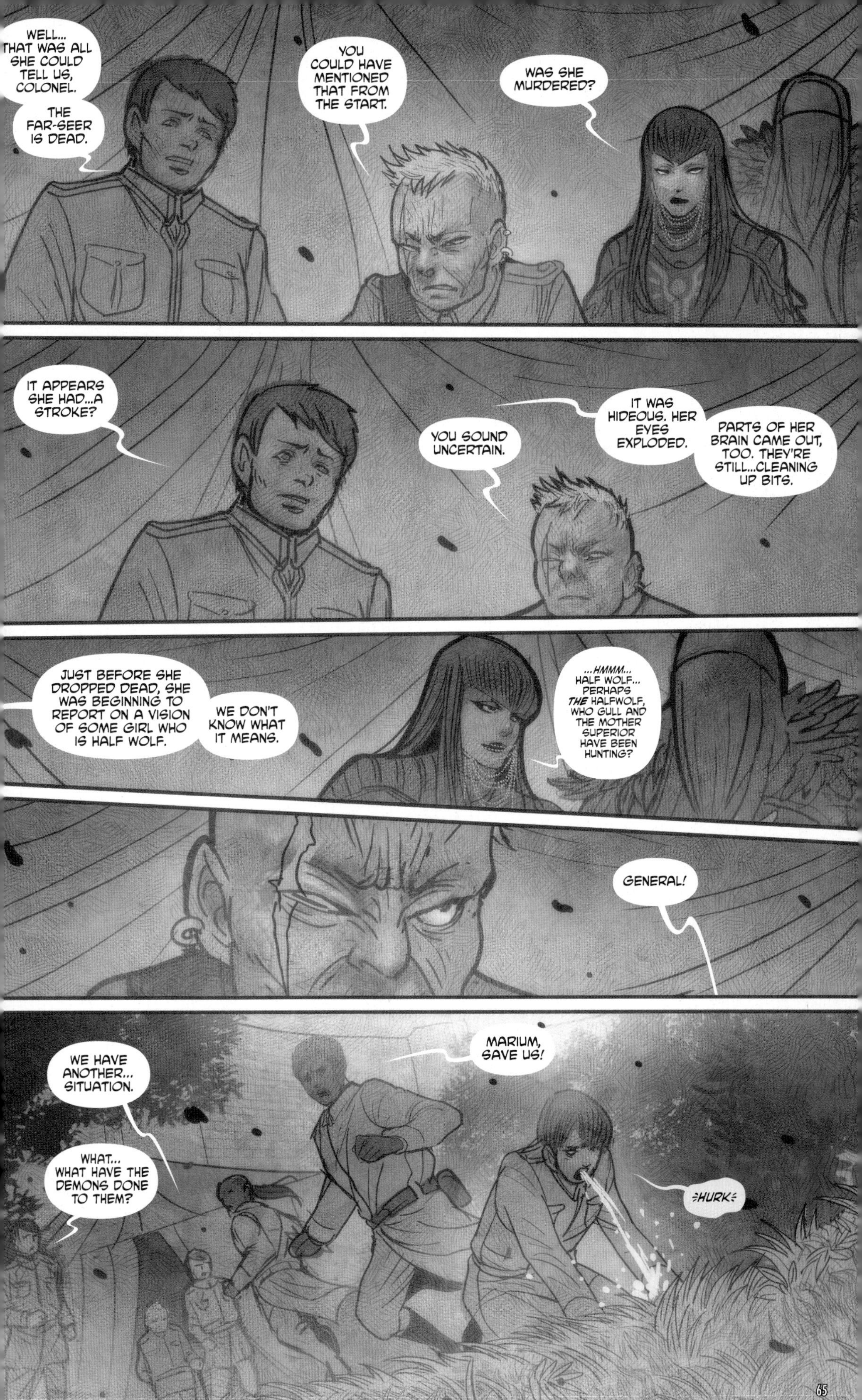
WELL... THAT WAS ALL SHE COULD TELL US, COLONEL.
THE FAR-SEER IS DEAD.
YOU COULD HAVE MENTIONED THAT FROM THE START.
WAS SHE MURDERED?
IT APPEARS SHE HAD...A STROKE?
YOU SOUND UNCERTAIN.
IT WAS HIDEOUS. HER EYES EXPLODED.
PARTS OF HER BRAIN CAME OUT, TOO. THEY'RE STILL...CLEANING UP BITS.
JUST BEFORE SHE DROPPED DEAD, SHE WAS BEGINNING TO REPORT ON A VISION OF SOME GIRL WHO IS HALF WOLF.
WE DON'T KNOW WHAT IT MEANS.
...HMMM... HALF WOLF... PERHAPS THE HALFWOLF, WHO GULL AND THE MOTHER SUPERIOR HAVE BEEN HUNTING?
GENERAL!
WE HAVE ANOTHER... SITUATION.
WHAT... WHAT HAVE THE DEMONS DONE TO THEM?
MARIUM, SAVE US!
HURK

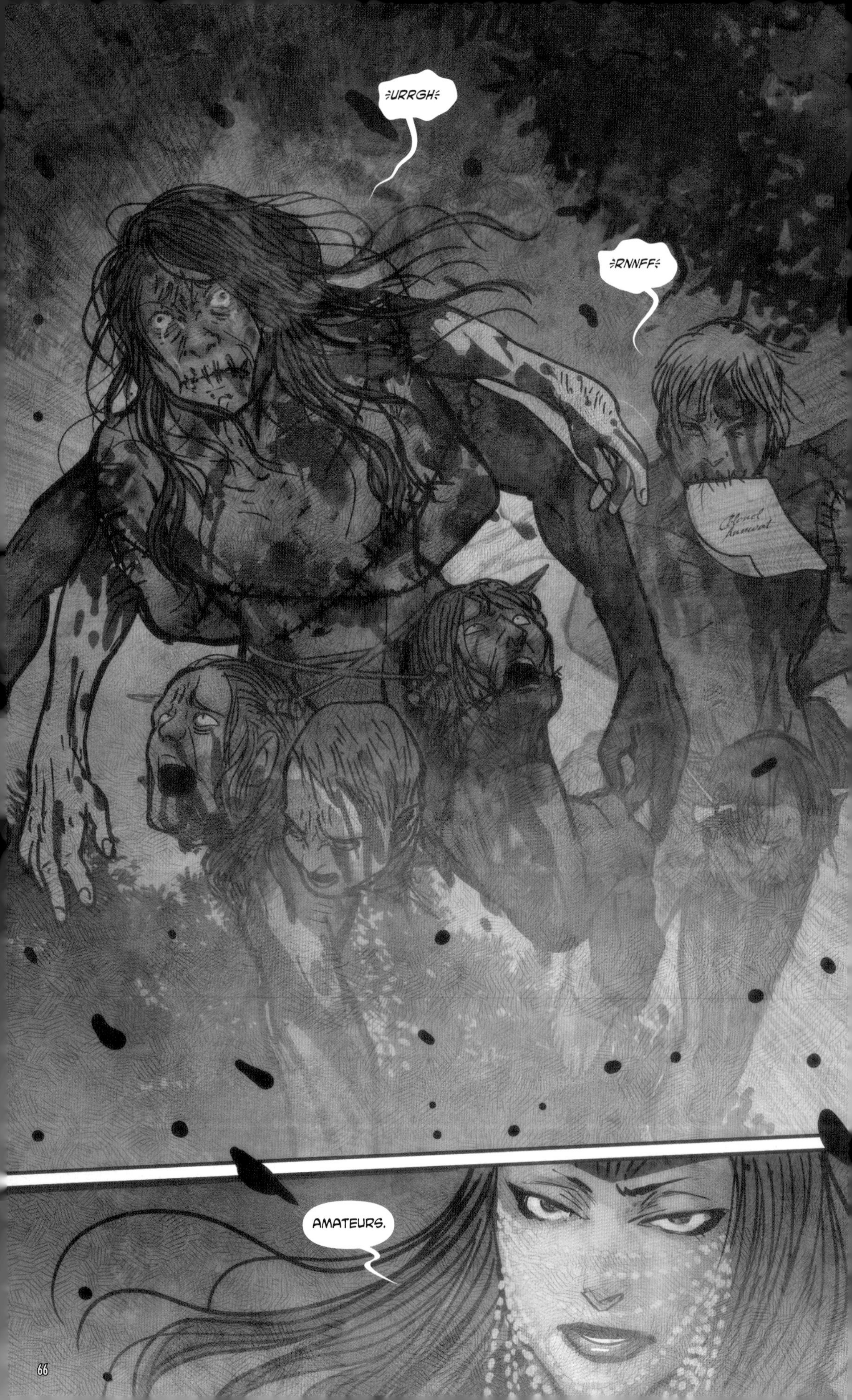
URRGH
RNNFF
AMATEURS.

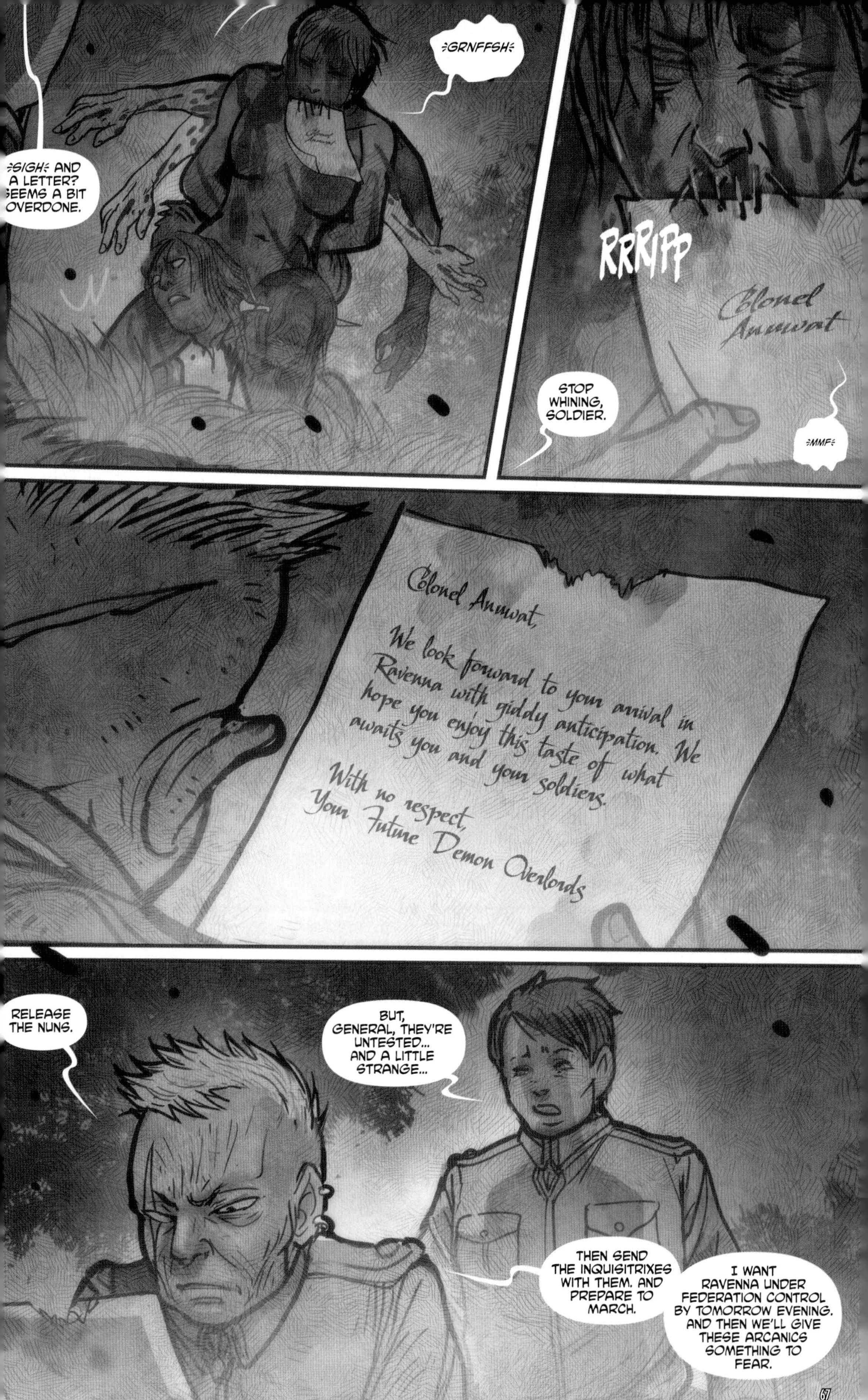

=SIGH= AND A LETTER? SEEMS A BIT OVERDONE.
=GRNFFSH=
RRRIPP
Colonel Anuwat
STOP WHINING, SOLDIER.
=MMF=
Colonel Anuwat,
We look forward to your arrival in Ravenna with giddy anticipation. We hope you enjoy this taste of what awaits you and your soldiers.
With no respect,
Your Future Demon Overlords
RELEASE THE NUNS.
BUT, GENERAL, THEY'RE UNTESTED... AND A LITTLE STRANGE...
THEN SEND THE INQUISITRIXES WITH THEM. AND PREPARE TO MARCH.
I WANT RAVENNA UNDER FEDERATION CONTROL BY TOMORROW EVENING. AND THEN WE'LL GIVE THESE ARCANICS SOMETHING TO FEAR.

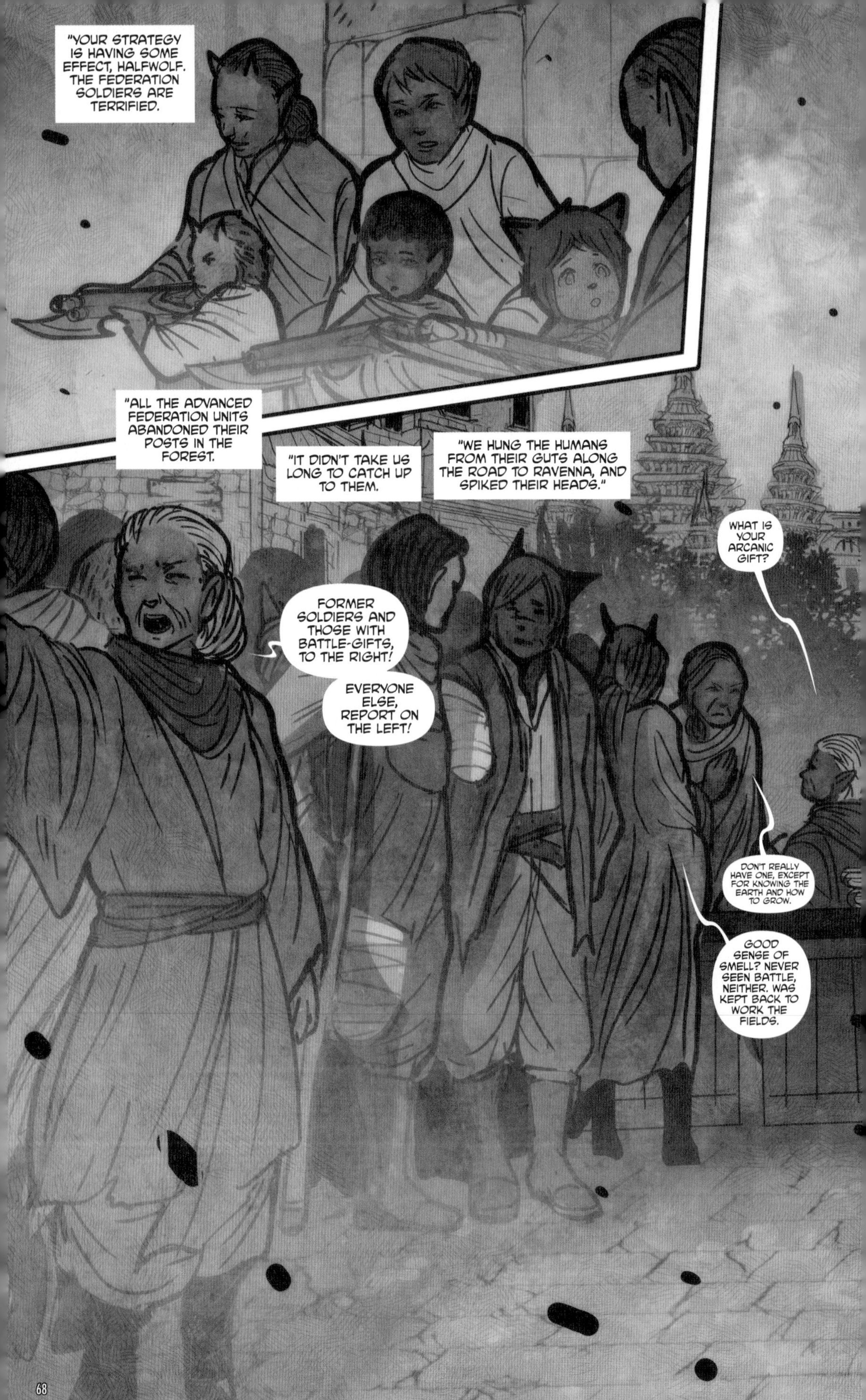
"YOUR STRATEGY IS HAVING SOME EFFECT, HALFWOLF. THE FEDERATION SOLDIERS ARE TERRIFIED.
"ALL THE ADVANCED FEDERATION UNITS ABANDONED THEIR POSTS IN THE FOREST.
"IT DIDN'T TAKE US LONG TO CATCH UP TO THEM.
"WE HUNG THE HUMANS FROM THEIR GUTS ALONG THE ROAD TO RAVENNA, AND SPIKED THEIR HEADS."
FORMER SOLDIERS AND THOSE WITH BATTLE-GIFTS, TO THE RIGHT!
EVERYONE ELSE, REPORT ON THE LEFT!
WHAT IS YOUR ARCANIC GIFT?
DON'T REALLY HAVE ONE, EXCEPT FOR KNOWING THE EARTH AND HOW TO GROW.
GOOD SENSE OF SMELL? NEVER SEEN BATTLE, NEITHER. WAS KEPT BACK TO WORK THE FIELDS.

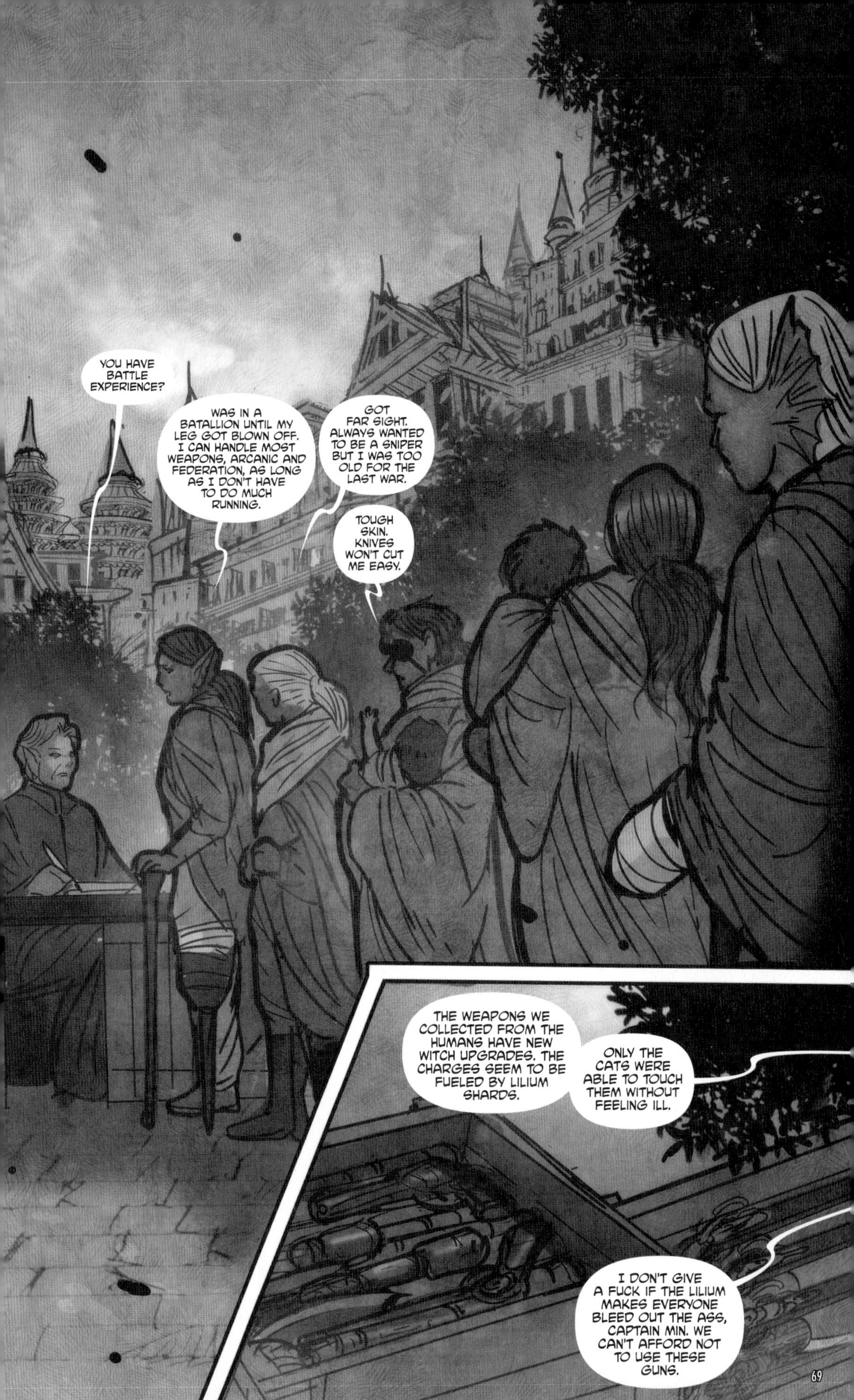
YOU HAVE BATTLE EXPERIENCE?
WAS IN A BATALLION UNTIL MY LEG GOT BLOWN OFF. I CAN HANDLE MOST WEAPONS, ARCANIC AND FEDERATION, AS LONG AS I DON'T HAVE TO DO MUCH RUNNING.
GOT FAR SIGHT. ALWAYS WANTED TO BE A SNIPER BUT I WAS TOO OLD FOR THE LAST WAR.
TOUGH SKIN. KNIVES WON'T CUT ME EASY.
THE WEAPONS WE COLLECTED FROM THE HUMANS HAVE NEW WITCH UPGRADES. THE CHARGES SEEM TO BE FUELED BY LILIUM SHARDS.
ONLY THE CATS WERE ABLE TO TOUCH THEM WITHOUT FEELING ILL.
I DON'T GIVE A FUCK IF THE LILIUM MAKES EVERYONE BLEED OUT THE ASS, CAPTAIN MIN. WE CAN'T AFFORD NOT TO USE THESE GUNS.

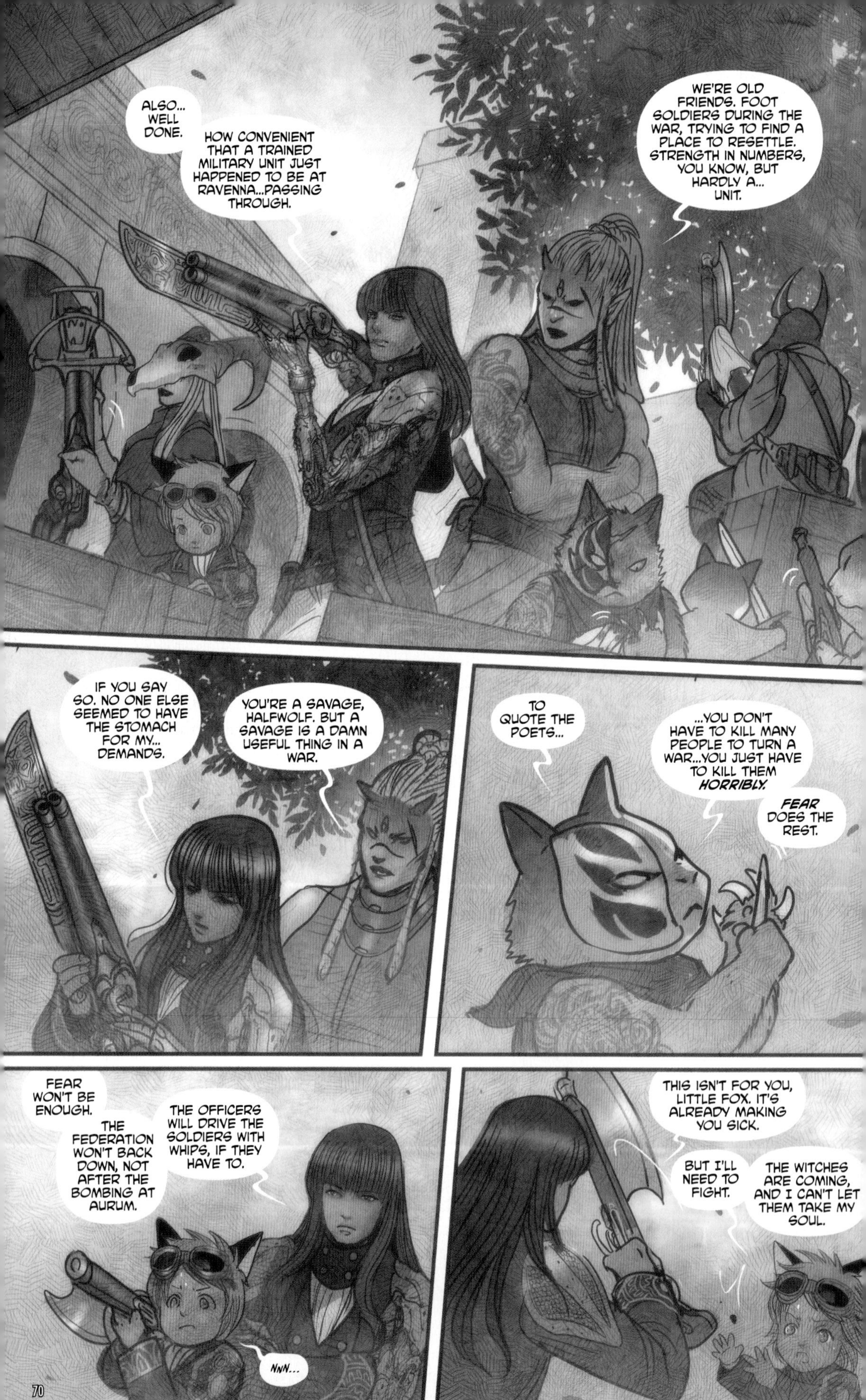
ALSO... WELL DONE.
HOW CONVENIENT THAT A TRAINED MILITARY UNIT JUST HAPPENED TO BE AT RAVENNA...PASSING THROUGH.
WE'RE OLD FRIENDS. FOOT SOLDIERS DURING THE WAR, TRYING TO FIND A PLACE TO RESETTLE. STRENGTH IN NUMBERS, YOU KNOW, BUT HARDLY A... UNIT.
IF YOU SAY SO. NO ONE ELSE SEEMED TO HAVE THE STOMACH FOR MY... DEMANDS.
YOU'RE A SAVAGE, HALFWOLF. BUT A SAVAGE IS A DAMN USEFUL THING IN A WAR.
TO QUOTE THE POETS...
...YOU DON'T HAVE TO KILL MANY PEOPLE TO TURN A WAR...YOU JUST HAVE TO KILL THEM *HORRIBLY.*
FEAR DOES THE REST.
FEAR WON'T BE ENOUGH.
THE FEDERATION WON'T BACK DOWN, NOT AFTER THE BOMBING AT AURUM.
THE OFFICERS WILL DRIVE THE SOLDIERS WITH WHIPS, IF THEY HAVE TO.
NNN...
THIS ISN'T FOR YOU, LITTLE FOX. IT'S ALREADY MAKING YOU SICK.
BUT I'LL NEED TO FIGHT.
THE WITCHES ARE COMING, AND I CAN'T LET THEM TAKE MY SOUL.

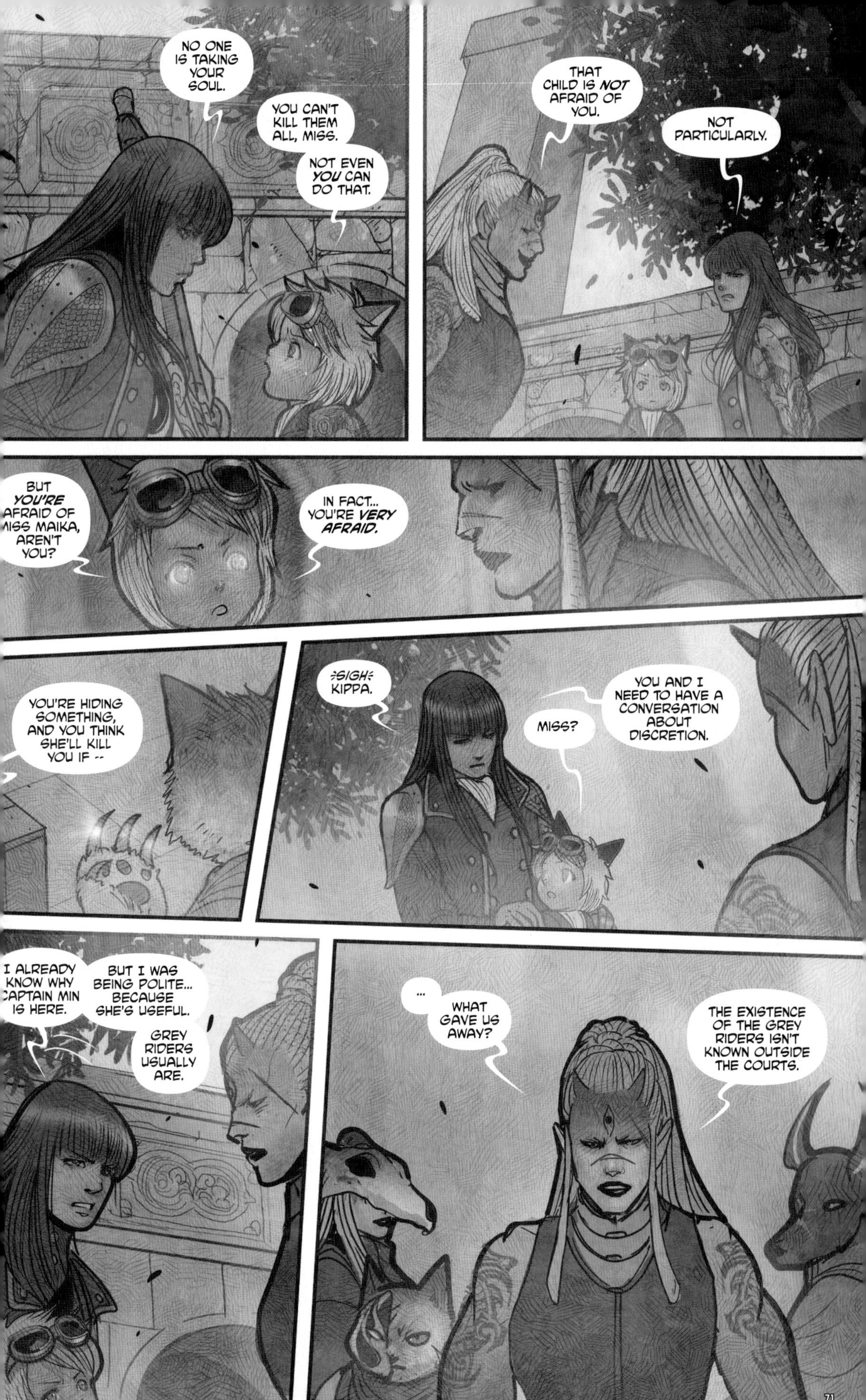
NO ONE IS TAKING YOUR SOUL.
YOU CAN'T KILL THEM ALL, MISS.
NOT EVEN YOU CAN DO THAT.
THAT CHILD IS NOT AFRAID OF YOU.
NOT PARTICULARLY.
BUT YOU'RE AFRAID OF MISS MAIKA, AREN'T YOU?
IN FACT... YOU'RE VERY AFRAID.
YOU'RE HIDING SOMETHING, AND YOU THINK SHE'LL KILL YOU IF --
SIGH KIPPA.
MISS?
YOU AND I NEED TO HAVE A CONVERSATION ABOUT DISCRETION.
I ALREADY KNOW WHY CAPTAIN MIN IS HERE.
BUT I WAS BEING POLITE... BECAUSE SHE'S USEFUL.
GREY RIDERS USUALLY ARE.
...
WHAT GAVE US AWAY?
THE EXISTENCE OF THE GREY RIDERS ISN'T KNOWN OUTSIDE THE COURTS.

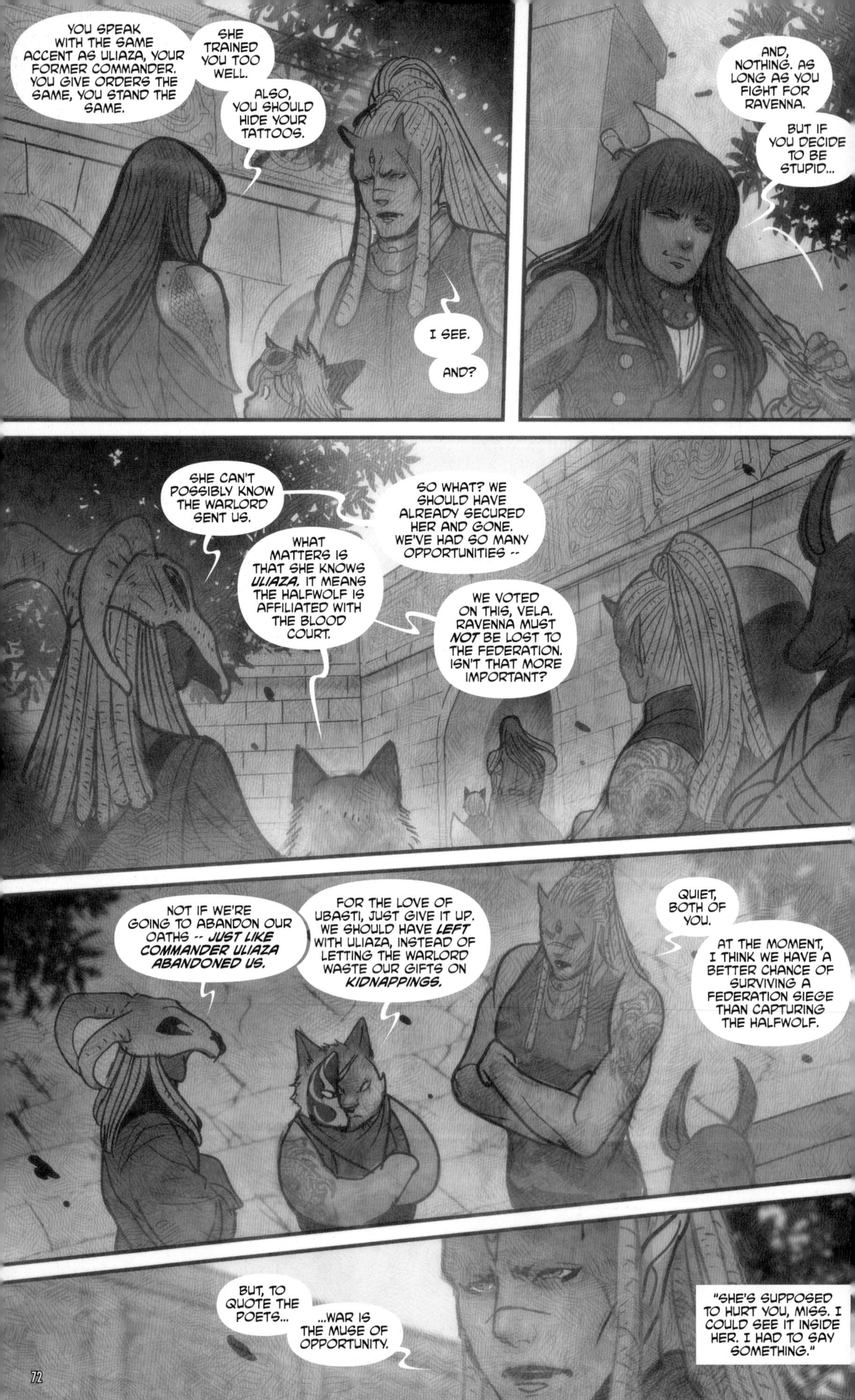
YOU SPEAK WITH THE SAME ACCENT AS ULIAZA, YOUR FORMER COMMANDER. YOU GIVE ORDERS THE SAME, YOU STAND THE SAME.
SHE TRAINED YOU TOO WELL.
ALSO, YOU SHOULD HIDE YOUR TATTOOS.
I SEE.
AND?
AND, NOTHING. AS LONG AS YOU FIGHT FOR RAVENNA.
BUT IF YOU DECIDE TO BE STUPID...
SHE CAN'T POSSIBLY KNOW THE WARLORD SENT US.
SO WHAT? WE SHOULD HAVE ALREADY SECURED HER AND GONE. WE'VE HAD SO MANY OPPORTUNITIES --
WHAT MATTERS IS THAT SHE KNOWS *ULIAZA.* IT MEANS THE HALFWOLF IS AFFILIATED WITH THE BLOOD COURT.
WE VOTED ON THIS, VELA. RAVENNA MUST ***NOT*** BE LOST TO THE FEDERATION. ISN'T THAT MORE IMPORTANT?
NOT IF WE'RE GOING TO ABANDON OUR OATHS -- ***JUST LIKE COMMANDER ULIAZA ABANDONED US.***
FOR THE LOVE OF UBASTI, JUST GIVE IT UP. WE SHOULD HAVE ***LEFT*** WITH ULIAZA, INSTEAD OF LETTING THE WARLORD WASTE OUR GIFTS ON ***KIDNAPPINGS.***
QUIET, BOTH OF YOU.
AT THE MOMENT, I THINK WE HAVE A BETTER CHANCE OF SURVIVING A FEDERATION SIEGE THAN CAPTURING THE HALFWOLF.
BUT, TO QUOTE THE POETS...
...WAR IS THE MUSE OF OPPORTUNITY.
"SHE'S SUPPOSED TO HURT YOU, MISS. I COULD SEE IT INSIDE HER. I HAD TO SAY SOMETHING."

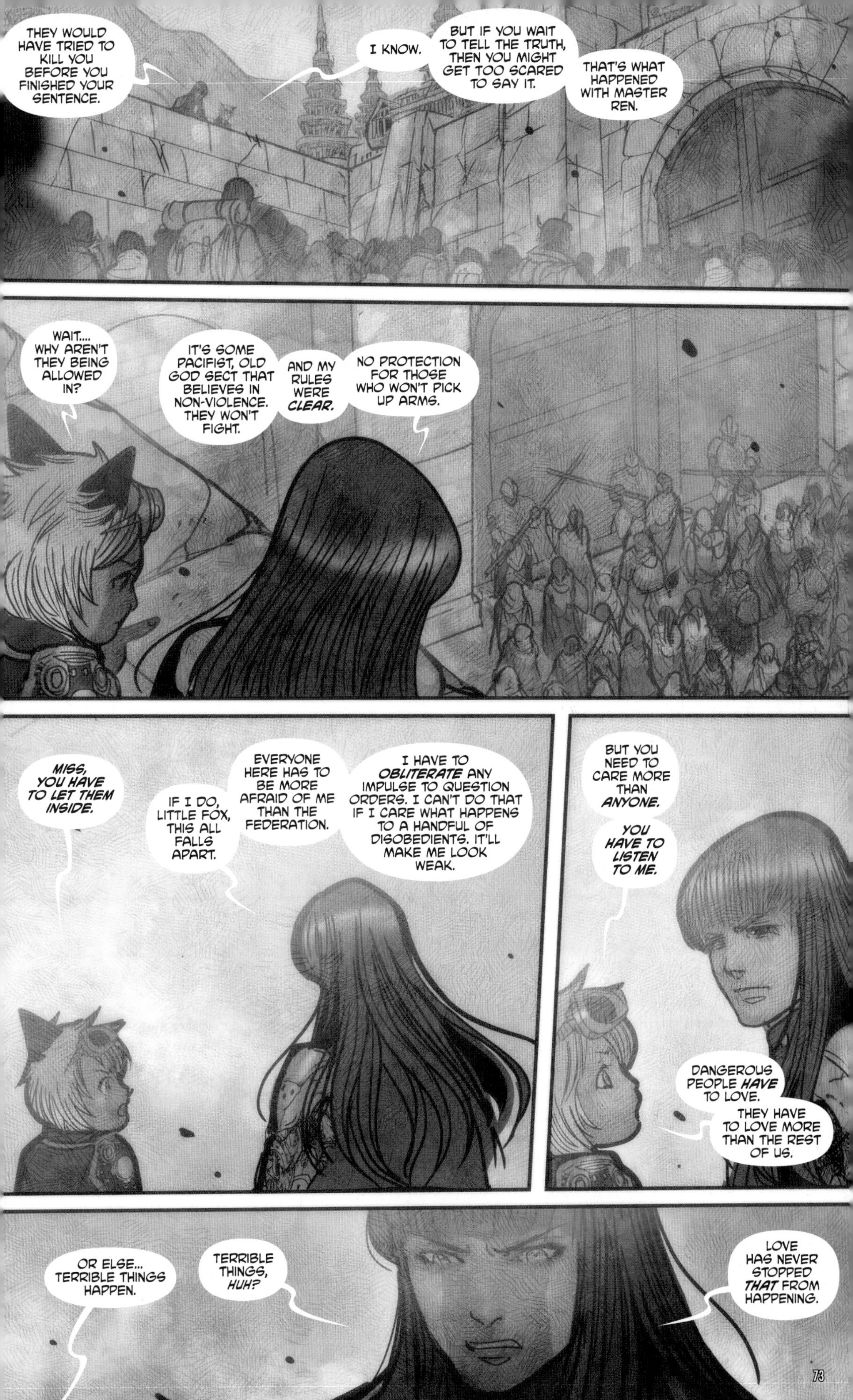

THEY WOULD HAVE TRIED TO KILL YOU BEFORE YOU FINISHED YOUR SENTENCE.
I KNOW.
BUT IF YOU WAIT TO TELL THE TRUTH, THEN YOU MIGHT GET TOO SCARED TO SAY IT.
THAT'S WHAT HAPPENED WITH MASTER REN.
WAIT.... WHY AREN'T THEY BEING ALLOWED IN?
IT'S SOME PACIFIST, OLD GOD SECT THAT BELIEVES IN NON-VIOLENCE. THEY WON'T FIGHT.
AND MY RULES WERE *CLEAR.*
NO PROTECTION FOR THOSE WHO WON'T PICK UP ARMS.
MISS, YOU HAVE TO LET THEM INSIDE.
IF I DO, LITTLE FOX, THIS ALL FALLS APART.
EVERYONE HERE HAS TO BE MORE AFRAID OF ME THAN THE FEDERATION.
I HAVE TO *OBLITERATE* ANY IMPULSE TO QUESTION ORDERS. I CAN'T DO THAT IF I CARE WHAT HAPPENS TO A HANDFUL OF DISOBEDIENTS. IT'LL MAKE ME LOOK WEAK.
BUT YOU NEED TO CARE MORE THAN *ANYONE.*
YOU HAVE TO LISTEN TO ME.
DANGEROUS PEOPLE *HAVE* TO LOVE.
THEY HAVE TO LOVE MORE THAN THE REST OF US.
OR ELSE... TERRIBLE THINGS HAPPEN.
TERRIBLE THINGS, *HUH?*
LOVE HAS NEVER STOPPED *THAT* FROM HAPPENING.

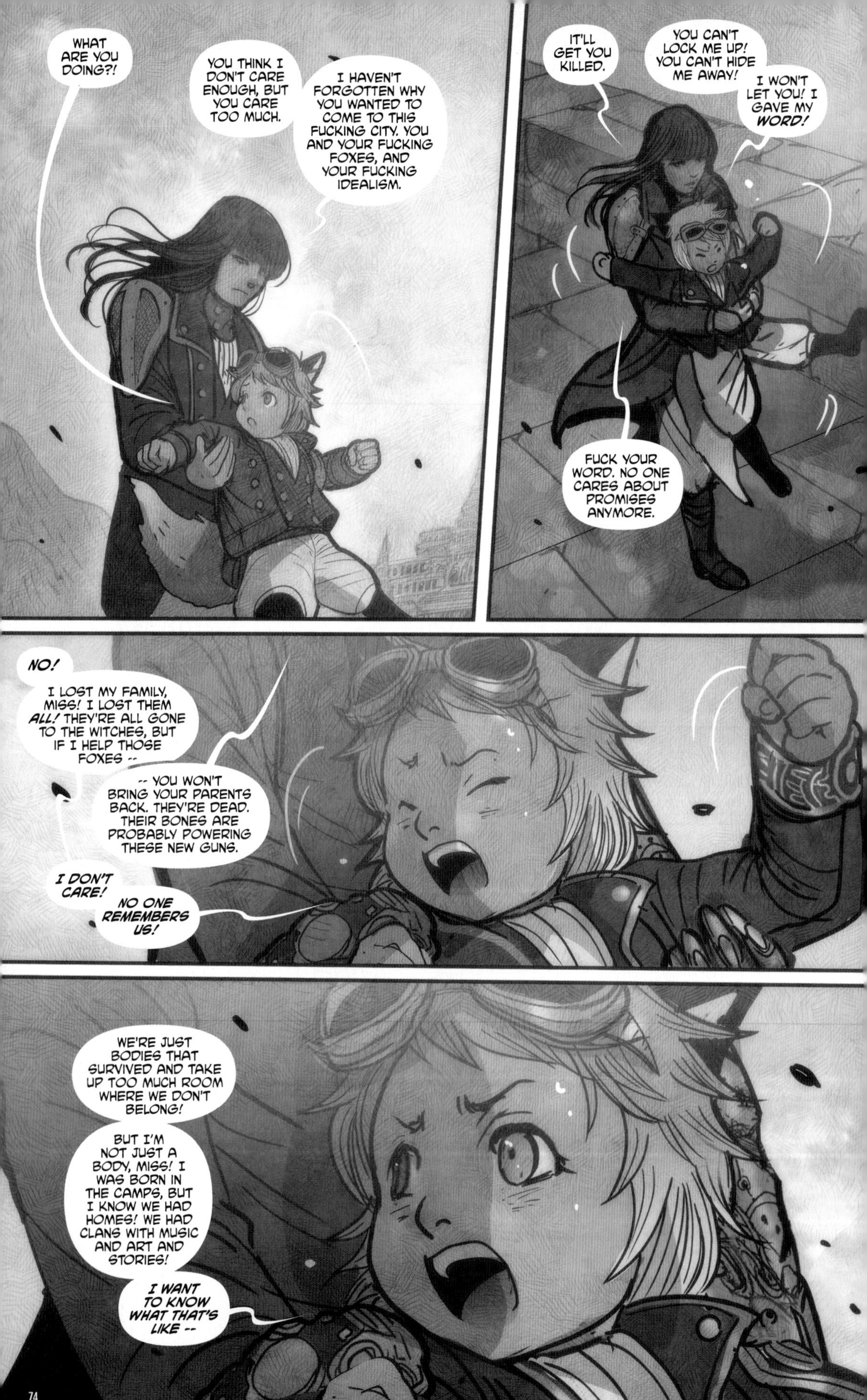
WHAT ARE YOU DOING?!
YOU THINK I DON'T CARE ENOUGH, BUT YOU CARE TOO MUCH.
I HAVEN'T FORGOTTEN WHY YOU WANTED TO COME TO THIS FUCKING CITY. YOU AND YOUR FUCKING FOXES, AND YOUR FUCKING IDEALISM.
IT'LL GET YOU KILLED.
YOU CAN'T LOCK ME UP! YOU CAN'T HIDE ME AWAY!
I WON'T LET YOU! I GAVE MY *WORD!*
FUCK YOUR WORD. NO ONE CARES ABOUT PROMISES ANYMORE.
NO!
I LOST MY FAMILY, MISS! I LOST THEM *ALL!* THEY'RE ALL GONE TO THE WITCHES, BUT IF I HELP THOSE FOXES --
-- YOU WON'T BRING YOUR PARENTS BACK. THEY'RE DEAD. THEIR BONES ARE PROBABLY POWERING THESE NEW GUNS.
I DON'T CARE!
NO ONE REMEMBERS US!
WE'RE JUST BODIES THAT SURVIVED AND TAKE UP TOO MUCH ROOM WHERE WE DON'T BELONG!
BUT I'M NOT JUST A BODY, MISS! I WAS BORN IN THE CAMPS, BUT I KNOW WE HAD HOMES! WE HAD CLANS WITH MUSIC AND ART AND STORIES!
I WANT TO KNOW WHAT THAT'S LIKE --

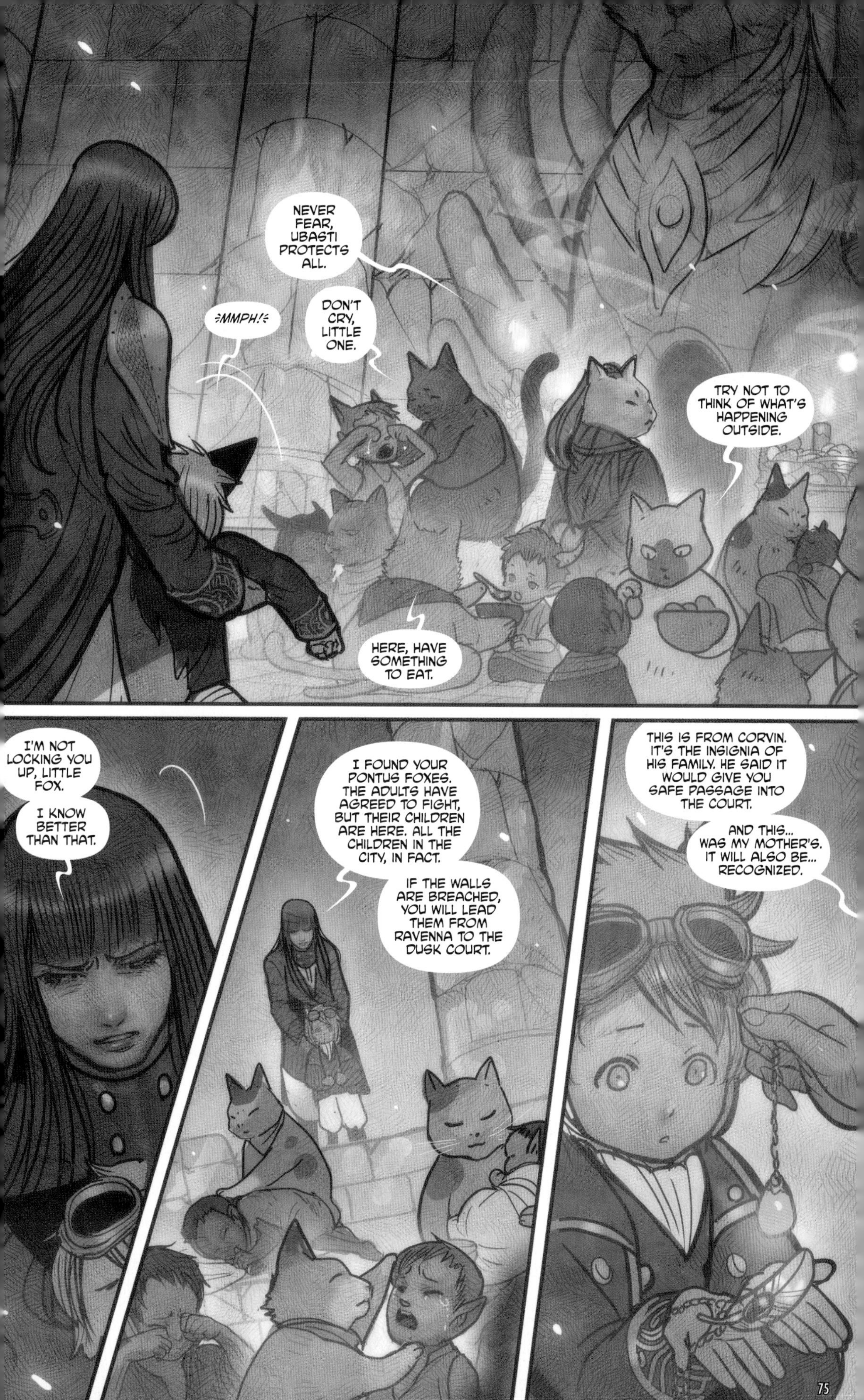
NEVER FEAR, UBASTI PROTECTS ALL.
MMPH!
DON'T CRY, LITTLE ONE.
TRY NOT TO THINK OF WHAT'S HAPPENING OUTSIDE.
HERE, HAVE SOMETHING TO EAT.
I'M NOT LOCKING YOU UP, LITTLE FOX.
I KNOW BETTER THAN THAT.
I FOUND YOUR PONTUS FOXES. THE ADULTS HAVE AGREED TO FIGHT, BUT THEIR CHILDREN ARE HERE. ALL THE CHILDREN IN THE CITY, IN FACT.
IF THE WALLS ARE BREACHED, YOU WILL LEAD THEM FROM RAVENNA TO THE DUSK COURT.
THIS IS FROM CORVIN. IT'S THE INSIGNIA OF HIS FAMILY. HE SAID IT WOULD GIVE YOU SAFE PASSAGE INTO THE COURT.
AND THIS... WAS MY MOTHER'S. IT WILL ALSO BE... RECOGNIZED.

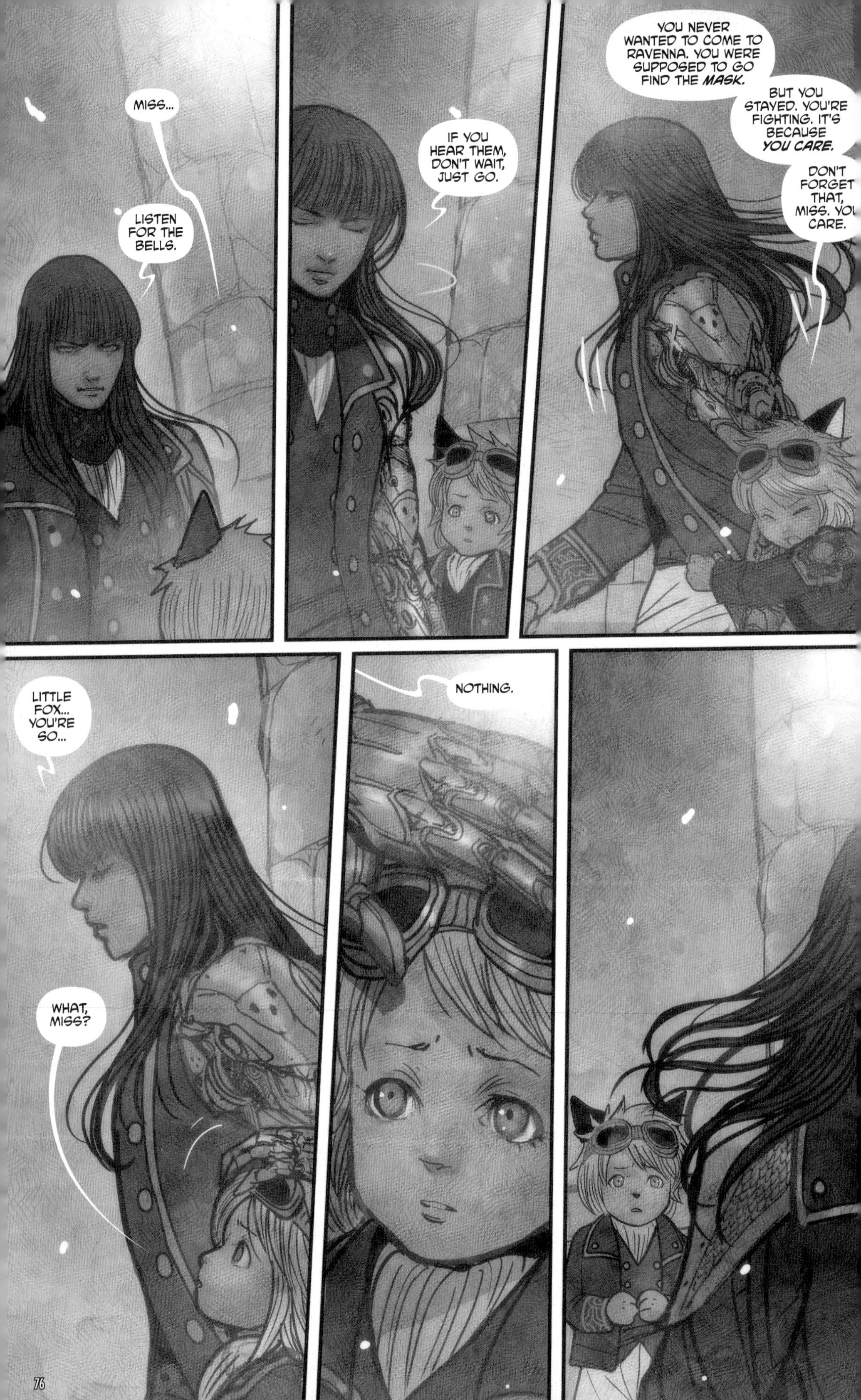
MISS...
LISTEN FOR THE BELLS.
IF YOU HEAR THEM, DON'T WAIT, JUST GO.
YOU NEVER WANTED TO COME TO RAVENNA. YOU WERE SUPPOSED TO GO FIND THE MASK.
BUT YOU STAYED. YOU'RE FIGHTING. IT'S BECAUSE YOU CARE.
DON'T FORGET THAT, MISS. YOU CARE.
LITTLE FOX... YOU'RE SO...
WHAT, MISS?
NOTHING.

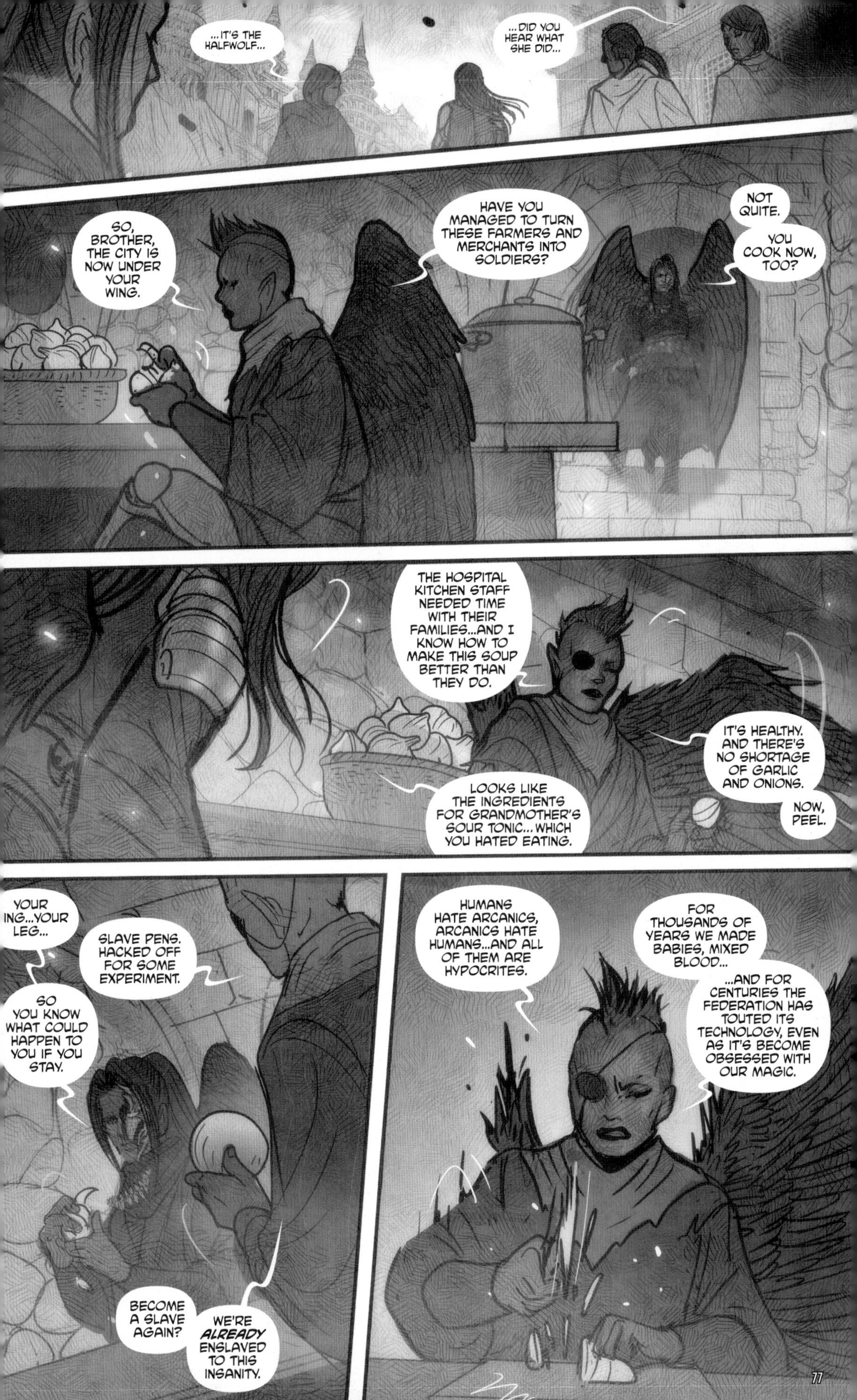
...IT'S THE HALFWOLF...
...DID YOU HEAR WHAT SHE DID...
SO, BROTHER, THE CITY IS NOW UNDER YOUR WING.
HAVE YOU MANAGED TO TURN THESE FARMERS AND MERCHANTS INTO SOLDIERS?
NOT QUITE.
YOU COOK NOW, TOO?
THE HOSPITAL KITCHEN STAFF NEEDED TIME WITH THEIR FAMILIES...AND I KNOW HOW TO MAKE THIS SOUP BETTER THAN THEY DO.
LOOKS LIKE THE INGREDIENTS FOR GRANDMOTHER'S SOUR TONIC...WHICH YOU HATED EATING.
IT'S HEALTHY. AND THERE'S NO SHORTAGE OF GARLIC AND ONIONS.
NOW, PEEL.
YOUR ING...YOUR LEG...
SLAVE PENS. HACKED OFF FOR SOME EXPERIMENT.
SO YOU KNOW WHAT COULD HAPPEN TO YOU IF YOU STAY.
BECOME A SLAVE AGAIN?
WE'RE *ALREADY* ENSLAVED TO THIS INSANITY.
HUMANS HATE ARCANICS, ARCANICS HATE HUMANS...AND ALL OF THEM ARE HYPOCRITES.
FOR THOUSANDS OF YEARS WE MADE BABIES, MIXED BLOOD...
...AND FOR CENTURIES THE FEDERATION HAS TOUTED ITS TECHNOLOGY, EVEN AS IT'S BECOME OBSESSED WITH OUR MAGIC.

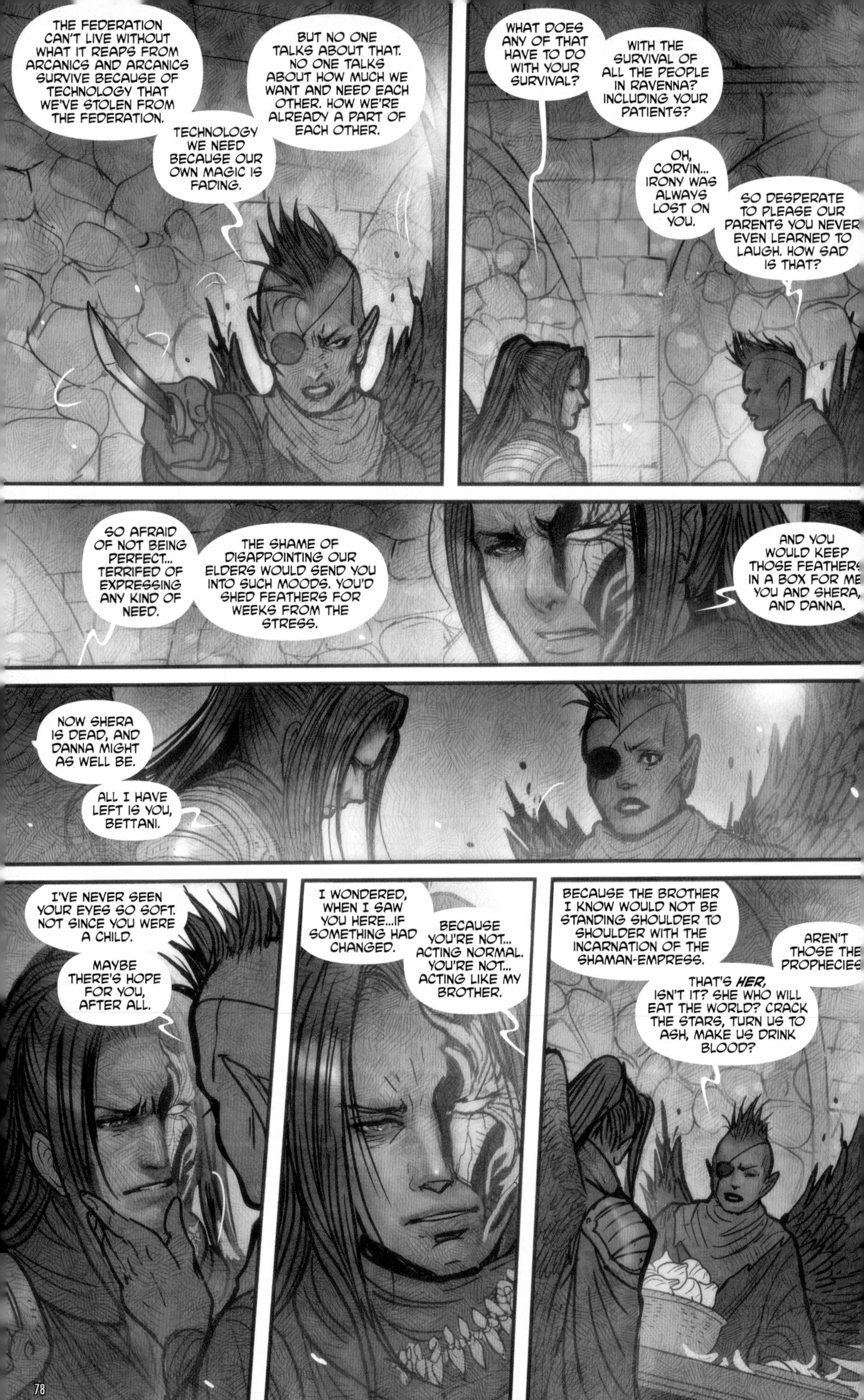
THE FEDERATION CAN'T LIVE WITHOUT WHAT IT REAPS FROM ARCANICS AND ARCANICS SURVIVE BECAUSE OF TECHNOLOGY THAT WE'VE STOLEN FROM THE FEDERATION.
TECHNOLOGY WE NEED BECAUSE OUR OWN MAGIC IS FADING.
BUT NO ONE TALKS ABOUT THAT. NO ONE TALKS ABOUT HOW MUCH WE WANT AND NEED EACH OTHER. HOW WE'RE ALREADY A PART OF EACH OTHER.
WHAT DOES ANY OF THAT HAVE TO DO WITH YOUR SURVIVAL?
WITH THE SURVIVAL OF ALL THE PEOPLE IN RAVENNA? INCLUDING YOUR PATIENTS?
OH, CORVIN... IRONY WAS ALWAYS LOST ON YOU.
SO DESPERATE TO PLEASE OUR PARENTS YOU NEVER EVEN LEARNED TO LAUGH. HOW SAD IS THAT?
SO AFRAID OF NOT BEING PERFECT... TERRIFIED OF EXPRESSING ANY KIND OF NEED.
THE SHAME OF DISAPPOINTING OUR ELDERS WOULD SEND YOU INTO SUCH MOODS. YOU'D SHED FEATHERS FOR WEEKS FROM THE STRESS.
AND YOU WOULD KEEP THOSE FEATHERS IN A BOX FOR ME, YOU AND SHERA, AND DANNA.
NOW SHERA IS DEAD, AND DANNA MIGHT AS WELL BE.
ALL I HAVE LEFT IS YOU, BETTANI.
I'VE NEVER SEEN YOUR EYES SO SOFT. NOT SINCE YOU WERE A CHILD.
MAYBE THERE'S HOPE FOR YOU, AFTER ALL.
I WONDERED, WHEN I SAW YOU HERE...IF SOMETHING HAD CHANGED.
BECAUSE YOU'RE NOT... ACTING NORMAL. YOU'RE NOT... ACTING LIKE MY BROTHER.
BECAUSE THE BROTHER I KNOW WOULD NOT BE STANDING SHOULDER TO SHOULDER WITH THE INCARNATION OF THE SHAMAN-EMPRESS.
THAT'S *HER,* ISN'T IT? SHE WHO WILL EAT THE WORLD? CRACK THE STARS, TURN US TO ASH, MAKE US DRINK BLOOD?
AREN'T THOSE THE PROPHECIES

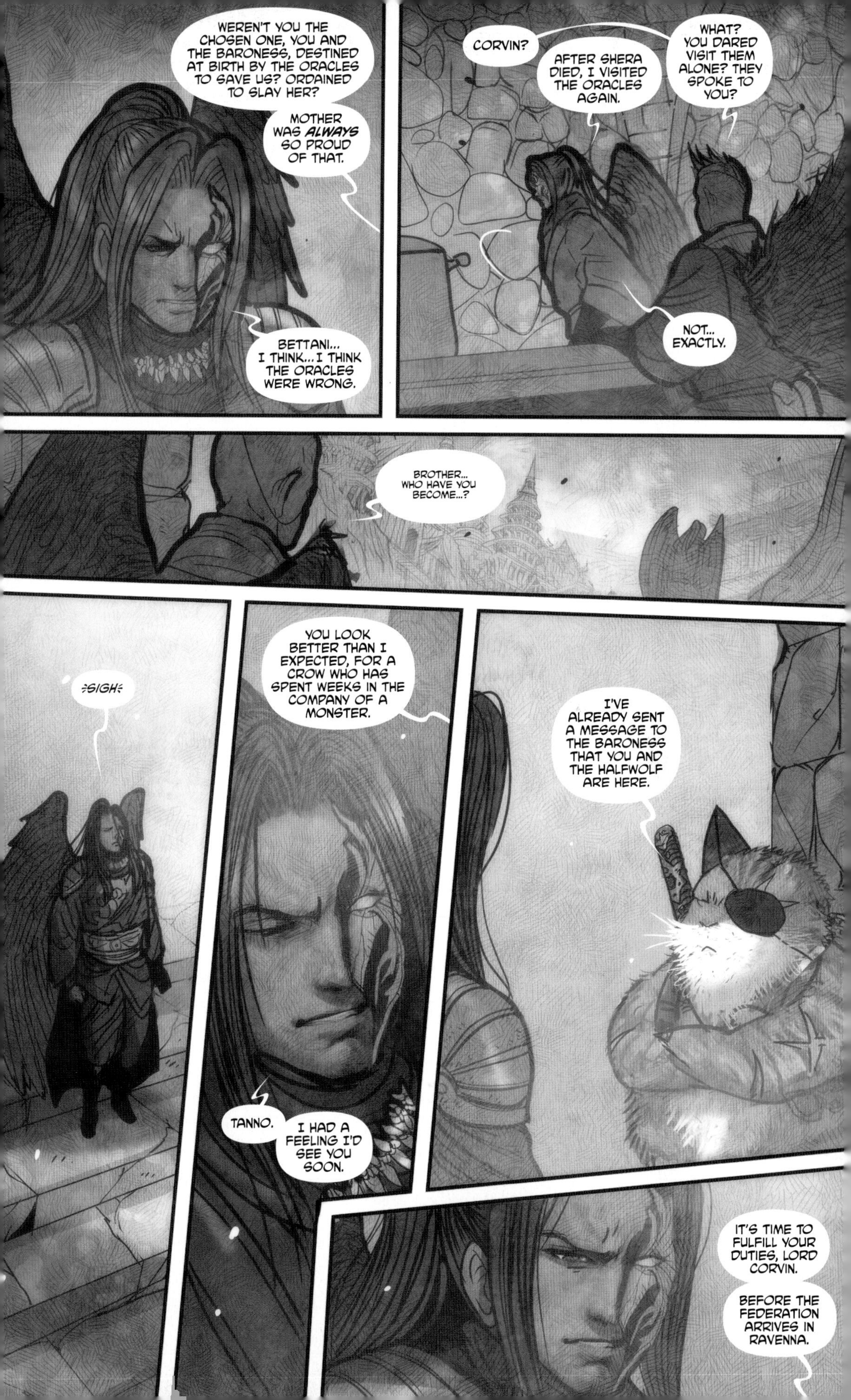
WEREN'T YOU THE CHOSEN ONE, YOU AND THE BARONESS, DESTINED AT BIRTH BY THE ORACLES TO SAVE US? ORDAINED TO SLAY HER?
MOTHER WAS ALWAYS SO PROUD OF THAT.
BETTANI... I THINK... I THINK THE ORACLES WERE WRONG.
CORVIN?
AFTER SHERA DIED, I VISITED THE ORACLES AGAIN.
WHAT? YOU DARED VISIT THEM ALONE? THEY SPOKE TO YOU?
NOT... EXACTLY.
BROTHER... WHO HAVE YOU BECOME...?
SIGH
YOU LOOK BETTER THAN I EXPECTED, FOR A CROW WHO HAS SPENT WEEKS IN THE COMPANY OF A MONSTER.
TANNO.
I HAD A FEELING I'D SEE YOU SOON.
I'VE ALREADY SENT A MESSAGE TO THE BARONESS THAT YOU AND THE HALFWOLF ARE HERE.
IT'S TIME TO FULFILL YOUR DUTIES, LORD CORVIN.
BEFORE THE FEDERATION ARRIVES IN RAVENNA.

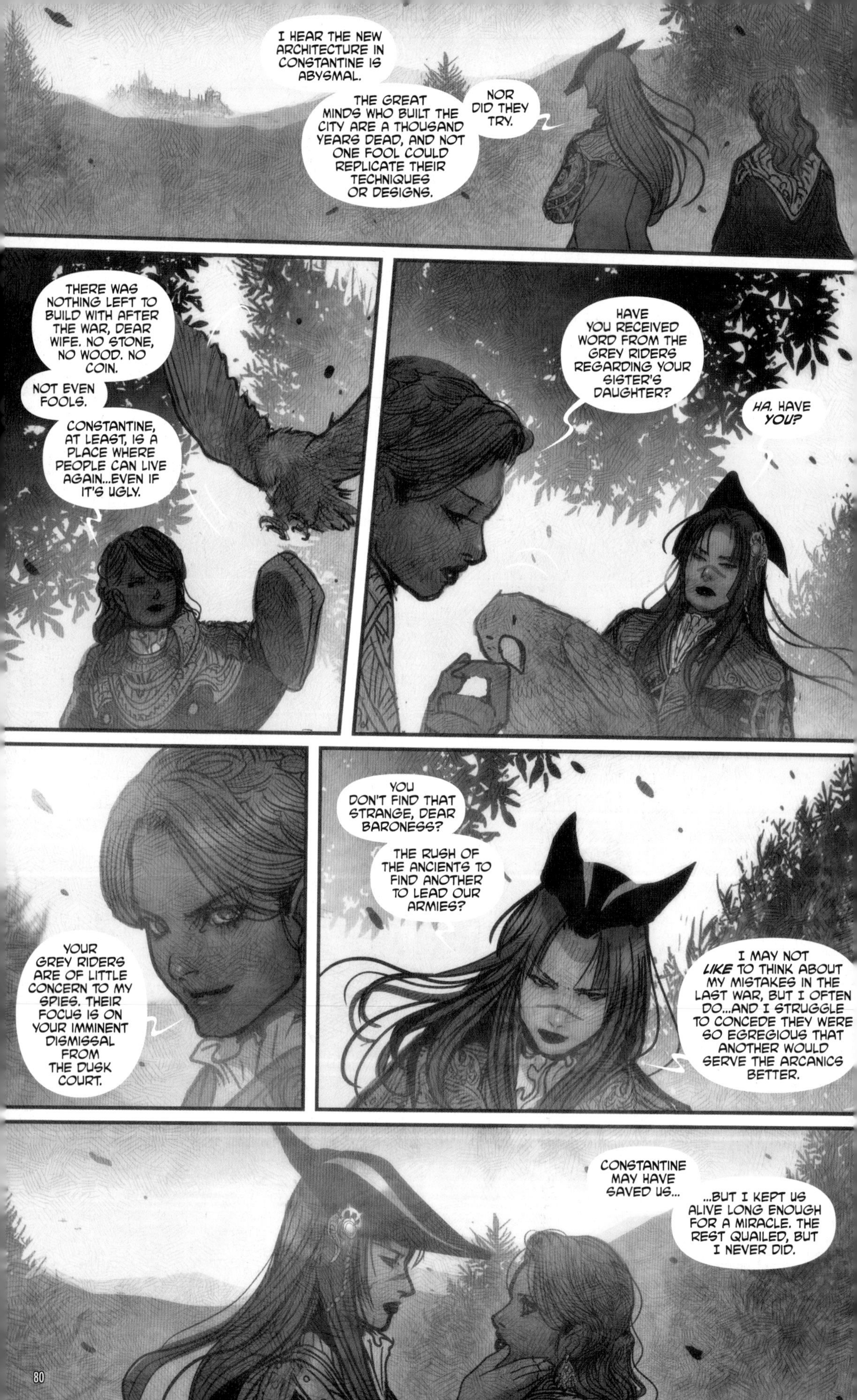
I HEAR THE NEW ARCHITECTURE IN CONSTANTINE IS ABYSMAL.
THE GREAT MINDS WHO BUILT THE CITY ARE A THOUSAND YEARS DEAD, AND NOT ONE FOOL COULD REPLICATE THEIR TECHNIQUES OR DESIGNS.
NOR DID THEY TRY.
THERE WAS NOTHING LEFT TO BUILD WITH AFTER THE WAR, DEAR WIFE. NO STONE, NO WOOD. NO COIN.
NOT EVEN FOOLS.
CONSTANTINE, AT LEAST, IS A PLACE WHERE PEOPLE CAN LIVE AGAIN...EVEN IF IT'S UGLY.
HAVE YOU RECEIVED WORD FROM THE GREY RIDERS REGARDING YOUR SISTER'S DAUGHTER?
HA. HAVE YOU?
YOUR GREY RIDERS ARE OF LITTLE CONCERN TO MY SPIES. THEIR FOCUS IS ON YOUR IMMINENT DISMISSAL FROM THE DUSK COURT.
YOU DON'T FIND THAT STRANGE, DEAR BARONESS?
THE RUSH OF THE ANCIENTS TO FIND ANOTHER TO LEAD OUR ARMIES?
I MAY NOT LIKE TO THINK ABOUT MY MISTAKES IN THE LAST WAR, BUT I OFTEN DO...AND I STRUGGLE TO CONCEDE THEY WERE SO EGREGIOUS THAT ANOTHER WOULD SERVE THE ARCANICS BETTER.
CONSTANTINE MAY HAVE SAVED US...
...BUT I KEPT US ALIVE LONG ENOUGH FOR A MIRACLE. THE REST QUAILED, BUT I NEVER DID.

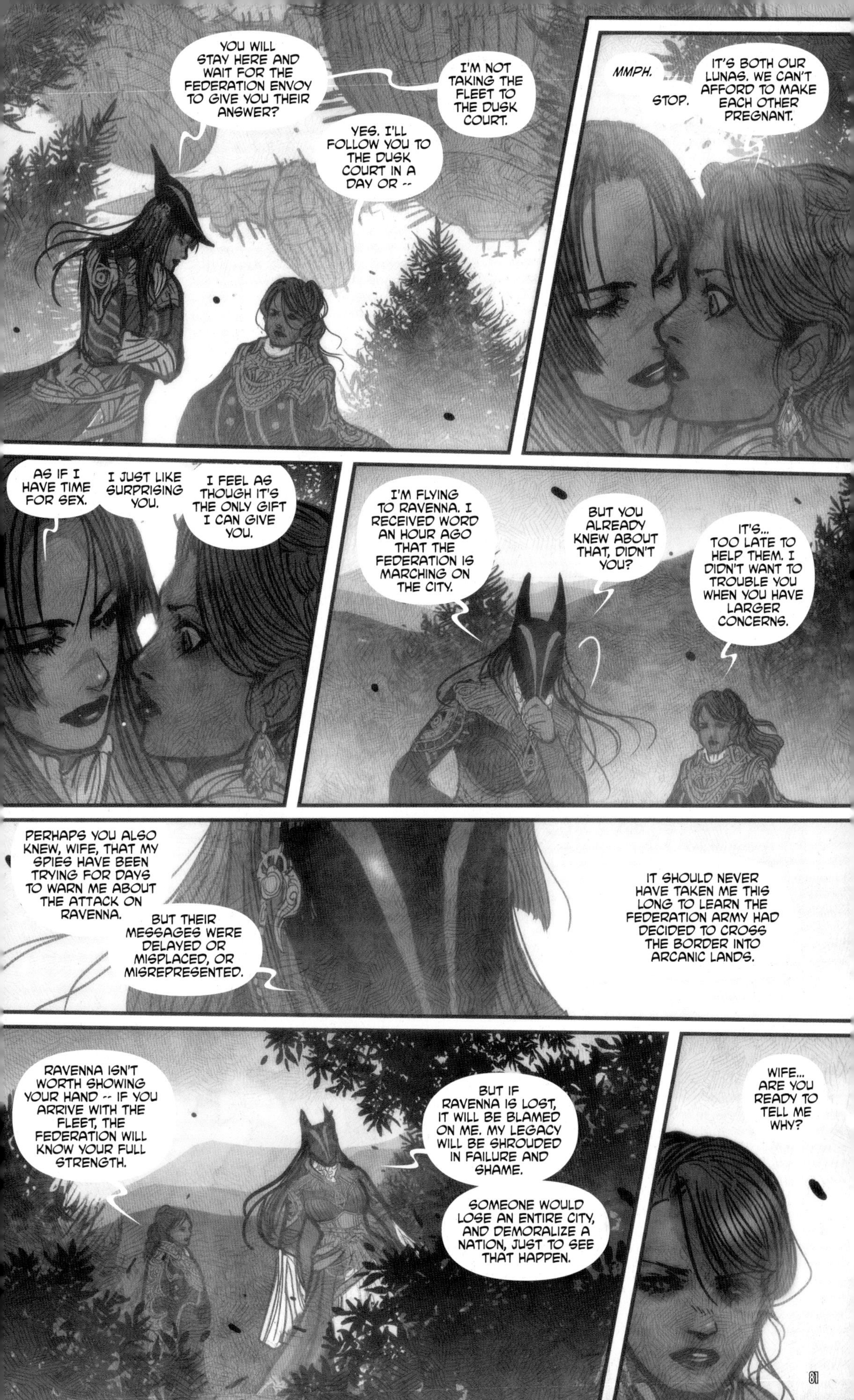
YOU WILL STAY HERE AND WAIT FOR THE FEDERATION ENVOY TO GIVE YOU THEIR ANSWER?
I'M NOT TAKING THE FLEET TO THE DUSK COURT.
YES. I'LL FOLLOW YOU TO THE DUSK COURT IN A DAY OR --
MMPH.
STOP.
IT'S BOTH OUR LUNAS. WE CAN'T AFFORD TO MAKE EACH OTHER PREGNANT.
AS IF I HAVE TIME FOR SEX.
I JUST LIKE SURPRISING YOU.
I FEEL AS THOUGH IT'S THE ONLY GIFT I CAN GIVE YOU.
I'M FLYING TO RAVENNA. I RECEIVED WORD AN HOUR AGO THAT THE FEDERATION IS MARCHING ON THE CITY.
BUT YOU ALREADY KNEW ABOUT THAT, DIDN'T YOU?
IT'S... TOO LATE TO HELP THEM. I DIDN'T WANT TO TROUBLE YOU WHEN YOU HAVE LARGER CONCERNS.
PERHAPS YOU ALSO KNEW, WIFE, THAT MY SPIES HAVE BEEN TRYING FOR DAYS TO WARN ME ABOUT THE ATTACK ON RAVENNA.
BUT THEIR MESSAGES WERE DELAYED OR MISPLACED, OR MISREPRESENTED.
IT SHOULD NEVER HAVE TAKEN ME THIS LONG TO LEARN THE FEDERATION ARMY HAD DECIDED TO CROSS THE BORDER INTO ARCANIC LANDS.
RAVENNA ISN'T WORTH SHOWING YOUR HAND -- IF YOU ARRIVE WITH THE FLEET, THE FEDERATION WILL KNOW YOUR FULL STRENGTH.
BUT IF RAVENNA IS LOST, IT WILL BE BLAMED ON ME. MY LEGACY WILL BE SHROUDED IN FAILURE AND SHAME.
SOMEONE WOULD LOSE AN ENTIRE CITY, AND DEMORALIZE A NATION, JUST TO SEE THAT HAPPEN.
WIFE... ARE YOU READY TO TELL ME WHY?

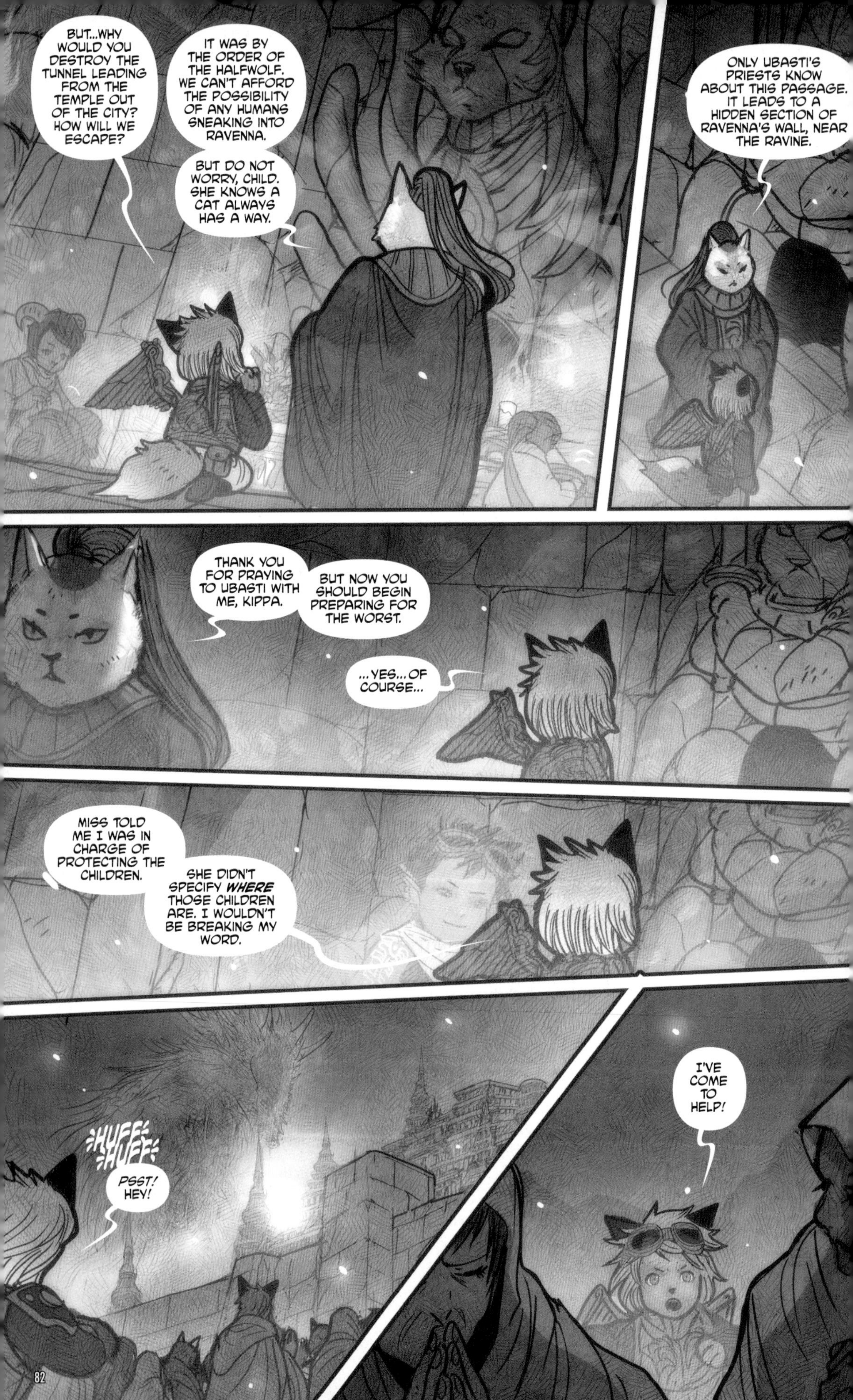
BUT...WHY WOULD YOU DESTROY THE TUNNEL LEADING FROM THE TEMPLE OUT OF THE CITY? HOW WILL WE ESCAPE?
IT WAS BY THE ORDER OF THE HALFWOLF. WE CAN'T AFFORD THE POSSIBILITY OF ANY HUMANS SNEAKING INTO RAVENNA.
BUT DO NOT WORRY, CHILD. SHE KNOWS A CAT ALWAYS HAS A WAY.
ONLY UBASTI'S PRIESTS KNOW ABOUT THIS PASSAGE. IT LEADS TO A HIDDEN SECTION OF RAVENNA'S WALL, NEAR THE RAVINE.
THANK YOU FOR PRAYING TO UBASTI WITH ME, KIPPA.
BUT NOW YOU SHOULD BEGIN PREPARING FOR THE WORST.
...YES...OF COURSE...
MISS TOLD ME I WAS IN CHARGE OF PROTECTING THE CHILDREN.
SHE DIDN'T SPECIFY ***WHERE*** THOSE CHILDREN ARE. I WOULDN'T BE BREAKING MY WORD.
HUFF HUFF
PSST! HEY!
I'VE COME TO HELP!

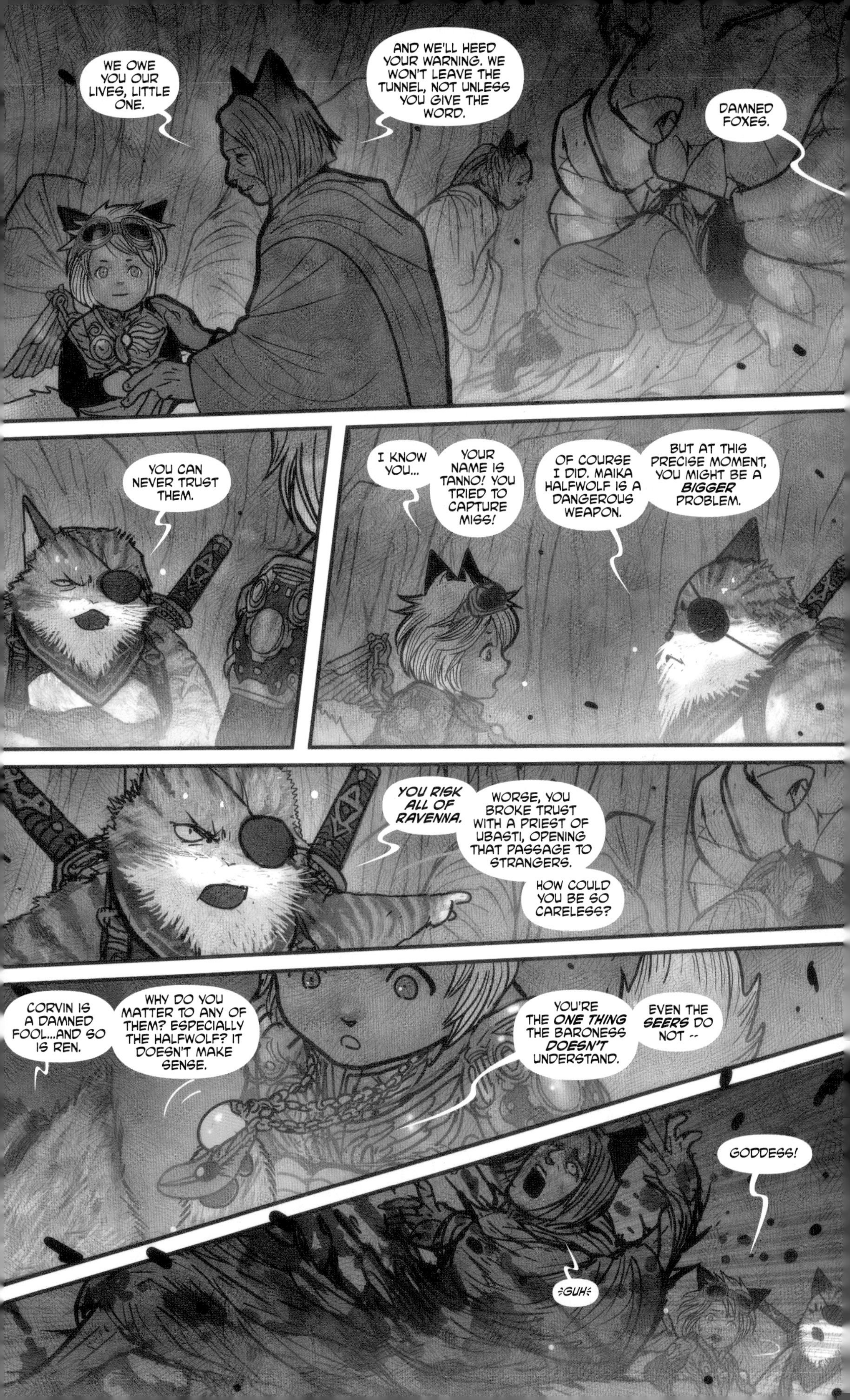
WE OWE YOU OUR LIVES, LITTLE ONE.
AND WE'LL HEED YOUR WARNING. WE WON'T LEAVE THE TUNNEL, NOT UNLESS YOU GIVE THE WORD.
DAMNED FOXES.
YOU CAN NEVER TRUST THEM.
I KNOW YOU...
YOUR NAME IS TANNO! YOU TRIED TO CAPTURE MISS!
OF COURSE I DID. MAIKA HALFWOLF IS A DANGEROUS WEAPON.
BUT AT THIS PRECISE MOMENT, YOU MIGHT BE A BIGGER PROBLEM.
YOU RISK ALL OF RAVENNA.
WORSE, YOU BROKE TRUST WITH A PRIEST OF UBASTI, OPENING THAT PASSAGE TO STRANGERS.
HOW COULD YOU BE SO CARELESS?
CORVIN IS A DAMNED FOOL...AND SO IS REN.
WHY DO YOU MATTER TO ANY OF THEM? ESPECIALLY THE HALFWOLF? IT DOESN'T MAKE SENSE.
YOU'RE THE ONE THING THE BARONESS DOESN'T UNDERSTAND.
EVEN THE SEERS DO NOT --
GODDESS!
GUH

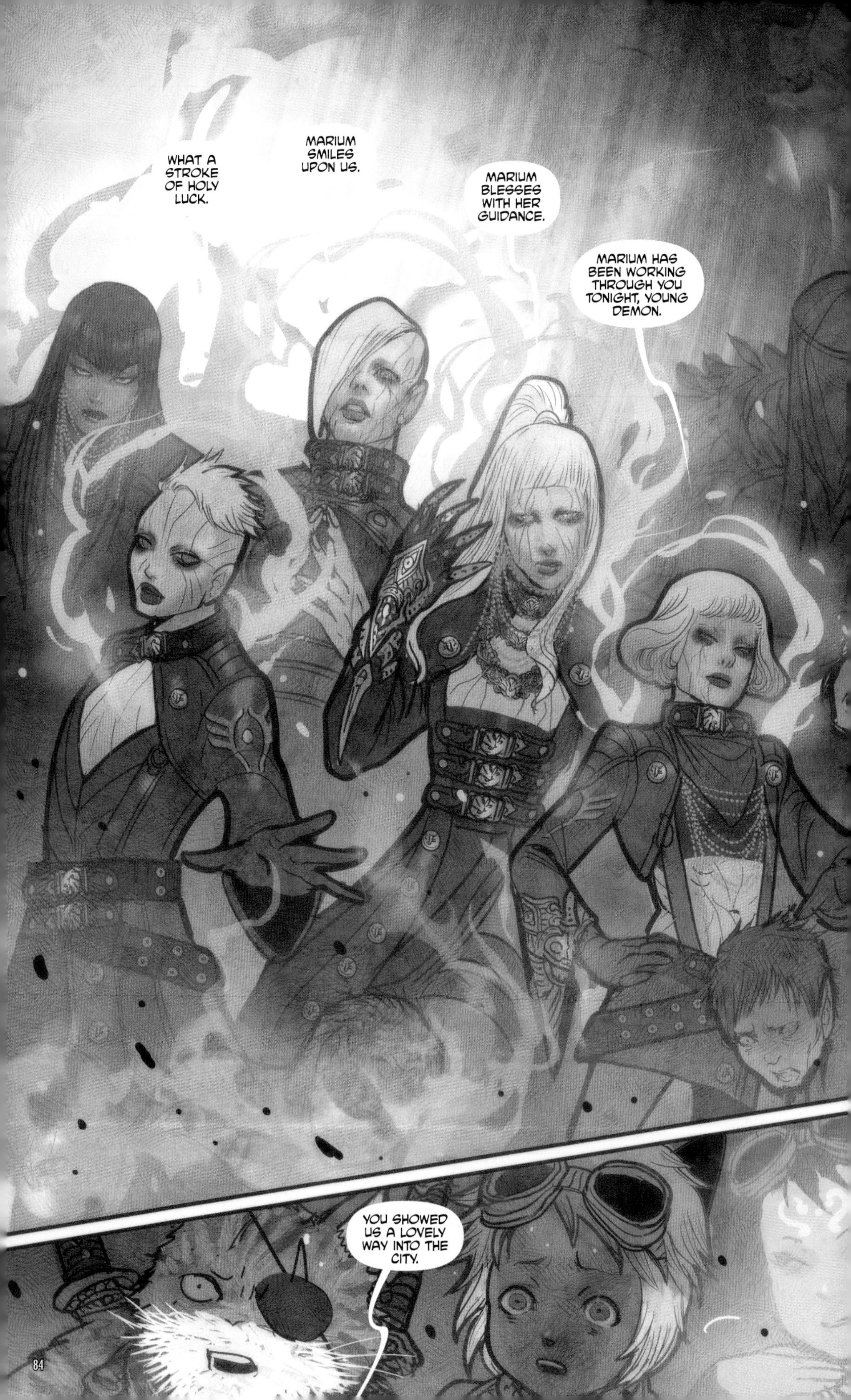
WHAT A STROKE OF HOLY LUCK.
MARIUM SMILES UPON US.
MARIUM BLESSES WITH HER GUIDANCE.
MARIUM HAS BEEN WORKING THROUGH YOU TONIGHT, YOUNG DEMON.
YOU SHOWED US A LOVELY WAY INTO THE CITY.

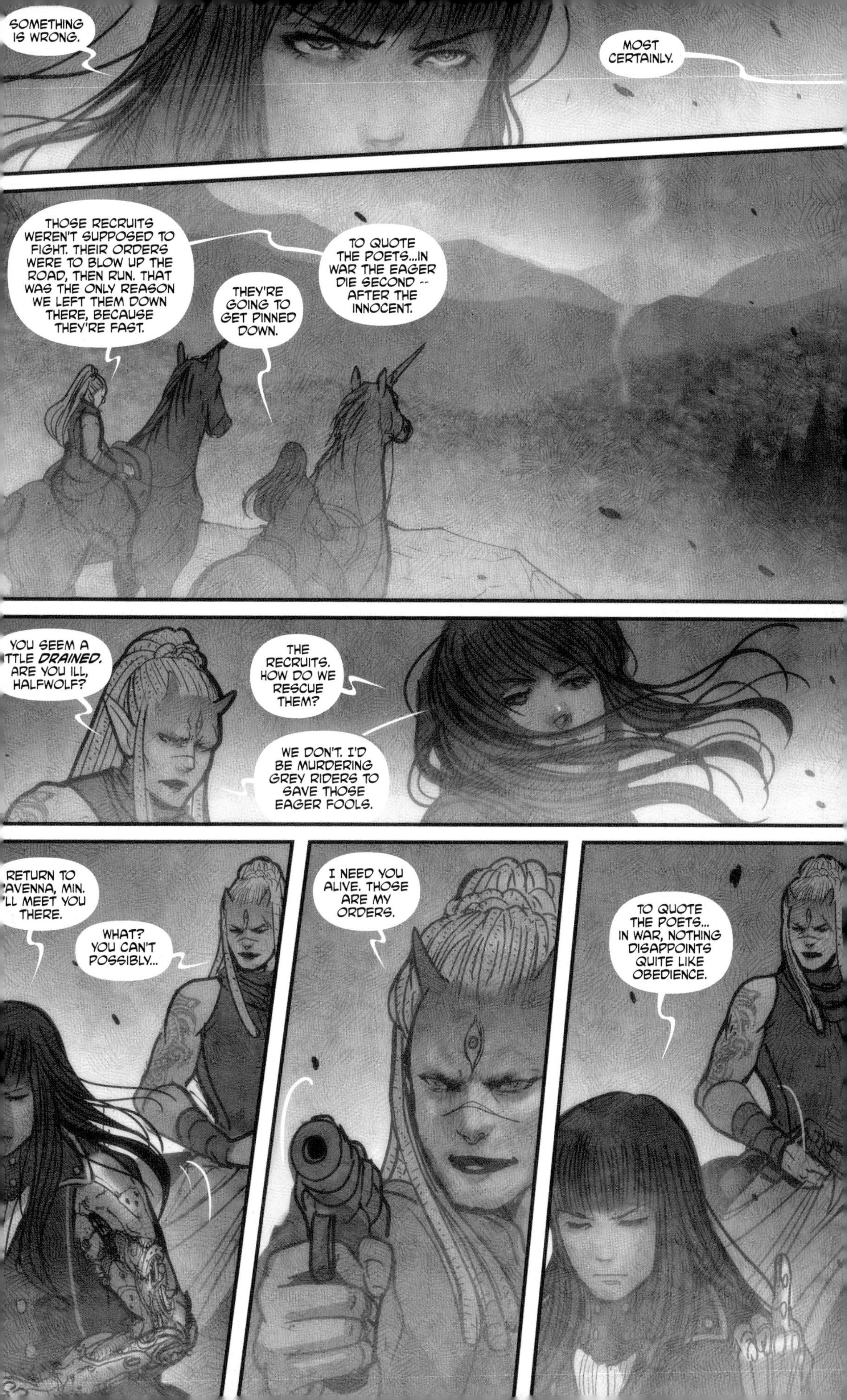

SOMETHING IS WRONG.
MOST CERTAINLY.
THOSE RECRUITS WEREN'T SUPPOSED TO FIGHT. THEIR ORDERS WERE TO BLOW UP THE ROAD, THEN RUN. THAT WAS THE ONLY REASON WE LEFT THEM DOWN THERE, BECAUSE THEY'RE FAST.
THEY'RE GOING TO GET PINNED DOWN.
TO QUOTE THE POETS...IN WAR THE EAGER DIE SECOND -- AFTER THE INNOCENT.
YOU SEEM A TTLE *DRAINED.* ARE YOU ILL, HALFWOLF?
THE RECRUITS. HOW DO WE RESCUE THEM?
WE DON'T. I'D BE MURDERING GREY RIDERS TO SAVE THOSE EAGER FOOLS.
RETURN TO AVENNA, MIN. 'LL MEET YOU THERE.
WHAT? YOU CAN'T POSSIBLY...
I NEED YOU ALIVE. THOSE ARE MY ORDERS.
TO QUOTE THE POETS... IN WAR, NOTHING DISAPPOINTS QUITE LIKE OBEDIENCE.

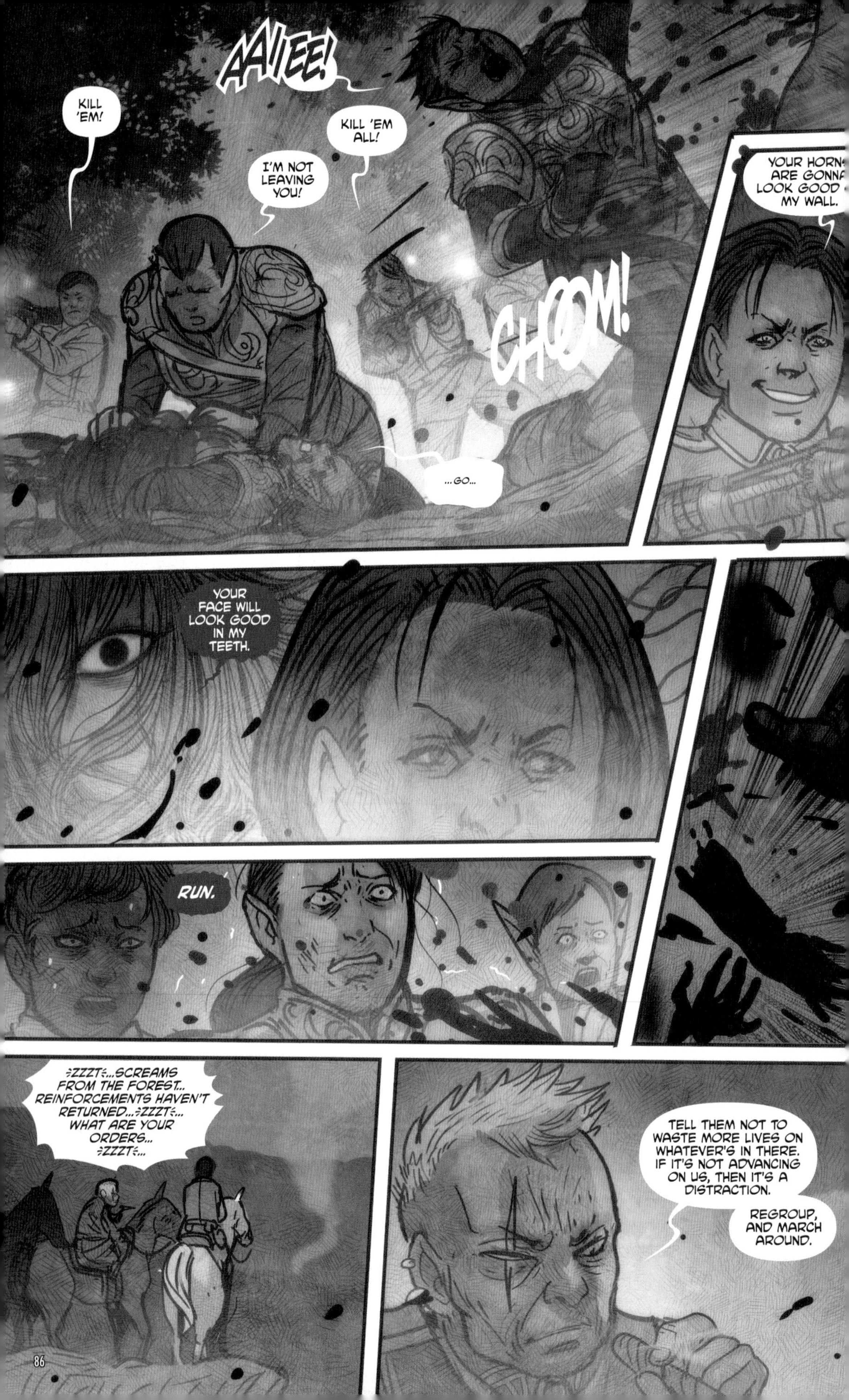
AAIIEE!
KILL 'EM!
I'M NOT LEAVING YOU!
KILL 'EM ALL!
CHOOM!
...GO...
YOUR HORNS ARE GONNA LOOK GOOD ON MY WALL.
YOUR FACE WILL LOOK GOOD IN MY TEETH.
RUN.
ZZZT...SCREAMS FROM THE FOREST.. REINFORCEMENTS HAVEN'T RETURNED...ZZZT... WHAT ARE YOUR ORDERS... ZZZT...
TELL THEM NOT TO WASTE MORE LIVES ON WHATEVER'S IN THERE. IF IT'S NOT ADVANCING ON US, THEN IT'S A DISTRACTION.
REGROUP, AND MARCH AROUND.

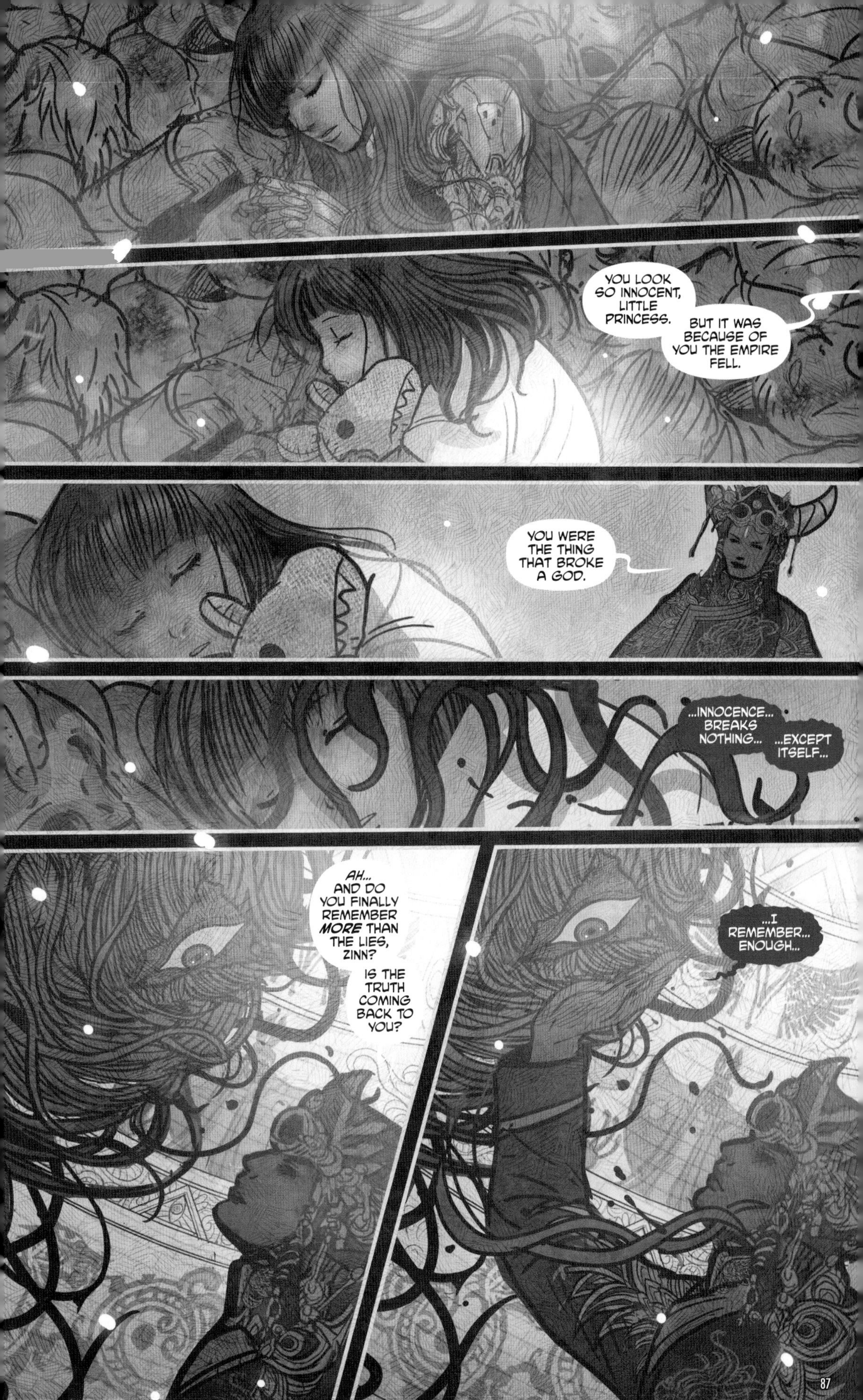
YOU LOOK SO INNOCENT, LITTLE PRINCESS.
BUT IT WAS BECAUSE OF YOU THE EMPIRE FELL.
YOU WERE THE THING THAT BROKE A GOD.
...INNOCENCE... BREAKS NOTHING...
...EXCEPT ITSELF...
AH... AND DO YOU FINALLY REMEMBER MORE THAN THE LIES, ZINN?
IS THE TRUTH COMING BACK TO YOU?
...I REMEMBER... ENOUGH...

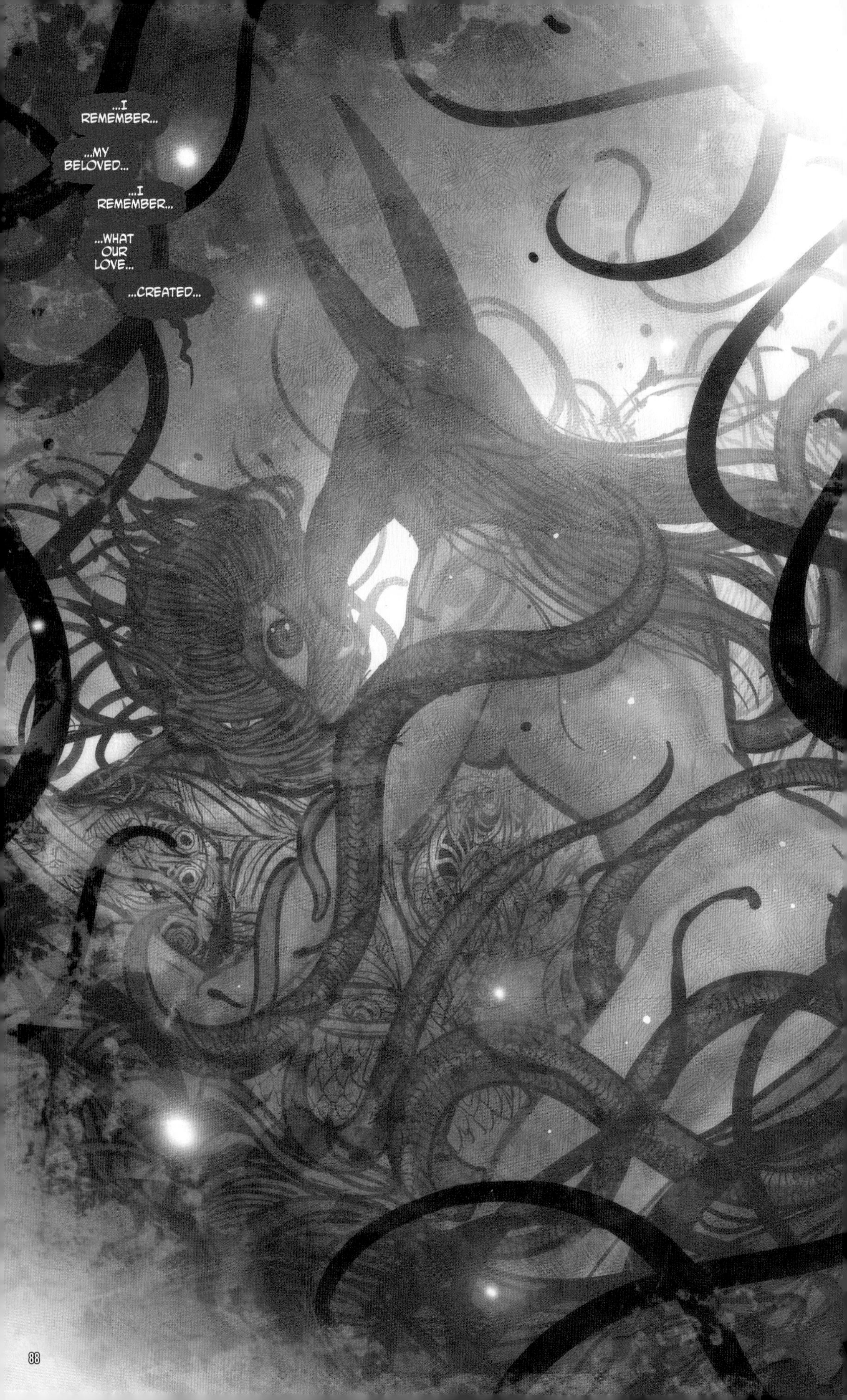
...I REMEMBER...
...MY BELOVED...
...I REMEMBER...
...WHAT OUR LOVE...
...CREATED...

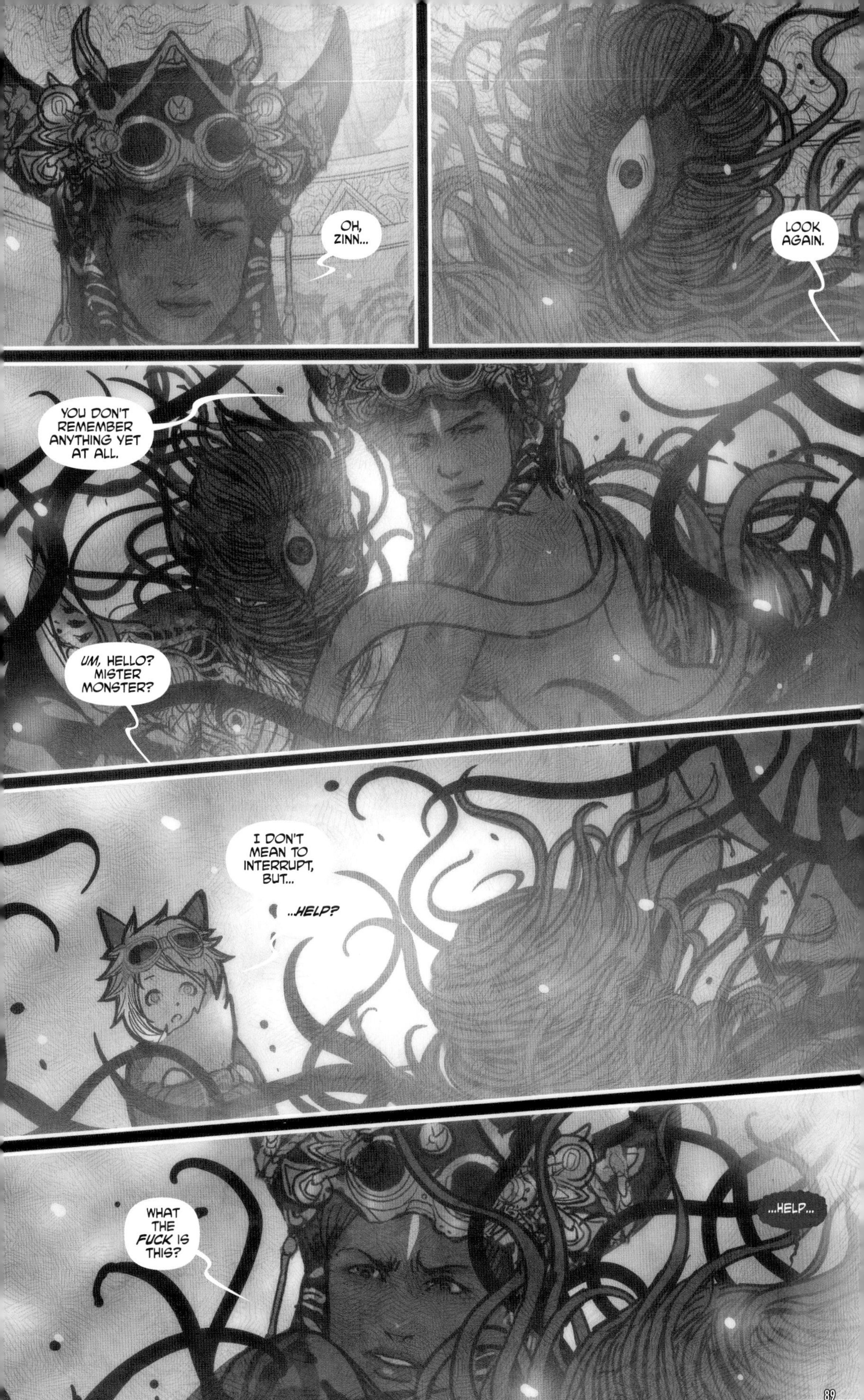
OH, ZINN...
LOOK AGAIN.
YOU DON'T REMEMBER ANYTHING YET AT ALL.
UM, HELLO? MISTER MONSTER?
I DON'T MEAN TO INTERRUPT, BUT...
...*HELP?*
WHAT THE *FUCK* IS THIS?
...HELP...

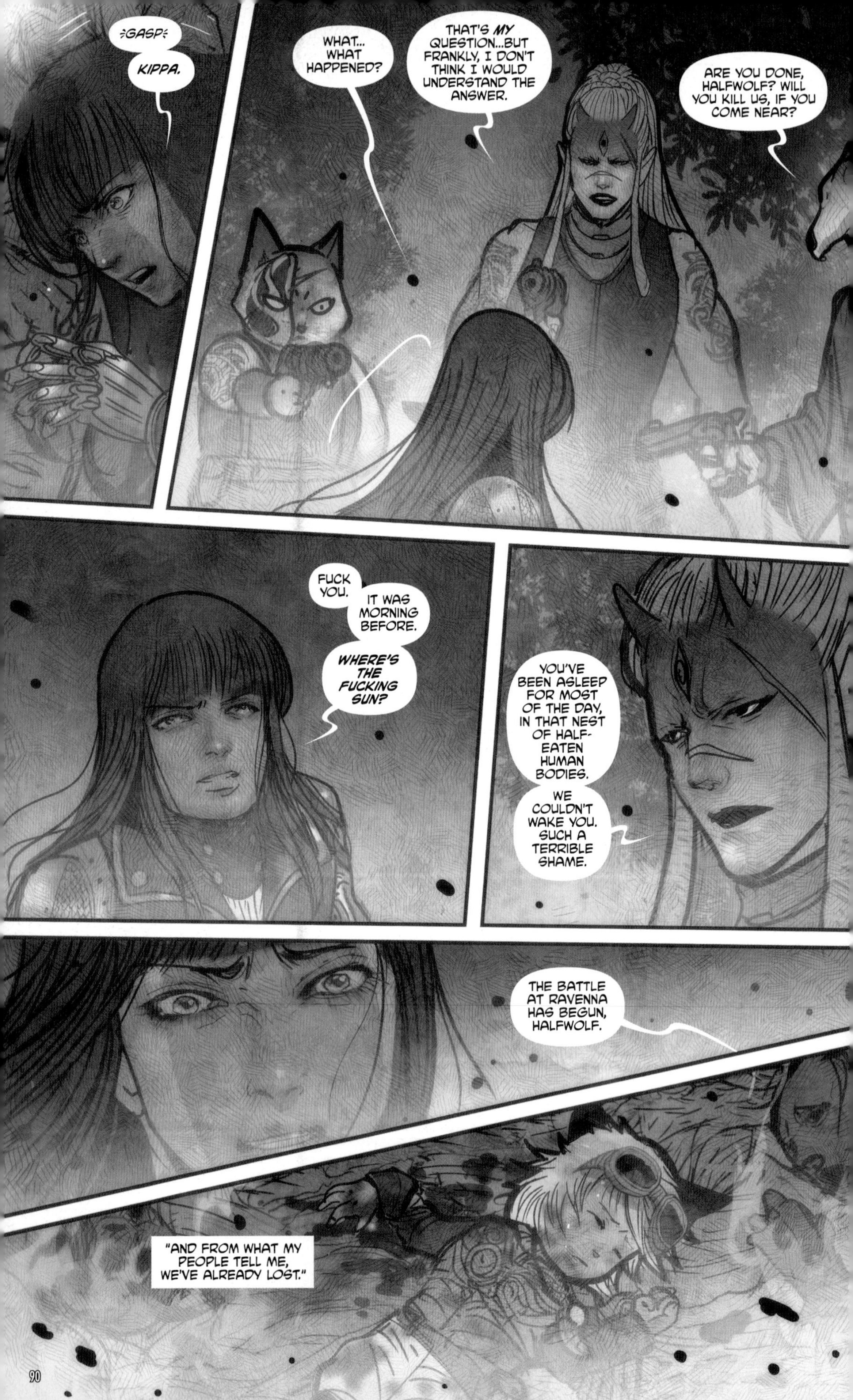

⇒GASP⇐
KIPPA.
WHAT... WHAT HAPPENED?
THAT'S MY QUESTION...BUT FRANKLY, I DON'T THINK I WOULD UNDERSTAND THE ANSWER.
ARE YOU DONE, HALFWOLF? WILL YOU KILL US, IF YOU COME NEAR?
FUCK YOU.
IT WAS MORNING BEFORE.
WHERE'S THE FUCKING SUN?
YOU'VE BEEN ASLEEP FOR MOST OF THE DAY, IN THAT NEST OF HALF-EATEN HUMAN BODIES.
WE COULDN'T WAKE YOU. SUCH A TERRIBLE SHAME.
THE BATTLE AT RAVENNA HAS BEGUN, HALFWOLF.
"AND FROM WHAT MY PEOPLE TELL ME, WE'VE ALREADY LOST."

CHAPTER TWENTY-EIGHT

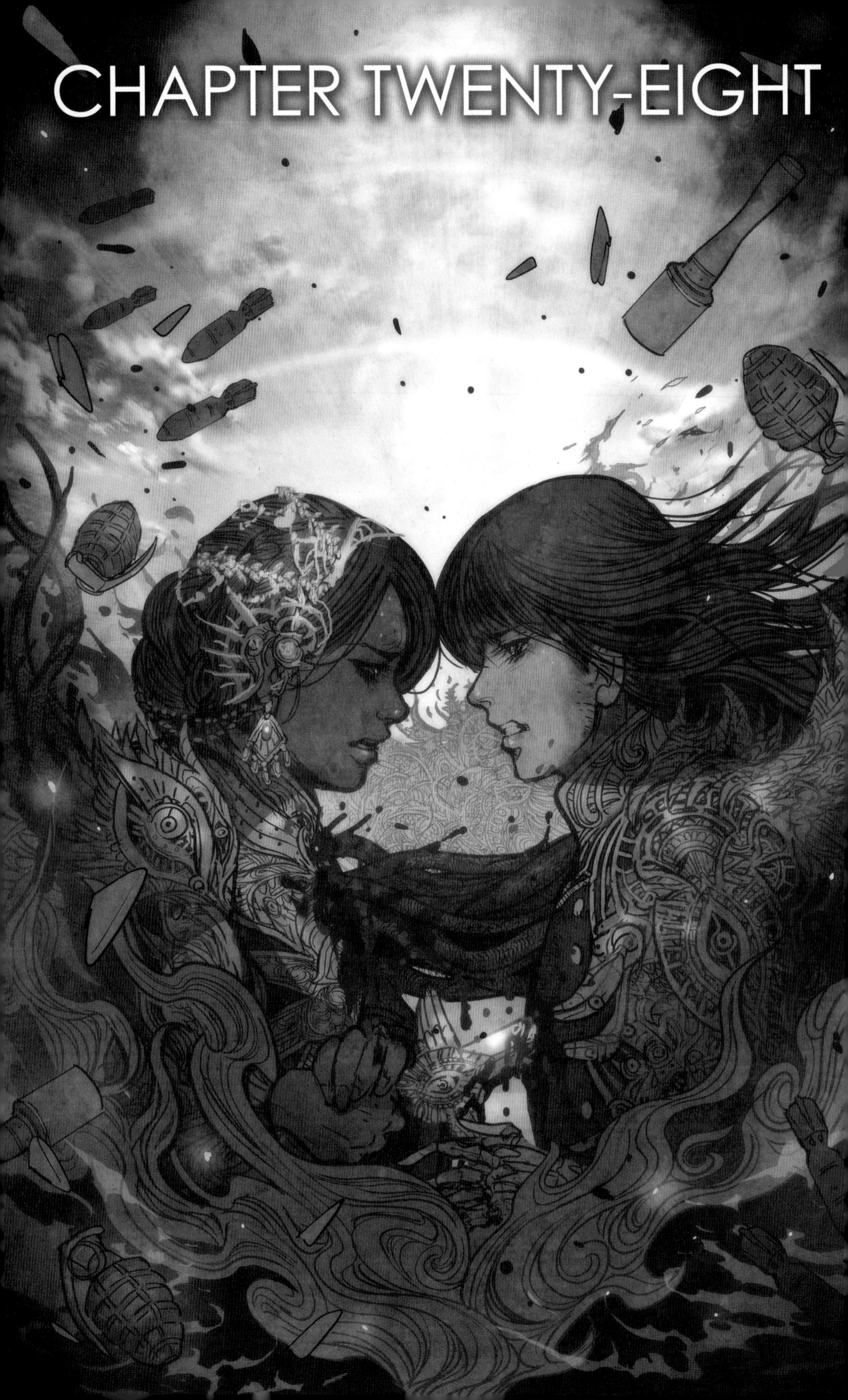

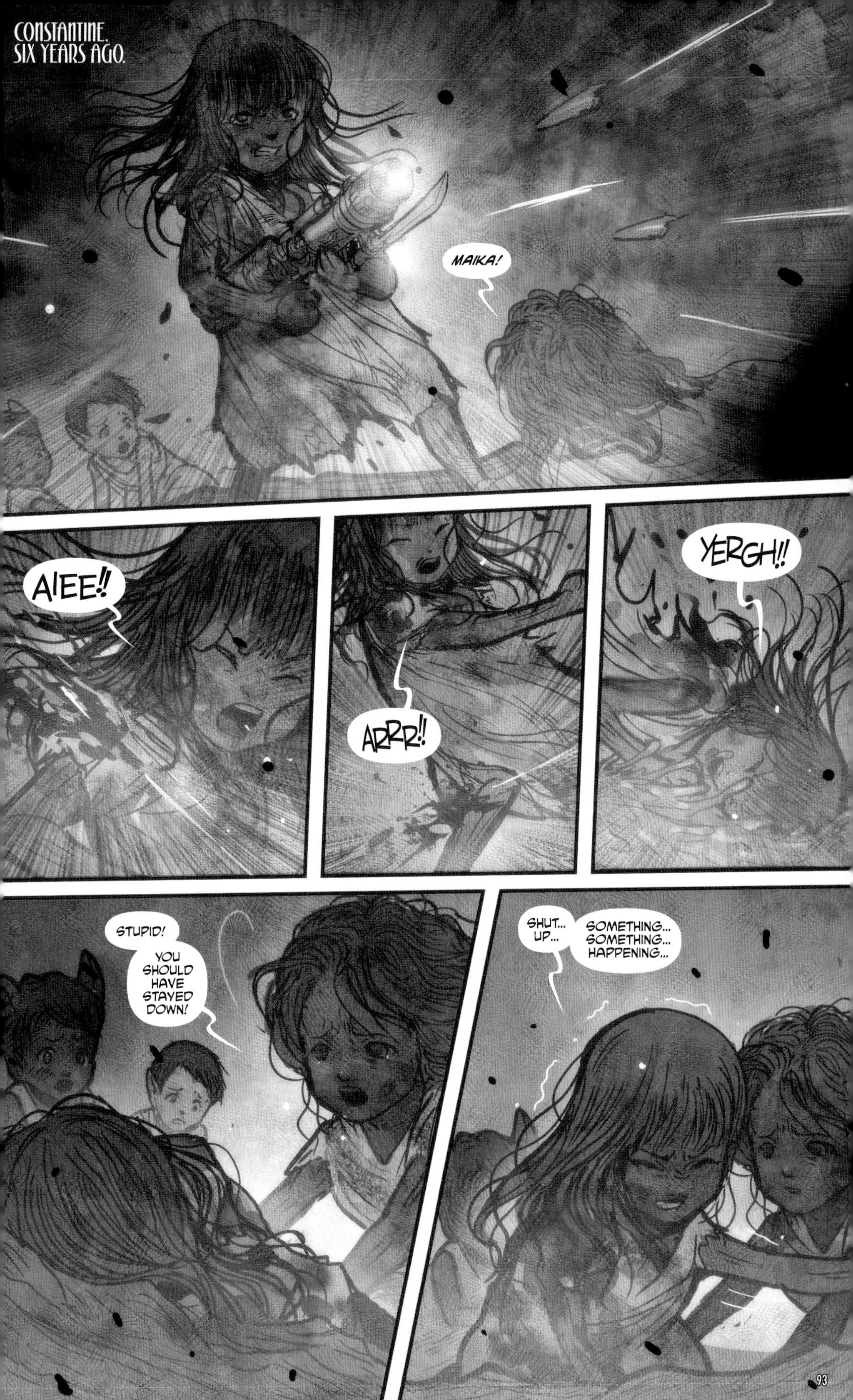
CONSTANTINE.
SIX YEARS AGO.
MAIKA!
AIEE!!
ARRR!!
YERGH!!
STUPID!
YOU SHOULD HAVE STAYED DOWN!
SHUT... UP...
SOMETHING... SOMETHING... HAPPENING...

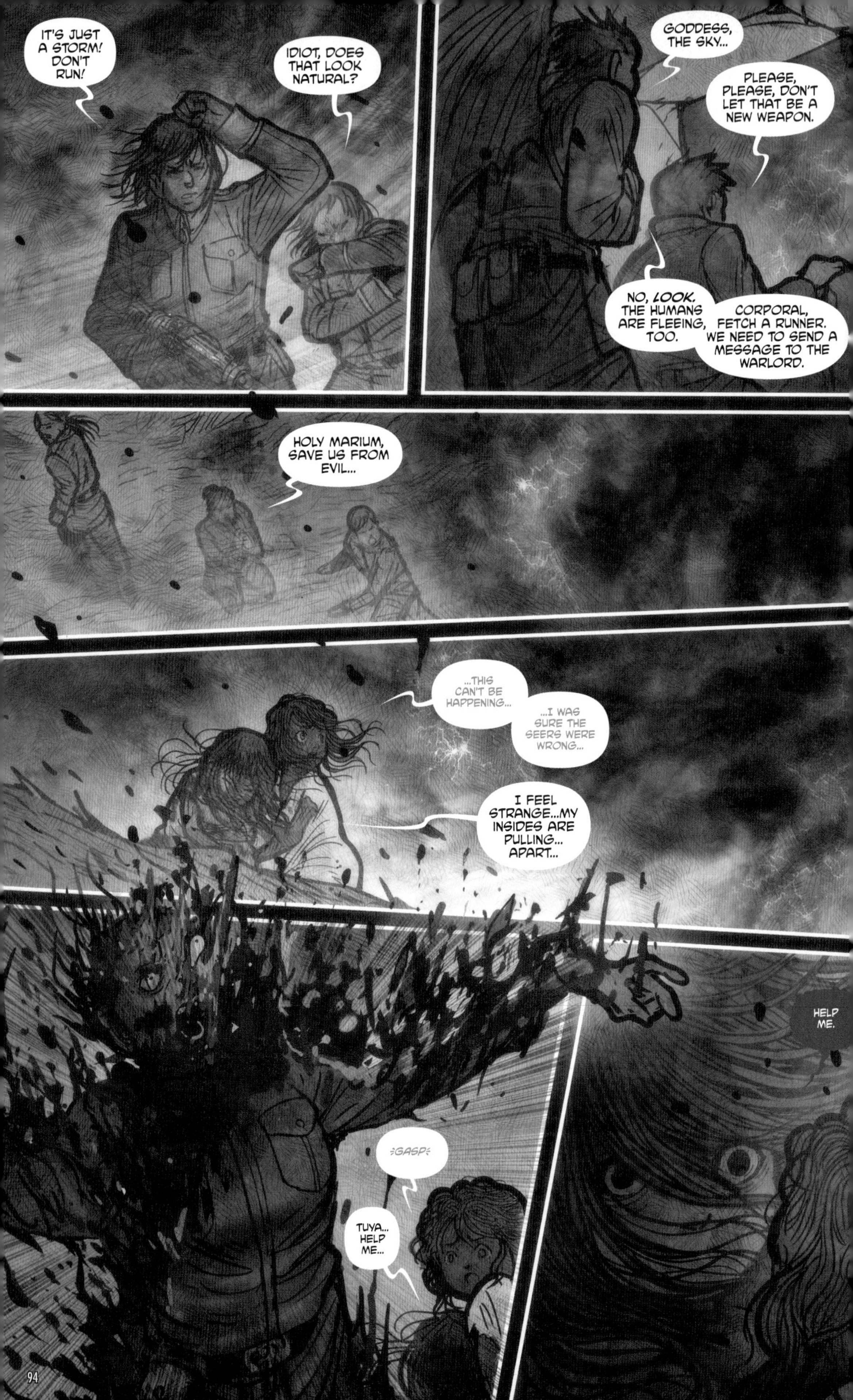
IT'S JUST A STORM! DON'T RUN!
IDIOT, DOES THAT LOOK NATURAL?
GODDESS, THE SKY...
PLEASE, PLEASE, DON'T LET THAT BE A NEW WEAPON.
NO, *LOOK.* THE HUMANS ARE FLEEING, TOO.
CORPORAL, FETCH A RUNNER. WE NEED TO SEND A MESSAGE TO THE WARLORD.
HOLY MARIUM, SAVE US FROM EVIL...
...THIS CAN'T BE HAPPENING...
...I WAS SURE THE SEERS WERE WRONG...
I FEEL STRANGE...MY INSIDES ARE PULLING... APART...
HELP ME.
GASP
TUYA... HELP ME...

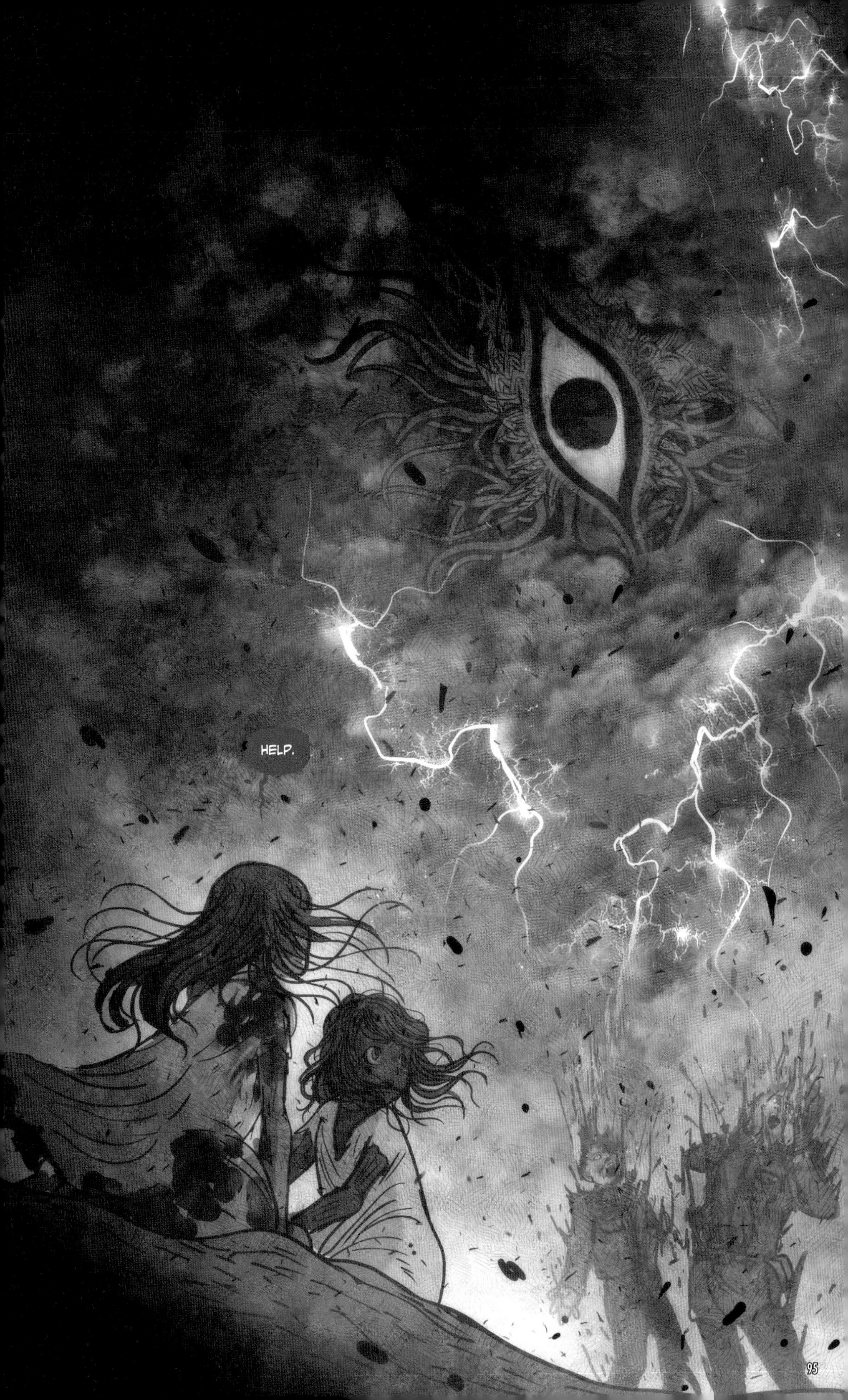
HELP.

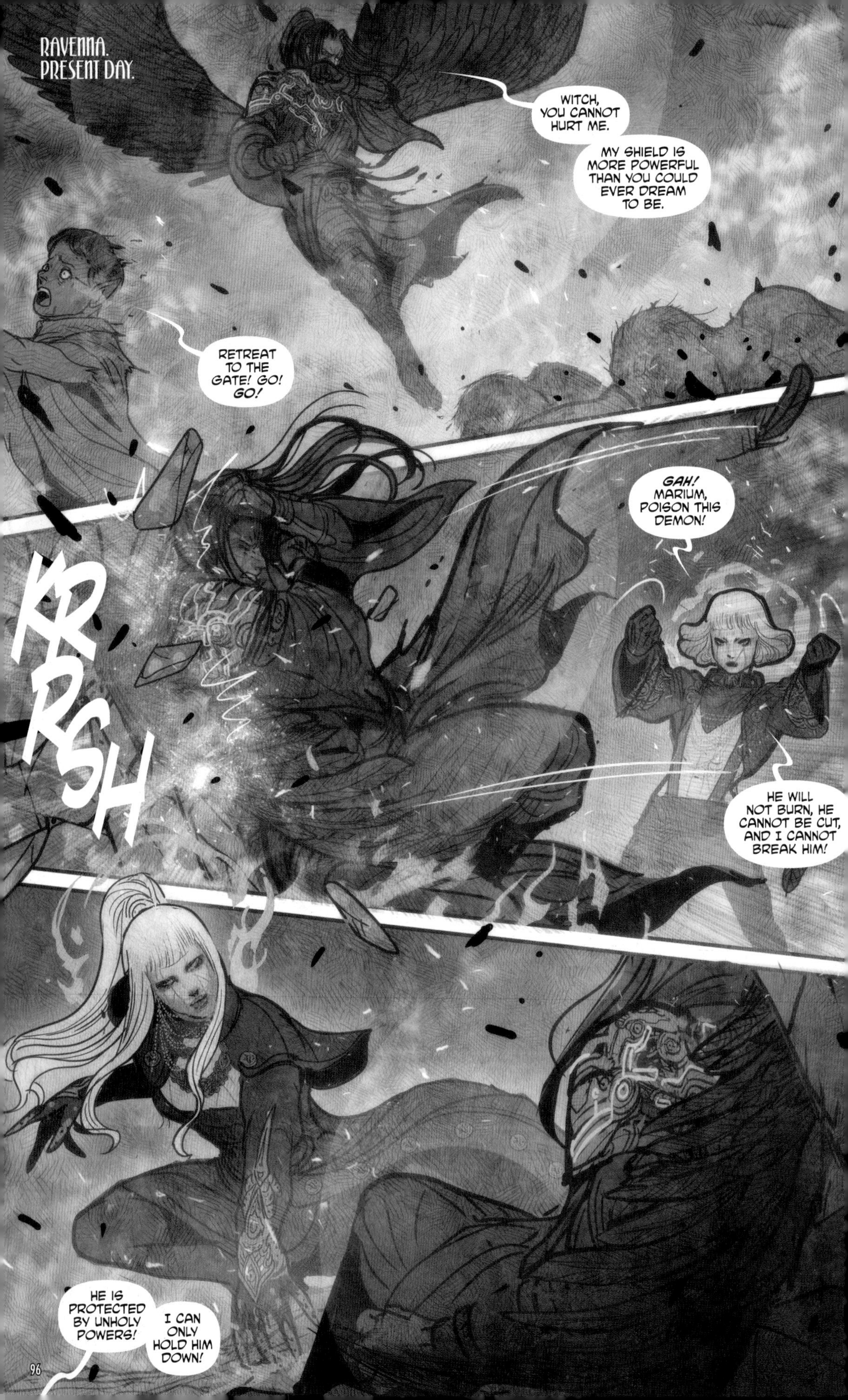
RAVENNA. PRESENT DAY.
WITCH, YOU CANNOT HURT ME.
MY SHIELD IS MORE POWERFUL THAN YOU COULD EVER DREAM TO BE.
RETREAT TO THE GATE! GO! GO!
KRRSH
GAH! MARIUM, POISON THIS DEMON!
HE WILL NOT BURN, HE CANNOT BE CUT, AND I CANNOT BREAK HIM!
HE IS PROTECTED BY UNHOLY POWERS!
I CAN ONLY HOLD HIM DOWN!
96

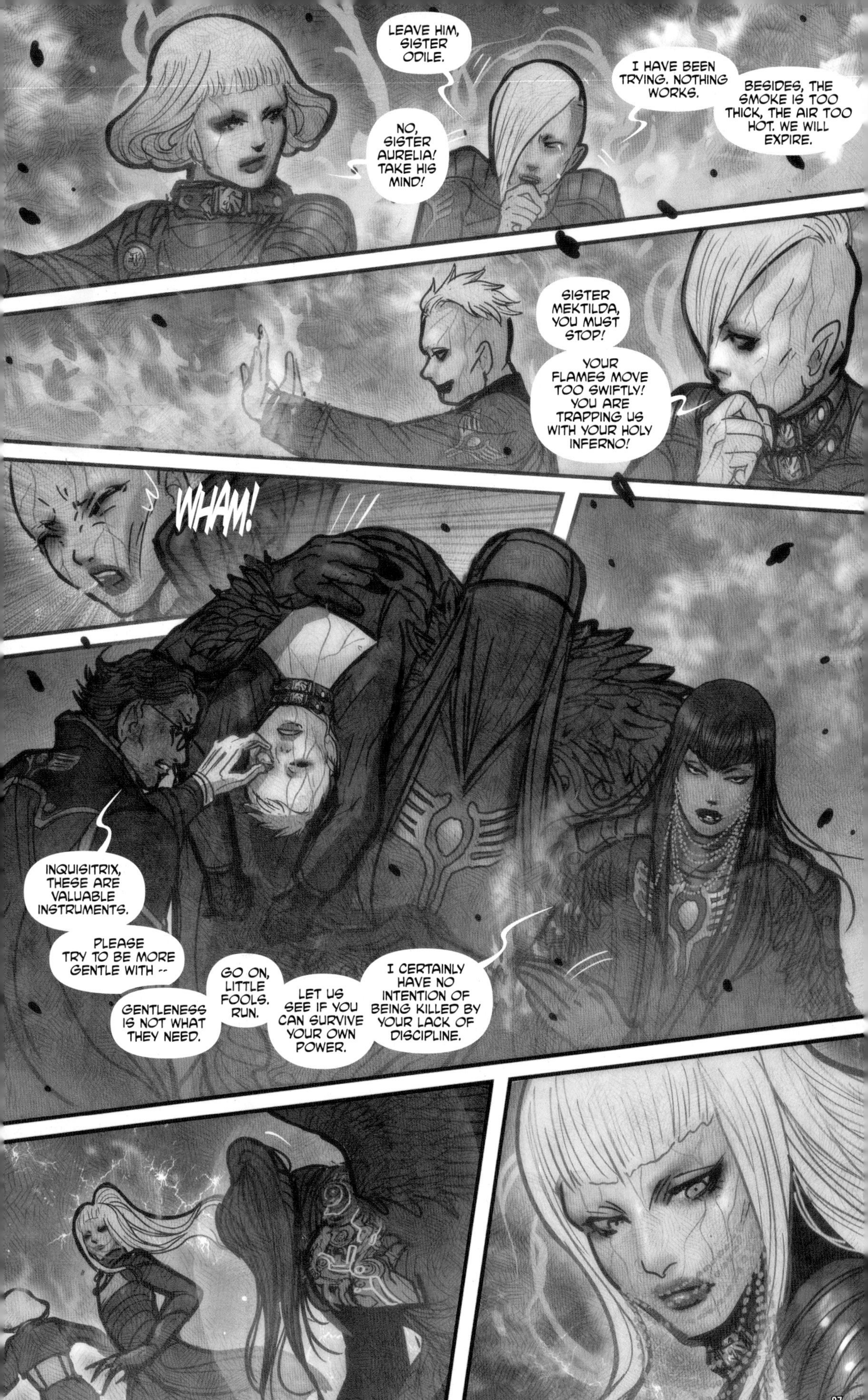
LEAVE HIM, SISTER ODILE.
NO, SISTER AURELIA! TAKE HIS MIND!
I HAVE BEEN TRYING. NOTHING WORKS.
BESIDES, THE SMOKE IS TOO THICK, THE AIR TOO HOT. WE WILL EXPIRE.
SISTER MEKTILDA, YOU MUST STOP!
YOUR FLAMES MOVE TOO SWIFTLY! YOU ARE TRAPPING US WITH YOUR HOLY INFERNO!
WHAM!
INQUISITRIX, THESE ARE VALUABLE INSTRUMENTS.
PLEASE TRY TO BE MORE GENTLE WITH --
GENTLENESS IS NOT WHAT THEY NEED.
GO ON, LITTLE FOOLS. RUN.
LET US SEE IF YOU CAN SURVIVE YOUR OWN POWER.
I CERTAINLY HAVE NO INTENTION OF BEING KILLED BY YOUR LACK OF DISCIPLINE.

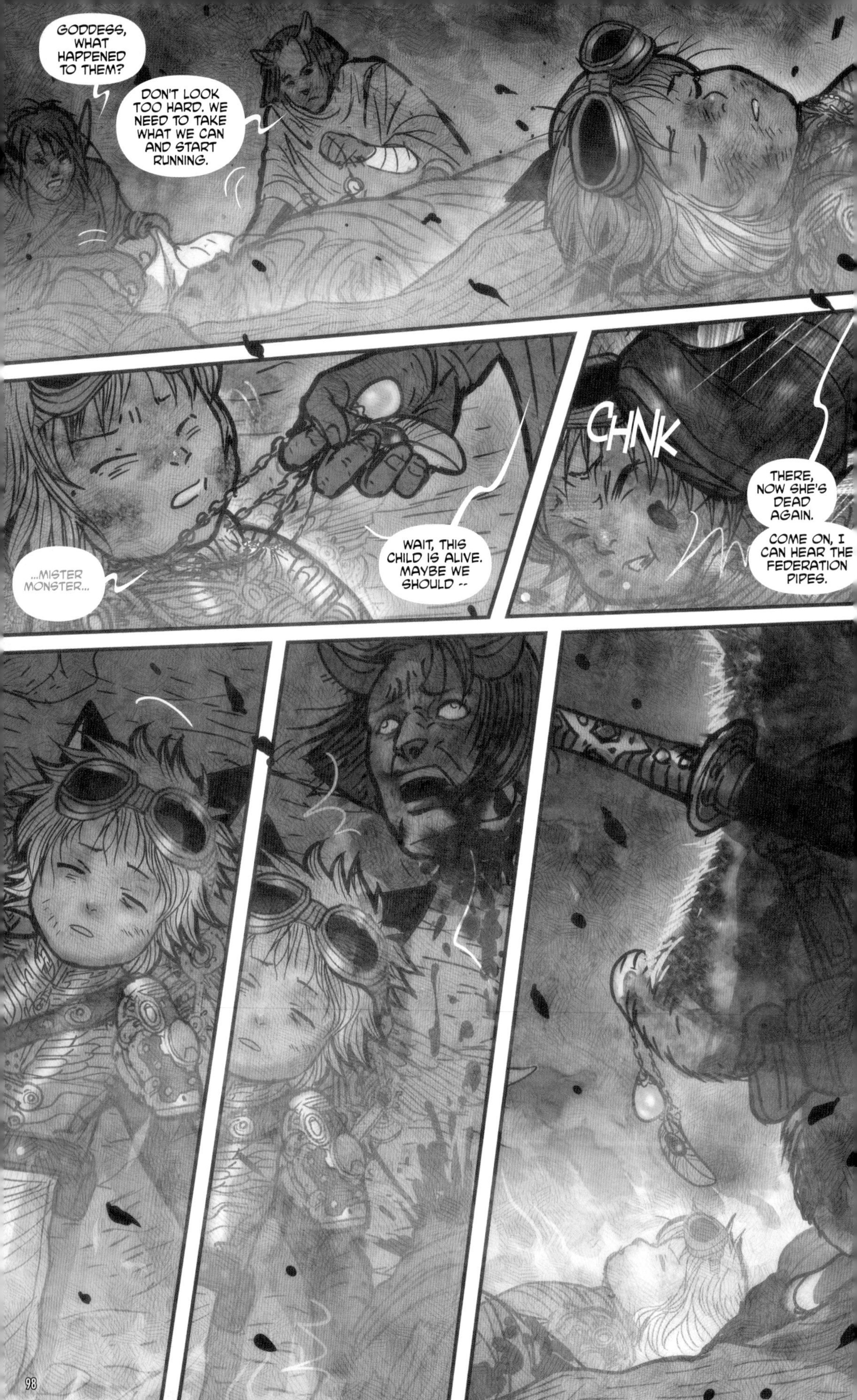

GODDESS, WHAT HAPPENED TO THEM?
DON'T LOOK TOO HARD. WE NEED TO TAKE WHAT WE CAN AND START RUNNING.
...MISTER MONSTER...
WAIT, THIS CHILD IS ALIVE. MAYBE WE SHOULD --
CHNK
THERE, NOW SHE'S DEAD AGAIN.
COME ON, I CAN HEAR THE FEDERATION PIPES.

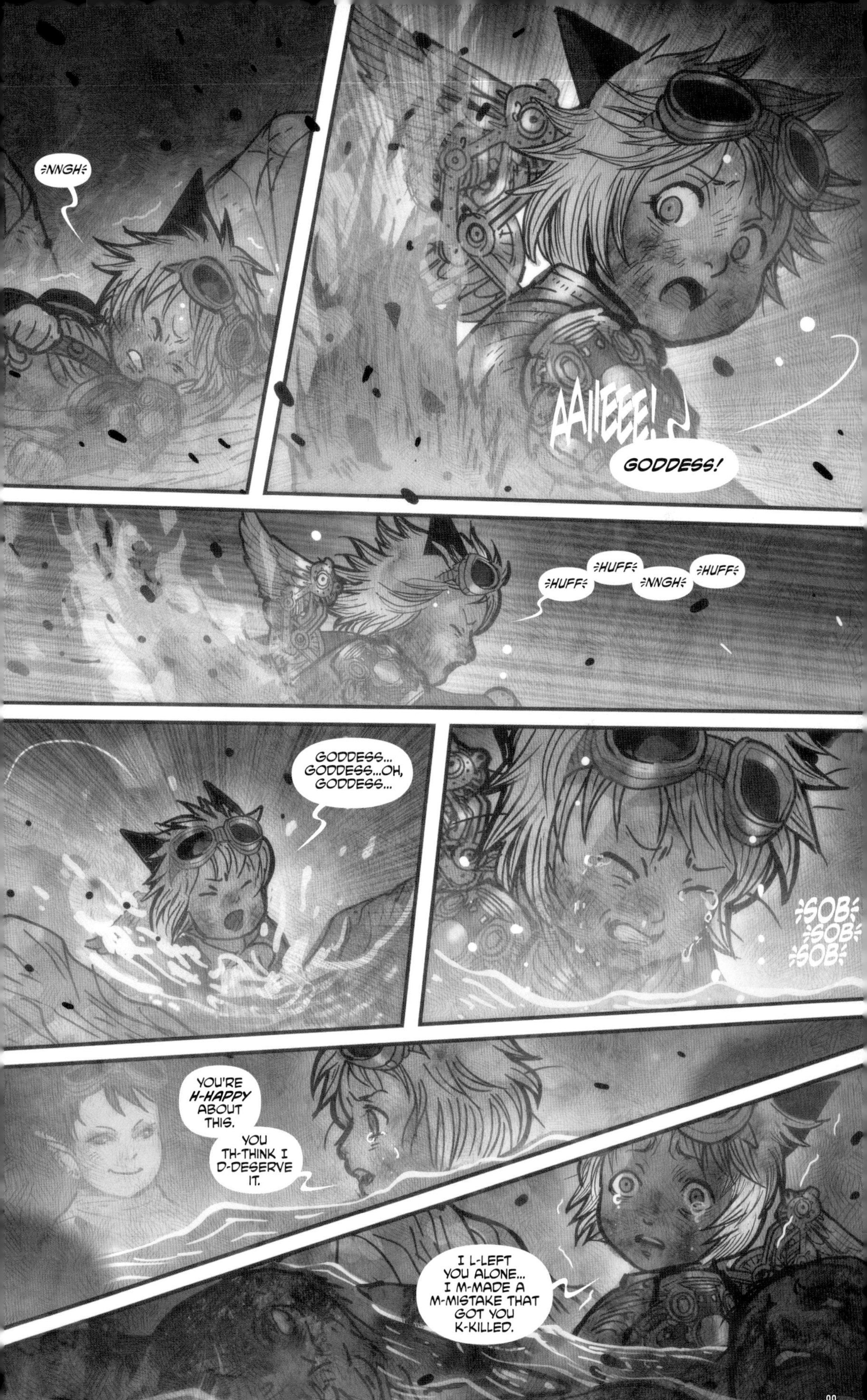
NNGH
AAIIEEE!
GODDESS!
HUFF
HUFF
NNGH
HUFF
GODDESS... GODDESS...OH, GODDESS...
SOB SOB SOB
YOU'RE *H-HAPPY* ABOUT THIS.
YOU TH-THINK I D-DESERVE IT.
I L-LEFT YOU ALONE... I M-MADE A M-MISTAKE THAT GOT YOU K-KILLED.

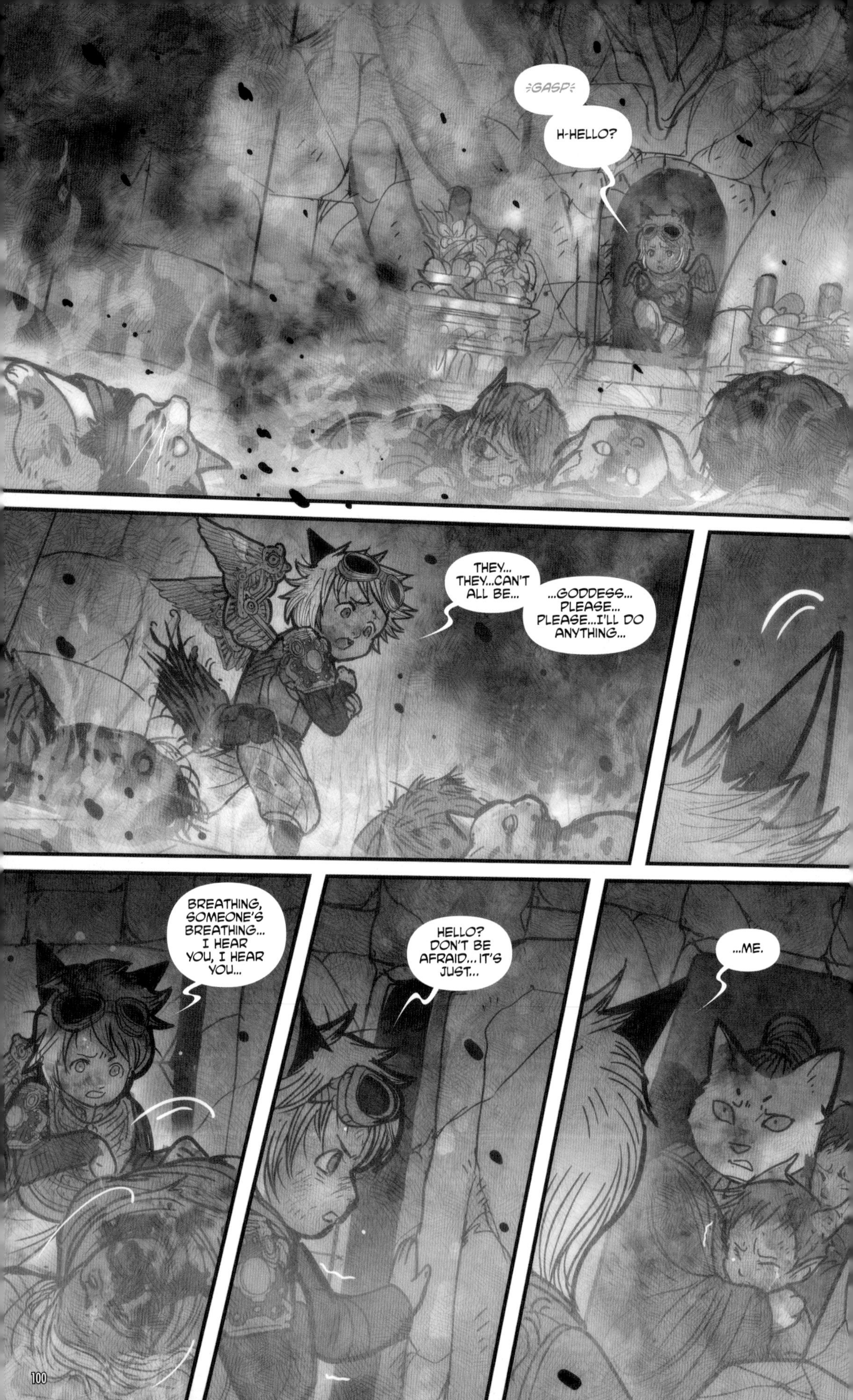

GASP
H-HELLO?
THEY... THEY...CAN'T ALL BE...
...GODDESS... PLEASE... PLEASE...I'LL DO ANYTHING...
BREATHING, SOMEONE'S BREATHING... I HEAR YOU, I HEAR YOU...
HELLO? DON'T BE AFRAID...IT'S JUST...
...ME.

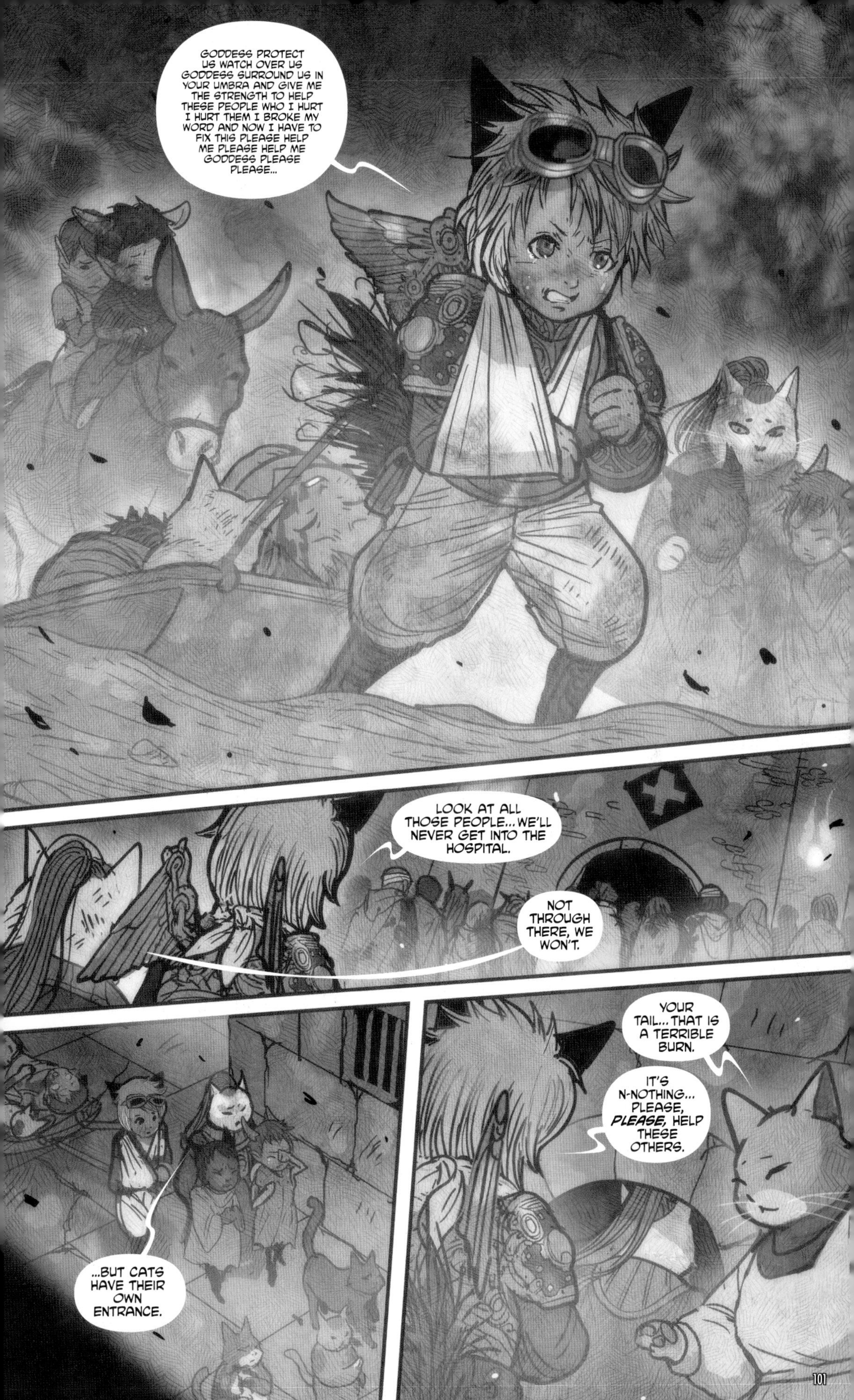
GODDESS PROTECT US WATCH OVER US GODDESS SURROUND US IN YOUR UMBRA AND GIVE ME THE STRENGTH TO HELP THESE PEOPLE WHO I HURT I HURT THEM I BROKE MY WORD AND NOW I HAVE TO FIX THIS PLEASE HELP ME PLEASE HELP ME GODDESS PLEASE PLEASE...
LOOK AT ALL THOSE PEOPLE... WE'LL NEVER GET INTO THE HOSPITAL.
NOT THROUGH THERE, WE WON'T.
...BUT CATS HAVE THEIR OWN ENTRANCE.
YOUR TAIL... THAT IS A TERRIBLE BURN.
IT'S N-NOTHING... PLEASE, *PLEASE,* HELP THESE OTHERS.

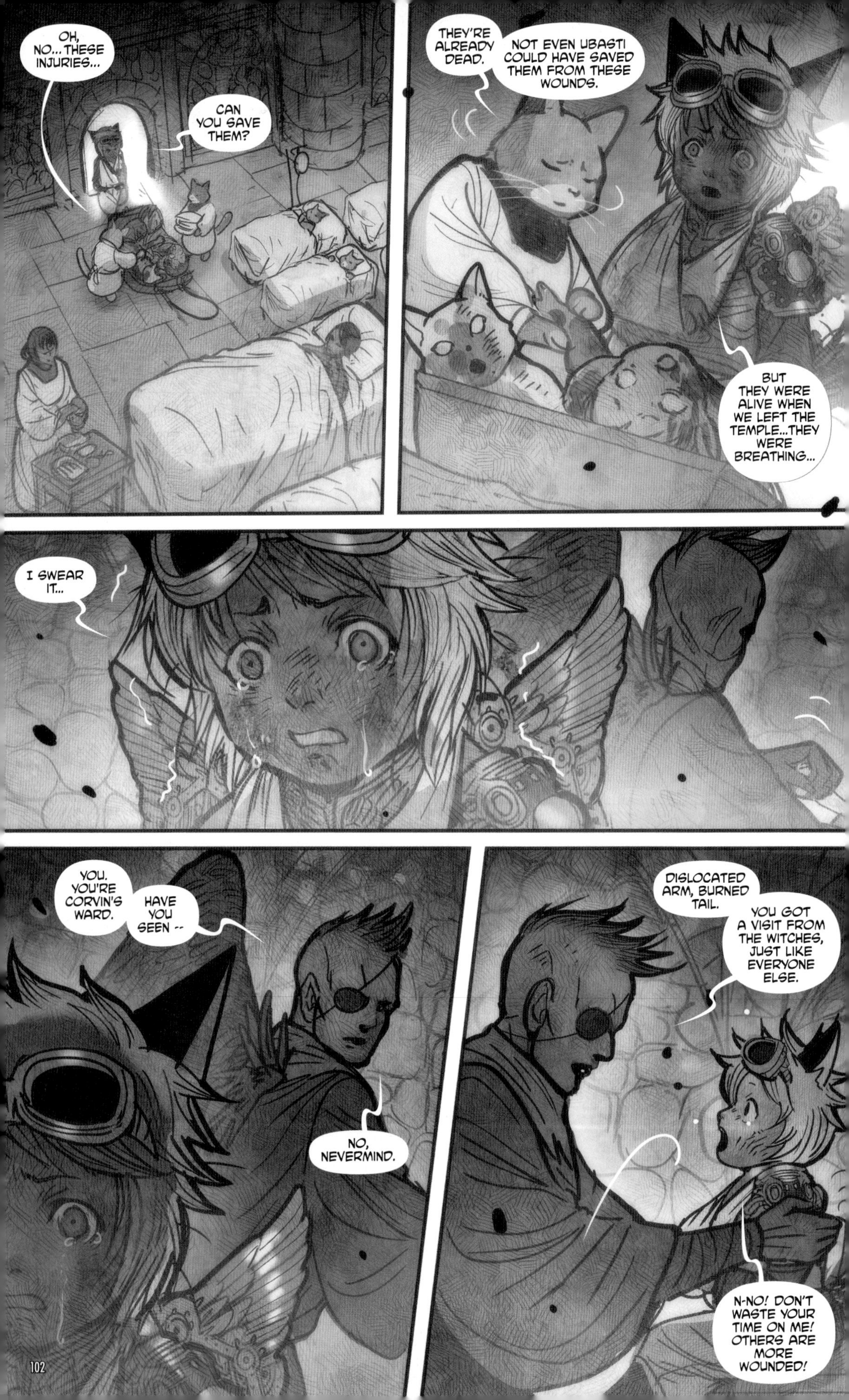
OH, NO... THESE INJURIES...
CAN YOU SAVE THEM?
THEY'RE ALREADY DEAD.
NOT EVEN UBASTI COULD HAVE SAVED THEM FROM THESE WOUNDS.
BUT THEY WERE ALIVE WHEN WE LEFT THE TEMPLE...THEY WERE BREATHING...
I SWEAR IT...
YOU. YOU'RE CORVIN'S WARD.
HAVE YOU SEEN --
NO, NEVERMIND.
DISLOCATED ARM, BURNED TAIL.
YOU GOT A VISIT FROM THE WITCHES, JUST LIKE EVERYONE ELSE.
N-NO! DON'T WASTE YOUR TIME ON ME! OTHERS ARE MORE WOUNDED!

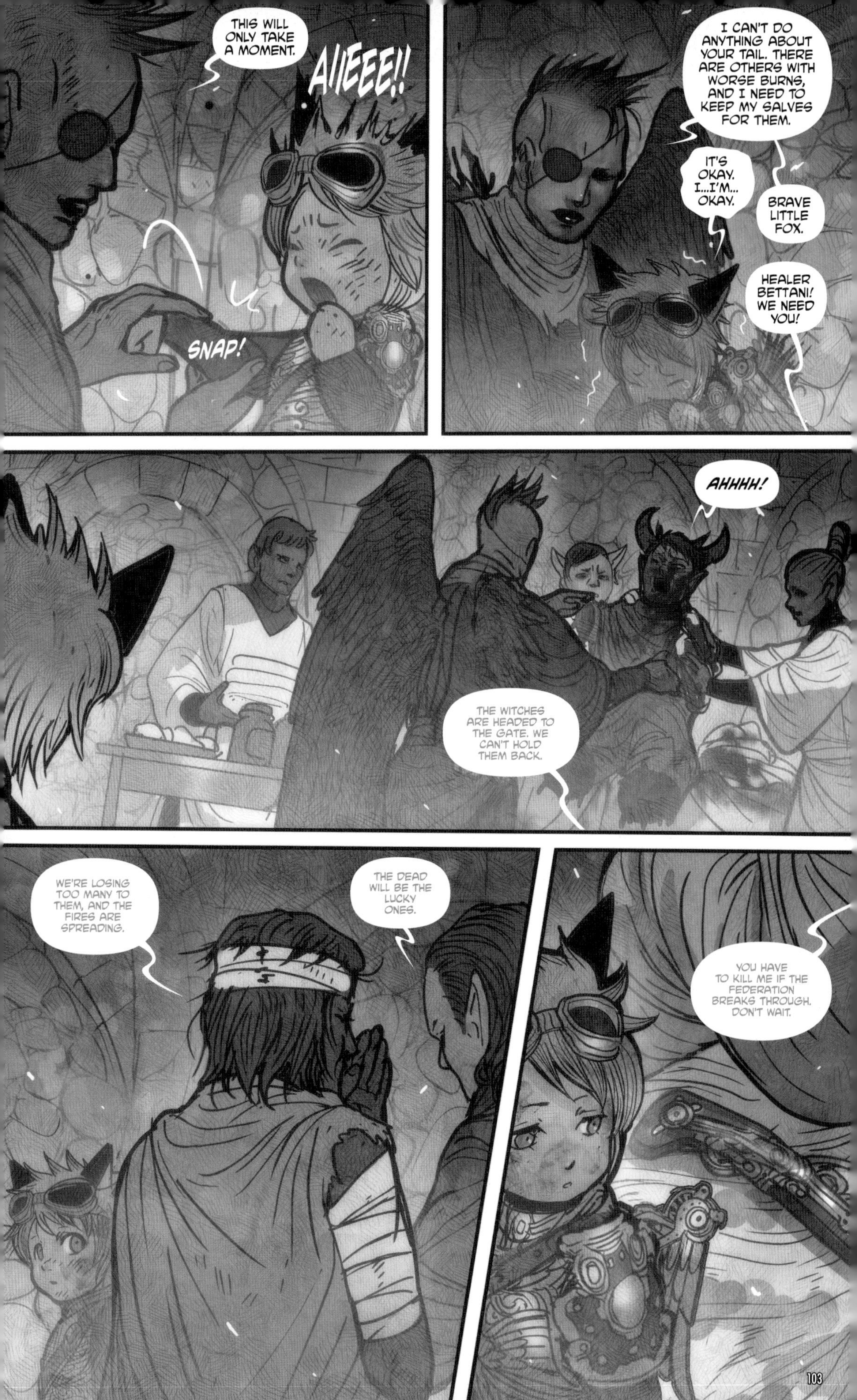
THIS WILL ONLY TAKE A MOMENT.
AIIEEE!!
SNAP!
I CAN'T DO ANYTHING ABOUT YOUR TAIL. THERE ARE OTHERS WITH WORSE BURNS, AND I NEED TO KEEP MY SALVES FOR THEM.
IT'S OKAY. I...I'M... OKAY.
BRAVE LITTLE FOX.
HEALER BETTANI! WE NEED YOU!
AHHHH!
THE WITCHES ARE HEADED TO THE GATE. WE CAN'T HOLD THEM BACK.
WE'RE LOSING TOO MANY TO THEM, AND THE FIRES ARE SPREADING.
THE DEAD WILL BE THE LUCKY ONES.
YOU HAVE TO KILL ME IF THE FEDERATION BREAKS THROUGH. DON'T WAIT.

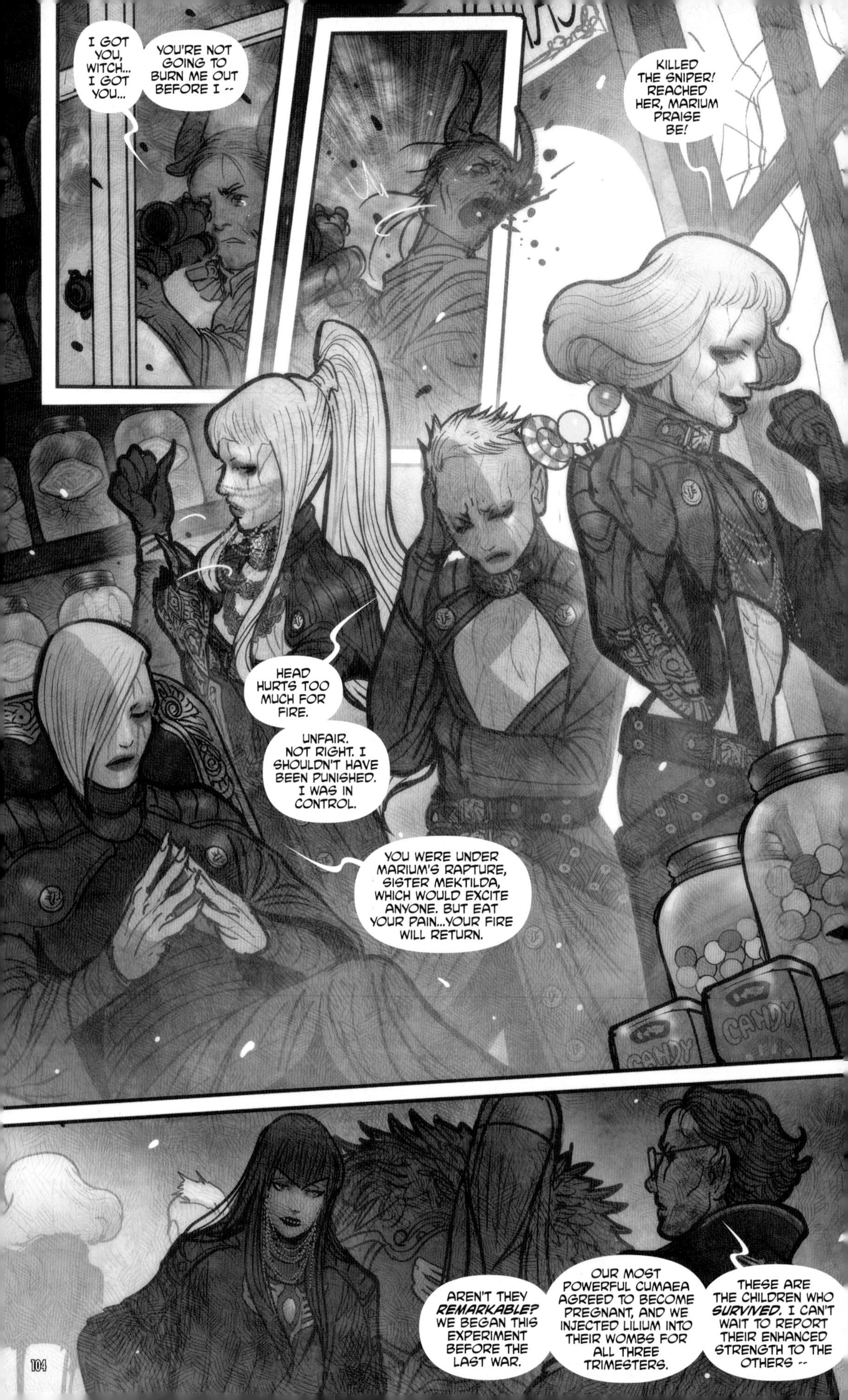
I GOT YOU, WITCH... I GOT YOU...
YOU'RE NOT GOING TO BURN ME OUT BEFORE I --
KILLED THE SNIPER! REACHED HER, MARIUM PRAISE BE!
HEAD HURTS TOO MUCH FOR FIRE.
UNFAIR. NOT RIGHT. I SHOULDN'T HAVE BEEN PUNISHED. I WAS IN CONTROL.
YOU WERE UNDER MARIUM'S RAPTURE, SISTER MEKTILDA, WHICH WOULD EXCITE ANYONE. BUT EAT YOUR PAIN...YOUR FIRE WILL RETURN.
CANDY
CANDY
AREN'T THEY *REMARKABLE?* WE BEGAN THIS EXPERIMENT BEFORE THE LAST WAR.
OUR MOST POWERFUL CUMAEA AGREED TO BECOME PREGNANT, AND WE INJECTED LILIUM INTO THEIR WOMBS FOR ALL THREE TRIMESTERS.
THESE ARE THE CHILDREN WHO *SURVIVED.* I CAN'T WAIT TO REPORT THEIR ENHANCED STRENGTH TO THE OTHERS --

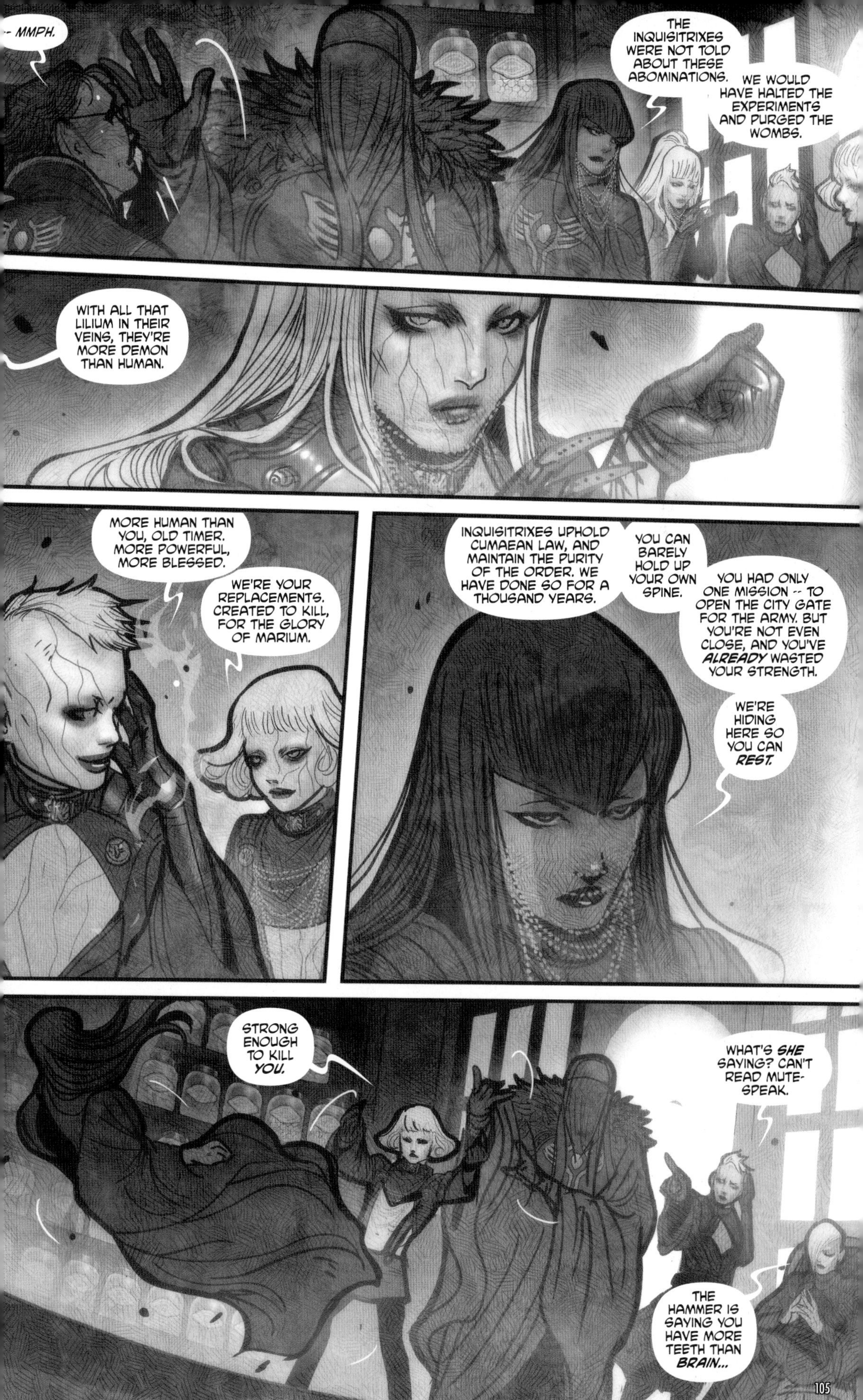
-- MMPH.
THE INQUISITRIXES WERE NOT TOLD ABOUT THESE ABOMINATIONS.
WE WOULD HAVE HALTED THE EXPERIMENTS AND PURGED THE WOMBS.
WITH ALL THAT LILIUM IN THEIR VEINS, THEY'RE MORE DEMON THAN HUMAN.
MORE HUMAN THAN YOU, OLD TIMER. MORE POWERFUL, MORE BLESSED.
WE'RE YOUR REPLACEMENTS. CREATED TO KILL, FOR THE GLORY OF MARIUM.
INQUISITRIXES UPHOLD CUMAEAN LAW, AND MAINTAIN THE PURITY OF THE ORDER. WE HAVE DONE SO FOR A THOUSAND YEARS.
YOU CAN BARELY HOLD UP YOUR OWN SPINE.
YOU HAD ONLY ONE MISSION -- TO OPEN THE CITY GATE FOR THE ARMY. BUT YOU'RE NOT EVEN CLOSE, AND YOU'VE ALREADY WASTED YOUR STRENGTH.
WE'RE HIDING HERE SO YOU CAN REST.
STRONG ENOUGH TO KILL YOU.
WHAT'S SHE SAYING? CAN'T READ MUTE-SPEAK.
THE HAMMER IS SAYING YOU HAVE MORE TEETH THAN BRAIN...

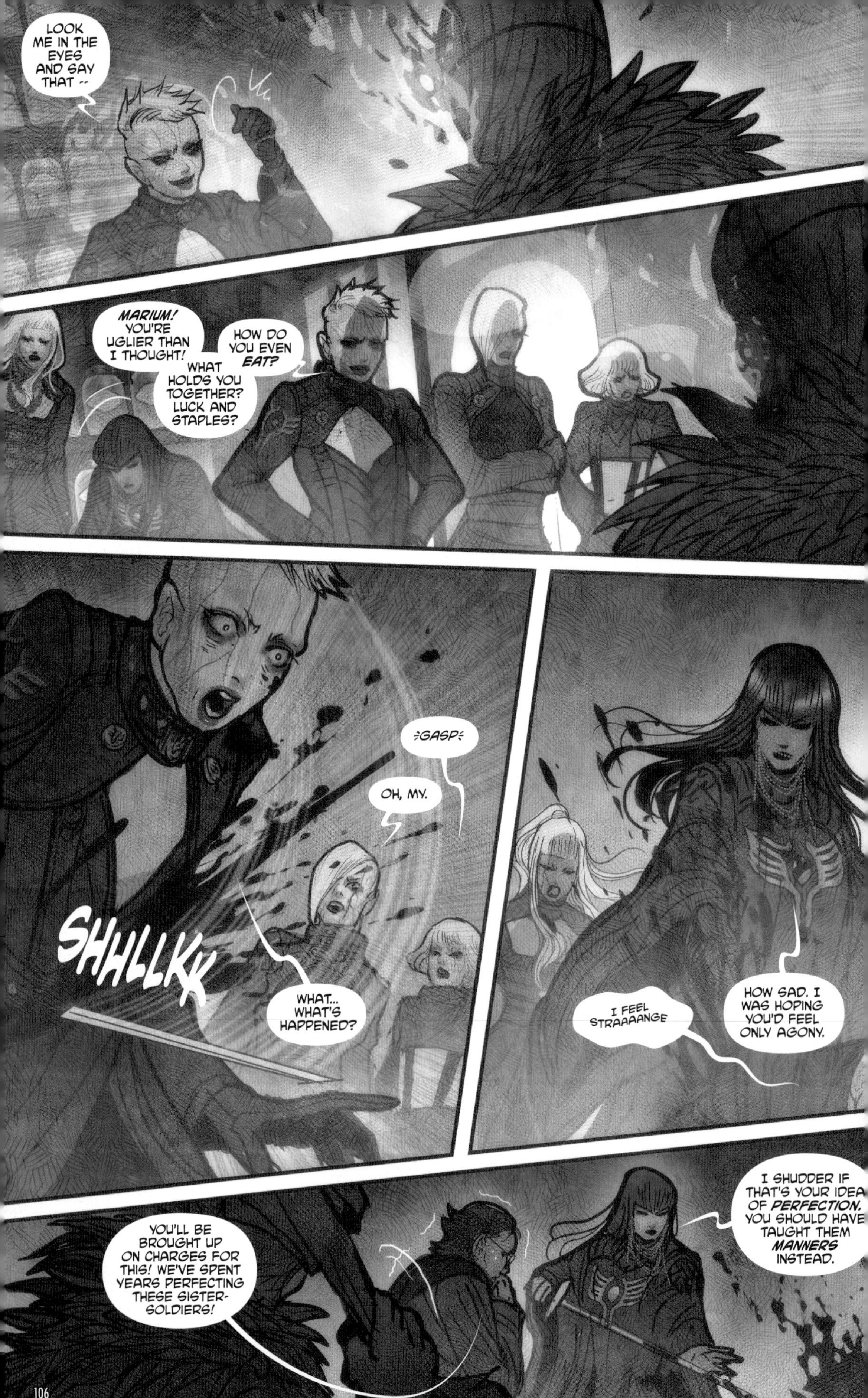

LOOK ME IN THE EYES AND SAY THAT --
MARIUM! YOU'RE UGLIER THAN I THOUGHT!
WHAT HOLDS YOU TOGETHER? LUCK AND STAPLES?
HOW DO YOU EVEN *EAT?*
SHHLLKK
-GASP-
OH, MY.
WHAT... WHAT'S HAPPENED?
I FEEL STRAAAANGE
HOW SAD. I WAS HOPING YOU'D FEEL ONLY AGONY.
YOU'LL BE BROUGHT UP ON CHARGES FOR THIS! WE'VE SPENT YEARS PERFECTING THESE SISTER-SOLDIERS!
I SHUDDER IF THAT'S YOUR IDEA OF *PERFECTION.* YOU SHOULD HAVE TAUGHT THEM *MANNERS* INSTEAD.

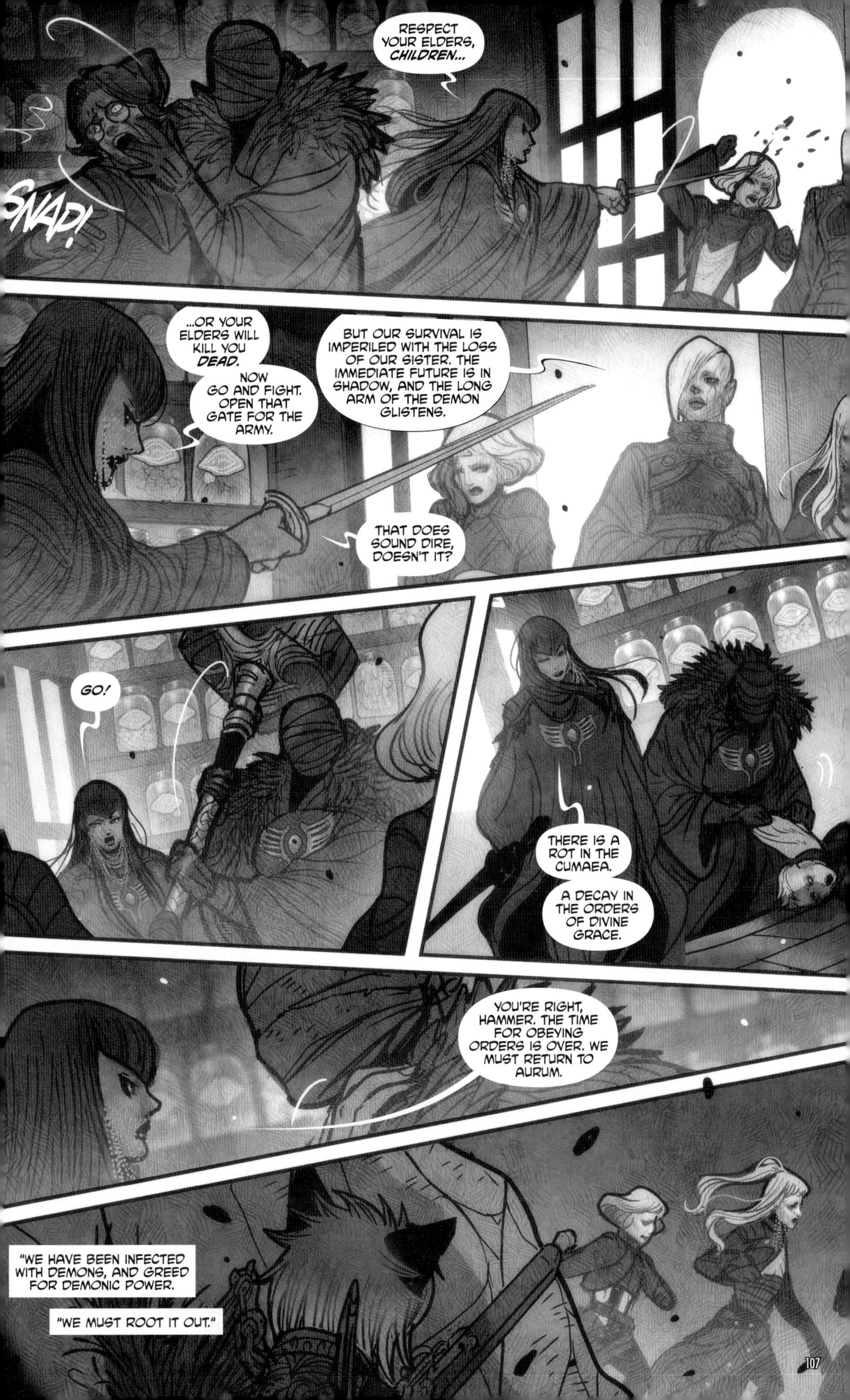

SNAP!
RESPECT YOUR ELDERS, CHILDREN...
...OR YOUR ELDERS WILL KILL YOU DEAD.
NOW GO AND FIGHT. OPEN THAT GATE FOR THE ARMY.
BUT OUR SURVIVAL IS IMPERILED WITH THE LOSS OF OUR SISTER. THE IMMEDIATE FUTURE IS IN SHADOW, AND THE LONG ARM OF THE DEMON GLISTENS.
THAT DOES SOUND DIRE, DOESN'T IT?
GO!
THERE IS A ROT IN THE CUMAEA.
A DECAY IN THE ORDERS OF DIVINE GRACE.
YOU'RE RIGHT, HAMMER. THE TIME FOR OBEYING ORDERS IS OVER. WE MUST RETURN TO AURUM.
"WE HAVE BEEN INFECTED WITH DEMONS, AND GREED FOR DEMONIC POWER.
"WE MUST ROOT IT OUT."

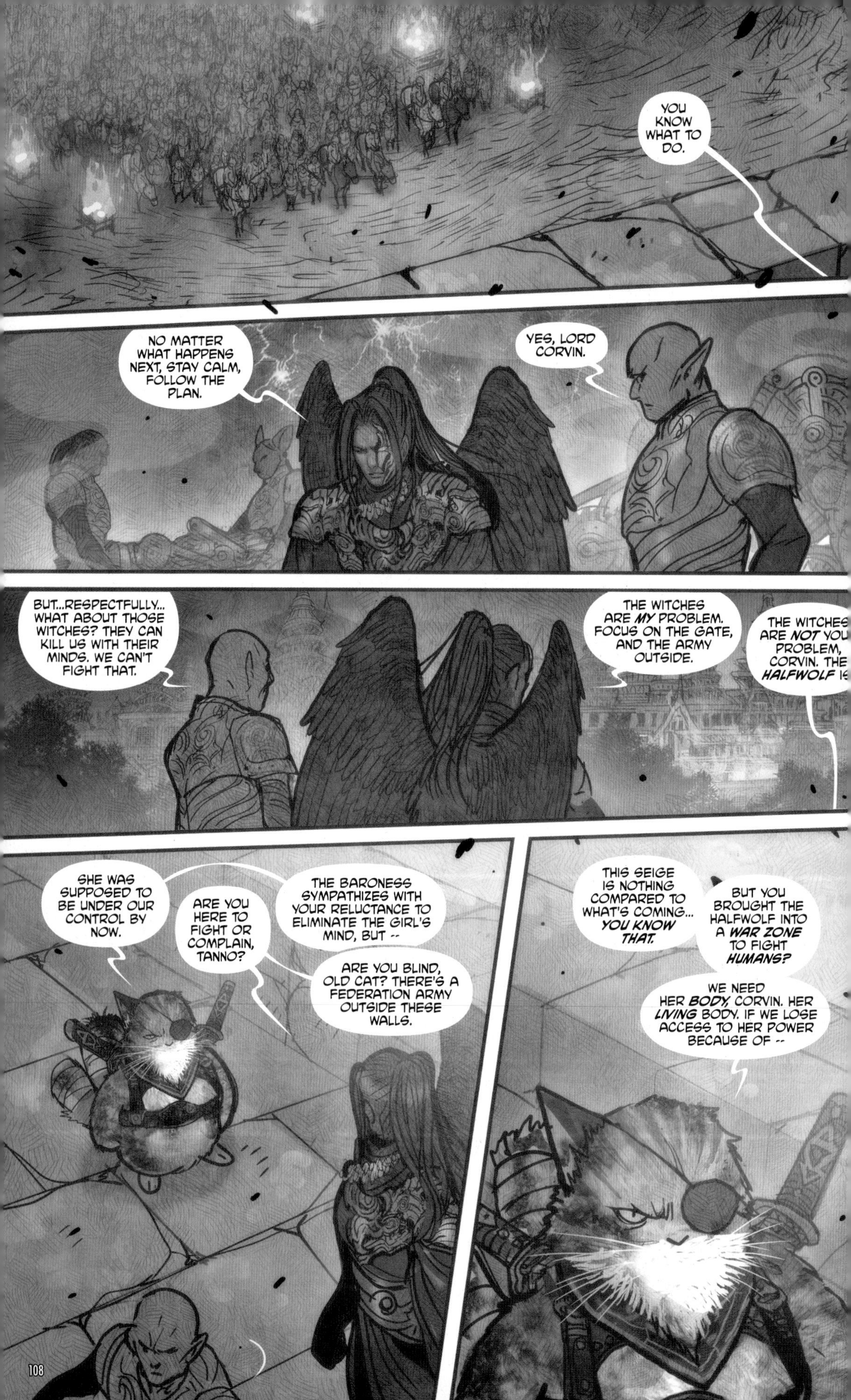
YOU KNOW WHAT TO DO.
NO MATTER WHAT HAPPENS NEXT, STAY CALM, FOLLOW THE PLAN.
YES, LORD CORVIN.
BUT...RESPECTFULLY... WHAT ABOUT THOSE WITCHES? THEY CAN KILL US WITH THEIR MINDS. WE CAN'T FIGHT THAT.
THE WITCHES ARE *MY* PROBLEM. FOCUS ON THE GATE, AND THE ARMY OUTSIDE.
THE WITCHES ARE *NOT* YOU PROBLEM, CORVIN. THE *HALFWOLF* IS
SHE WAS SUPPOSED TO BE UNDER OUR CONTROL BY NOW.
ARE YOU HERE TO FIGHT OR COMPLAIN, TANNO?
THE BARONESS SYMPATHIZES WITH YOUR RELUCTANCE TO ELIMINATE THE GIRL'S MIND, BUT --
ARE YOU BLIND, OLD CAT? THERE'S A FEDERATION ARMY OUTSIDE THESE WALLS.
THIS SEIGE IS NOTHING COMPARED TO WHAT'S COMING... *YOU KNOW THAT.*
BUT YOU BROUGHT THE HALFWOLF INTO A *WAR ZONE* TO FIGHT *HUMANS?*
WE NEED HER *BODY,* CORVIN. HER *LIVING* BODY. IF WE LOSE ACCESS TO HER POWER BECAUSE OF --

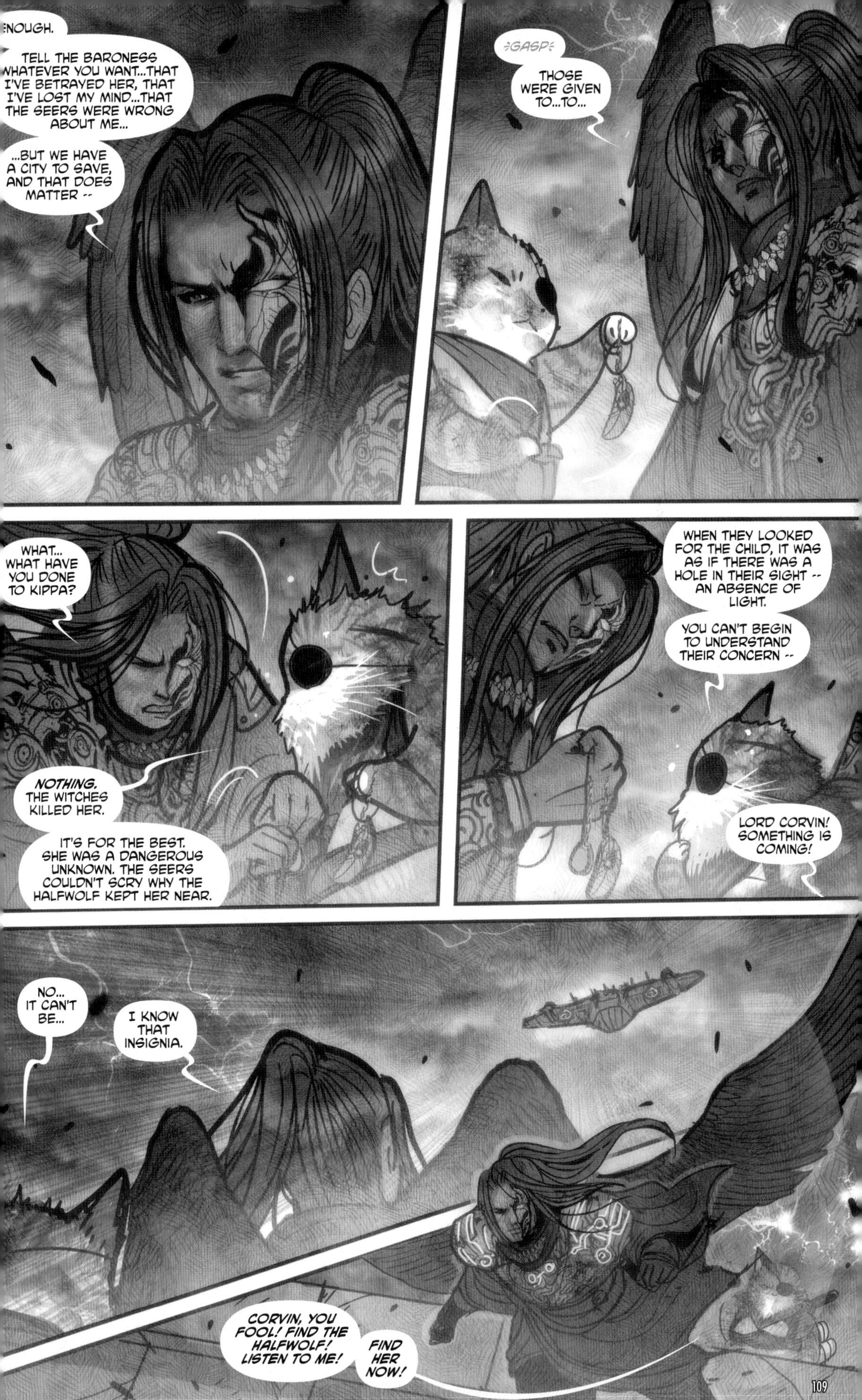
ENOUGH.
TELL THE BARONESS WHATEVER YOU WANT...THAT I'VE BETRAYED HER, THAT I'VE LOST MY MIND...THAT THE SEERS WERE WRONG ABOUT ME...
...BUT WE HAVE A CITY TO SAVE, AND THAT DOES MATTER --
GASP
THOSE WERE GIVEN TO...TO...
WHAT... WHAT HAVE YOU DONE TO KIPPA?
NOTHING. THE WITCHES KILLED HER.
IT'S FOR THE BEST. SHE WAS A DANGEROUS UNKNOWN. THE SEERS COULDN'T SCRY WHY THE HALFWOLF KEPT HER NEAR.
WHEN THEY LOOKED FOR THE CHILD, IT WAS AS IF THERE WAS A HOLE IN THEIR SIGHT -- AN ABSENCE OF LIGHT.
YOU CAN'T BEGIN TO UNDERSTAND THEIR CONCERN --
LORD CORVIN! SOMETHING IS COMING!
NO... IT CAN'T BE...
I KNOW THAT INSIGNIA.
CORVIN, YOU FOOL! FIND THE HALFWOLF! LISTEN TO ME!
FIND HER NOW!

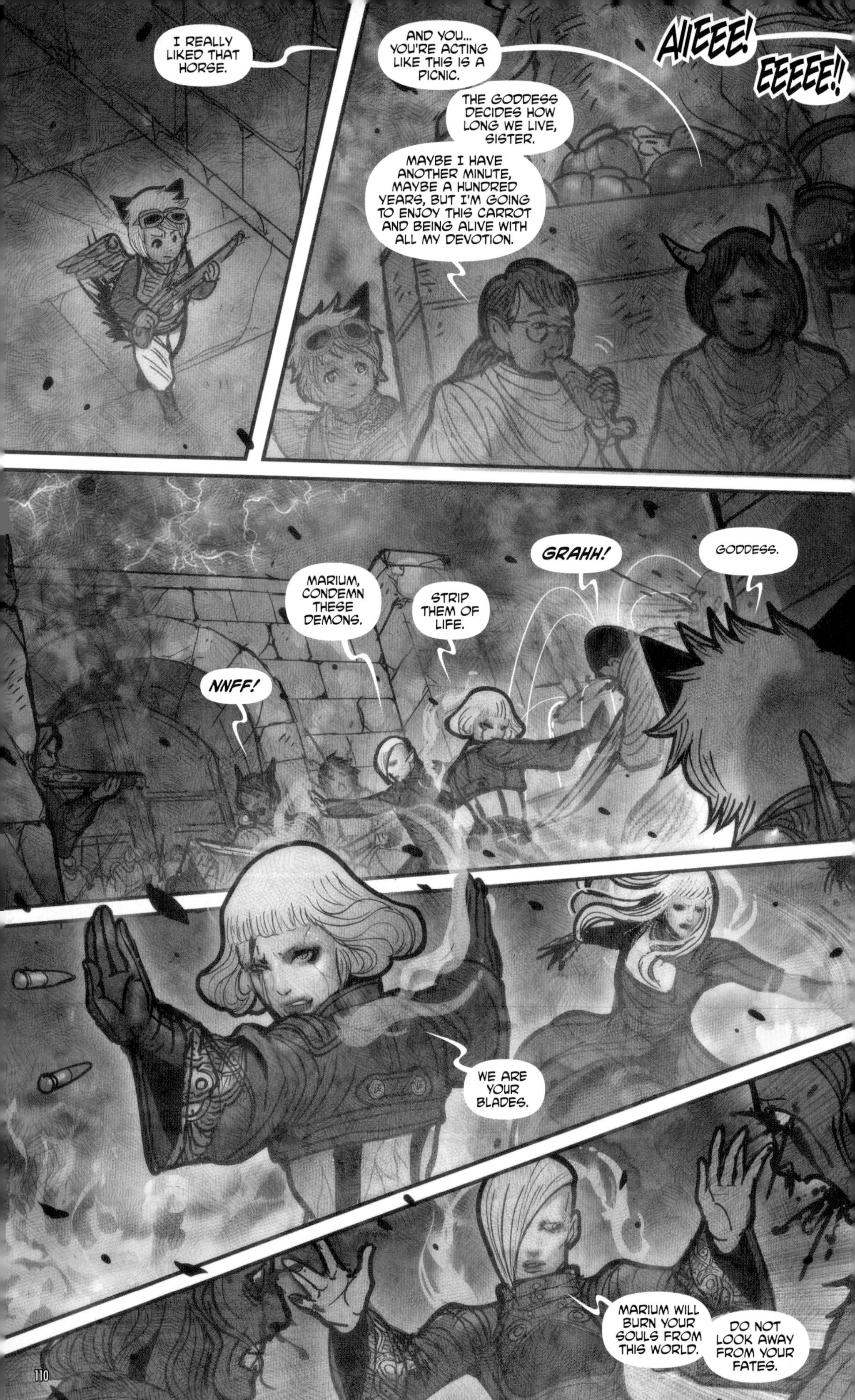
I REALLY LIKED THAT HORSE.
AND YOU... YOU'RE ACTING LIKE THIS IS A PICNIC.
AIIEEE! EEEEE!!
THE GODDESS DECIDES HOW LONG WE LIVE, SISTER.
MAYBE I HAVE ANOTHER MINUTE, MAYBE A HUNDRED YEARS, BUT I'M GOING TO ENJOY THIS CARROT AND BEING ALIVE WITH ALL MY DEVOTION.
NNFF!
MARIUM, CONDEMN THESE DEMONS.
STRIP THEM OF LIFE.
GRAHH!
GODDESS.
WE ARE YOUR BLADES.
MARIUM WILL BURN YOUR SOULS FROM THIS WORLD.
DO NOT LOOK AWAY FROM YOUR FATES.

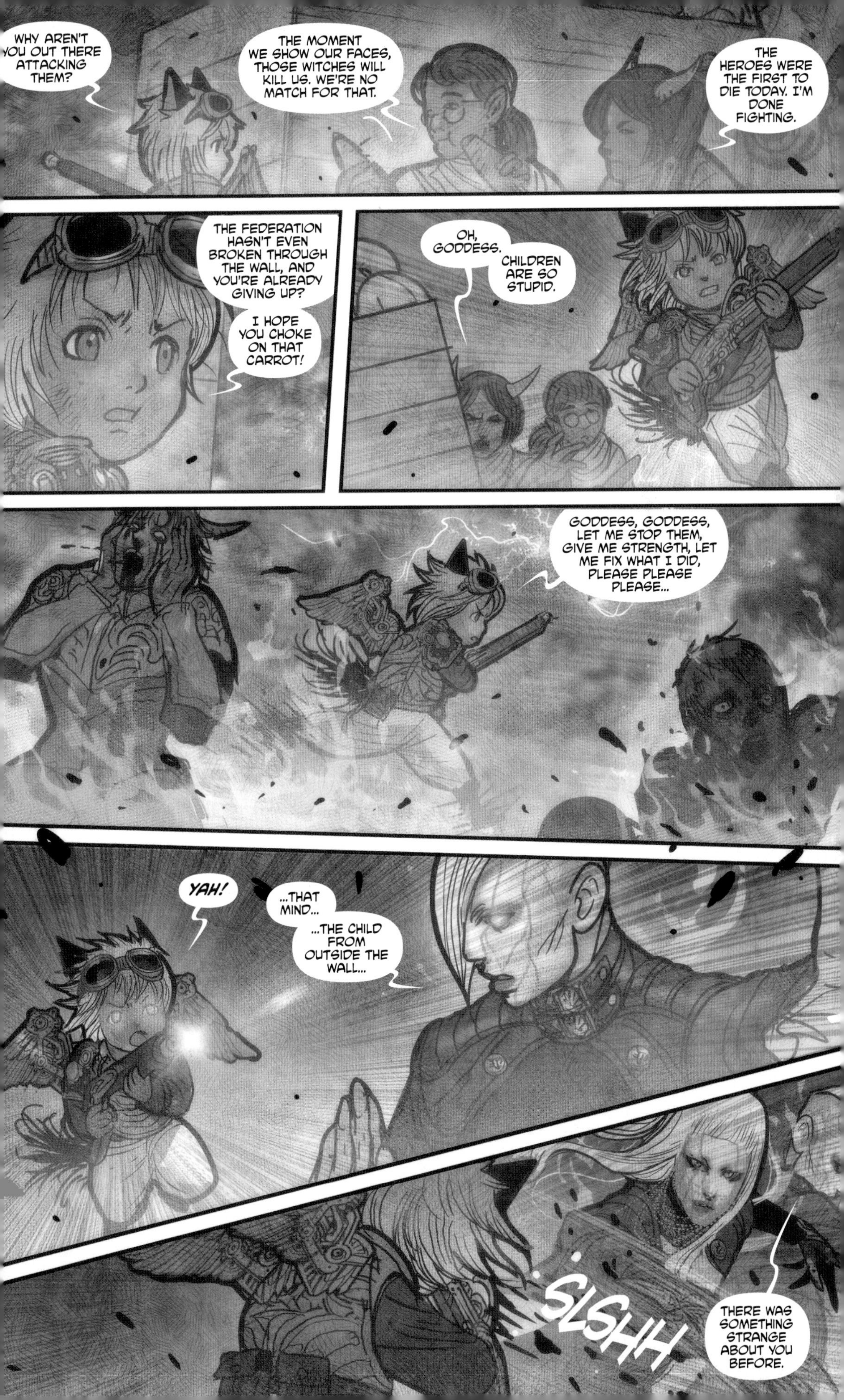
WHY AREN'T YOU OUT THERE ATTACKING THEM?
THE MOMENT WE SHOW OUR FACES, THOSE WITCHES WILL KILL US. WE'RE NO MATCH FOR THAT.
THE HEROES WERE THE FIRST TO DIE TODAY. I'M DONE FIGHTING.
THE FEDERATION HASN'T EVEN BROKEN THROUGH THE WALL, AND YOU'RE ALREADY GIVING UP?
I HOPE YOU CHOKE ON THAT CARROT!
OH, GODDESS.
CHILDREN ARE SO STUPID.
GODDESS, GODDESS, LET ME STOP THEM, GIVE ME STRENGTH, LET ME FIX WHAT I DID, PLEASE PLEASE PLEASE...
YAH!
...THAT MIND...
...THE CHILD FROM OUTSIDE THE WALL...
SLSHH
THERE WAS SOMETHING STRANGE ABOUT YOU BEFORE.

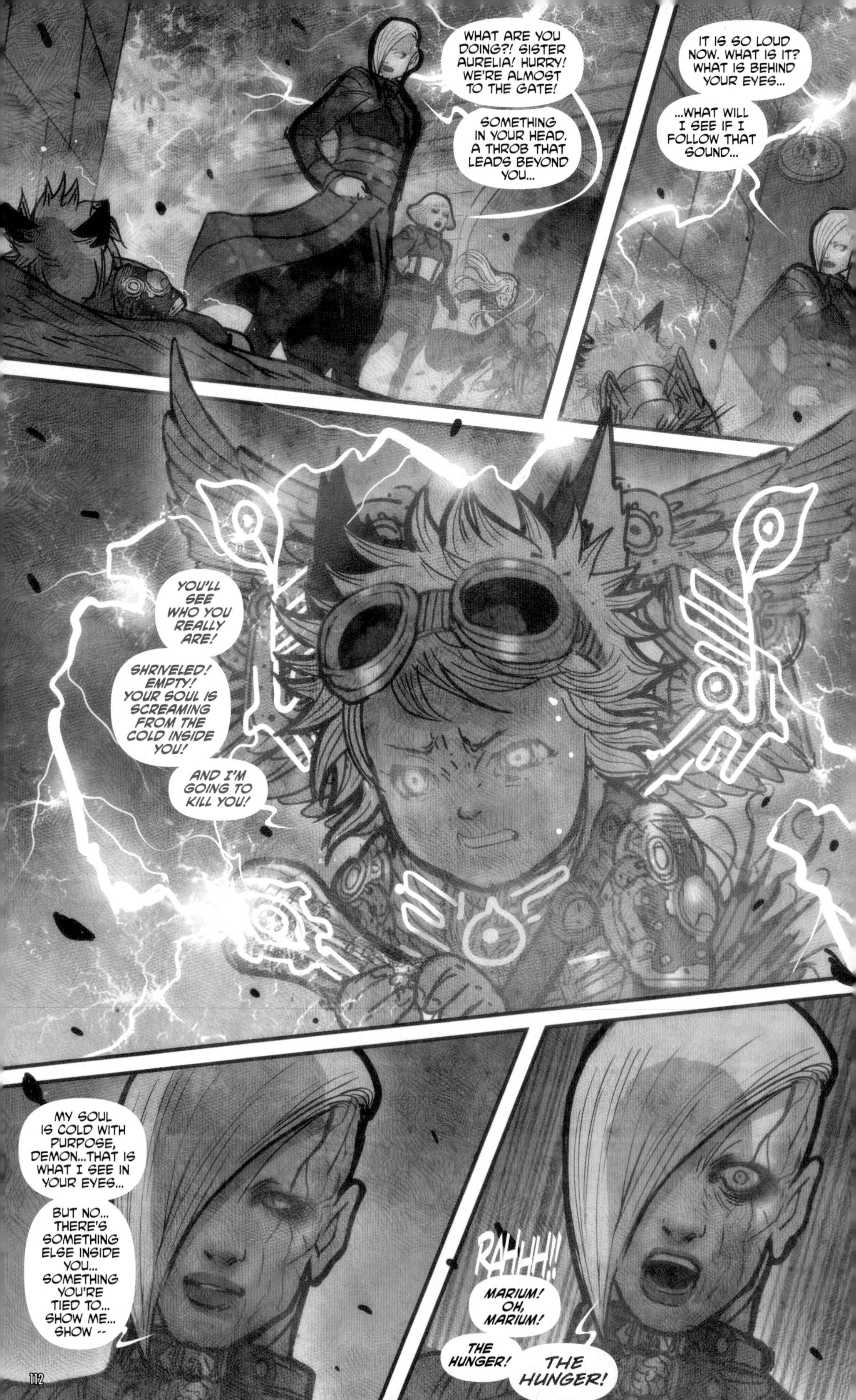
WHAT ARE YOU DOING?! SISTER AURELIA! HURRY! WE'RE ALMOST TO THE GATE!
SOMETHING IN YOUR HEAD. A THROB THAT LEADS BEYOND YOU...
IT IS SO LOUD NOW. WHAT IS IT? WHAT IS BEHIND YOUR EYES...
...WHAT WILL I SEE IF I FOLLOW THAT SOUND...
YOU'LL SEE WHO YOU REALLY ARE!
SHRIVELED! EMPTY! YOUR SOUL IS SCREAMING FROM THE COLD INSIDE YOU!
AND I'M GOING TO KILL YOU!
MY SOUL IS COLD WITH PURPOSE, DEMON...THAT IS WHAT I SEE IN YOUR EYES...
BUT NO... THERE'S SOMETHING ELSE INSIDE YOU... SOMETHING YOU'RE TIED TO... SHOW ME... SHOW --
RAHHH!!
MARIUM! OH, MARIUM!
THE HUNGER!
THE HUNGER!

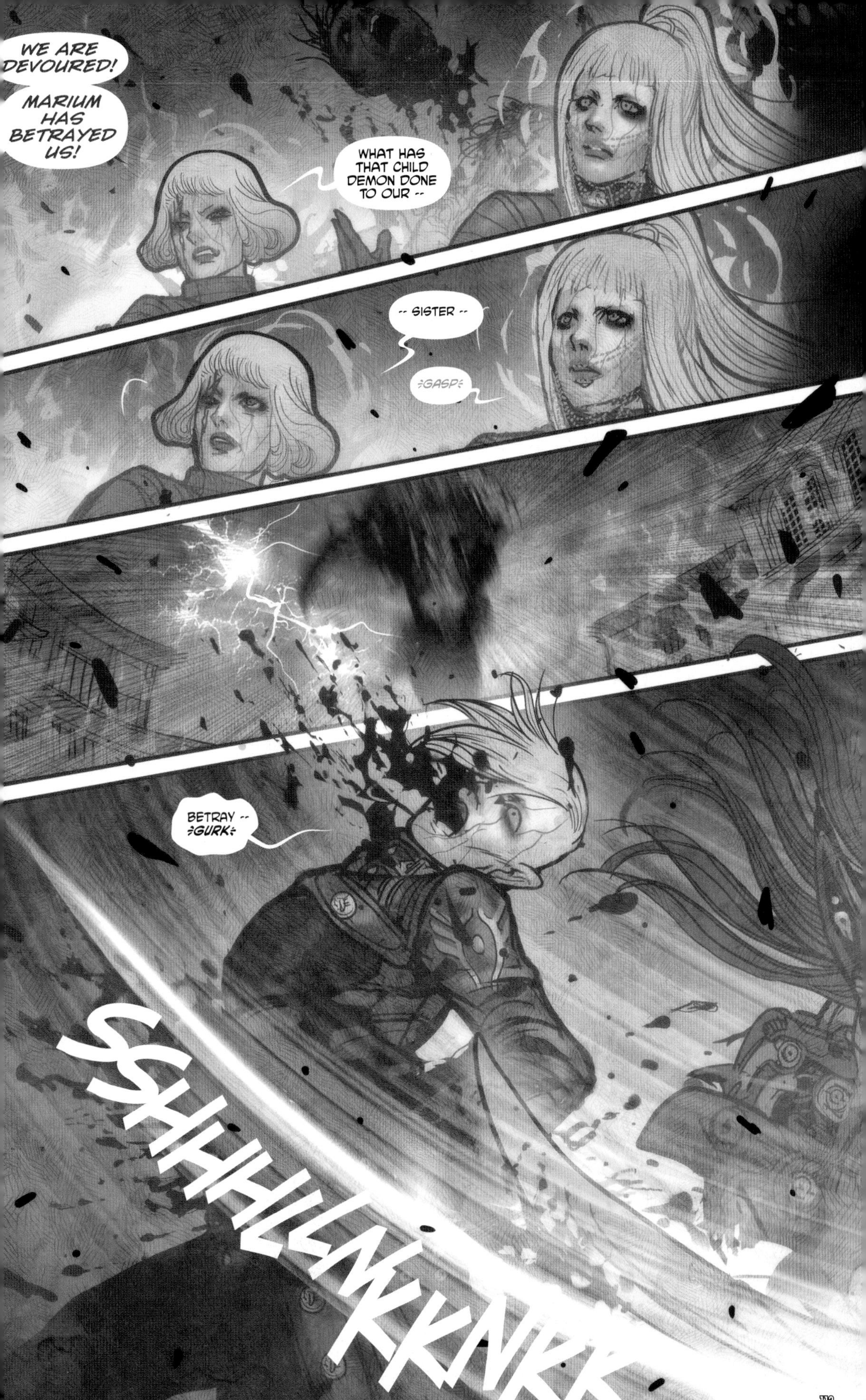
WE ARE DEVOURED!
MARIUM HAS BETRAYED US!
WHAT HAS THAT CHILD DEMON DONE TO OUR --
-- SISTER --
GASP
BETRAY -- GURK
SSHHLNKKNRK

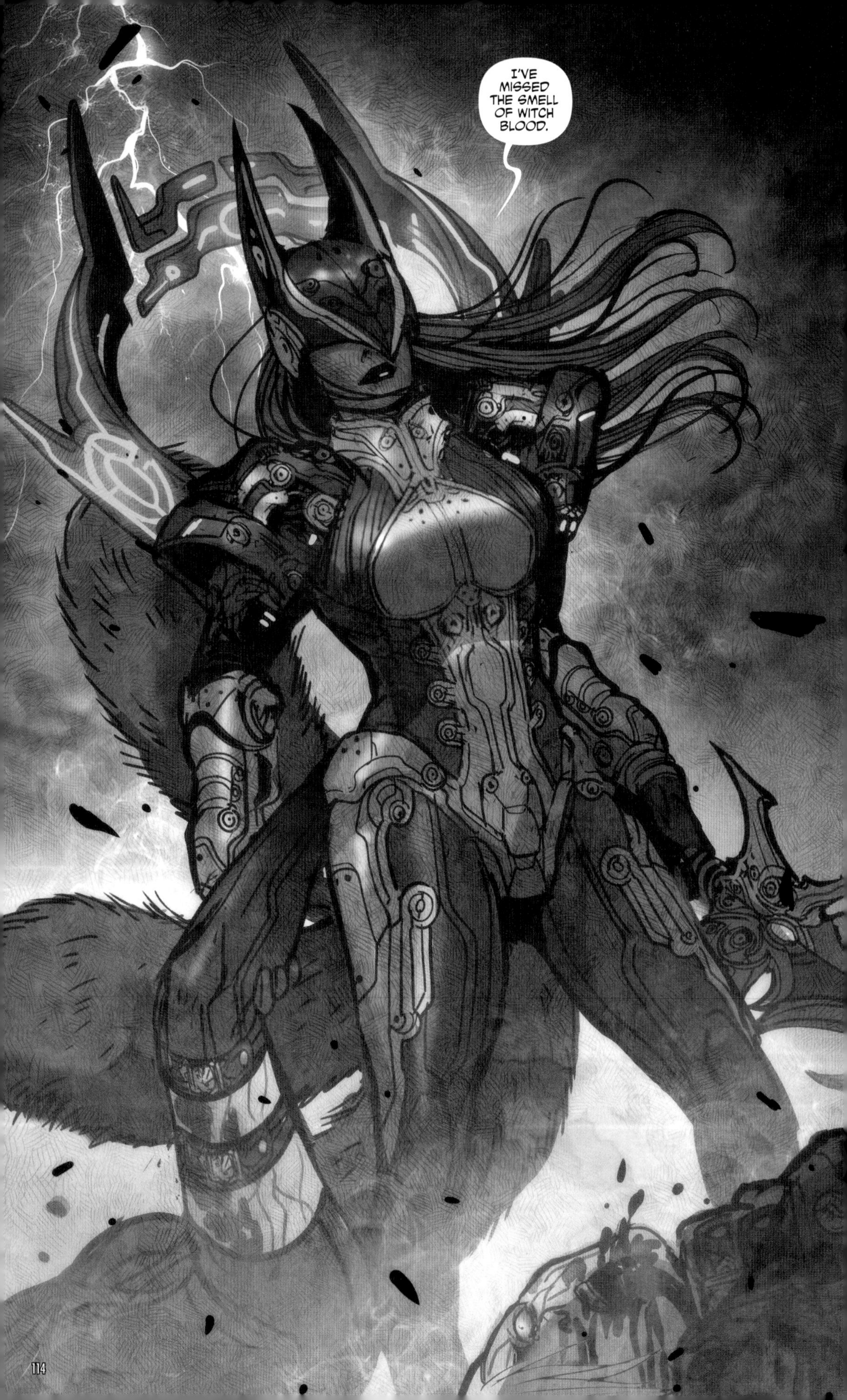
I'VE MISSED THE SMELL OF WITCH BLOOD.

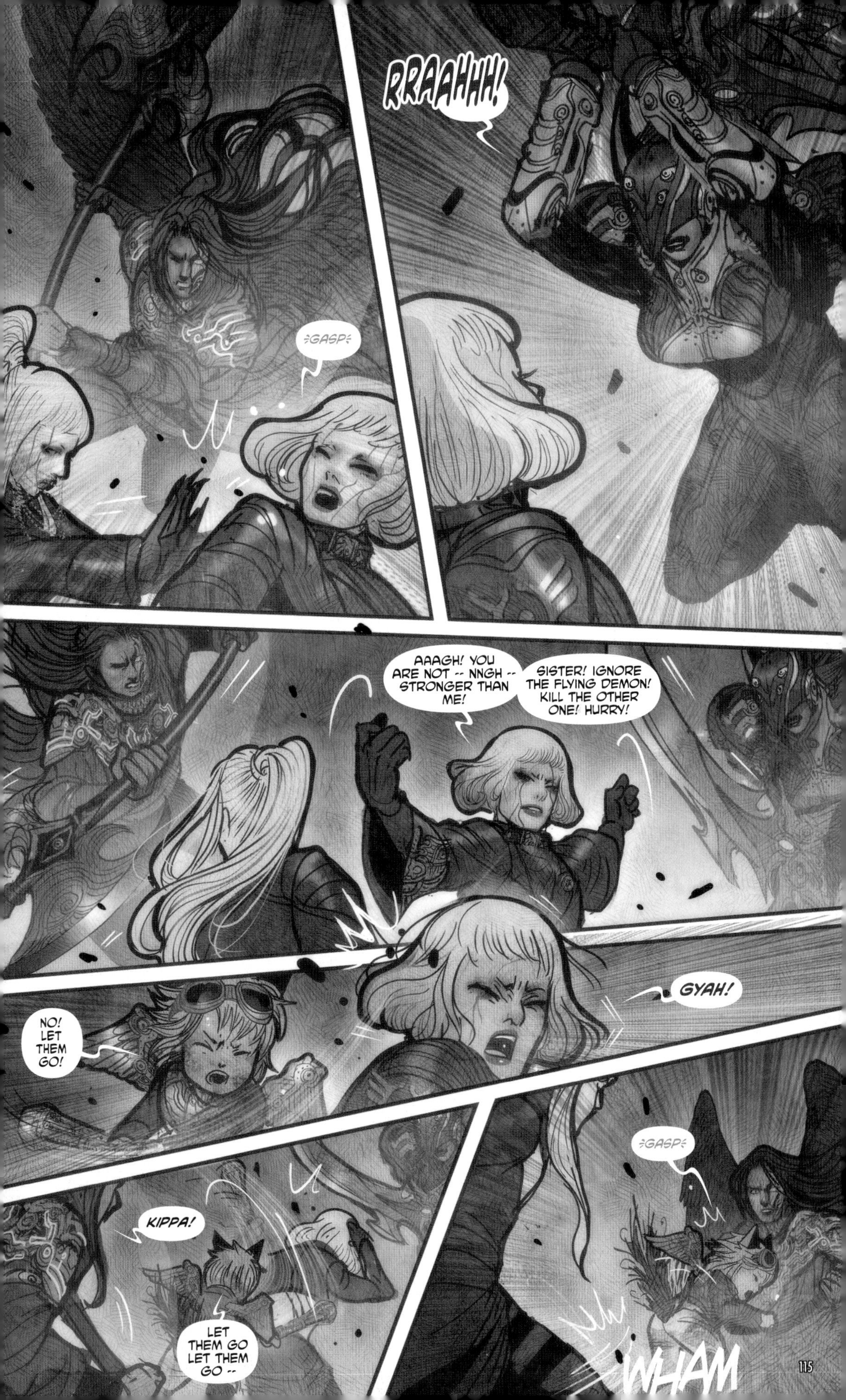
GASP
RRAAHHH!
AAAGH! YOU ARE NOT -- NNGH -- STRONGER THAN ME!
SISTER! IGNORE THE FLYING DEMON! KILL THE OTHER ONE! HURRY!
NO! LET THEM GO!
GYAH!
KIPPA!
LET THEM GO LET THEM GO --
GASP
WHAM

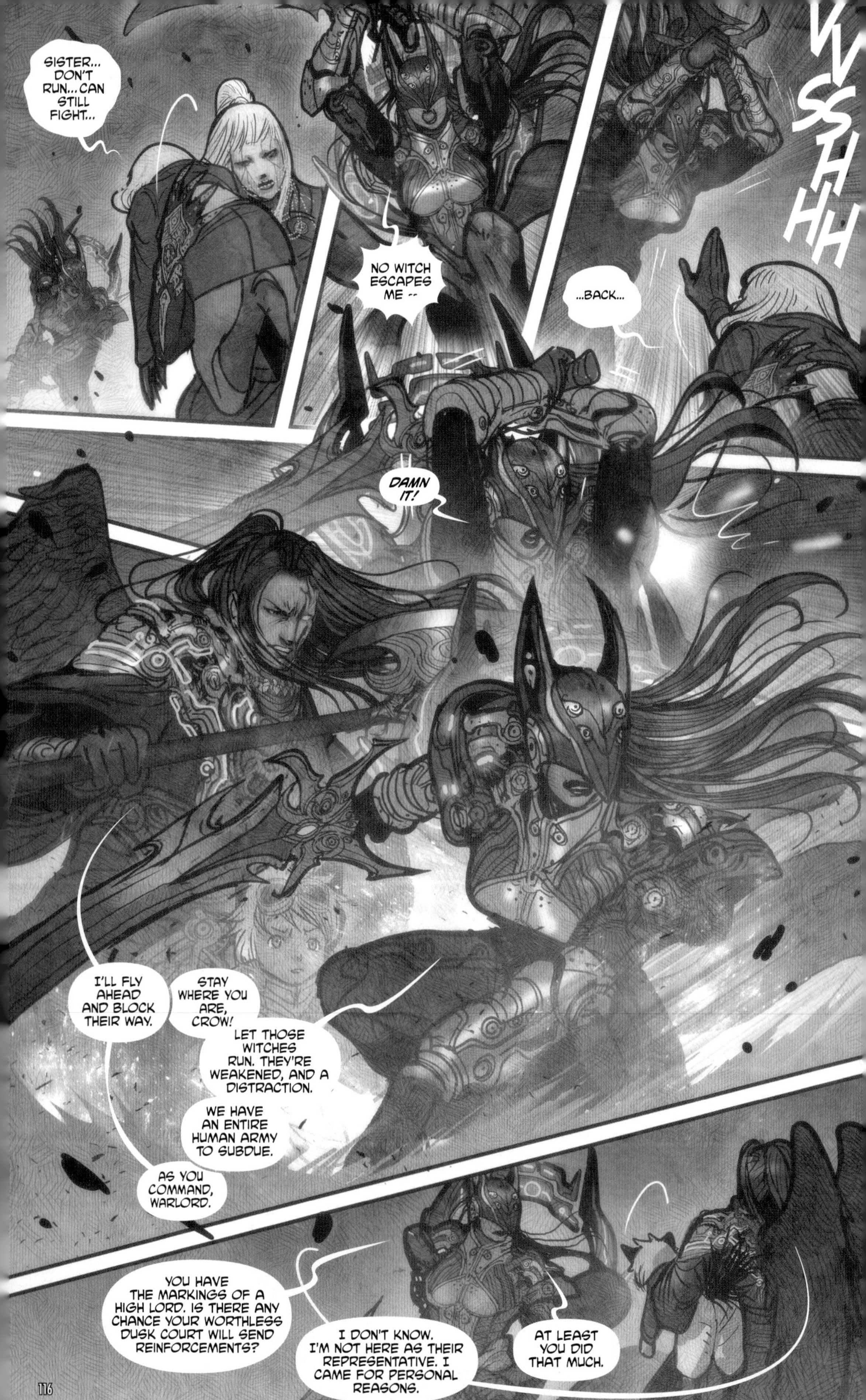
SISTER... DON'T RUN... CAN STILL FIGHT...
NO WITCH ESCAPES ME --
...BACK...
VVSSHHH
DAMN IT!
I'LL FLY AHEAD AND BLOCK THEIR WAY.
STAY WHERE YOU ARE, CROW!
LET THOSE WITCHES RUN. THEY'RE WEAKENED, AND A DISTRACTION.
WE HAVE AN ENTIRE HUMAN ARMY TO SUBDUE.
AS YOU COMMAND, WARLORD.
YOU HAVE THE MARKINGS OF A HIGH LORD. IS THERE ANY CHANCE YOUR WORTHLESS DUSK COURT WILL SEND REINFORCEMENTS?
I DON'T KNOW. I'M NOT HERE AS THEIR REPRESENTATIVE. I CAME FOR PERSONAL REASONS.
AT LEAST YOU DID THAT MUCH.

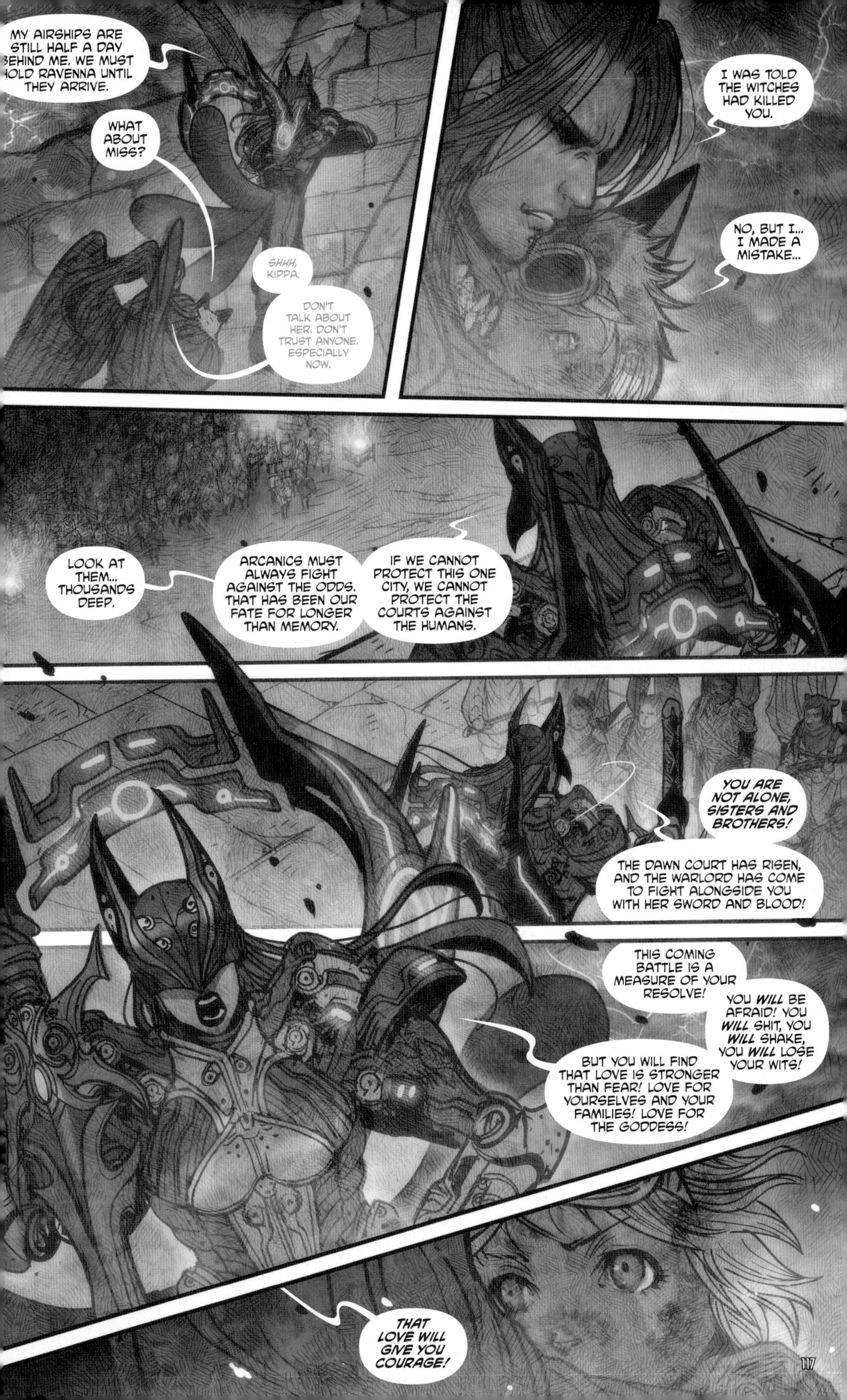
MY AIRSHIPS ARE STILL HALF A DAY BEHIND ME. WE MUST HOLD RAVENNA UNTIL THEY ARRIVE.
WHAT ABOUT MISS?
SHHH, KIPPA.
DON'T TALK ABOUT HER. DON'T TRUST ANYONE. ESPECIALLY NOW.
I WAS TOLD THE WITCHES HAD KILLED YOU.
NO, BUT I... I MADE A MISTAKE...
LOOK AT THEM... THOUSANDS DEEP.
ARCANICS MUST ALWAYS FIGHT AGAINST THE ODDS. THAT HAS BEEN OUR FATE FOR LONGER THAN MEMORY.
IF WE CANNOT PROTECT THIS ONE CITY, WE CANNOT PROTECT THE COURTS AGAINST THE HUMANS.
YOU ARE NOT ALONE, SISTERS AND BROTHERS!
THE DAWN COURT HAS RISEN, AND THE WARLORD HAS COME TO FIGHT ALONGSIDE YOU WITH HER SWORD AND BLOOD!
THIS COMING BATTLE IS A MEASURE OF YOUR RESOLVE!
YOU WILL BE AFRAID! YOU WILL SHIT, YOU WILL SHAKE, YOU WILL LOSE YOUR WITS!
BUT YOU WILL FIND THAT LOVE IS STRONGER THAN FEAR! LOVE FOR YOURSELVES AND YOUR FAMILIES! LOVE FOR THE GODDESS!
THAT LOVE WILL GIVE YOU COURAGE!

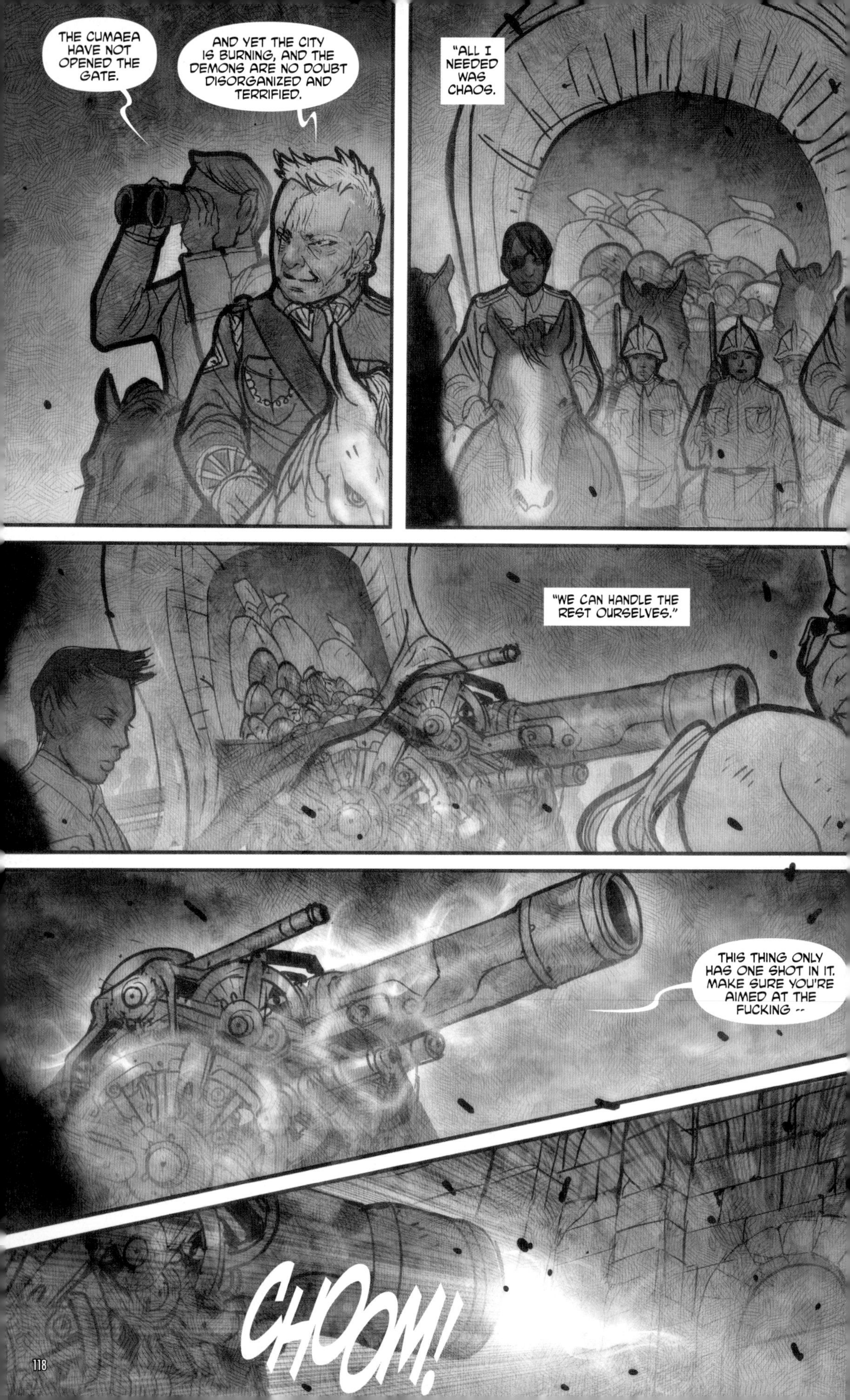
THE CUMAEA HAVE NOT OPENED THE GATE.
AND YET THE CITY IS BURNING, AND THE DEMONS ARE NO DOUBT DISORGANIZED AND TERRIFIED.
"ALL I NEEDED WAS CHAOS.
"WE CAN HANDLE THE REST OURSELVES."
THIS THING ONLY HAS ONE SHOT IN IT. MAKE SURE YOU'RE AIMED AT THE FUCKING --
CHOOM!

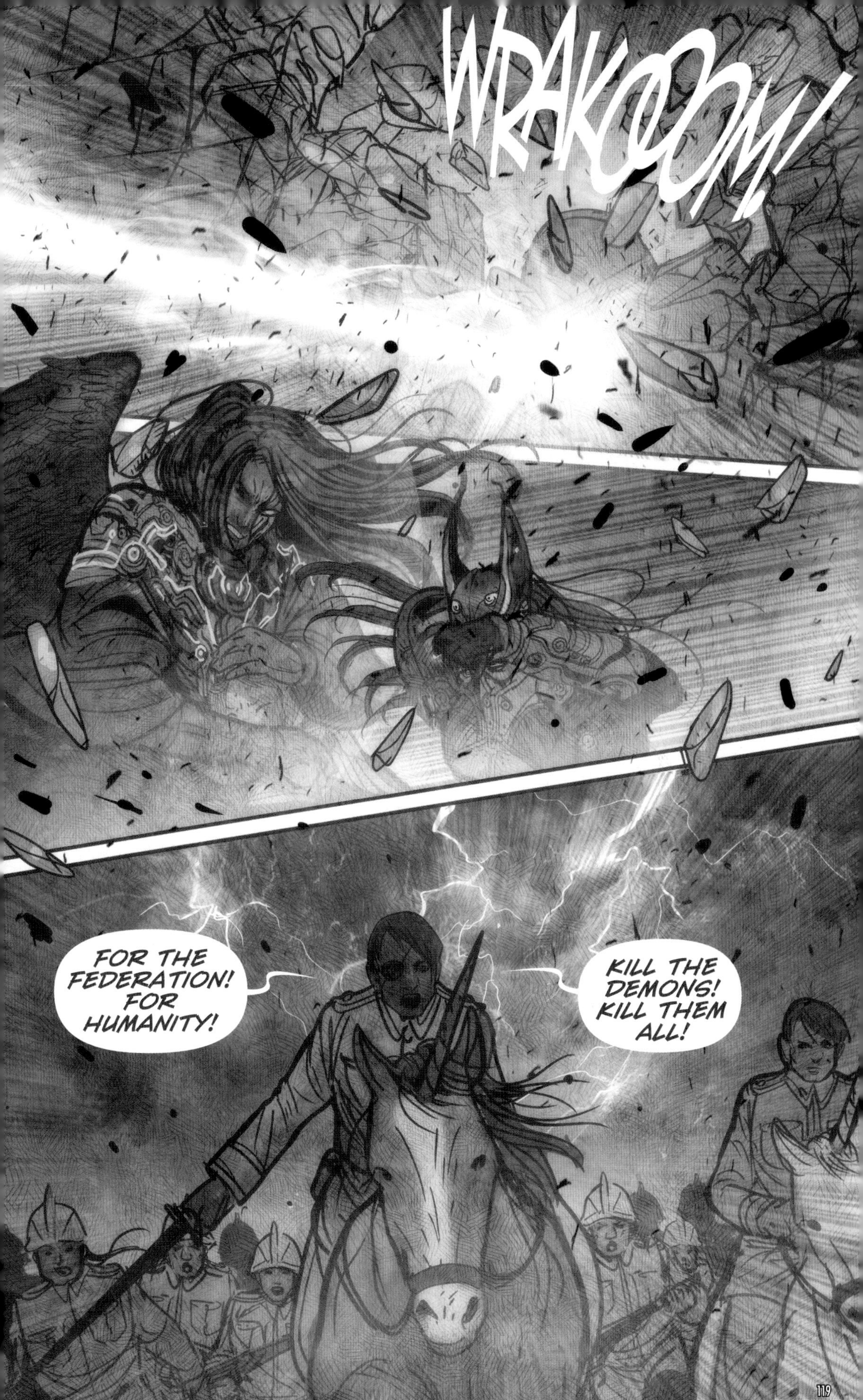
WRAKOOOM!
FOR THE FEDERATION! FOR HUMANITY!
KILL THE DEMONS! KILL THEM ALL!

CHAPTER TWENTY-NINE

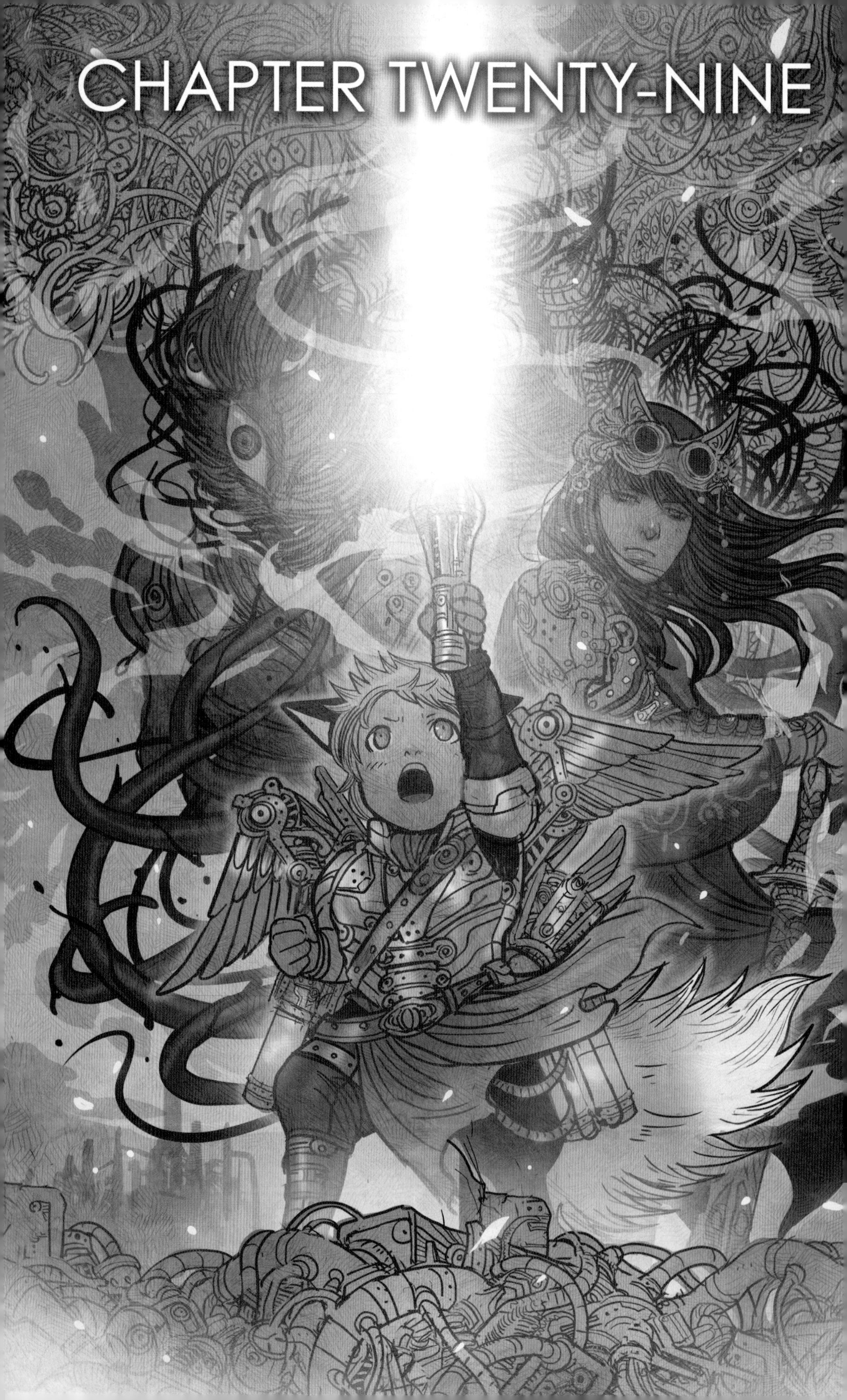

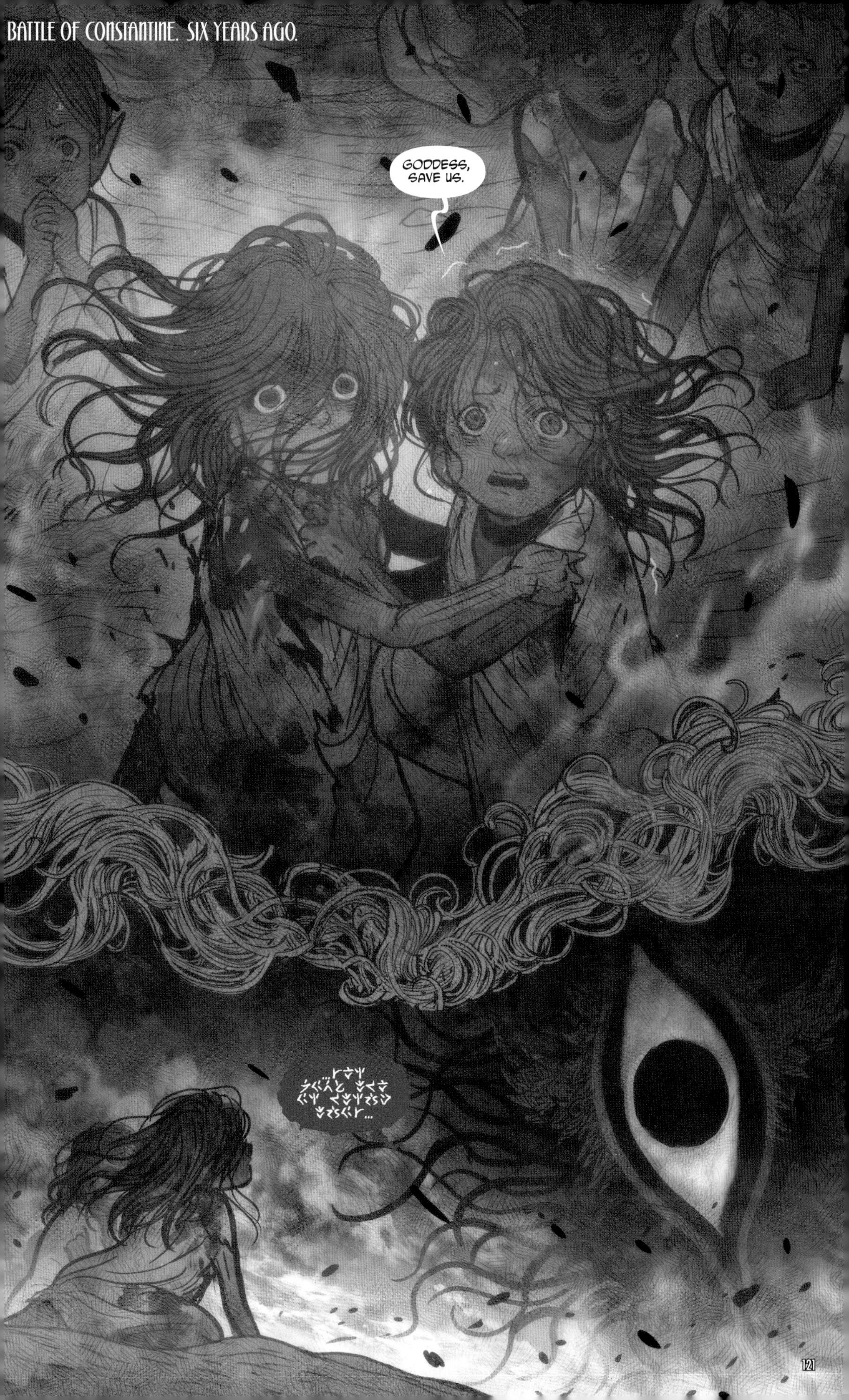
BATTLE OF CONSTANTINE. SIX YEARS AGO.
GODDESS, SAVE US.

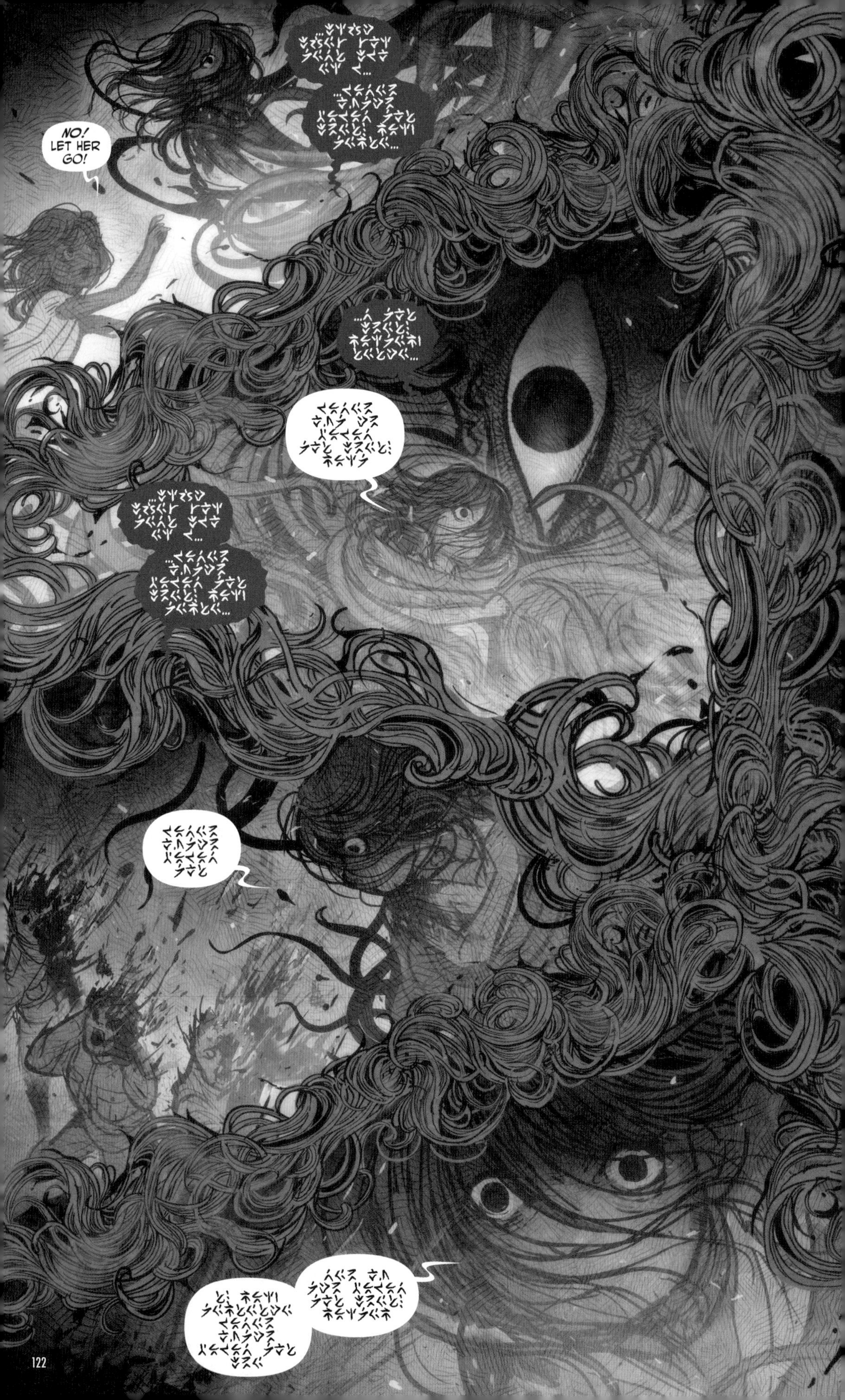
NO! LET HER GO!

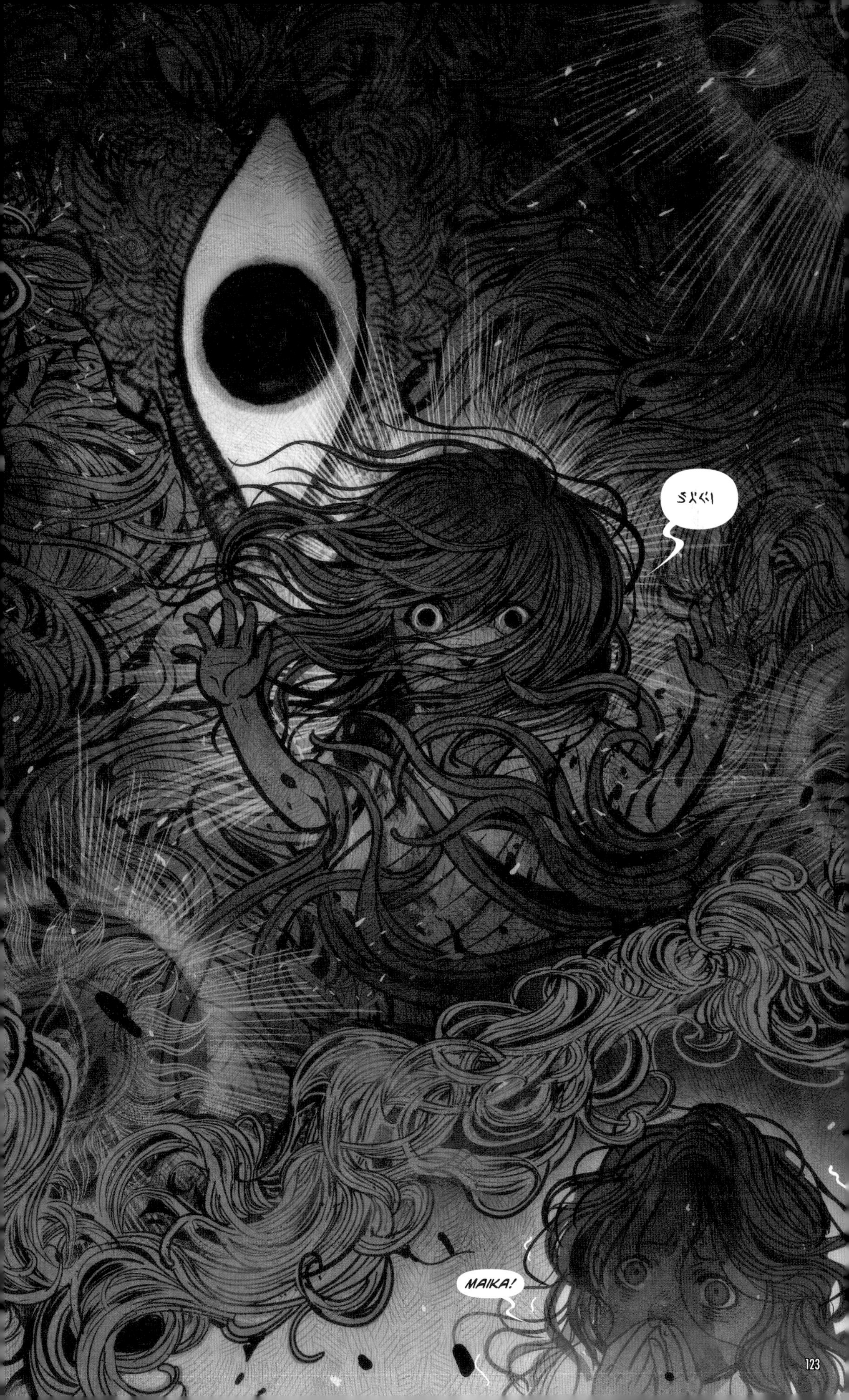
MAIKA!

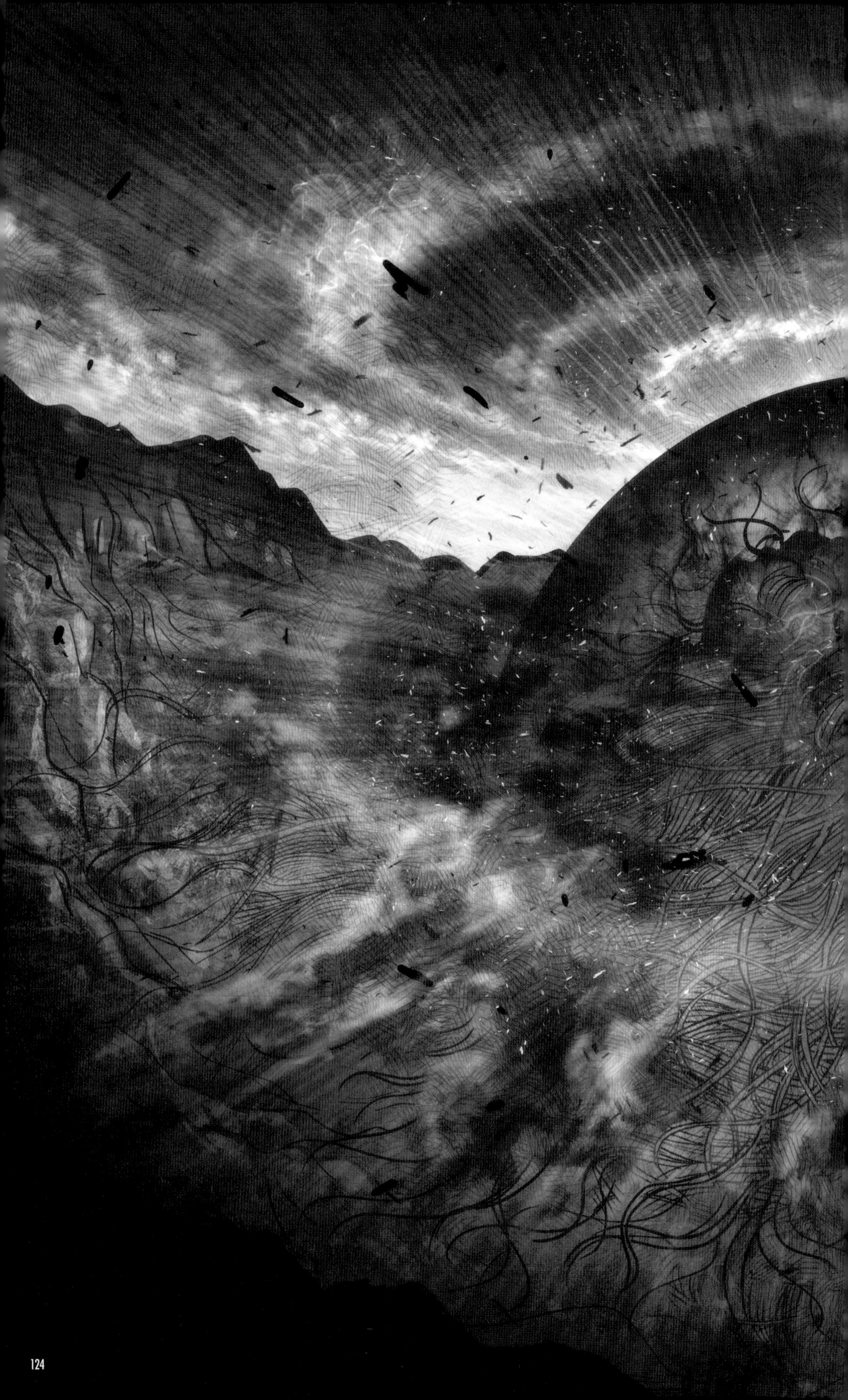

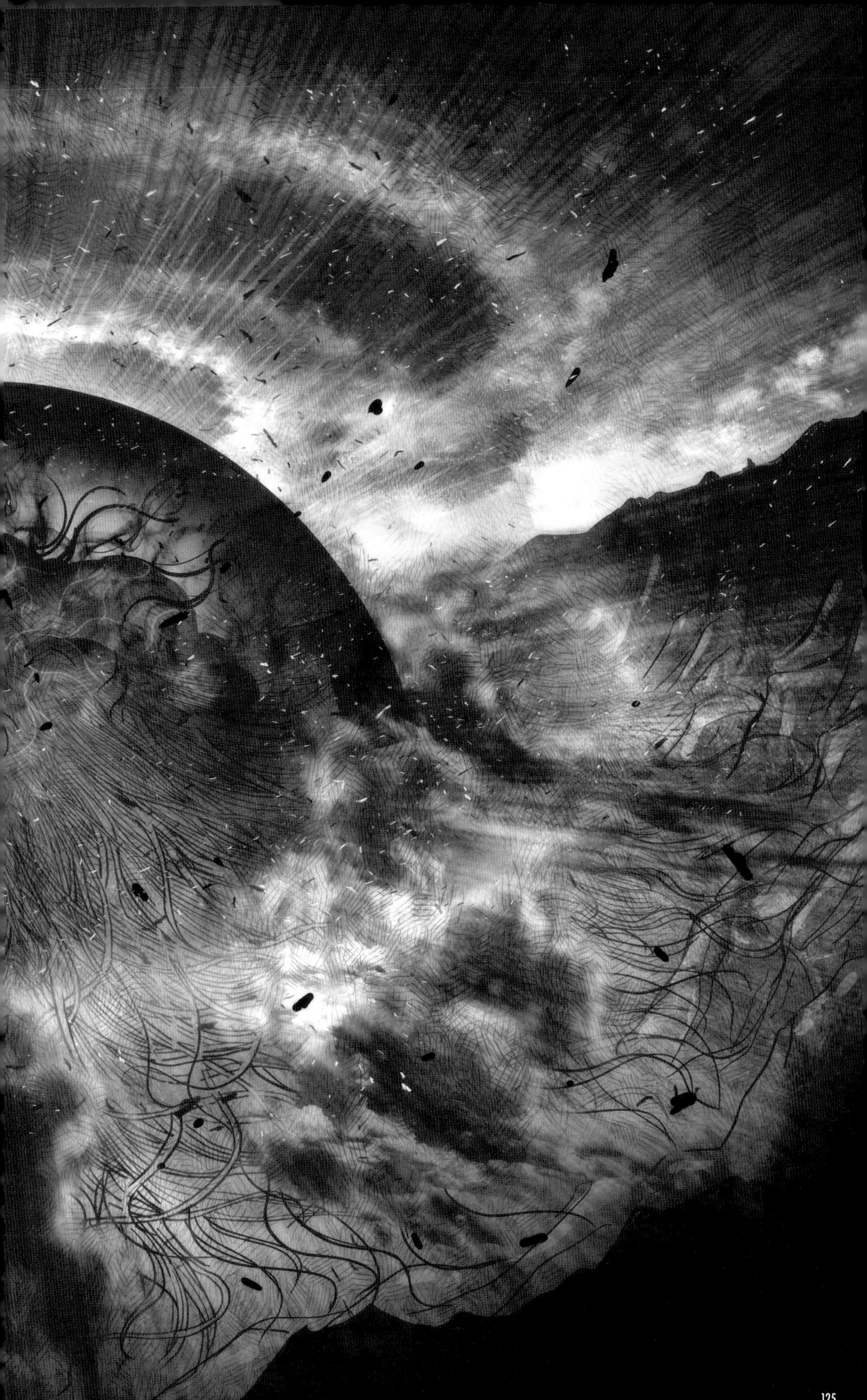

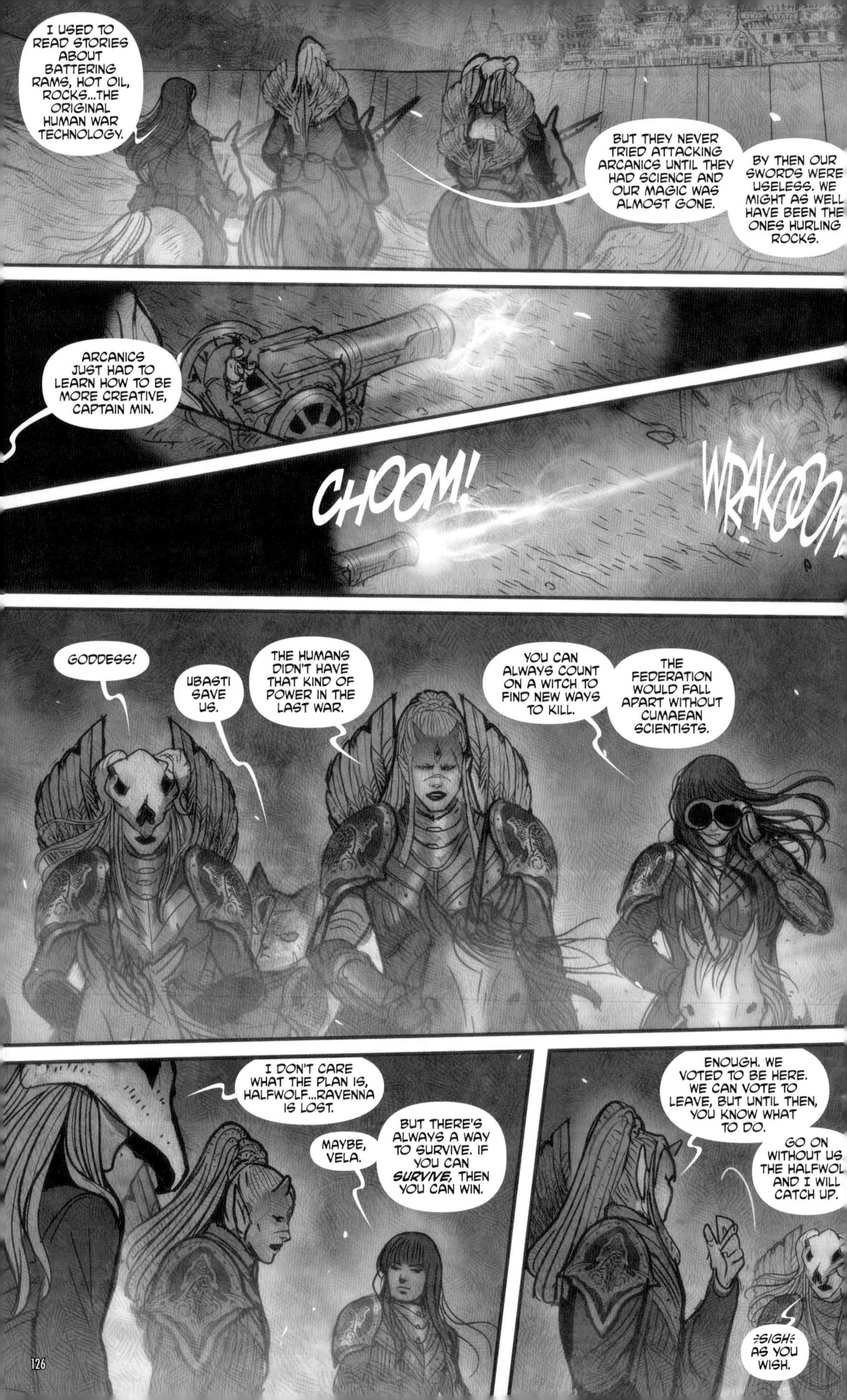
I USED TO READ STORIES ABOUT BATTERING RAMS, HOT OIL, ROCKS...THE ORIGINAL HUMAN WAR TECHNOLOGY.
BUT THEY NEVER TRIED ATTACKING ARCANICS UNTIL THEY HAD SCIENCE AND OUR MAGIC WAS ALMOST GONE.
BY THEN OUR SWORDS WERE USELESS. WE MIGHT AS WELL HAVE BEEN THE ONES HURLING ROCKS.
ARCANICS JUST HAD TO LEARN HOW TO BE MORE CREATIVE, CAPTAIN MIN.
CHOOM!
WRAKOOOM
GODDESS!
UBASTI SAVE US.
THE HUMANS DIDN'T HAVE THAT KIND OF POWER IN THE LAST WAR.
YOU CAN ALWAYS COUNT ON A WITCH TO FIND NEW WAYS TO KILL.
THE FEDERATION WOULD FALL APART WITHOUT CUMAEAN SCIENTISTS.
I DON'T CARE WHAT THE PLAN IS, HALFWOLF...RAVENNA IS LOST.
MAYBE, VELA.
BUT THERE'S ALWAYS A WAY TO SURVIVE. IF YOU CAN SURVIVE, THEN YOU CAN WIN.
ENOUGH. WE VOTED TO BE HERE. WE CAN VOTE TO LEAVE, BUT UNTIL THEN, YOU KNOW WHAT TO DO.
GO ON WITHOUT US. THE HALFWOL AND I WILL CATCH UP.
SIGH AS YOU WISH.

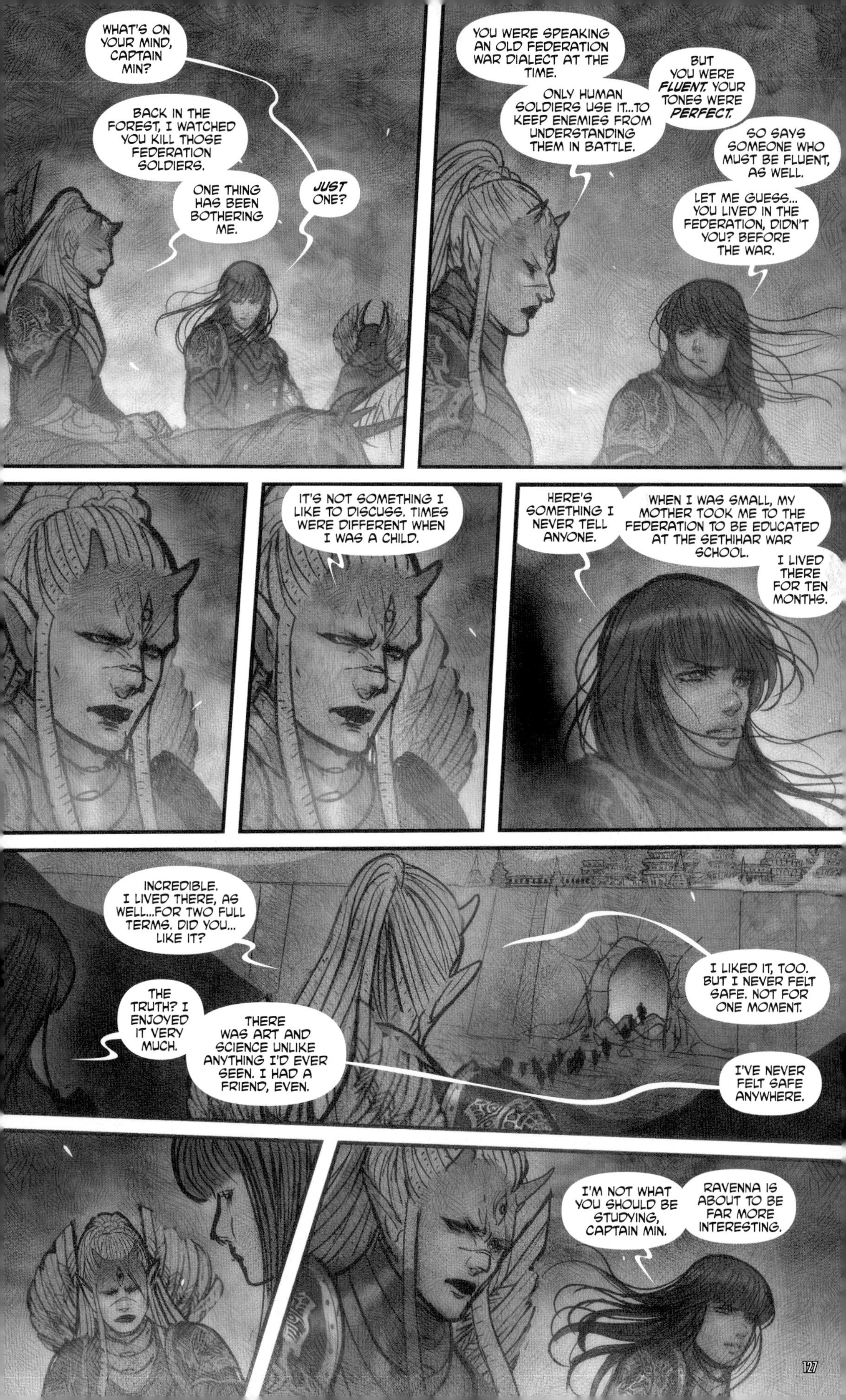
WHAT'S ON YOUR MIND, CAPTAIN MIN?
BACK IN THE FOREST, I WATCHED YOU KILL THOSE FEDERATION SOLDIERS.
ONE THING HAS BEEN BOTHERING ME.
JUST ONE?
YOU WERE SPEAKING AN OLD FEDERATION WAR DIALECT AT THE TIME.
ONLY HUMAN SOLDIERS USE IT...TO KEEP ENEMIES FROM UNDERSTANDING THEM IN BATTLE.
BUT YOU WERE FLUENT. YOUR TONES WERE PERFECT.
SO SAYS SOMEONE WHO MUST BE FLUENT, AS WELL.
LET ME GUESS... YOU LIVED IN THE FEDERATION, DIDN'T YOU? BEFORE THE WAR.
IT'S NOT SOMETHING I LIKE TO DISCUSS. TIMES WERE DIFFERENT WHEN I WAS A CHILD.
HERE'S SOMETHING I NEVER TELL ANYONE.
WHEN I WAS SMALL, MY MOTHER TOOK ME TO THE FEDERATION TO BE EDUCATED AT THE SETHIHAR WAR SCHOOL.
I LIVED THERE FOR TEN MONTHS.
INCREDIBLE. I LIVED THERE, AS WELL...FOR TWO FULL TERMS. DID YOU... LIKE IT?
THE TRUTH? I ENJOYED IT VERY MUCH.
THERE WAS ART AND SCIENCE UNLIKE ANYTHING I'D EVER SEEN. I HAD A FRIEND, EVEN.
I LIKED IT, TOO. BUT I NEVER FELT SAFE. NOT FOR ONE MOMENT.
I'VE NEVER FELT SAFE ANYWHERE.
I'M NOT WHAT YOU SHOULD BE STUDYING, CAPTAIN MIN.
RAVENNA IS ABOUT TO BE FAR MORE INTERESTING.

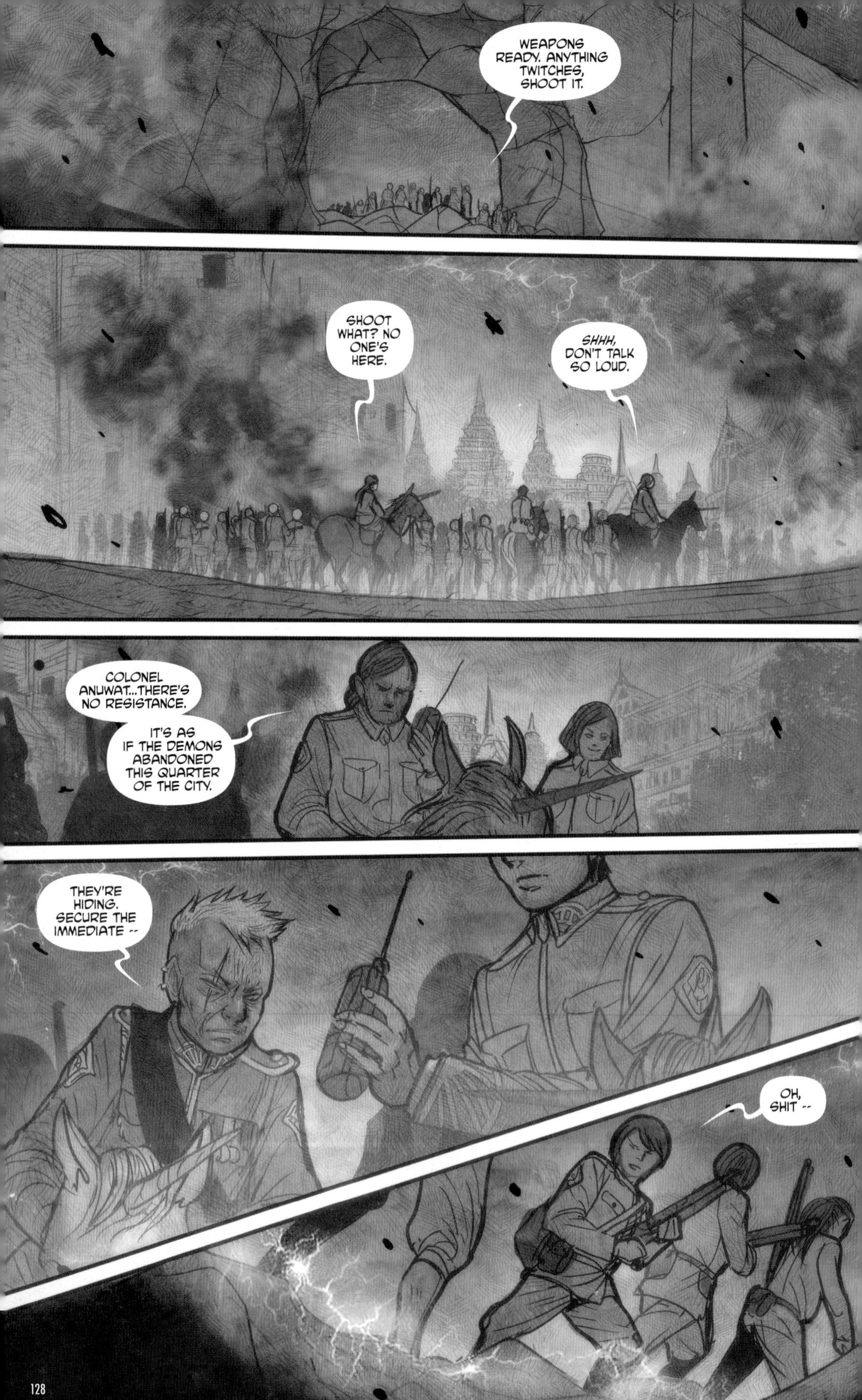
WEAPONS READY. ANYTHING TWITCHES, SHOOT IT.
SHOOT WHAT? NO ONE'S HERE.
SHHH, DON'T TALK SO LOUD.
COLONEL ANUWAT...THERE'S NO RESISTANCE.
IT'S AS IF THE DEMONS ABANDONED THIS QUARTER OF THE CITY.
THEY'RE HIDING. SECURE THE IMMEDIATE --
OH, SHIT --

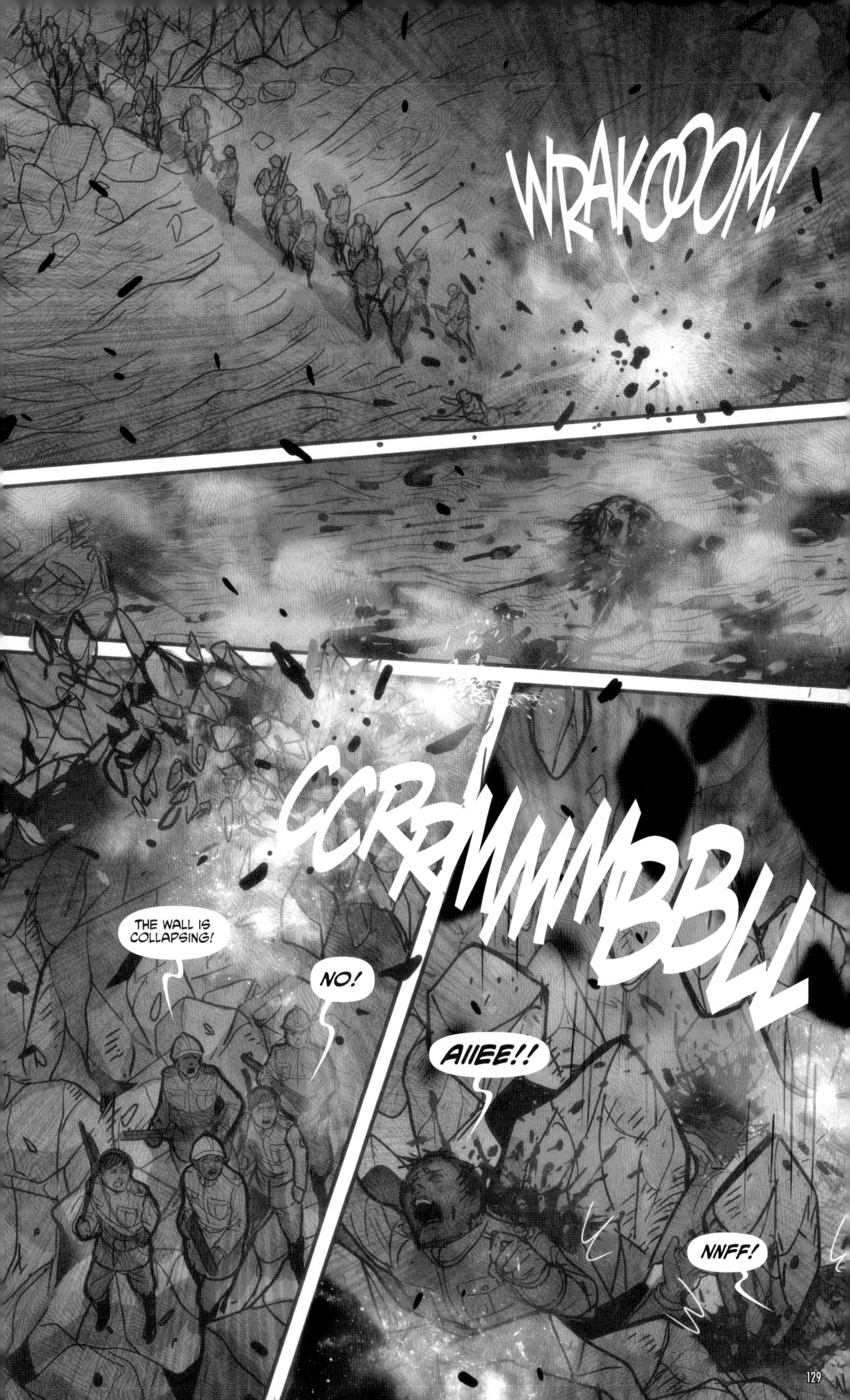
WRAKOOOM!
CCRRMMMMBBLL
THE WALL IS COLLAPSING!
NO!
AIIEE!!
NNFF!

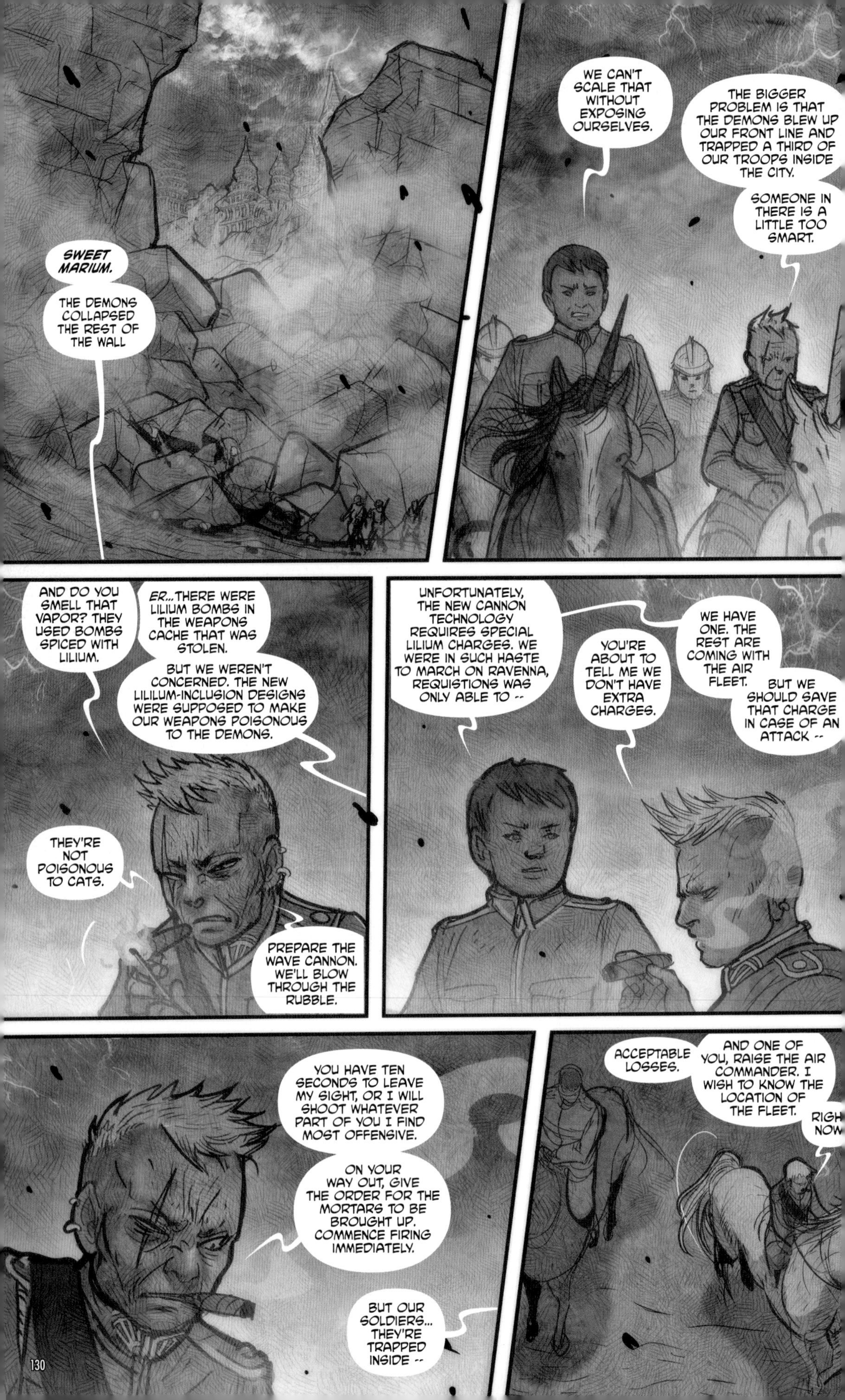
SWEET MARIUM.
THE DEMONS COLLAPSED THE REST OF THE WALL
WE CAN'T SCALE THAT WITHOUT EXPOSING OURSELVES.
THE BIGGER PROBLEM IS THAT THE DEMONS BLEW UP OUR FRONT LINE AND TRAPPED A THIRD OF OUR TROOPS INSIDE THE CITY.
SOMEONE IN THERE IS A LITTLE TOO SMART.
AND DO YOU SMELL THAT VAPOR? THEY USED BOMBS SPICED WITH LILIUM.
ER...THERE WERE LILIUM BOMBS IN THE WEAPONS CACHE THAT WAS STOLEN.
BUT WE WEREN'T CONCERNED. THE NEW LILILUM-INCLUSION DESIGNS WERE SUPPOSED TO MAKE OUR WEAPONS POISONOUS TO THE DEMONS.
THEY'RE NOT POISONOUS TO CATS.
PREPARE THE WAVE CANNON. WE'LL BLOW THROUGH THE RUBBLE.
UNFORTUNATELY, THE NEW CANNON TECHNOLOGY REQUIRES SPECIAL LILIUM CHARGES. WE WERE IN SUCH HASTE TO MARCH ON RAVENNA, REQUISTIONS WAS ONLY ABLE TO --
YOU'RE ABOUT TO TELL ME WE DON'T HAVE EXTRA CHARGES.
WE HAVE ONE. THE REST ARE COMING WITH THE AIR FLEET.
BUT WE SHOULD SAVE THAT CHARGE IN CASE OF AN ATTACK --
YOU HAVE TEN SECONDS TO LEAVE MY SIGHT, OR I WILL SHOOT WHATEVER PART OF YOU I FIND MOST OFFENSIVE.
ON YOUR WAY OUT, GIVE THE ORDER FOR THE MORTARS TO BE BROUGHT UP. COMMENCE FIRING IMMEDIATELY.
BUT OUR SOLDIERS... THEY'RE TRAPPED INSIDE --
ACCEPTABLE LOSSES.
AND ONE OF YOU, RAISE THE AIR COMMANDER. I WISH TO KNOW THE LOCATION OF THE FLEET.
RIGH NOW

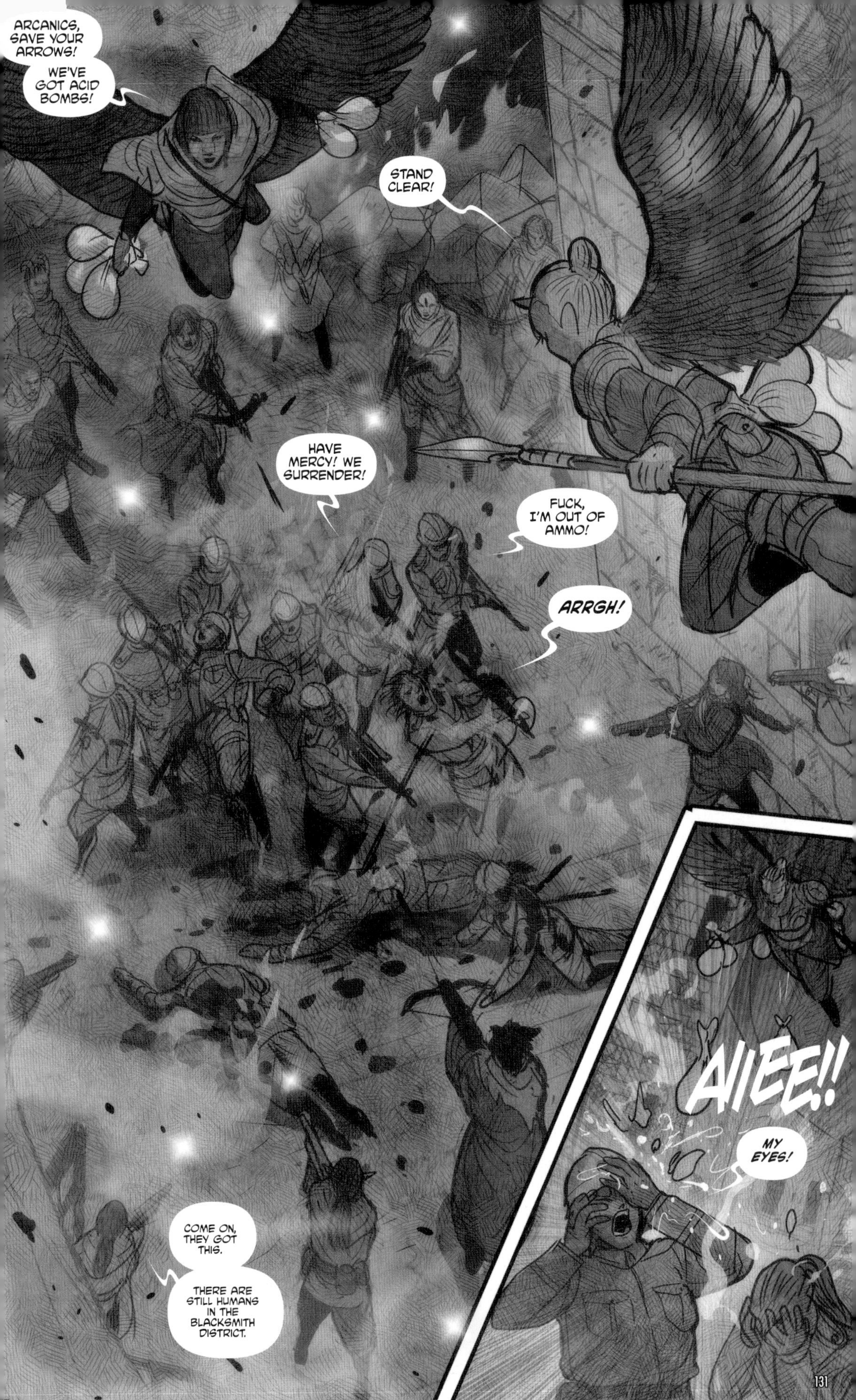
ARCANICS, SAVE YOUR ARROWS!
WE'VE GOT ACID BOMBS!
STAND CLEAR!
HAVE MERCY! WE SURRENDER!
FUCK, I'M OUT OF AMMO!
ARRGH!
COME ON, THEY GOT THIS.
THERE ARE STILL HUMANS IN THE BLACKSMITH DISTRICT.
AIIEE!!
MY EYES!

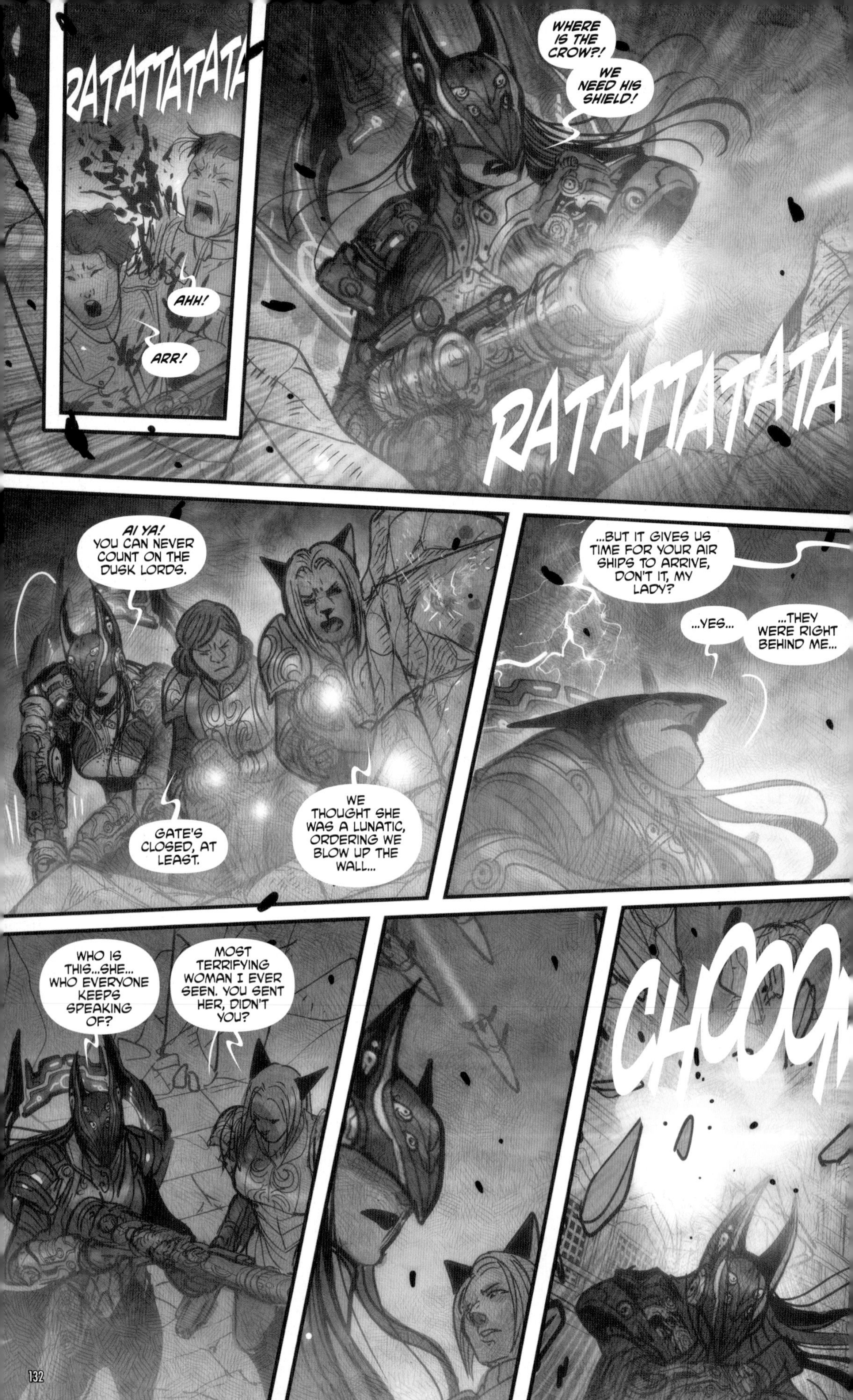
RATATTATATA
AHH!
ARR!
WHERE IS THE CROW?!
WE NEED HIS SHIELD!
RATATTATATA
AI YA! YOU CAN NEVER COUNT ON THE DUSK LORDS.
GATE'S CLOSED, AT LEAST.
WE THOUGHT SHE WAS A LUNATIC, ORDERING WE BLOW UP THE WALL...
...BUT IT GIVES US TIME FOR YOUR AIR SHIPS TO ARRIVE, DON'T IT, MY LADY?
...YES...
...THEY WERE RIGHT BEHIND ME...
WHO IS THIS...SHE... WHO EVERYONE KEEPS SPEAKING OF?
MOST TERRIFYING WOMAN I EVER SEEN. YOU SENT HER, DIDN'T YOU?
CHOOO

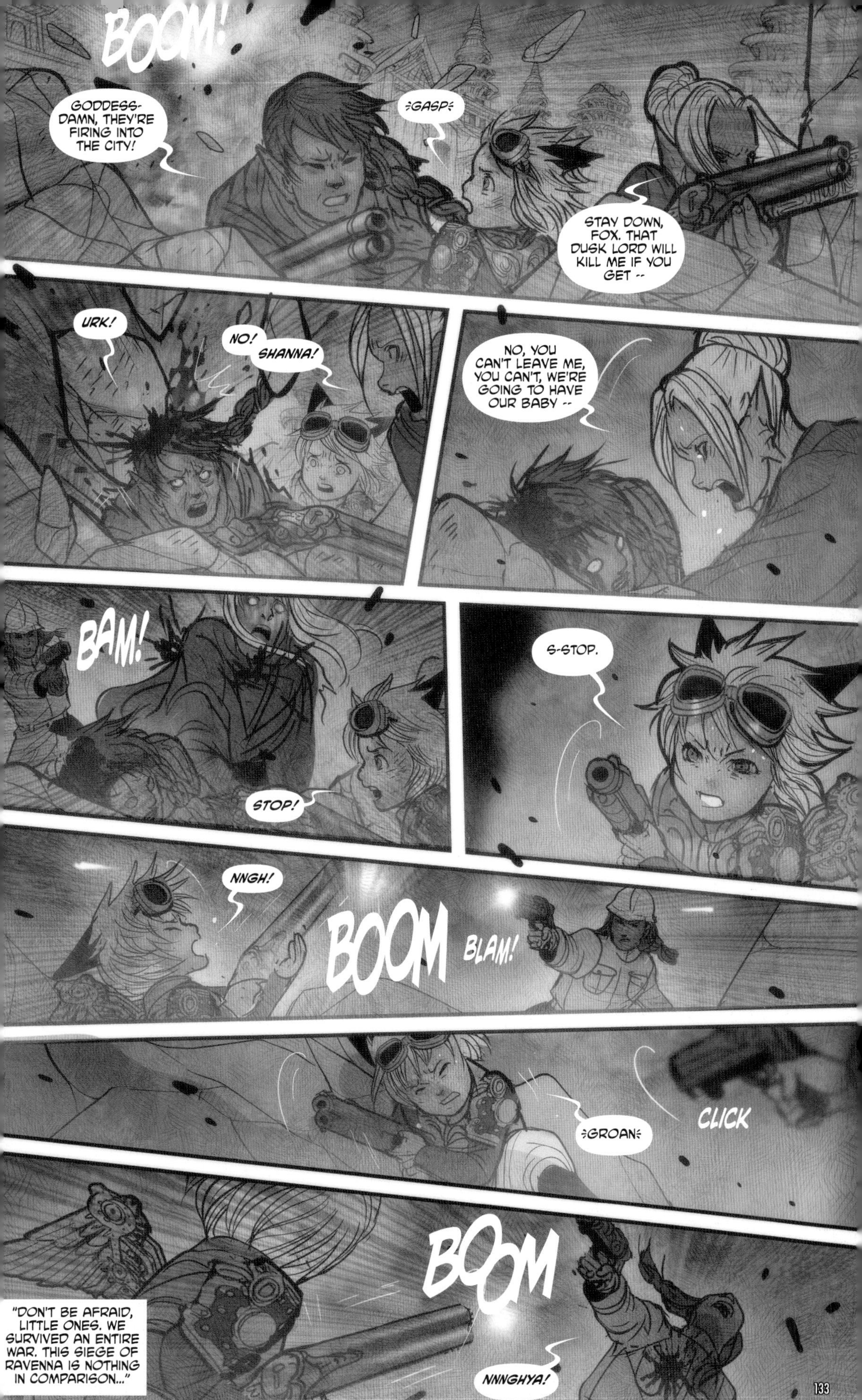
BOOM!
GODDESS-DAMN, THEY'RE FIRING INTO THE CITY!
GASP
STAY DOWN, FOX. THAT DUSK LORD WILL KILL ME IF YOU GET --
URK!
NO!
SHANNA!
NO, YOU CAN'T LEAVE ME, YOU CAN'T, WE'RE GOING TO HAVE OUR BABY --
BAM!
STOP!
S-STOP.
NNGH!
BOOM
BLAM!
GROAN
CLICK
BOOM
"DON'T BE AFRAID, LITTLE ONES. WE SURVIVED AN ENTIRE WAR. THIS SIEGE OF RAVENNA IS NOTHING IN COMPARISON..."
NNNGHYA!

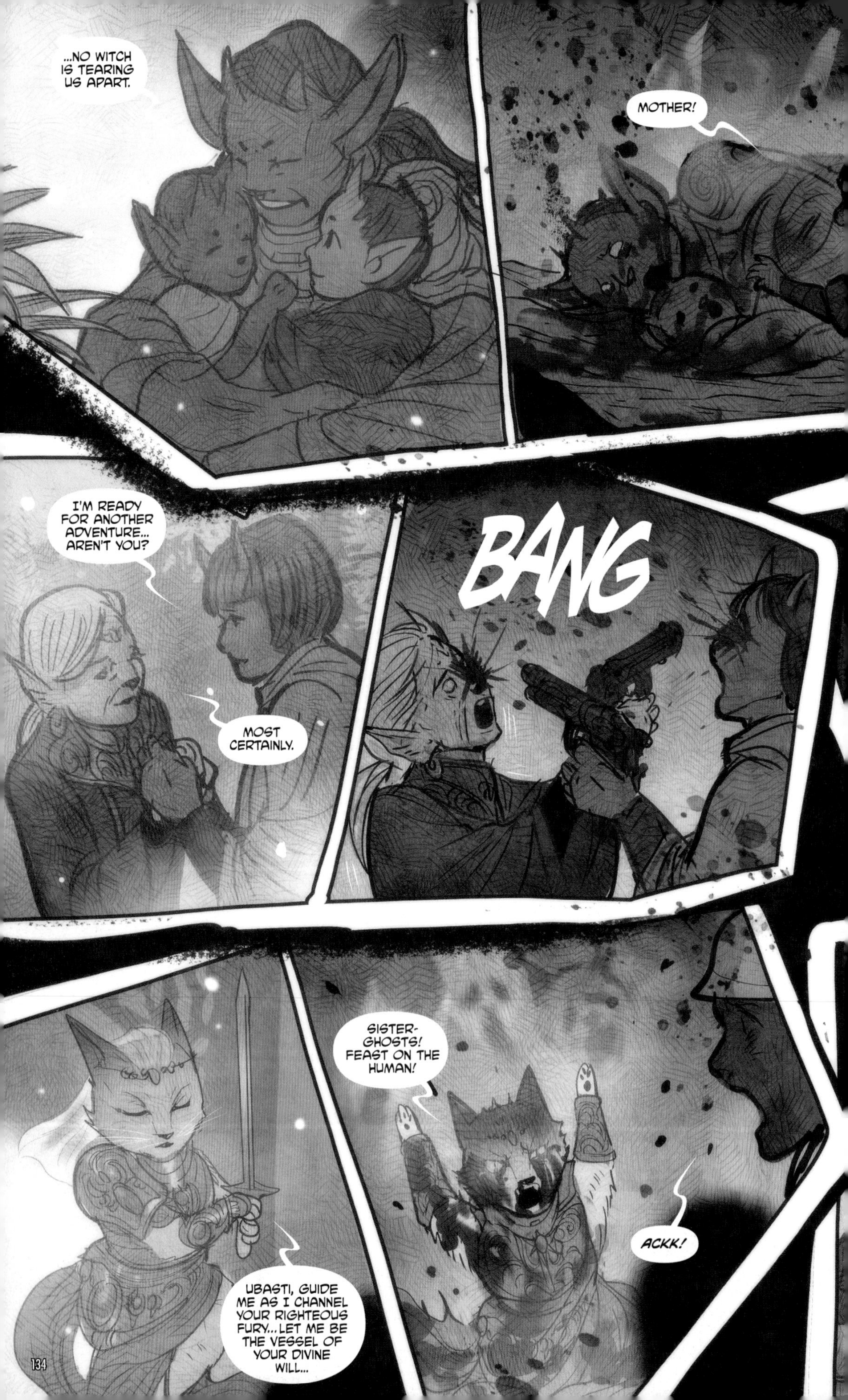
...NO WITCH IS TEARING US APART.
MOTHER!
I'M READY FOR ANOTHER ADVENTURE... AREN'T YOU?
MOST CERTAINLY.
BANG
UBASTI, GUIDE ME AS I CHANNEL YOUR RIGHTEOUS FURY...LET ME BE THE VESSEL OF YOUR DIVINE WILL...
SISTER-GHOSTS! FEAST ON THE HUMAN!
ACKK!

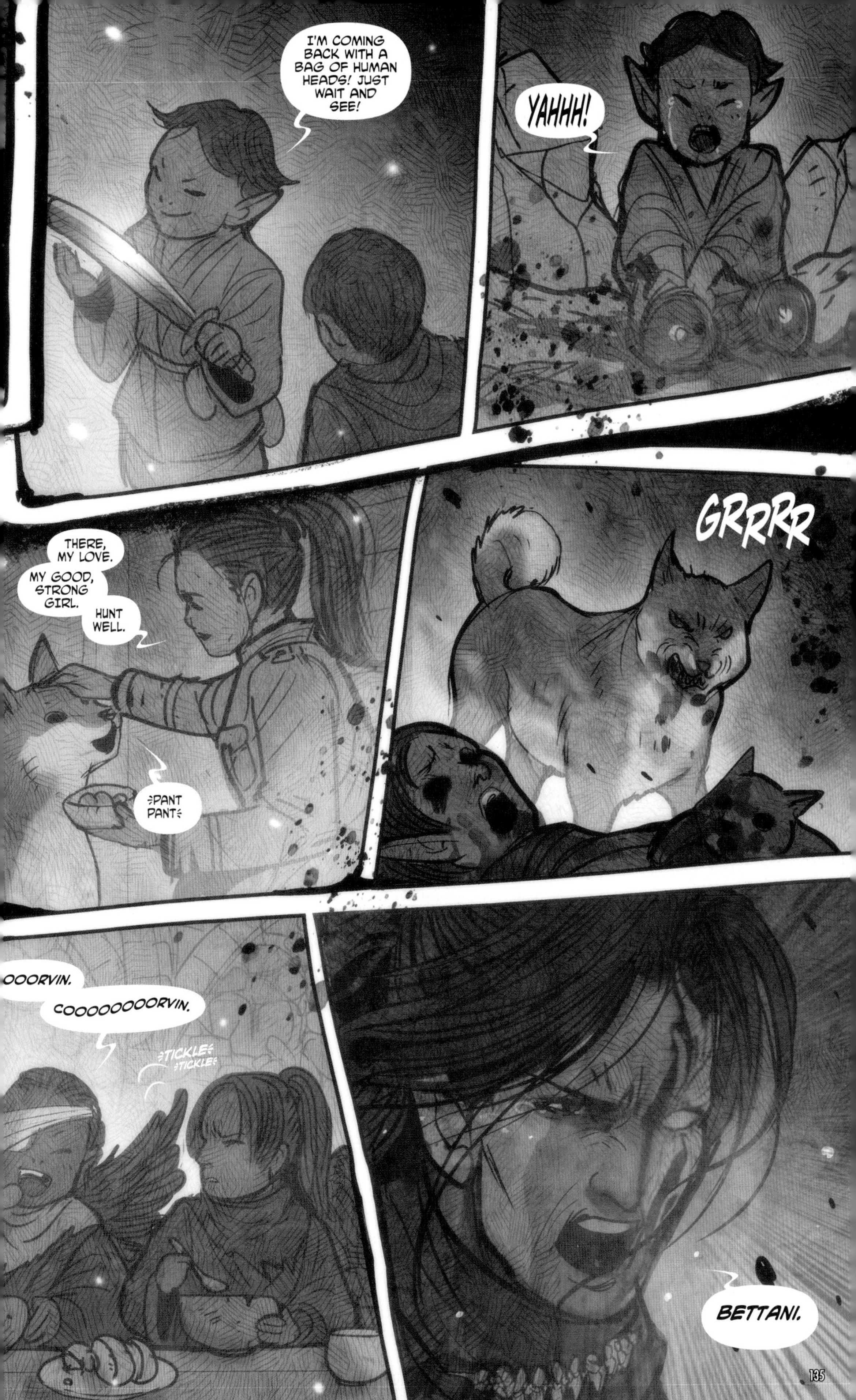
I'M COMING BACK WITH A BAG OF HUMAN HEADS! JUST WAIT AND SEE!
YAHHH!
THERE, MY LOVE.
MY GOOD, STRONG GIRL.
HUNT WELL.
PANT PANT
GRRRR
OOORVIN.
COOOOOOOORVIN.
TICKLE TICKLE
BETTANI.

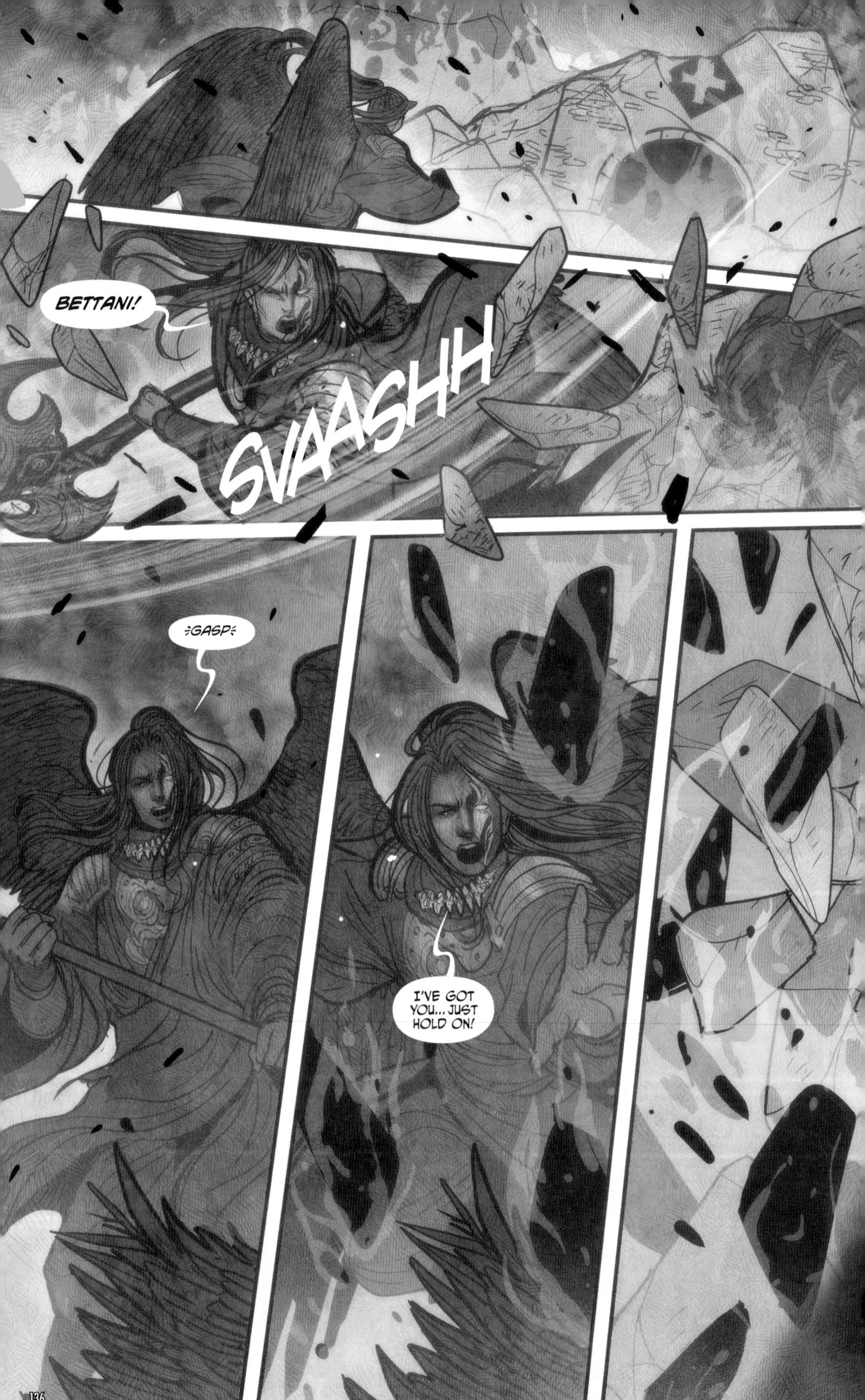
BETTANI!
SVAASHH
GASP
I'VE GOT YOU... JUST HOLD ON!

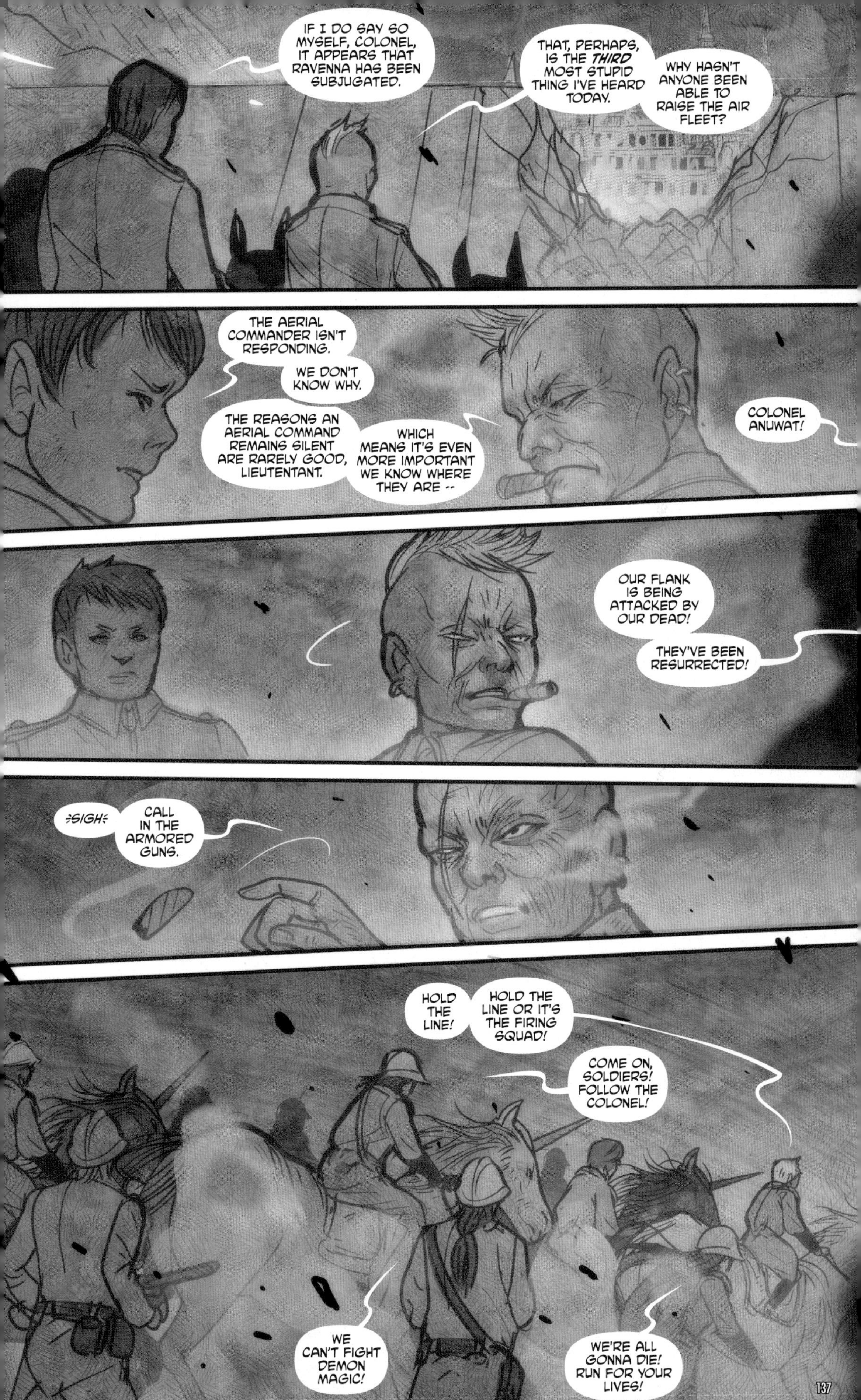
IF I DO SAY SO MYSELF, COLONEL, IT APPEARS THAT RAVENNA HAS BEEN SUBJUGATED.
THAT, PERHAPS, IS THE *THIRD* MOST STUPID THING I'VE HEARD TODAY.
WHY HASN'T ANYONE BEEN ABLE TO RAISE THE AIR FLEET?
THE AERIAL COMMANDER ISN'T RESPONDING.
WE DON'T KNOW WHY.
THE REASONS AN AERIAL COMMAND REMAINS SILENT ARE RARELY GOOD, LIEUTENTANT.
WHICH MEANS IT'S EVEN MORE IMPORTANT WE KNOW WHERE THEY ARE --
COLONEL ANUWAT!
OUR FLANK IS BEING ATTACKED BY OUR DEAD!
THEY'VE BEEN RESURRECTED!
SIGH
CALL IN THE ARMORED GUNS.
HOLD THE LINE!
HOLD THE LINE OR IT'S THE FIRING SQUAD!
COME ON, SOLDIERS! FOLLOW THE COLONEL!
WE CAN'T FIGHT DEMON MAGIC!
WE'RE ALL GONNA DIE! RUN FOR YOUR LIVES!

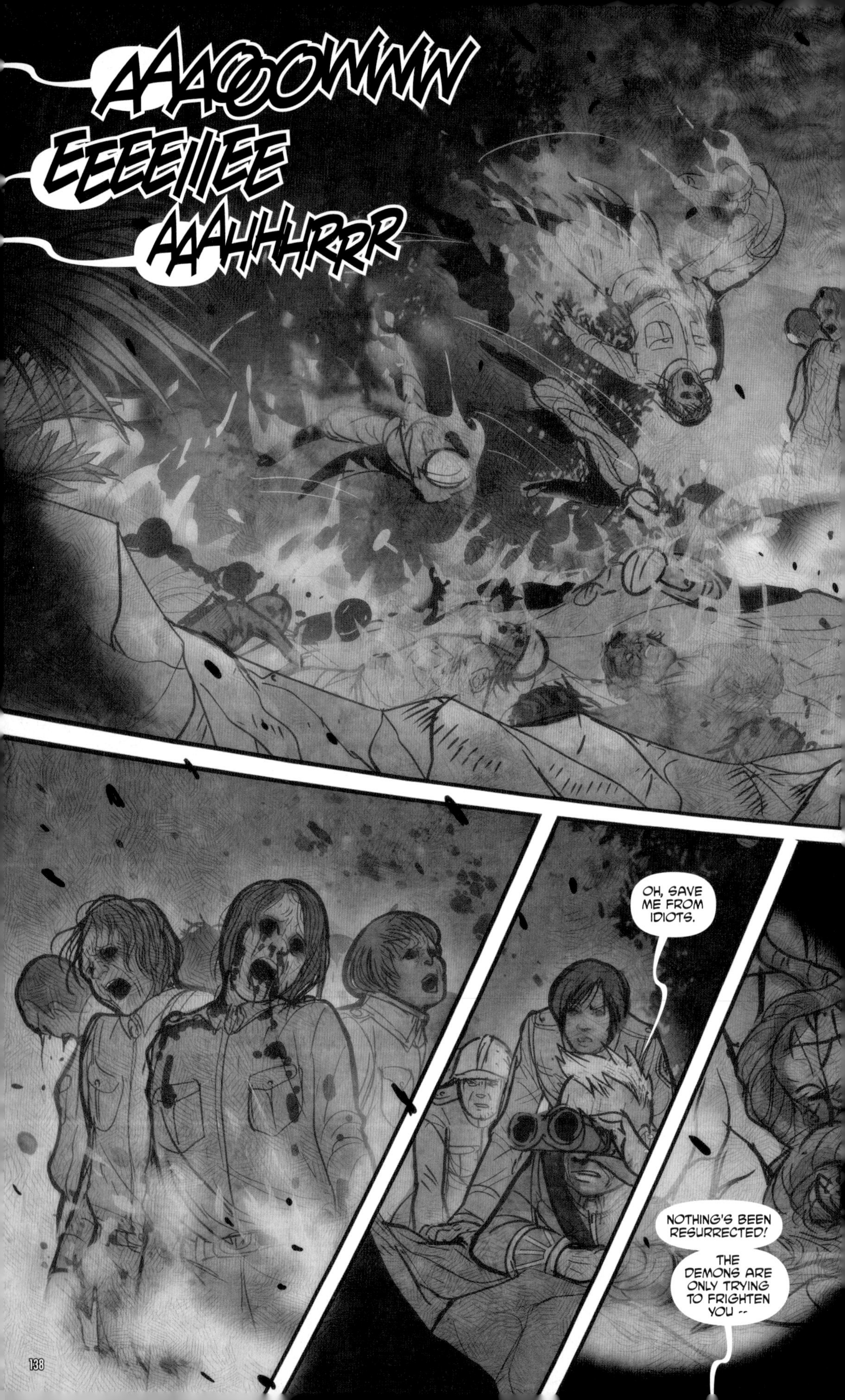
AAAOOOWWW
EEEEIIIEE
AAAHHRRR
OH, SAVE ME FROM IDIOTS.
NOTHING'S BEEN RESURRECTED!
THE DEMONS ARE ONLY TRYING TO FRIGHTEN YOU --

WE'RE FUCKED. I'M NOT ENDING UP LIKE THAT.
SEE THAT BADGE? THAT'S THE UNIT THAT DISAPPEARED IN THE FOREST!
WHY ARE THEY SO... *WITHERED?*

BLAM
BLAM
BLAM
BLAM
ARRGH!
YARR!
CHK
GYAH!
CHK
CHK

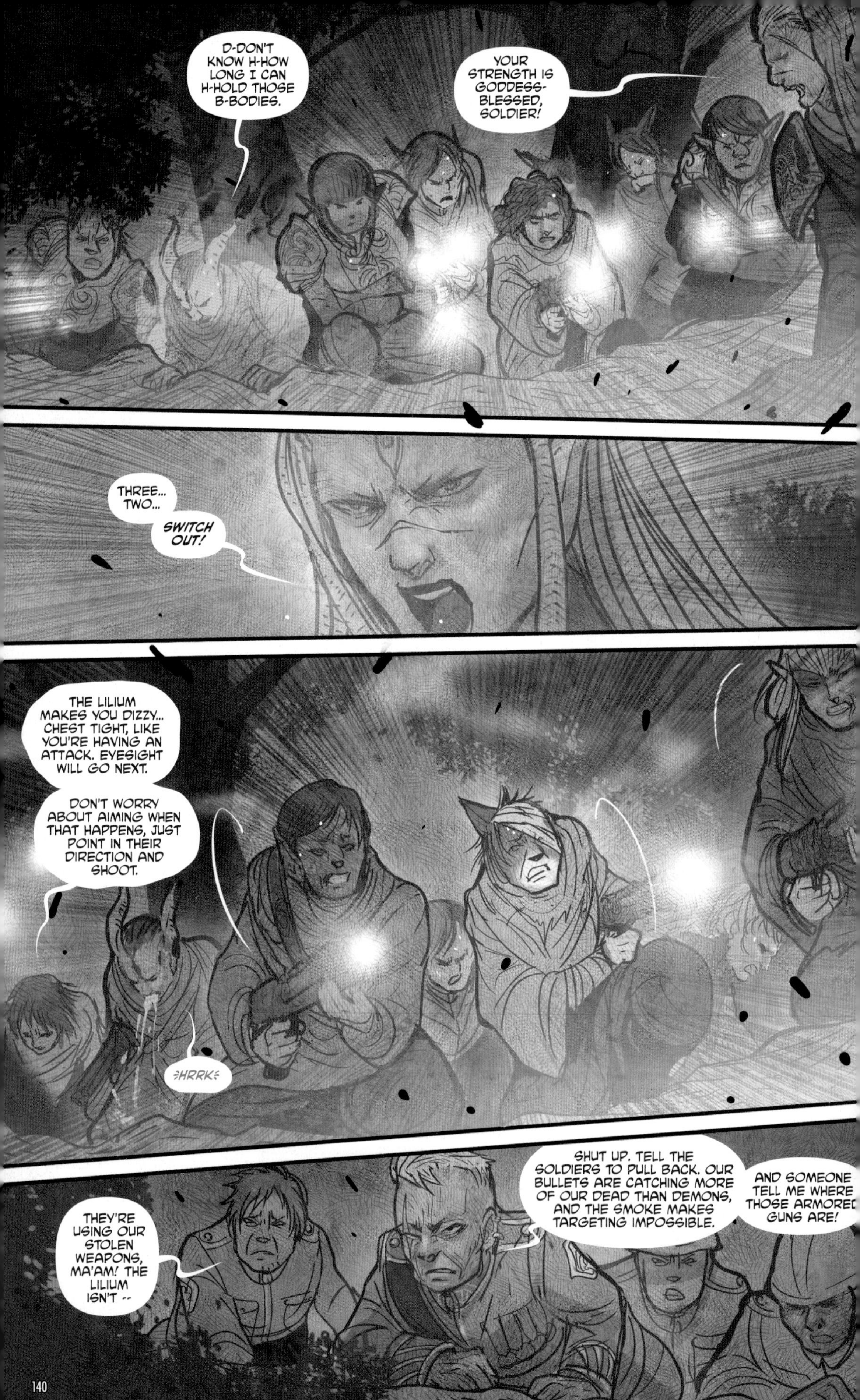
D-DON'T KNOW H-HOW LONG I CAN H-HOLD THOSE B-BODIES.
YOUR STRENGTH IS GODDESS-BLESSED, SOLDIER!
THREE... TWO...
SWITCH OUT!
THE LILIUM MAKES YOU DIZZY... CHEST TIGHT, LIKE YOU'RE HAVING AN ATTACK. EYESIGHT WILL GO NEXT.
DON'T WORRY ABOUT AIMING WHEN THAT HAPPENS, JUST POINT IN THEIR DIRECTION AND SHOOT.
HRRK
THEY'RE USING OUR STOLEN WEAPONS, MA'AM! THE LILIUM ISN'T --
SHUT UP. TELL THE SOLDIERS TO PULL BACK. OUR BULLETS ARE CATCHING MORE OF OUR DEAD THAN DEMONS, AND THE SMOKE MAKES TARGETING IMPOSSIBLE.
AND SOMEONE TELL ME WHERE THOSE ARMORED GUNS ARE!

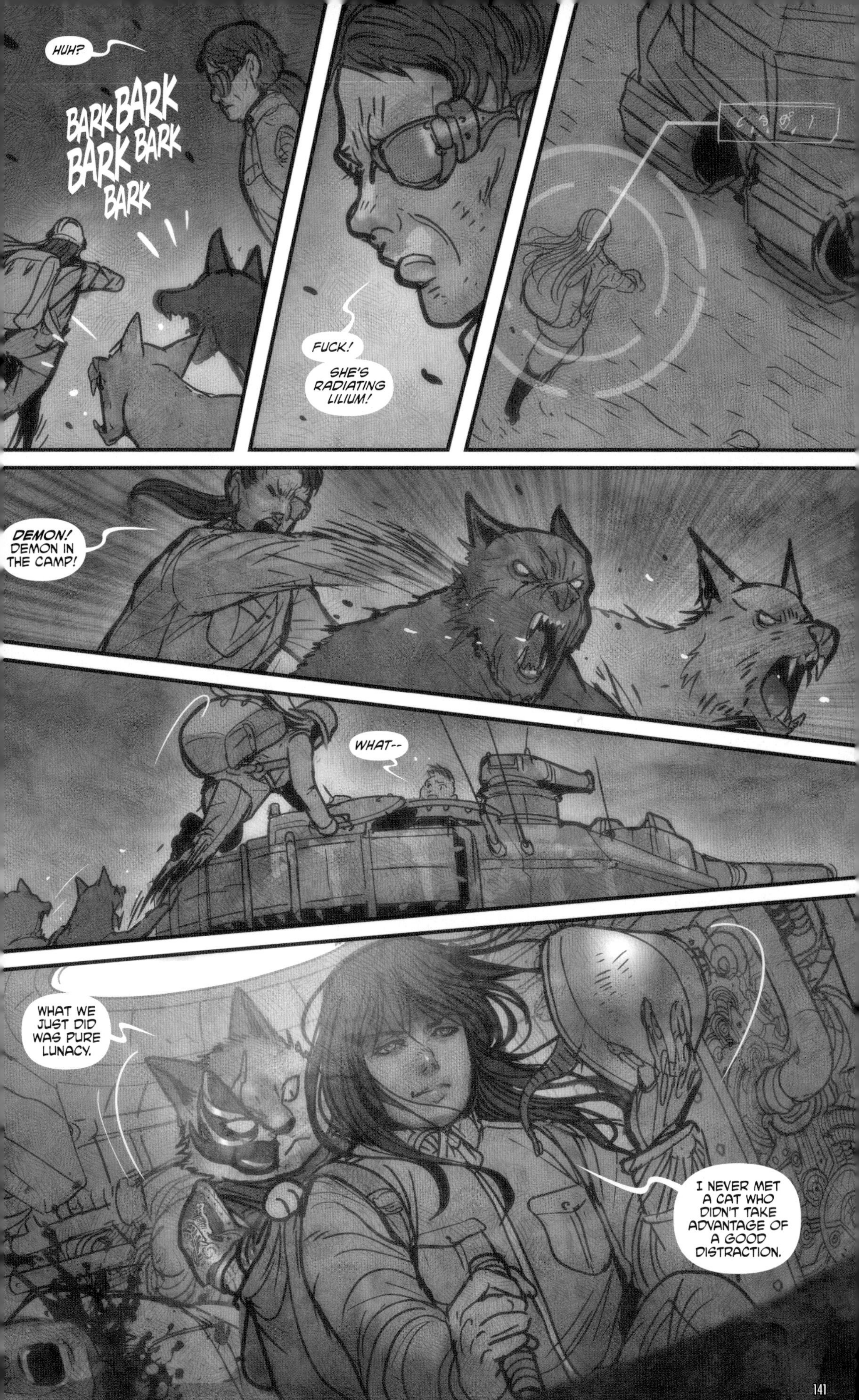
HUH?
BARK BARK
BARK BARK
BARK
FUCK!
SHE'S RADIATING LILIUM!
DEMON! DEMON IN THE CAMP!
WHAT--
WHAT WE JUST DID WAS PURE LUNACY.
I NEVER MET A CAT WHO DIDN'T TAKE ADVANTAGE OF A GOOD DISTRACTION.

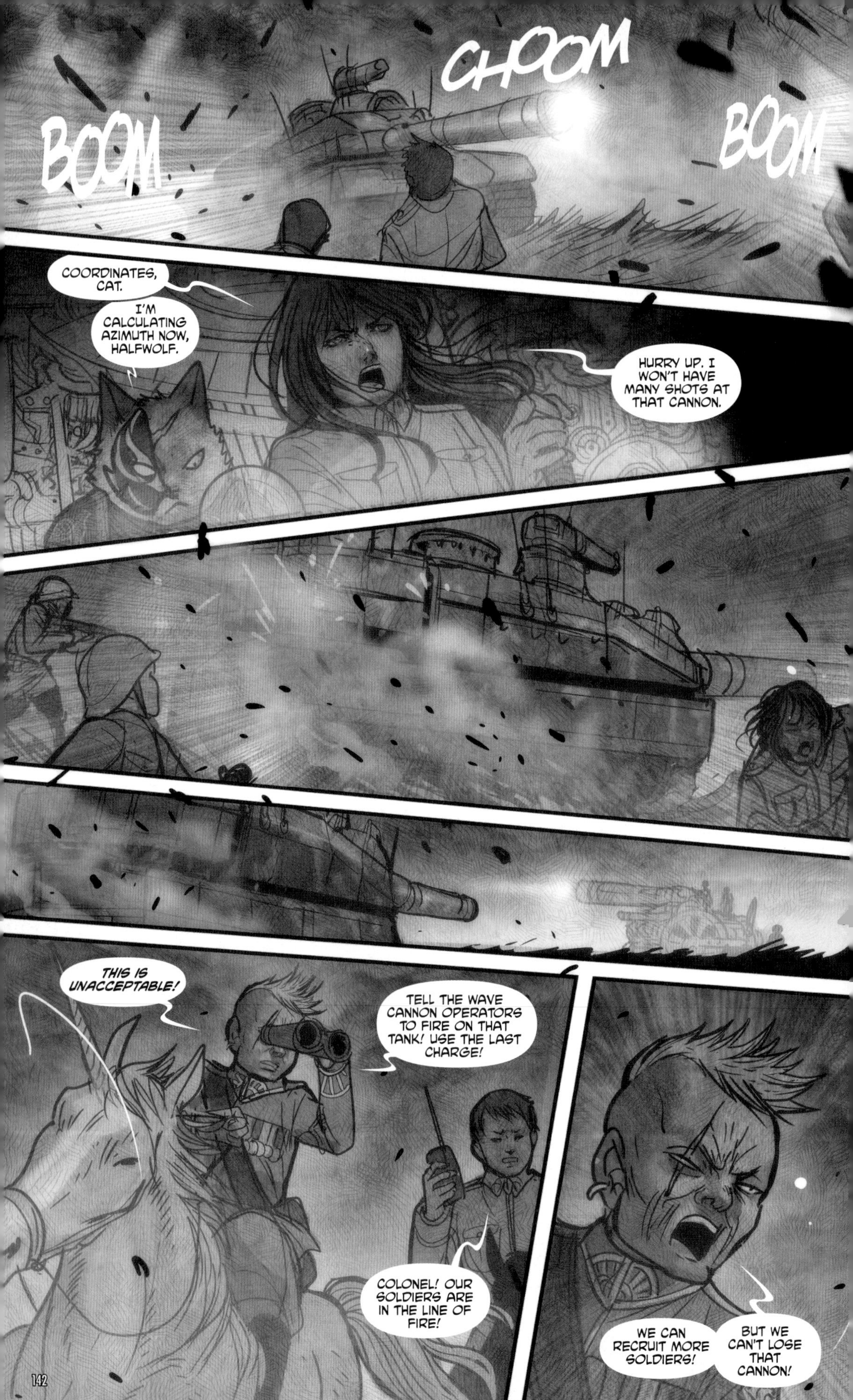
BOOM
CHOOM
BOOM
COORDINATES, CAT.
I'M CALCULATING AZIMUTH NOW, HALFWOLF.
HURRY UP. I WON'T HAVE MANY SHOTS AT THAT CANNON.
THIS IS UNACCEPTABLE!
TELL THE WAVE CANNON OPERATORS TO FIRE ON THAT TANK! USE THE LAST CHARGE!
COLONEL! OUR SOLDIERS ARE IN THE LINE OF FIRE!
WE CAN RECRUIT MORE SOLDIERS!
BUT WE CAN'T LOSE THAT CANNON!

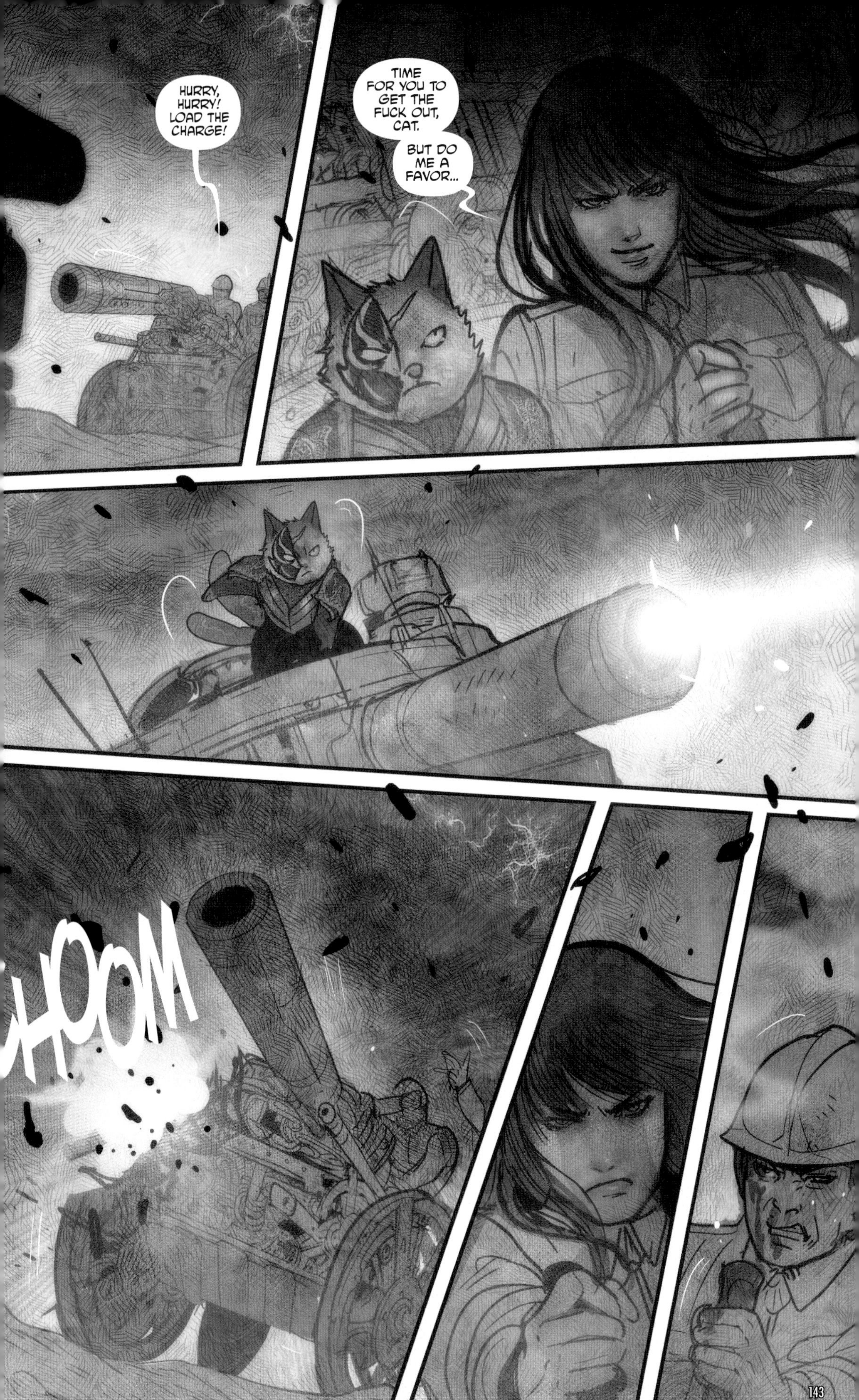
HURRY, HURRY! LOAD THE CHARGE!
TIME FOR YOU TO GET THE FUCK OUT, CAT.
BUT DO ME A FAVOR...
HOOM

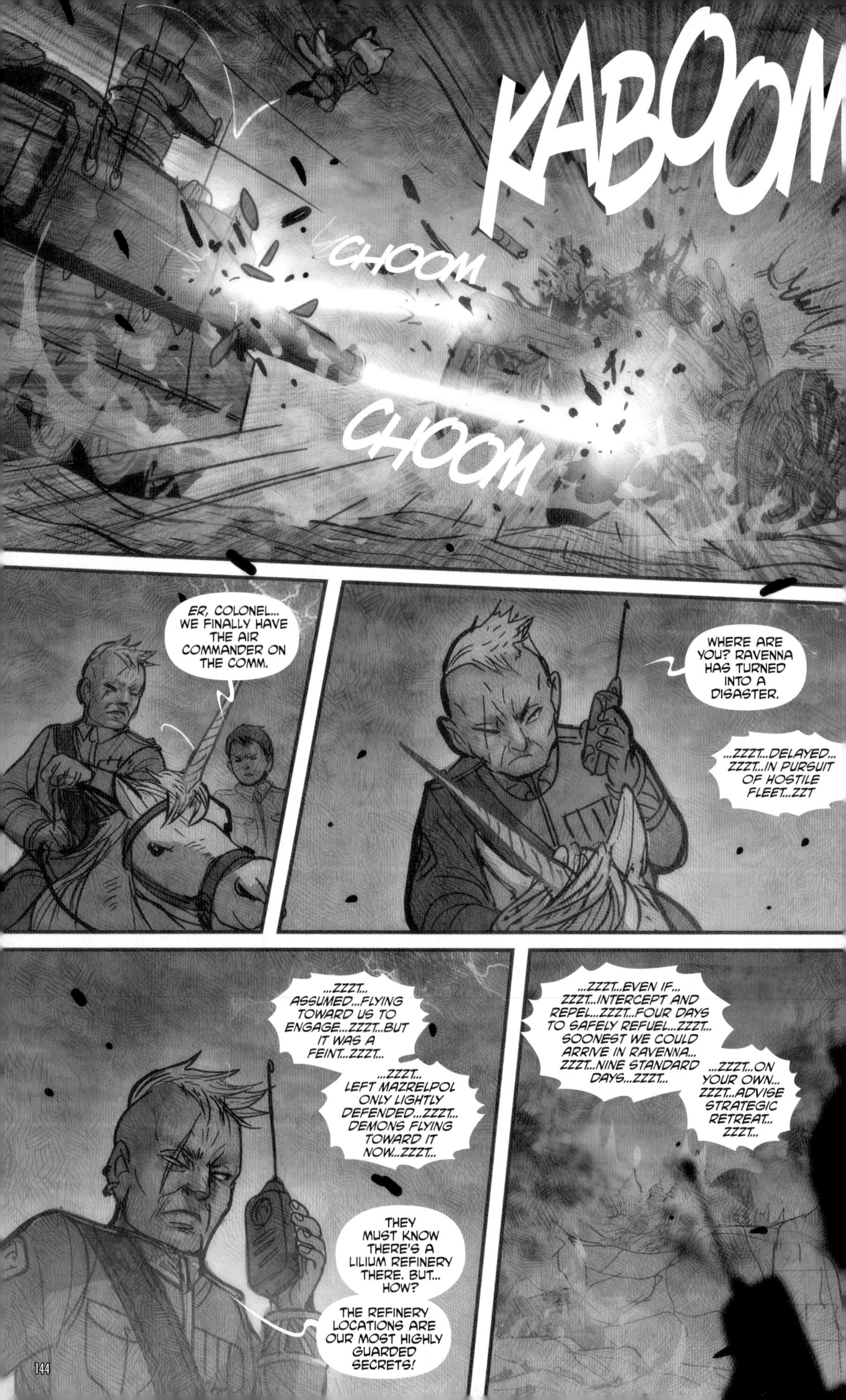
KABOOM
CHOOM
CHOOM
ER, COLONEL... WE FINALLY HAVE THE AIR COMMANDER ON THE COMM.
WHERE ARE YOU? RAVENNA HAS TURNED INTO A DISASTER.
...ZZZT...DELAYED... ZZZT...IN PURSUIT OF HOSTILE FLEET...ZZT
...ZZZT... ASSUMED...FLYING TOWARD US TO ENGAGE...ZZZT...BUT IT WAS A FEINT...ZZZT...
...ZZZT... LEFT MAZRELPOL ONLY LIGHTLY DEFENDED...ZZZT... DEMONS FLYING TOWARD IT NOW...ZZZT...
THEY MUST KNOW THERE'S A LILIUM REFINERY THERE. BUT... HOW?
THE REFINERY LOCATIONS ARE OUR MOST HIGHLY GUARDED SECRETS!
...ZZZT...EVEN IF... ZZZT...INTERCEPT AND REPEL...ZZZT...FOUR DAYS TO SAFELY REFUEL...ZZZT... SOONEST WE COULD ARRIVE IN RAVENNA... ZZZT...NINE STANDARD DAYS...ZZZT...
...ZZZT...ON YOUR OWN... ZZZT...ADVISE STRATEGIC RETREAT... ZZZT...

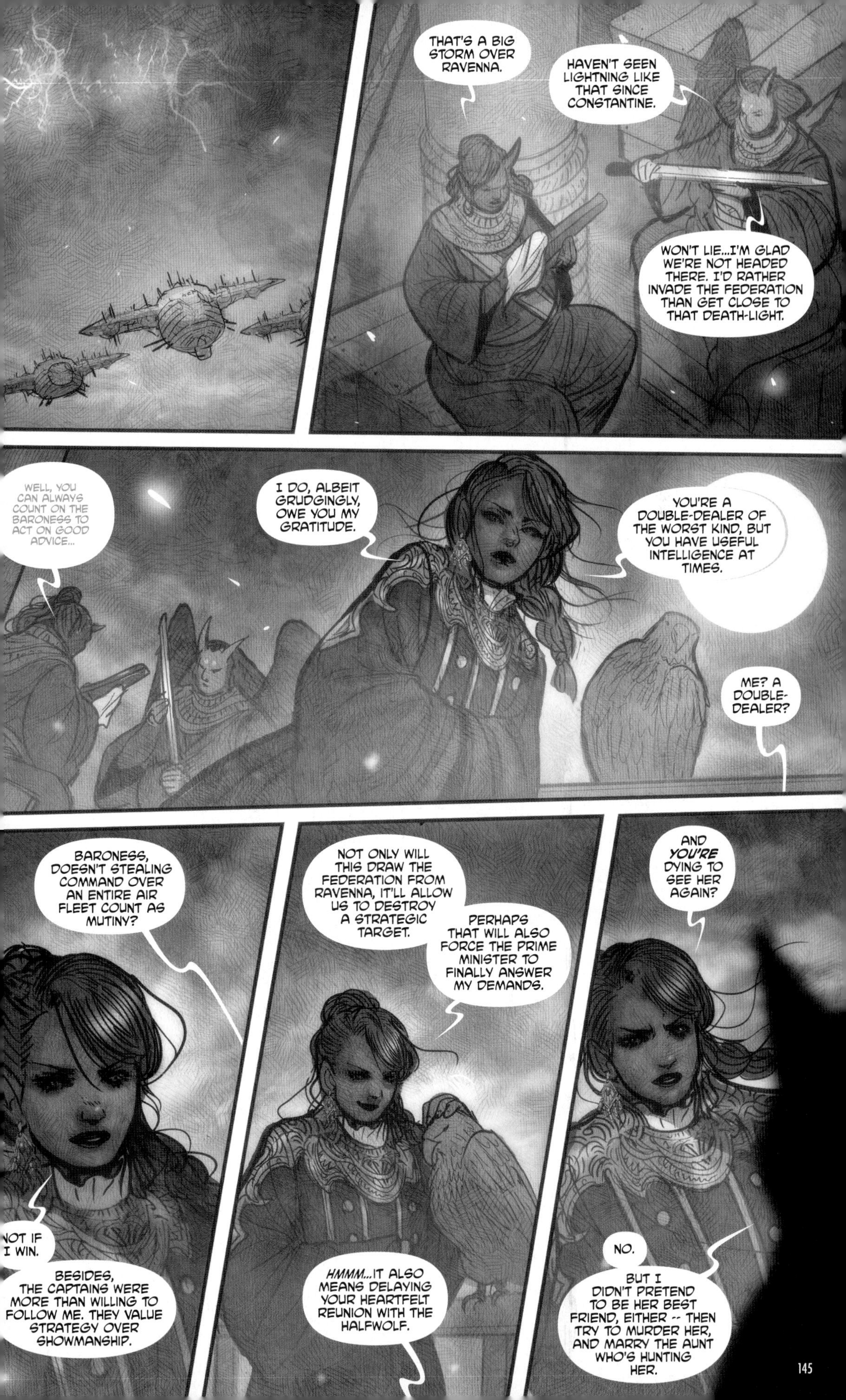
THAT'S A BIG STORM OVER RAVENNA.
HAVEN'T SEEN LIGHTNING LIKE THAT SINCE CONSTANTINE.
WON'T LIE...I'M GLAD WE'RE NOT HEADED THERE. I'D RATHER INVADE THE FEDERATION THAN GET CLOSE TO THAT DEATH-LIGHT.
WELL, YOU CAN ALWAYS COUNT ON THE BARONESS TO ACT ON GOOD ADVICE...
I DO, ALBEIT GRUDGINGLY, OWE YOU MY GRATITUDE.
YOU'RE A DOUBLE-DEALER OF THE WORST KIND, BUT YOU HAVE USEFUL INTELLIGENCE AT TIMES.
ME? A DOUBLE-DEALER?
BARONESS, DOESN'T STEALING COMMAND OVER AN ENTIRE AIR FLEET COUNT AS MUTINY?
NOT IF I WIN.
BESIDES, THE CAPTAINS WERE MORE THAN WILLING TO FOLLOW ME. THEY VALUE STRATEGY OVER SHOWMANSHIP.
NOT ONLY WILL THIS DRAW THE FEDERATION FROM RAVENNA, IT'LL ALLOW US TO DESTROY A STRATEGIC TARGET.
PERHAPS THAT WILL ALSO FORCE THE PRIME MINISTER TO FINALLY ANSWER MY DEMANDS.
HMMM...IT ALSO MEANS DELAYING YOUR HEARTFELT REUNION WITH THE HALFWOLF.
AND *YOU'RE* DYING TO SEE HER AGAIN?
NO.
BUT I DIDN'T PRETEND TO BE HER BEST FRIEND, EITHER -- THEN TRY TO MURDER HER, AND MARRY THE AUNT WHO'S HUNTING HER.

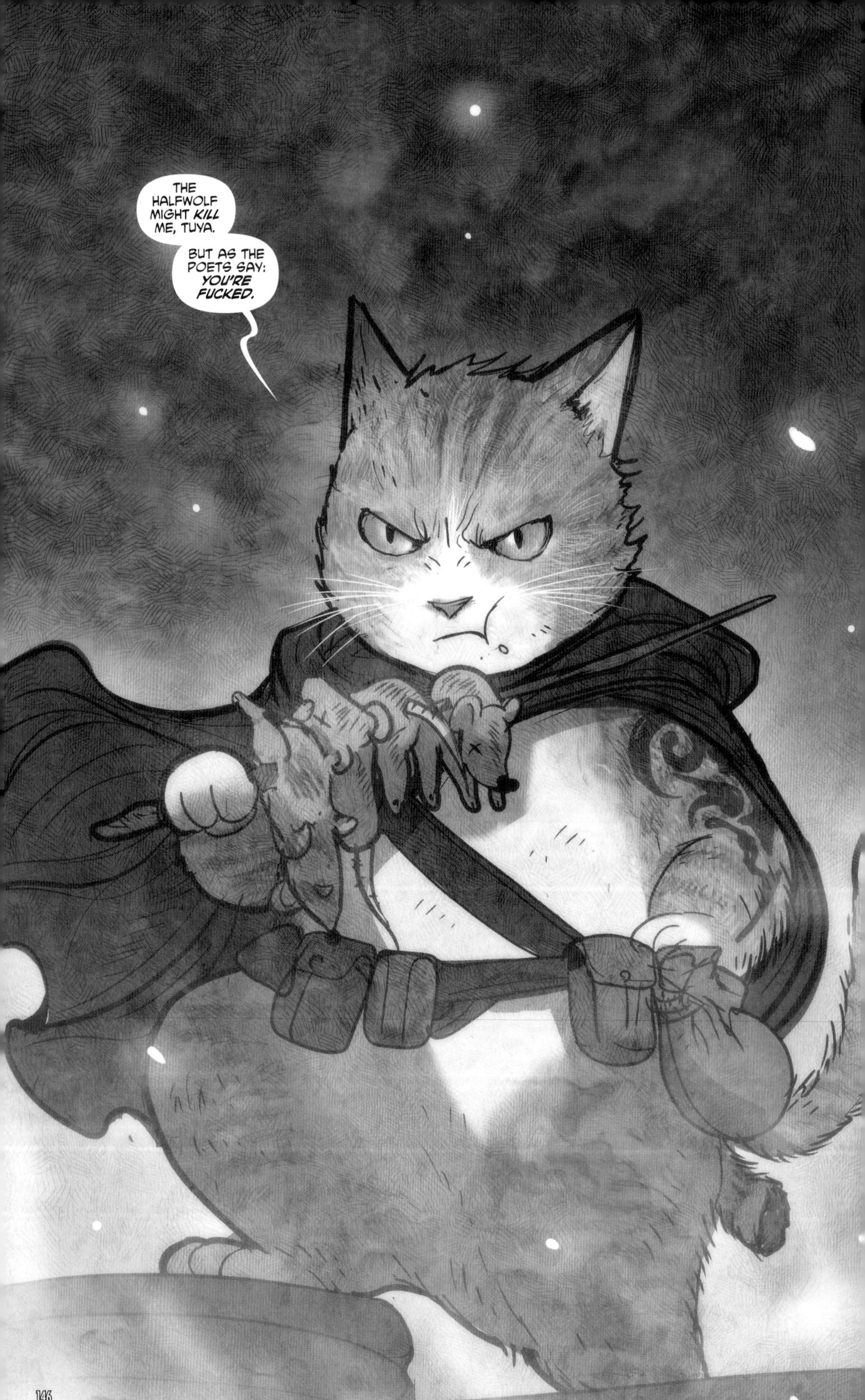
THE HALFWOLF MIGHT *KILL* ME, TUYA.
BUT AS THE POETS SAY: ***YOU'RE FUCKED.***

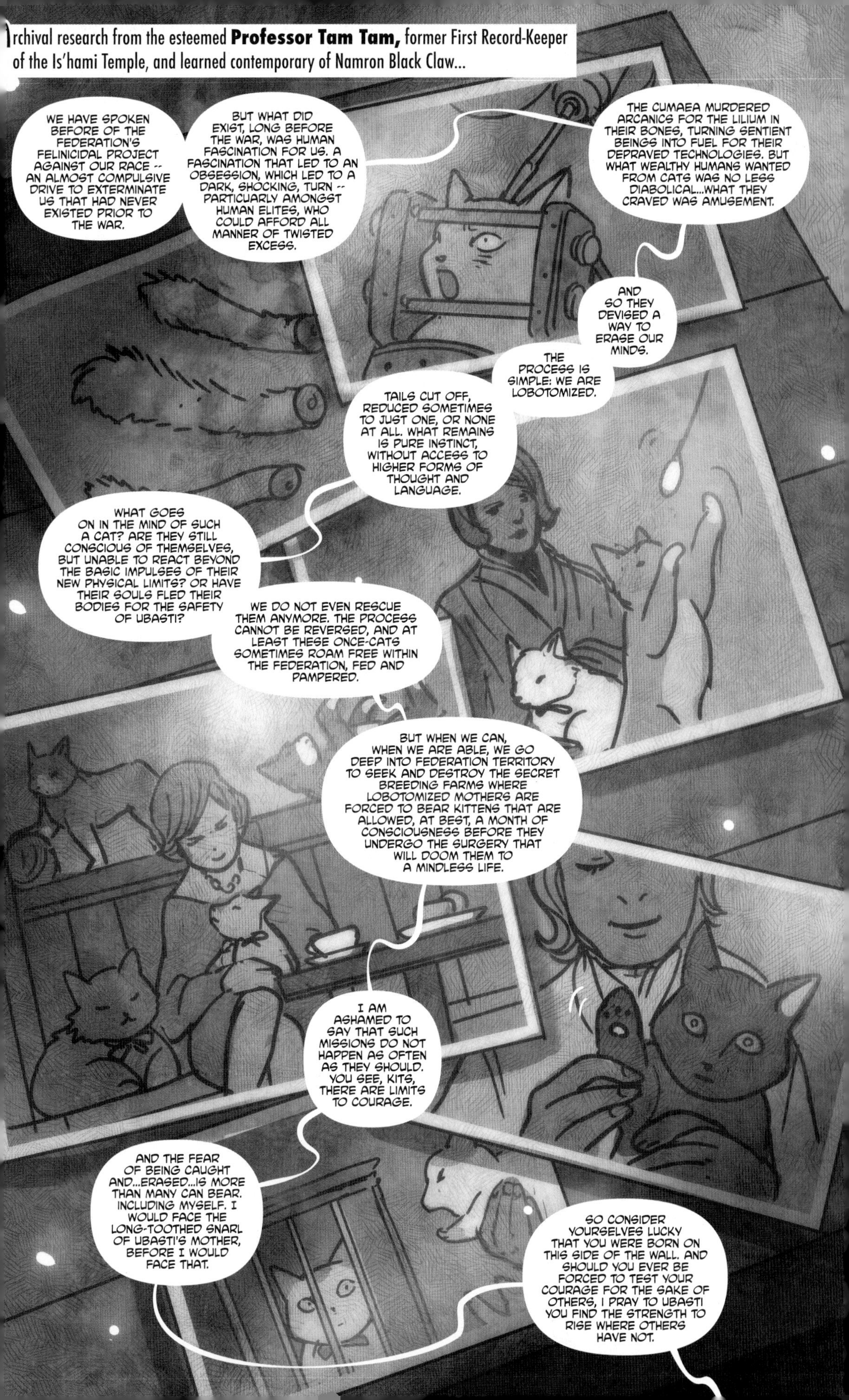
Archival research from the esteemed **Professor Tam Tam,** former First Record-Keeper of the Is'hami Temple, and learned contemporary of Namron Black Claw...
WE HAVE SPOKEN BEFORE OF THE FEDERATION'S FELINICIDAL PROJECT AGAINST OUR RACE -- AN ALMOST COMPULSIVE DRIVE TO EXTERMINATE US THAT HAD NEVER EXISTED PRIOR TO THE WAR.
BUT WHAT DID EXIST, LONG BEFORE THE WAR, WAS HUMAN FASCINATION FOR US. A FASCINATION THAT LED TO AN OBSESSION, WHICH LED TO A DARK, SHOCKING, TURN -- PARTICULARLY AMONGST HUMAN ELITES, WHO COULD AFFORD ALL MANNER OF TWISTED EXCESS.
THE CUMAEA MURDERED ARCANICS FOR THE LILIUM IN THEIR BONES, TURNING SENTIENT BEINGS INTO FUEL FOR THEIR DEPRAVED TECHNOLOGIES. BUT WHAT WEALTHY HUMANS WANTED FROM CATS WAS NO LESS DIABOLICAL...WHAT THEY CRAVED WAS AMUSEMENT.
AND SO THEY DEVISED A WAY TO ERASE OUR MINDS.
THE PROCESS IS SIMPLE: WE ARE LOBOTOMIZED.
TAILS CUT OFF, REDUCED SOMETIMES TO JUST ONE, OR NONE AT ALL. WHAT REMAINS IS PURE INSTINCT, WITHOUT ACCESS TO HIGHER FORMS OF THOUGHT AND LANGUAGE.
WHAT GOES ON IN THE MIND OF SUCH A CAT? ARE THEY STILL CONSCIOUS OF THEMSELVES, BUT UNABLE TO REACT BEYOND THE BASIC IMPULSES OF THEIR NEW PHYSICAL LIMITS? OR HAVE THEIR SOULS FLED THEIR BODIES FOR THE SAFETY OF UBASTI?
WE DO NOT EVEN RESCUE THEM ANYMORE. THE PROCESS CANNOT BE REVERSED, AND AT LEAST THESE ONCE-CATS SOMETIMES ROAM FREE WITHIN THE FEDERATION, FED AND PAMPERED.
BUT WHEN WE CAN, WHEN WE ARE ABLE, WE GO DEEP INTO FEDERATION TERRITORY TO SEEK AND DESTROY THE SECRET BREEDING FARMS WHERE LOBOTOMIZED MOTHERS ARE FORCED TO BEAR KITTENS THAT ARE ALLOWED, AT BEST, A MONTH OF CONSCIOUSNESS BEFORE THEY UNDERGO THE SURGERY THAT WILL DOOM THEM TO A MINDLESS LIFE.
I AM ASHAMED TO SAY THAT SUCH MISSIONS DO NOT HAPPEN AS OFTEN AS THEY SHOULD. YOU SEE, KITS, THERE ARE LIMITS TO COURAGE.
AND THE FEAR OF BEING CAUGHT AND...ERASED...IS MORE THAN MANY CAN BEAR. INCLUDING MYSELF. I WOULD FACE THE LONG-TOOTHED SNARL OF UBASTI'S MOTHER, BEFORE I WOULD FACE THAT.
SO CONSIDER YOURSELVES LUCKY THAT YOU WERE BORN ON THIS SIDE OF THE WALL. AND SHOULD YOU EVER BE FORCED TO TEST YOUR COURAGE FOR THE SAKE OF OTHERS, I PRAY TO UBASTI YOU FIND THE STRENGTH TO RISE WHERE OTHERS HAVE NOT.

CHAPTER THIRTY

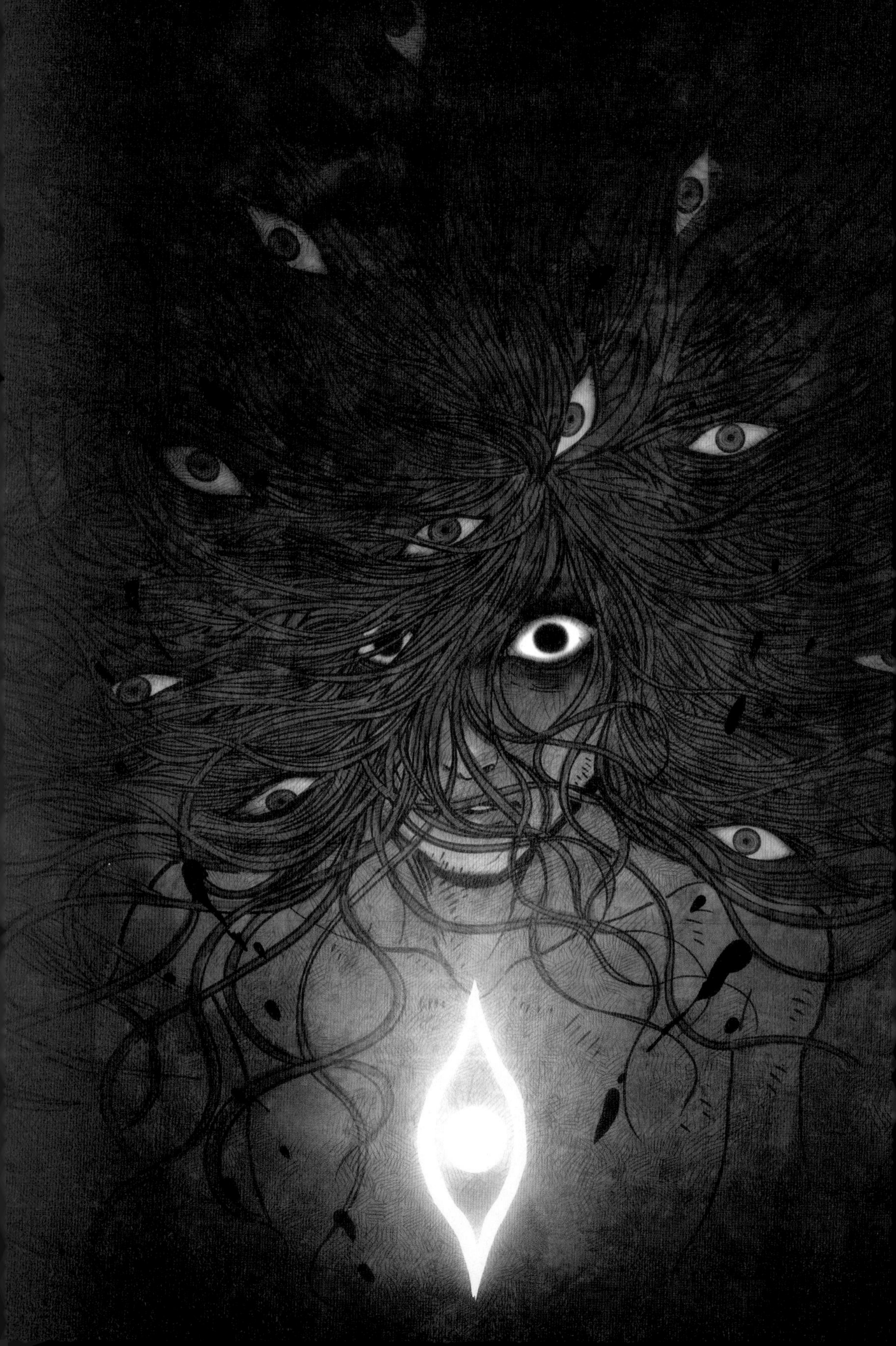

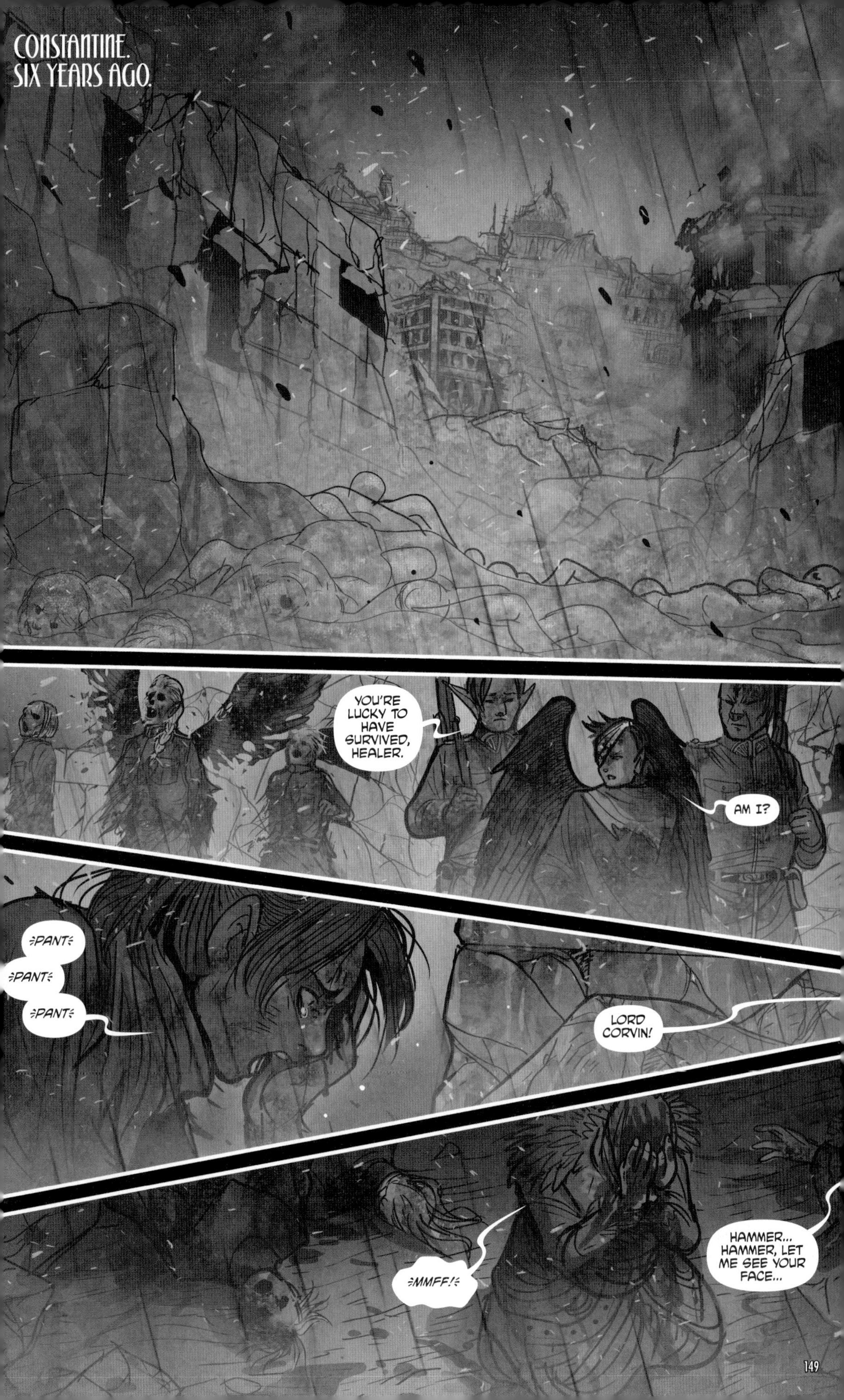
CONSTANTINE.
SIX YEARS AGO.
YOU'RE LUCKY TO HAVE SURVIVED, HEALER.
AM I?
PANT
PANT
PANT
LORD CORVIN!
MMFF!
HAMMER... HAMMER, LET ME SEE YOUR FACE...

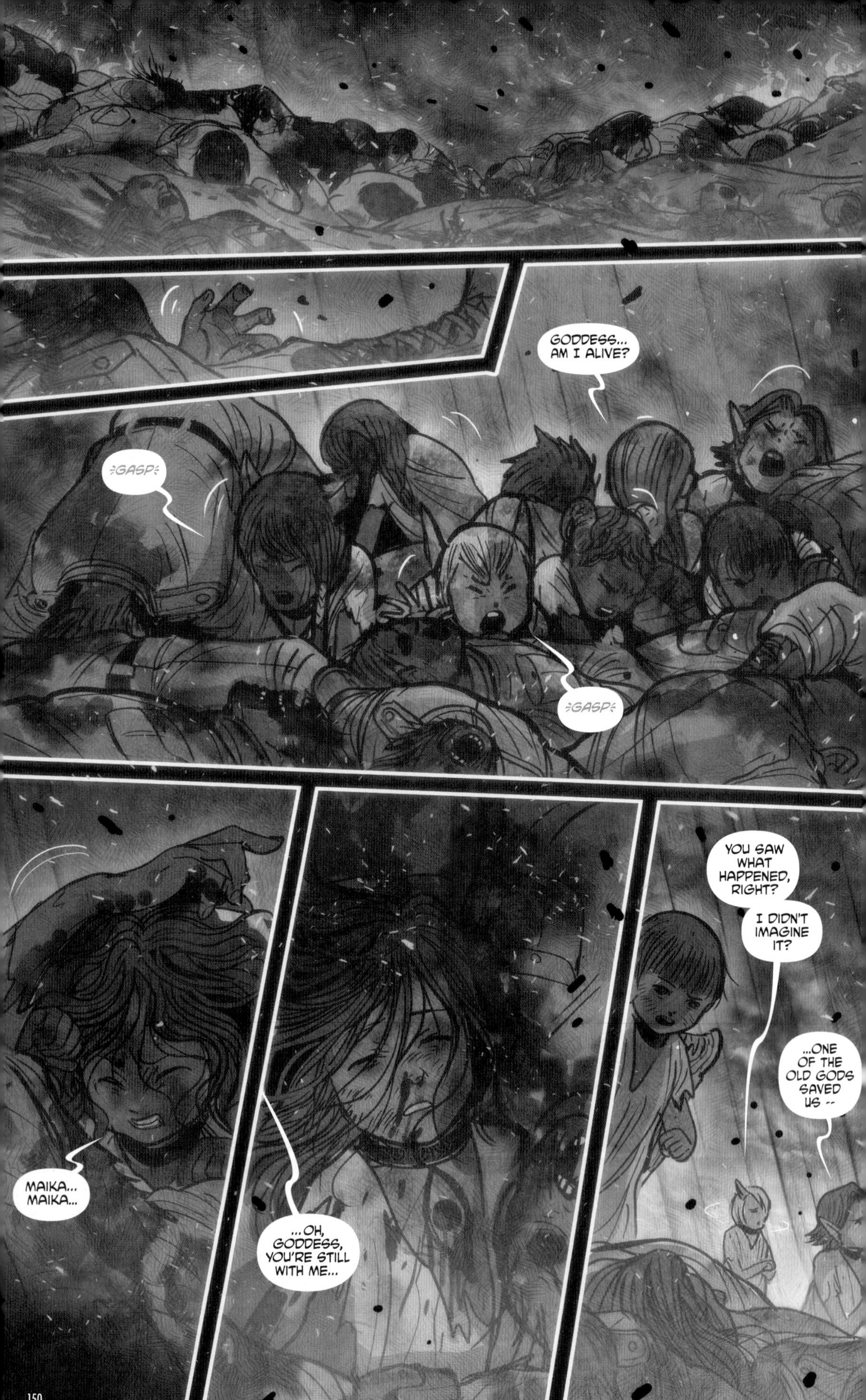
GODDESS... AM I ALIVE?
GASP
GASP
MAIKA... MAIKA...
...OH, GODDESS, YOU'RE STILL WITH ME...
YOU SAW WHAT HAPPENED, RIGHT?
I DIDN'T IMAGINE IT?
...ONE OF THE OLD GODS SAVED US --

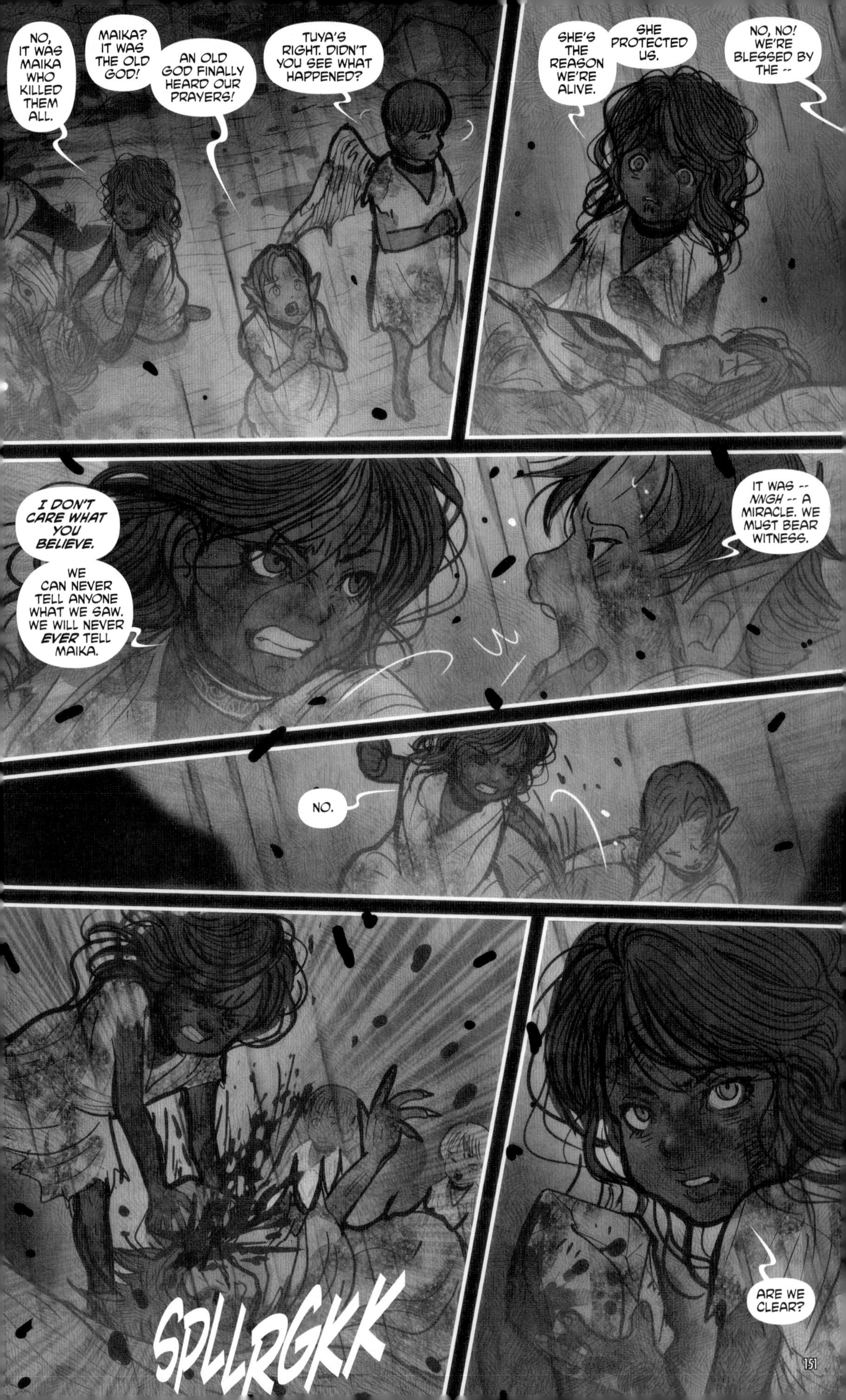
NO, IT WAS MAIKA WHO KILLED THEM ALL.
MAIKA? IT WAS THE OLD GOD!
AN OLD GOD FINALLY HEARD OUR PRAYERS!
TUYA'S RIGHT. DIDN'T YOU SEE WHAT HAPPENED?
SHE'S THE REASON WE'RE ALIVE.
SHE PROTECTED US.
NO, NO! WE'RE BLESSED BY THE --
I DON'T CARE WHAT YOU BELIEVE.
WE CAN NEVER TELL ANYONE WHAT WE SAW. WE WILL NEVER EVER TELL MAIKA.
IT WAS -- NNGH -- A MIRACLE. WE MUST BEAR WITNESS.
NO.
SPLLRGKK
ARE WE CLEAR?

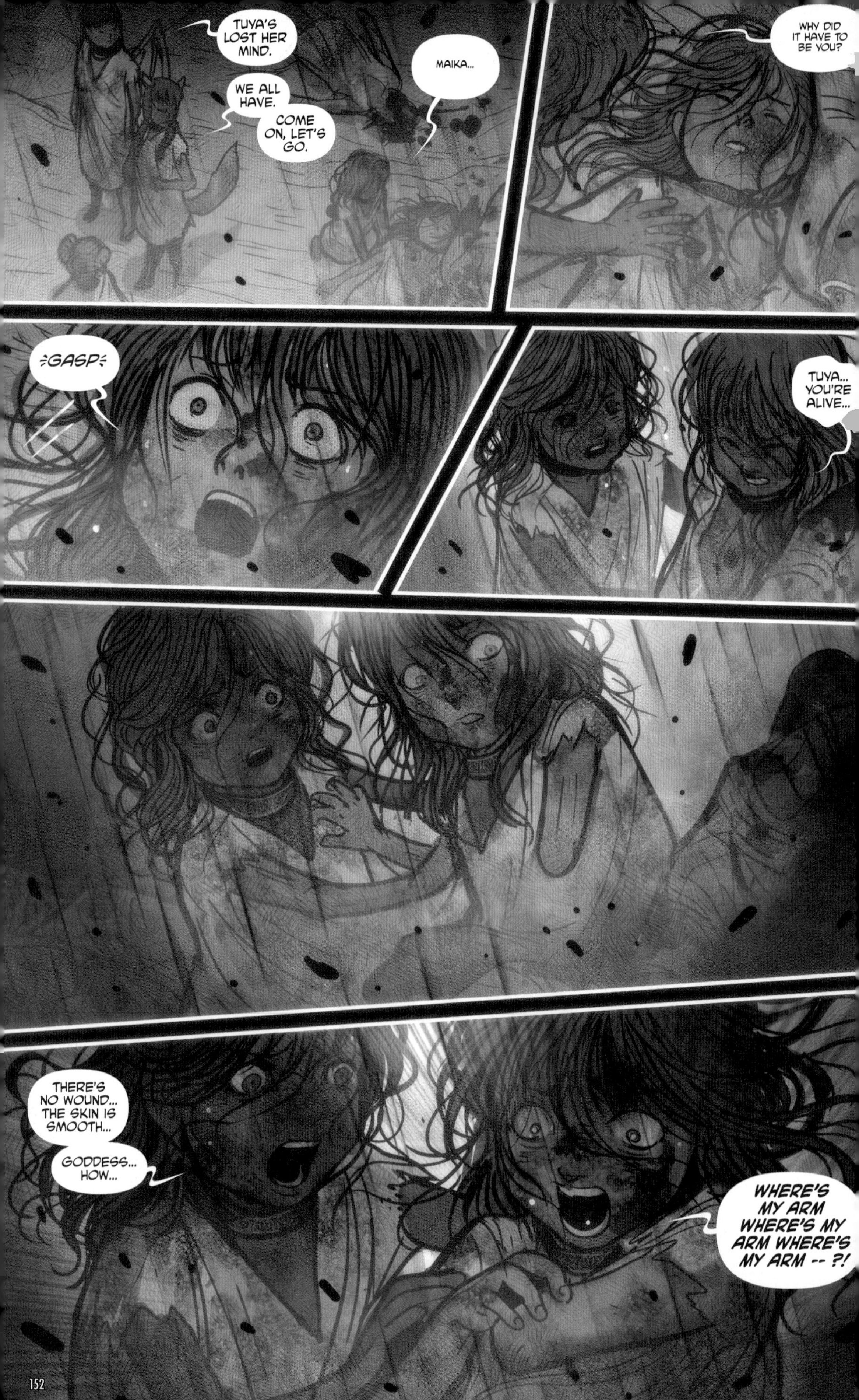
TUYA'S LOST HER MIND.
WE ALL HAVE.
COME ON, LET'S GO.
MAIKA...
WHY DID IT HAVE TO BE YOU?
GASP
TUYA... YOU'RE ALIVE...
THERE'S NO WOUND... THE SKIN IS SMOOTH...
GODDESS... HOW...
WHERE'S MY ARM WHERE'S MY ARM WHERE'S MY ARM -- ?!

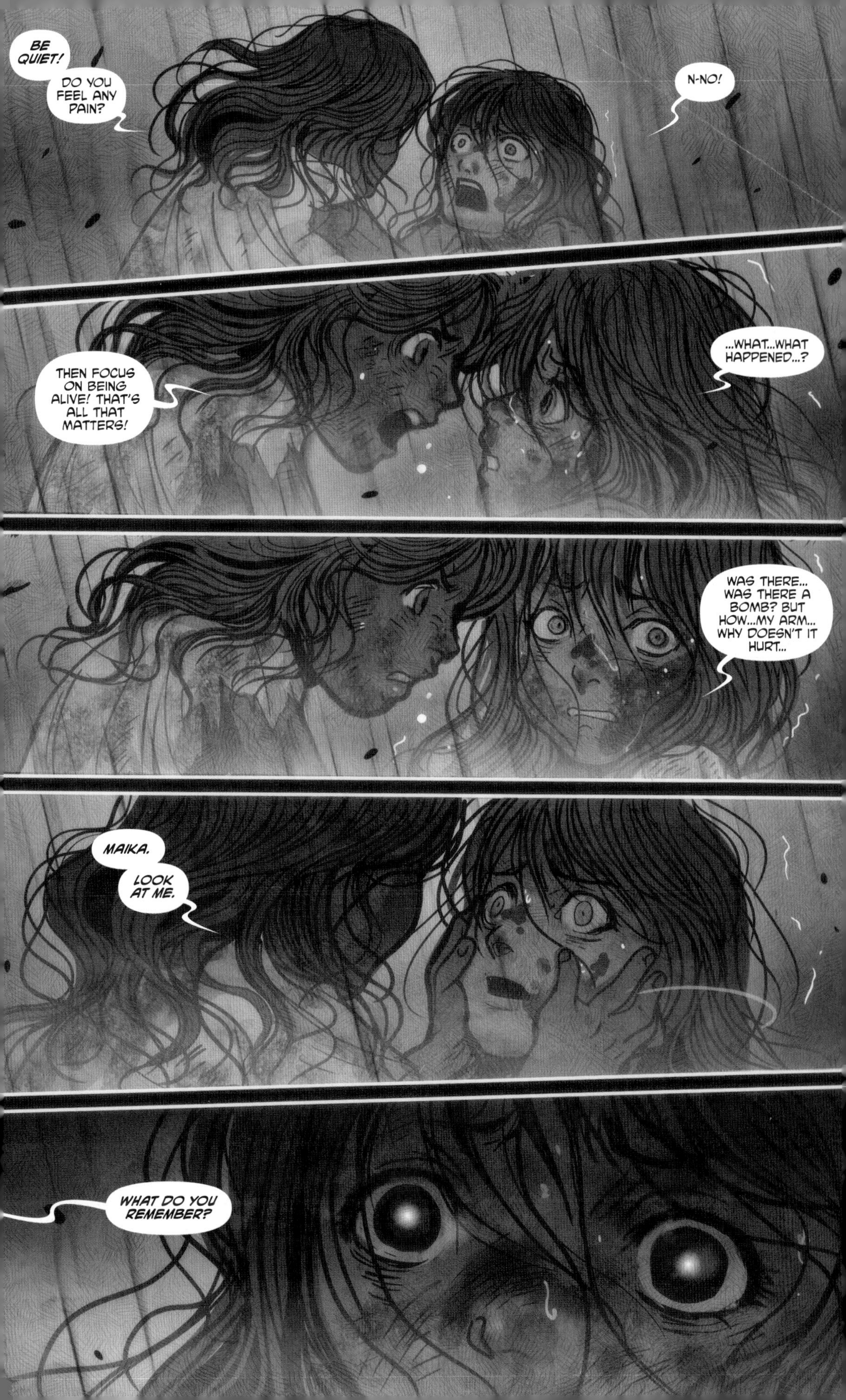
BE QUIET!
DO YOU FEEL ANY PAIN?
N-NO!
THEN FOCUS ON BEING ALIVE! THAT'S ALL THAT MATTERS!
...WHAT...WHAT HAPPENED...?
WAS THERE... WAS THERE A BOMB? BUT HOW...MY ARM... WHY DOESN'T IT HURT...
MAIKA.
LOOK AT ME.
WHAT DO YOU REMEMBER?

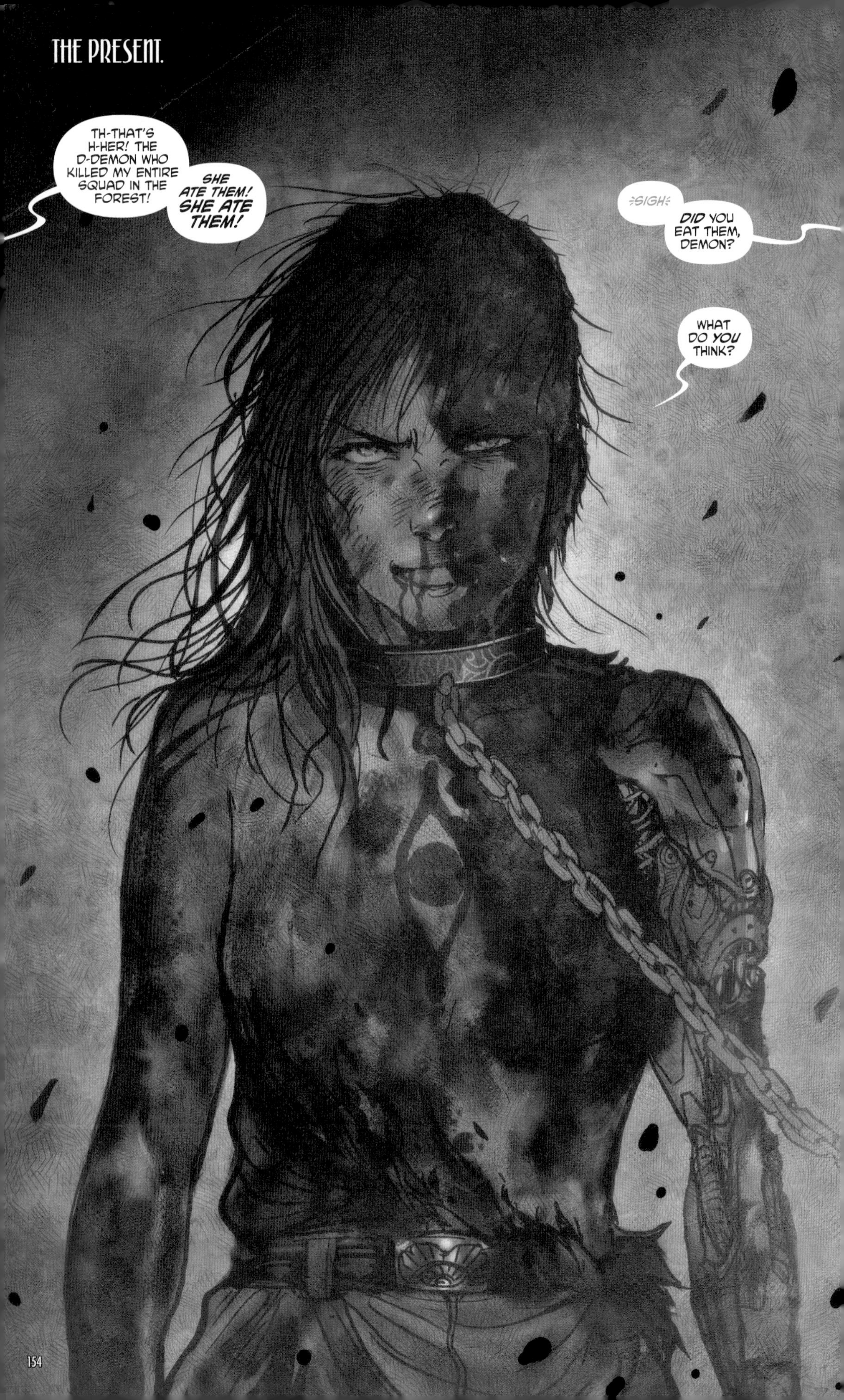
THE PRESENT.
TH-THAT'S H-HER! THE D-DEMON WHO KILLED MY ENTIRE SQUAD IN THE FOREST!
SHE ATE THEM! SHE ATE THEM!
SIGH
DID YOU EAT THEM, DEMON?
WHAT DO YOU THINK?

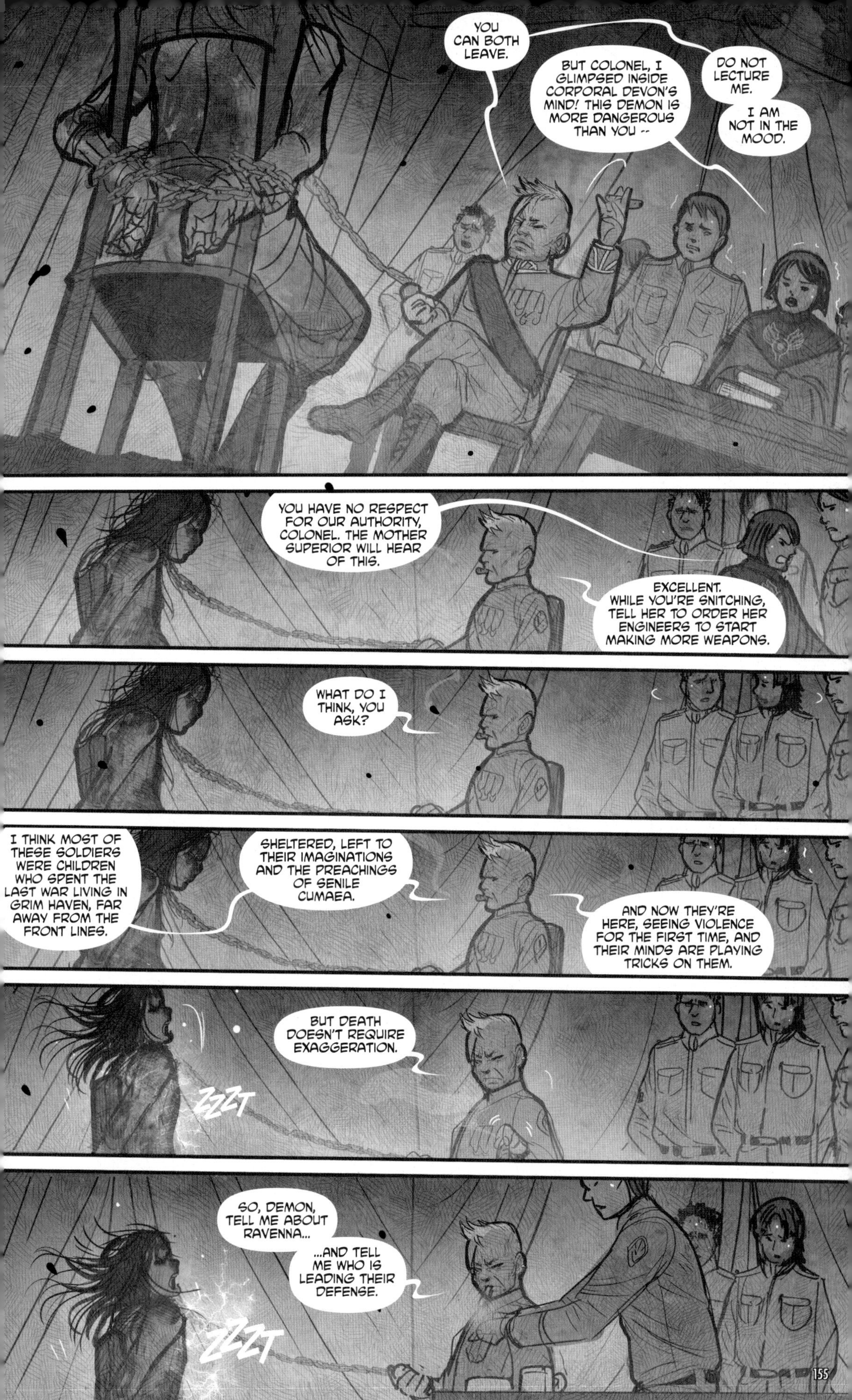
YOU CAN BOTH LEAVE.
BUT COLONEL, I GLIMPSED INSIDE CORPORAL DEVON'S MIND! THIS DEMON IS MORE DANGEROUS THAN YOU --
DO NOT LECTURE ME.
I AM NOT IN THE MOOD.
YOU HAVE NO RESPECT FOR OUR AUTHORITY, COLONEL. THE MOTHER SUPERIOR WILL HEAR OF THIS.
EXCELLENT. WHILE YOU'RE SNITCHING, TELL HER TO ORDER HER ENGINEERS TO START MAKING MORE WEAPONS.
WHAT DO I THINK, YOU ASK?
I THINK MOST OF THESE SOLDIERS WERE CHILDREN WHO SPENT THE LAST WAR LIVING IN GRIM HAVEN, FAR AWAY FROM THE FRONT LINES.
SHELTERED, LEFT TO THEIR IMAGINATIONS AND THE PREACHINGS OF SENILE CUMAEA.
AND NOW THEY'RE HERE, SEEING VIOLENCE FOR THE FIRST TIME, AND THEIR MINDS ARE PLAYING TRICKS ON THEM.
BUT DEATH DOESN'T REQUIRE EXAGGERATION.
ZZZT
SO, DEMON, TELL ME ABOUT RAVENNA...
...AND TELL ME WHO IS LEADING THEIR DEFENSE.
ZZZT

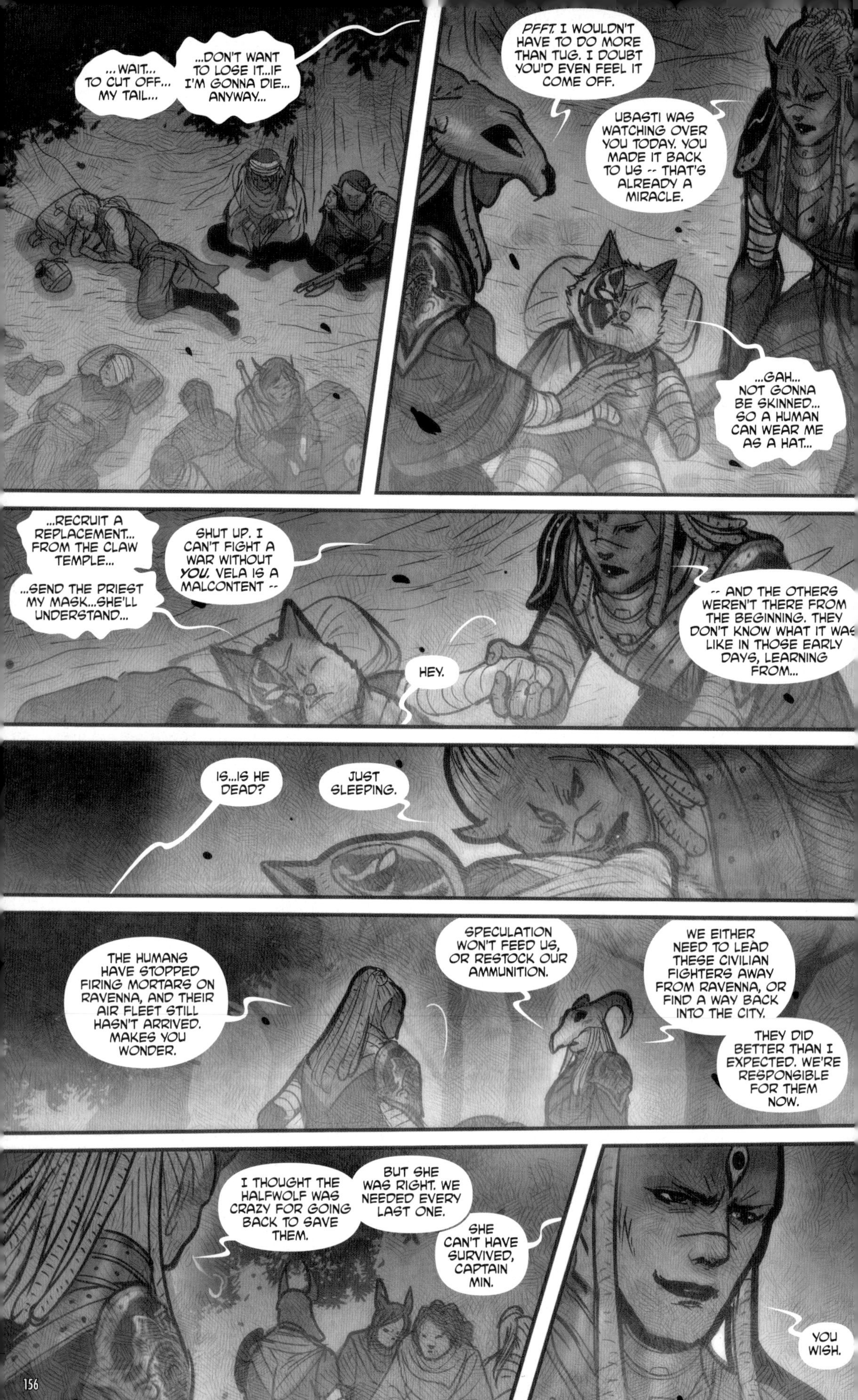
...WAIT... TO CUT OFF... MY TAIL...
...DON'T WANT TO LOSE IT...IF I'M GONNA DIE... ANYWAY...
PFFT. I WOULDN'T HAVE TO DO MORE THAN TUG. I DOUBT YOU'D EVEN FEEL IT COME OFF.
UBASTI WAS WATCHING OVER YOU TODAY. YOU MADE IT BACK TO US -- THAT'S ALREADY A MIRACLE.
...GAH... NOT GONNA BE SKINNED... SO A HUMAN CAN WEAR ME AS A HAT...
...RECRUIT A REPLACEMENT... FROM THE CLAW TEMPLE...
...SEND THE PRIEST MY MASK...SHE'LL UNDERSTAND...
SHUT UP. I CAN'T FIGHT A WAR WITHOUT YOU. VELA IS A MALCONTENT --
-- AND THE OTHERS WEREN'T THERE FROM THE BEGINNING. THEY DON'T KNOW WHAT IT WAS LIKE IN THOSE EARLY DAYS, LEARNING FROM...
HEY.
IS...IS HE DEAD?
JUST SLEEPING.
THE HUMANS HAVE STOPPED FIRING MORTARS ON RAVENNA, AND THEIR AIR FLEET STILL HASN'T ARRIVED. MAKES YOU WONDER.
SPECULATION WON'T FEED US, OR RESTOCK OUR AMMUNITION.
WE EITHER NEED TO LEAD THESE CIVILIAN FIGHTERS AWAY FROM RAVENNA, OR FIND A WAY BACK INTO THE CITY.
THEY DID BETTER THAN I EXPECTED. WE'RE RESPONSIBLE FOR THEM NOW.
I THOUGHT THE HALFWOLF WAS CRAZY FOR GOING BACK TO SAVE THEM.
BUT SHE WAS RIGHT. WE NEEDED EVERY LAST ONE.
SHE CAN'T HAVE SURVIVED, CAPTAIN MIN.
YOU WISH.

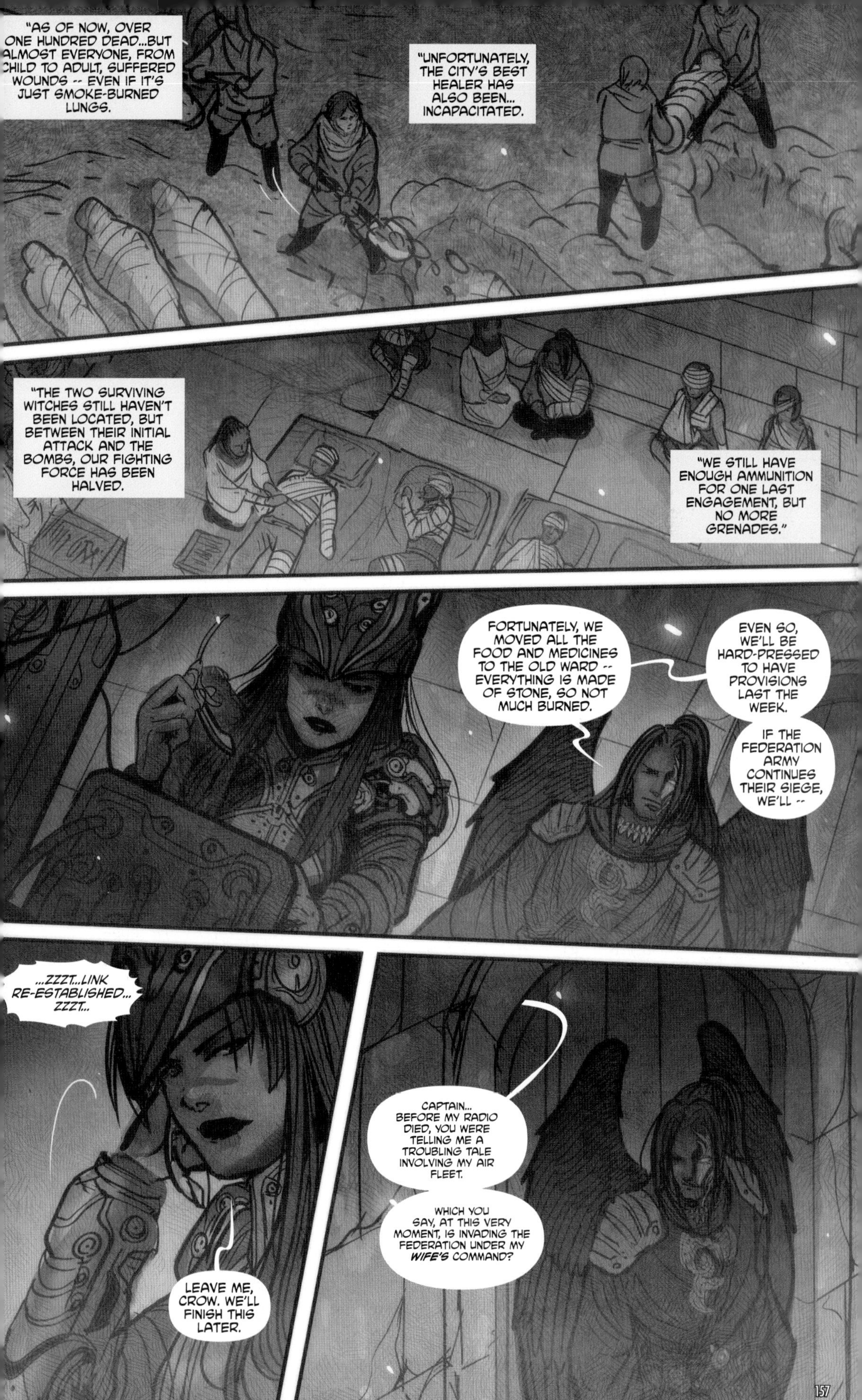
"AS OF NOW, OVER ONE HUNDRED DEAD...BUT ALMOST EVERYONE, FROM CHILD TO ADULT, SUFFERED WOUNDS -- EVEN IF IT'S JUST SMOKE-BURNED LUNGS.
"UNFORTUNATELY, THE CITY'S BEST HEALER HAS ALSO BEEN... INCAPACITATED.
"THE TWO SURVIVING WITCHES STILL HAVEN'T BEEN LOCATED, BUT BETWEEN THEIR INITIAL ATTACK AND THE BOMBS, OUR FIGHTING FORCE HAS BEEN HALVED.
"WE STILL HAVE ENOUGH AMMUNITION FOR ONE LAST ENGAGEMENT, BUT NO MORE GRENADES."
FORTUNATELY, WE MOVED ALL THE FOOD AND MEDICINES TO THE OLD WARD -- EVERYTHING IS MADE OF STONE, SO NOT MUCH BURNED.
EVEN SO, WE'LL BE HARD-PRESSED TO HAVE PROVISIONS LAST THE WEEK.
IF THE FEDERATION ARMY CONTINUES THEIR SIEGE, WE'LL --
...ZZZT...LINK RE-ESTABLISHED... ZZZT...
CAPTAIN... BEFORE MY RADIO DIED, YOU WERE TELLING ME A TROUBLING TALE INVOLVING MY AIR FLEET.
WHICH YOU SAY, AT THIS VERY MOMENT, IS INVADING THE FEDERATION UNDER MY *WIFE'S* COMMAND?
LEAVE ME, CROW. WE'LL FINISH THIS LATER.

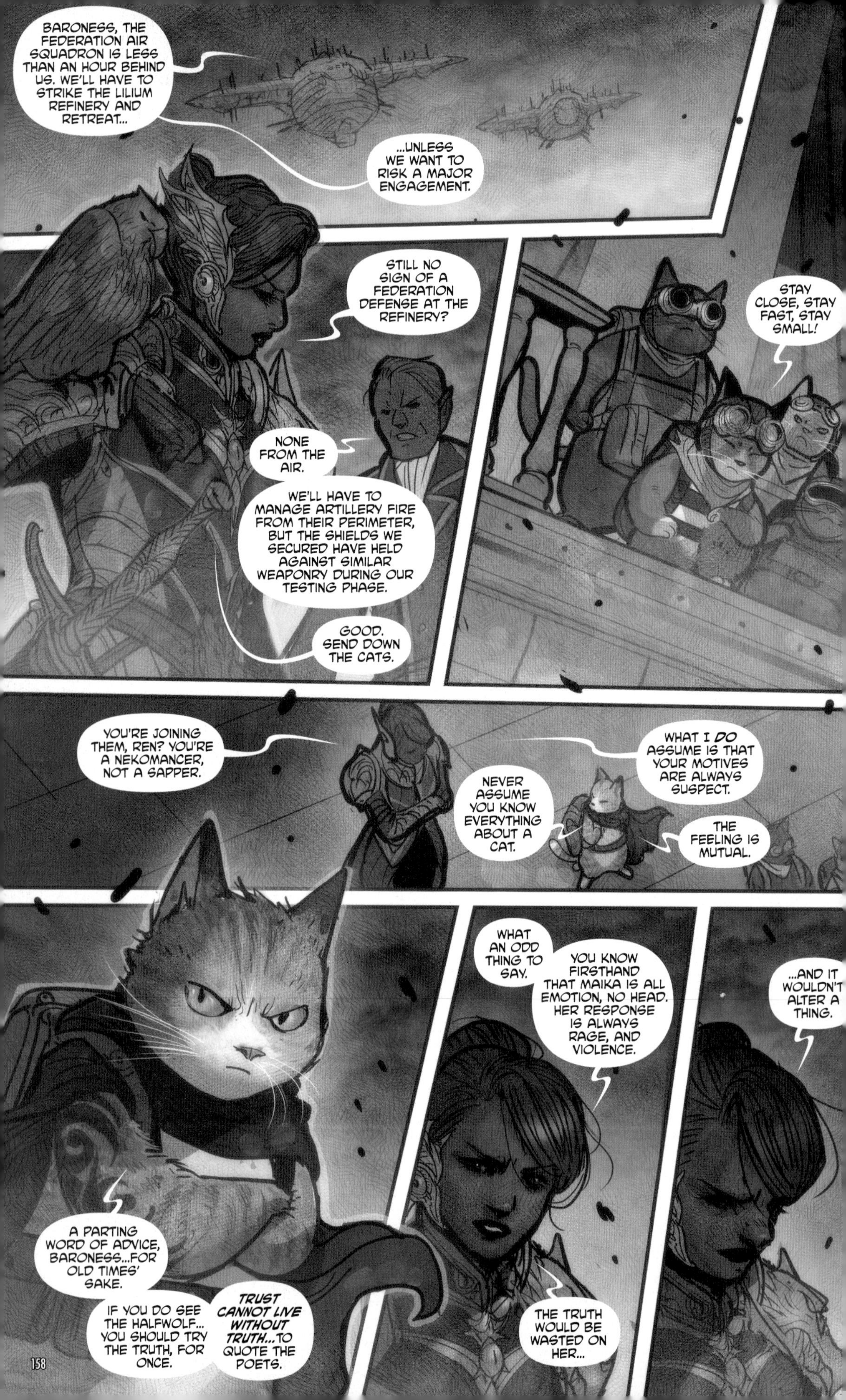

BARONESS, THE FEDERATION AIR SQUADRON IS LESS THAN AN HOUR BEHIND US. WE'LL HAVE TO STRIKE THE LILIUM REFINERY AND RETREAT...
...UNLESS WE WANT TO RISK A MAJOR ENGAGEMENT.
STILL NO SIGN OF A FEDERATION DEFENSE AT THE REFINERY?
NONE FROM THE AIR.
WE'LL HAVE TO MANAGE ARTILLERY FIRE FROM THEIR PERIMETER, BUT THE SHIELDS WE SECURED HAVE HELD AGAINST SIMILAR WEAPONRY DURING OUR TESTING PHASE.
GOOD. SEND DOWN THE CATS.
STAY CLOSE, STAY FAST, STAY SMALL!
YOU'RE JOINING THEM, REN? YOU'RE A NEKOMANCER, NOT A SAPPER.
NEVER ASSUME YOU KNOW EVERYTHING ABOUT A CAT.
WHAT I *DO* ASSUME IS THAT YOUR MOTIVES ARE ALWAYS SUSPECT.
THE FEELING IS MUTUAL.
A PARTING WORD OF ADVICE, BARONESS...FOR OLD TIMES' SAKE.
IF YOU DO SEE THE HALFWOLF... YOU SHOULD TRY THE TRUTH, FOR ONCE.
TRUST CANNOT LIVE WITHOUT TRUTH... TO QUOTE THE POETS.
WHAT AN ODD THING TO SAY.
YOU KNOW FIRSTHAND THAT MAIKA IS ALL EMOTION, NO HEAD. HER RESPONSE IS ALWAYS RAGE, AND VIOLENCE.
THE TRUTH WOULD BE WASTED ON HER...
...AND IT WOULDN'T ALTER A THING.

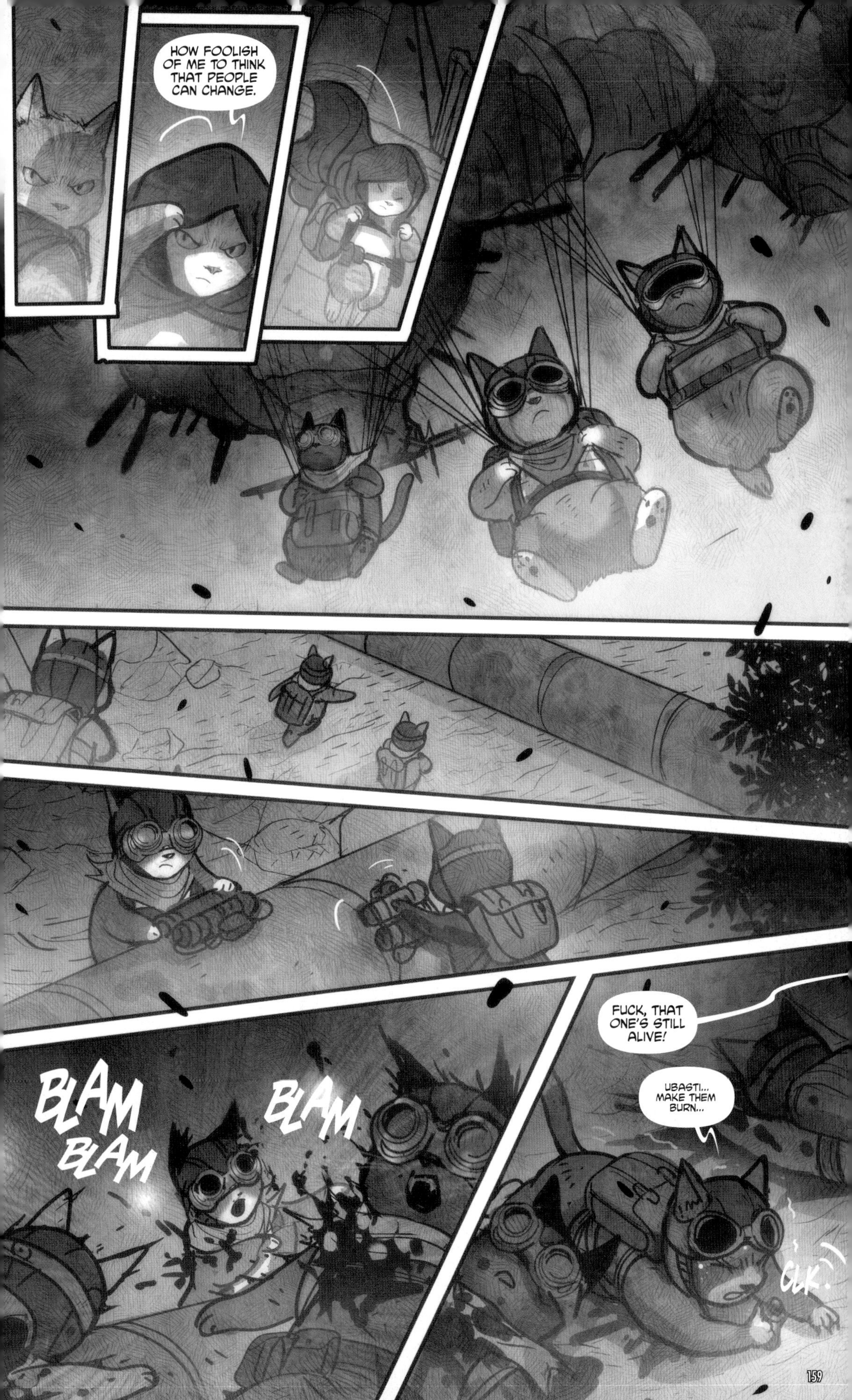

HOW FOOLISH OF ME TO THINK THAT PEOPLE CAN CHANGE.
BLAM
BLAM
BLAM
FUCK, THAT ONE'S STILL ALIVE!
UBASTI... MAKE THEM BURN...
GLK

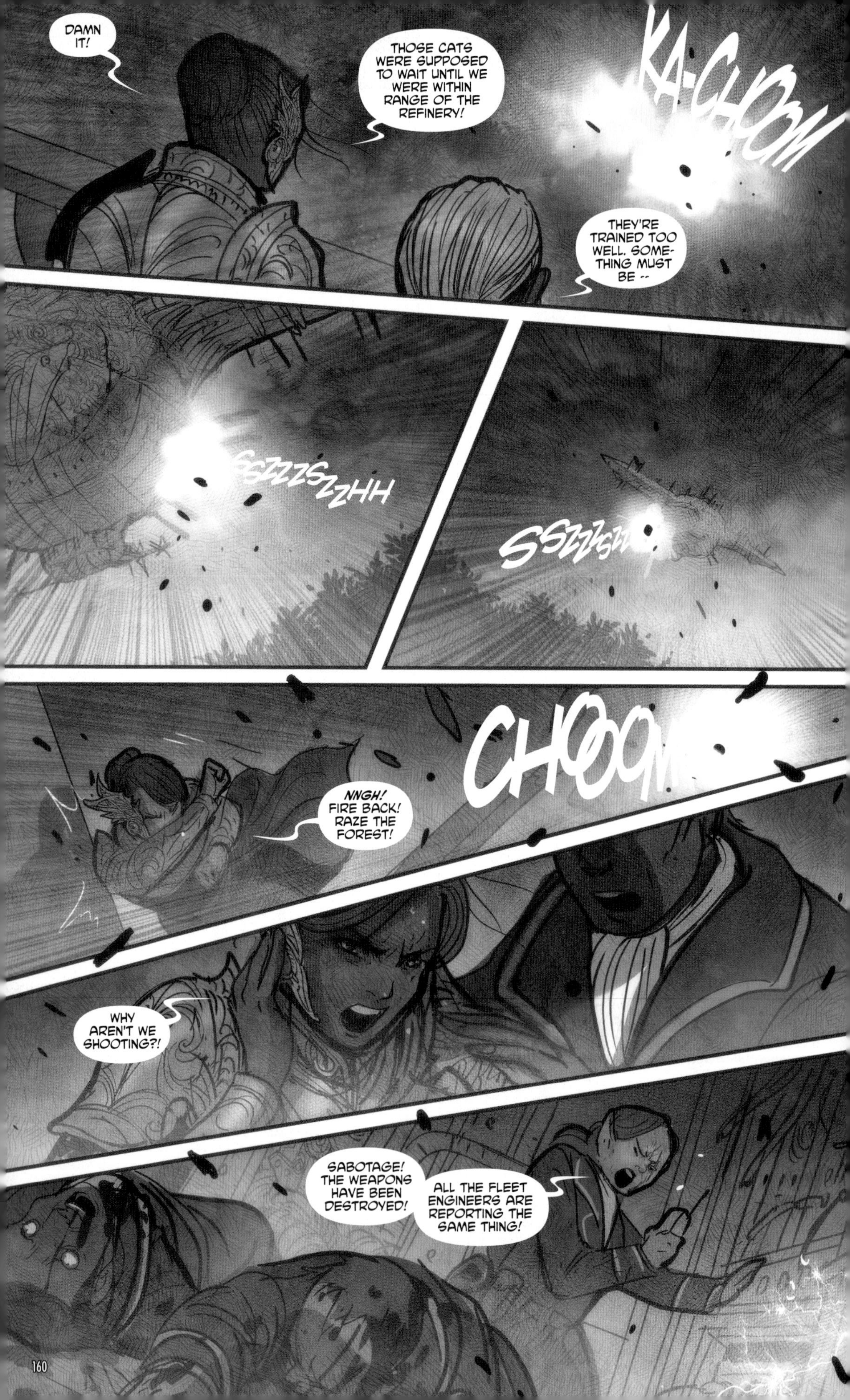
DAMN IT!
THOSE CATS WERE SUPPOSED TO WAIT UNTIL WE WERE WITHIN RANGE OF THE REFINERY!
KA-CHOOM
THEY'RE TRAINED TOO WELL. SOMETHING MUST BE --
SSZZZSZZZHH
CHOOM
NNGH! FIRE BACK! RAZE THE FOREST!
WHY AREN'T WE SHOOTING?!
SABOTAGE! THE WEAPONS HAVE BEEN DESTROYED!
ALL THE FLEET ENGINEERS ARE REPORTING THE SAME THING!

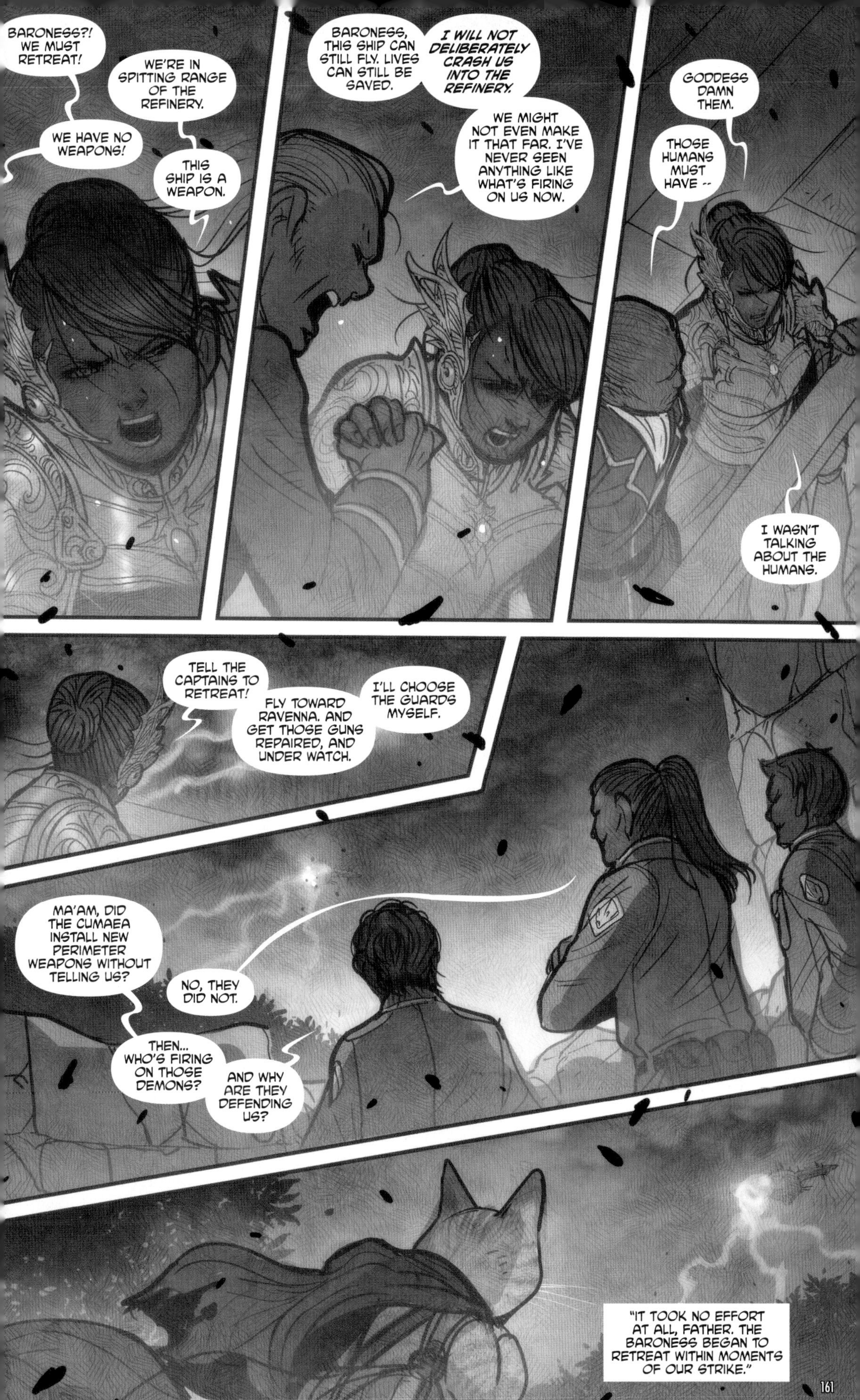
BARONESS?! WE MUST RETREAT!
WE'RE IN SPITTING RANGE OF THE REFINERY.
WE HAVE NO WEAPONS!
THIS SHIP IS A WEAPON.
BARONESS, THIS SHIP CAN STILL FLY. LIVES CAN STILL BE SAVED.
I WILL NOT DELIBERATELY CRASH US INTO THE REFINERY.
WE MIGHT NOT EVEN MAKE IT THAT FAR. I'VE NEVER SEEN ANYTHING LIKE WHAT'S FIRING ON US NOW.
GODDESS DAMN THEM.
THOSE HUMANS MUST HAVE --
I WASN'T TALKING ABOUT THE HUMANS.
TELL THE CAPTAINS TO RETREAT!
FLY TOWARD RAVENNA. AND GET THOSE GUNS REPAIRED, AND UNDER WATCH.
I'LL CHOOSE THE GUARDS MYSELF.
MA'AM, DID THE CUMAEA INSTALL NEW PERIMETER WEAPONS WITHOUT TELLING US?
NO, THEY DID NOT.
THEN... WHO'S FIRING ON THOSE DEMONS?
AND WHY ARE THEY DEFENDING US?
"IT TOOK NO EFFORT AT ALL, FATHER. THE BARONESS BEGAN TO RETREAT WITHIN MOMENTS OF OUR STRIKE."

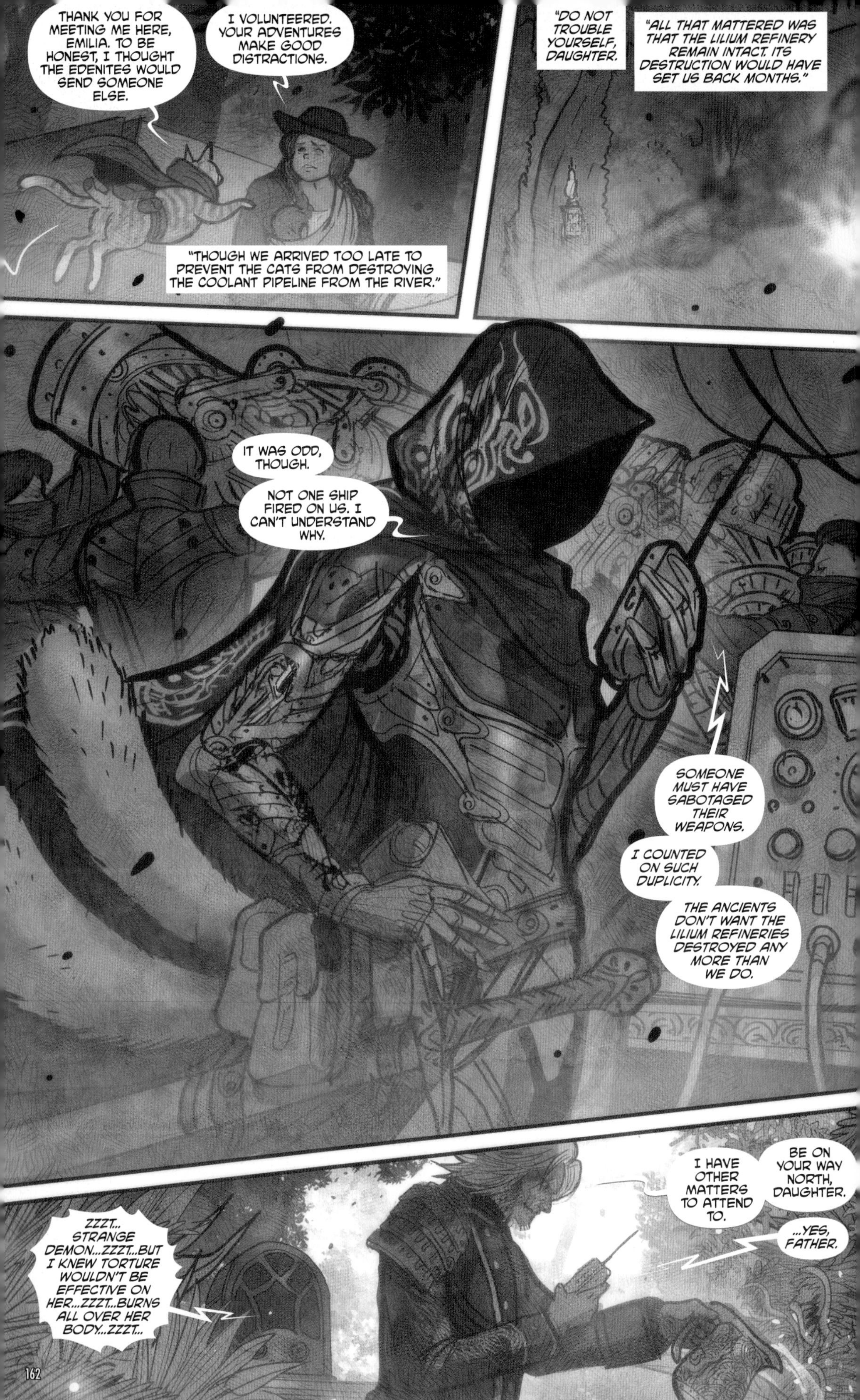
THANK YOU FOR MEETING ME HERE, EMILIA. TO BE HONEST, I THOUGHT THE EDENITES WOULD SEND SOMEONE ELSE.
I VOLUNTEERED. YOUR ADVENTURES MAKE GOOD DISTRACTIONS.
"THOUGH WE ARRIVED TOO LATE TO PREVENT THE CATS FROM DESTROYING THE COOLANT PIPELINE FROM THE RIVER."
"DO NOT TROUBLE YOURSELF, DAUGHTER.
"ALL THAT MATTERED WAS THAT THE LILIUM REFINERY REMAIN INTACT. ITS DESTRUCTION WOULD HAVE SET US BACK MONTHS."
IT WAS ODD, THOUGH.
NOT ONE SHIP FIRED ON US. I CAN'T UNDERSTAND WHY.
SOMEONE MUST HAVE SABOTAGED THEIR WEAPONS.
I COUNTED ON SUCH DUPLICITY.
THE ANCIENTS DON'T WANT THE LILIUM REFINERIES DESTROYED ANY MORE THAN WE DO.
ZZZT... STRANGE DEMON...ZZZT...BUT I KNEW TORTURE WOULDN'T BE EFFECTIVE ON HER...ZZZT...BURNS ALL OVER HER BODY...ZZZT...
I HAVE OTHER MATTERS TO ATTEND TO.
BE ON YOUR WAY NORTH, DAUGHTER.
...YES, FATHER.

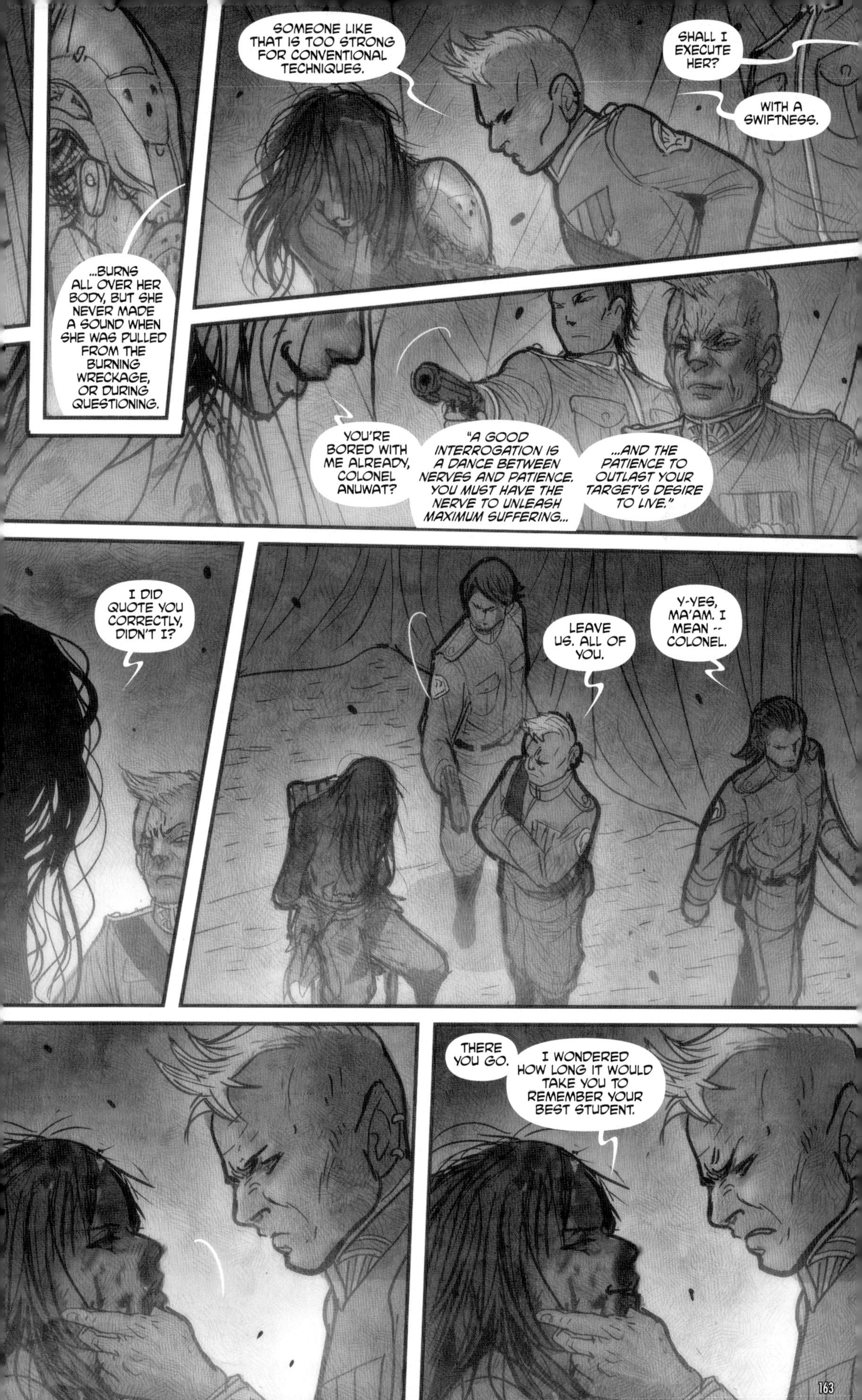

SOMEONE LIKE THAT IS TOO STRONG FOR CONVENTIONAL TECHNIQUES.
SHALL I EXECUTE HER?
WITH A SWIFTNESS.
...BURNS ALL OVER HER BODY, BUT SHE NEVER MADE A SOUND WHEN SHE WAS PULLED FROM THE BURNING WRECKAGE, OR DURING QUESTIONING.
YOU'RE BORED WITH ME ALREADY, COLONEL ANUWAT?
"A GOOD INTERROGATION IS A DANCE BETWEEN NERVES AND PATIENCE. YOU MUST HAVE THE NERVE TO UNLEASH MAXIMUM SUFFERING...
...AND THE PATIENCE TO OUTLAST YOUR TARGET'S DESIRE TO LIVE."
I DID QUOTE YOU CORRECTLY, DIDN'T I?
LEAVE US. ALL OF YOU.
Y-YES, MA'AM. I MEAN -- COLONEL.
THERE YOU GO.
I WONDERED HOW LONG IT WOULD TAKE YOU TO REMEMBER YOUR BEST STUDENT.

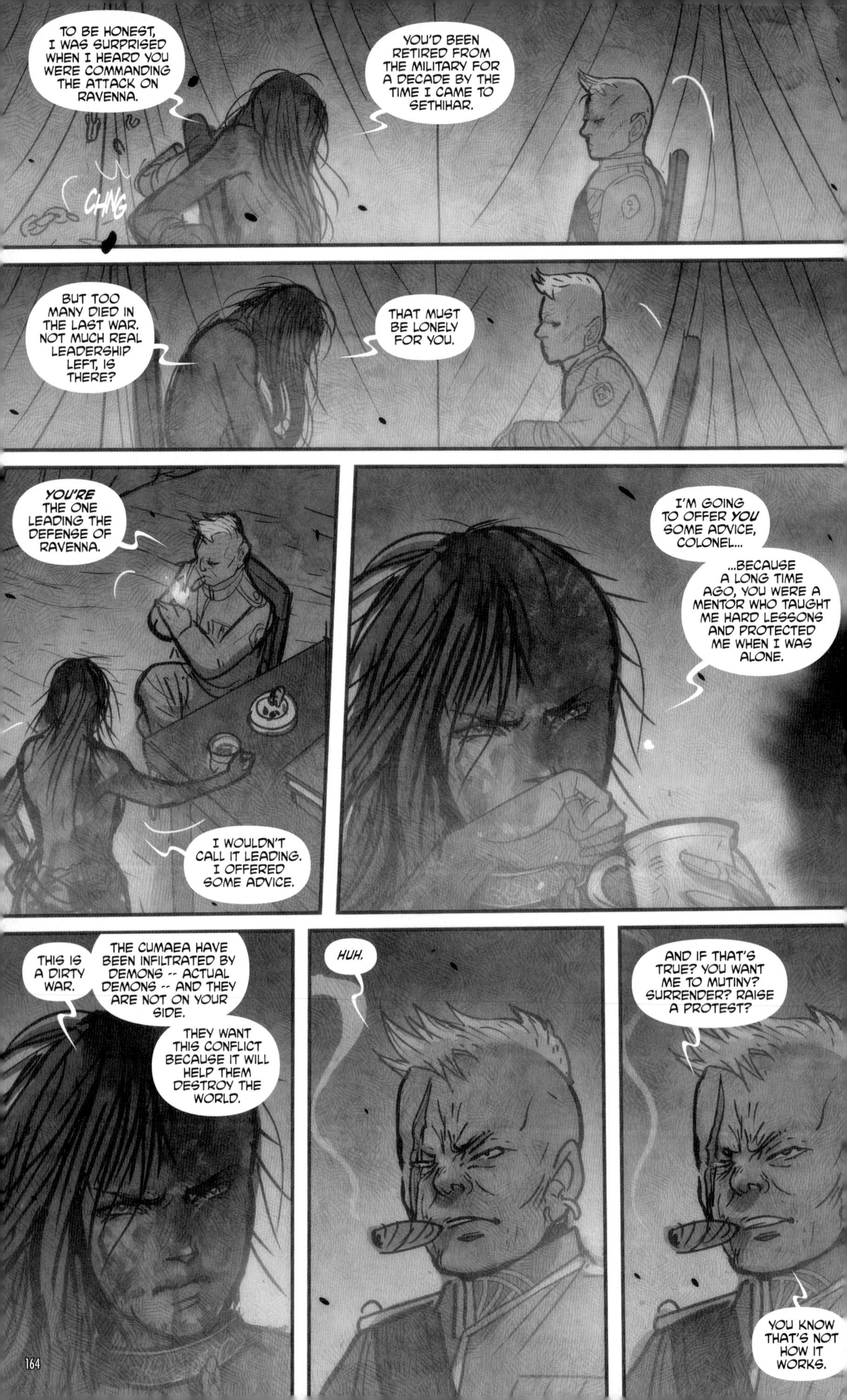

TO BE HONEST, I WAS SURPRISED WHEN I HEARD YOU WERE COMMANDING THE ATTACK ON RAVENNA.
YOU'D BEEN RETIRED FROM THE MILITARY FOR A DECADE BY THE TIME I CAME TO SETHIHAR.
CHING
BUT TOO MANY DIED IN THE LAST WAR. NOT MUCH REAL LEADERSHIP LEFT, IS THERE?
THAT MUST BE LONELY FOR YOU.
YOU'RE THE ONE LEADING THE DEFENSE OF RAVENNA.
I WOULDN'T CALL IT LEADING. I OFFERED SOME ADVICE.
I'M GOING TO OFFER YOU SOME ADVICE, COLONEL...
...BECAUSE A LONG TIME AGO, YOU WERE A MENTOR WHO TAUGHT ME HARD LESSONS AND PROTECTED ME WHEN I WAS ALONE.
THIS IS A DIRTY WAR.
THE CUMAEA HAVE BEEN INFILTRATED BY DEMONS -- ACTUAL DEMONS -- AND THEY ARE NOT ON YOUR SIDE.
THEY WANT THIS CONFLICT BECAUSE IT WILL HELP THEM DESTROY THE WORLD.
HUH.
AND IF THAT'S TRUE? YOU WANT ME TO MUTINY? SURRENDER? RAISE A PROTEST?
YOU KNOW THAT'S NOT HOW IT WORKS.

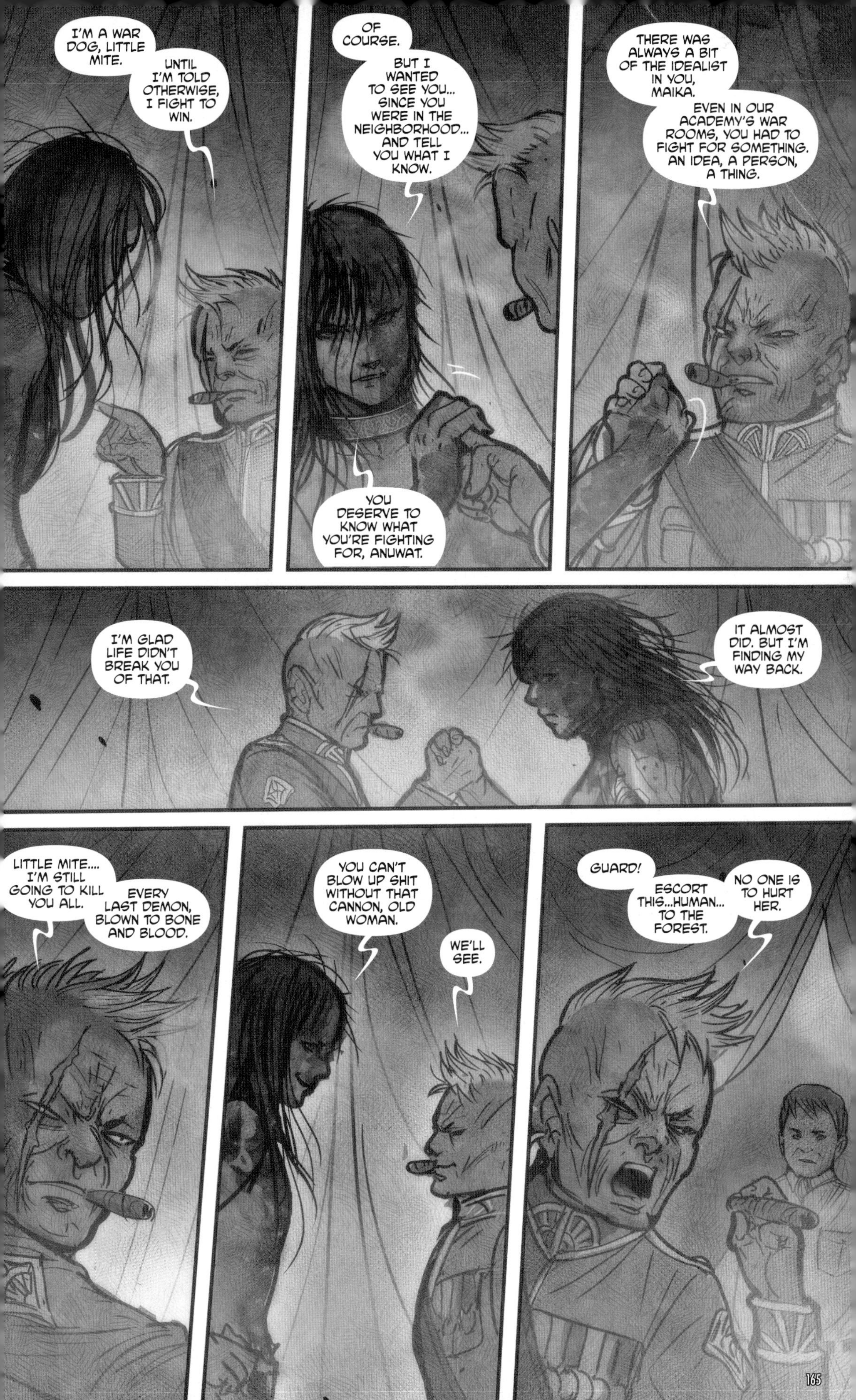
I'M A WAR DOG, LITTLE MITE.
UNTIL I'M TOLD OTHERWISE, I FIGHT TO WIN.
OF COURSE.
BUT I WANTED TO SEE YOU... SINCE YOU WERE IN THE NEIGHBORHOOD... AND TELL YOU WHAT I KNOW.
YOU DESERVE TO KNOW WHAT YOU'RE FIGHTING FOR, ANUWAT.
THERE WAS ALWAYS A BIT OF THE IDEALIST IN YOU, MAIKA.
EVEN IN OUR ACADEMY'S WAR ROOMS, YOU HAD TO FIGHT FOR SOMETHING. AN IDEA, A PERSON, A THING.
I'M GLAD LIFE DIDN'T BREAK YOU OF THAT.
IT ALMOST DID. BUT I'M FINDING MY WAY BACK.
LITTLE MITE.... I'M STILL GOING TO KILL YOU ALL.
EVERY LAST DEMON, BLOWN TO BONE AND BLOOD.
YOU CAN'T BLOW UP SHIT WITHOUT THAT CANNON, OLD WOMAN.
WE'LL SEE.
GUARD!
ESCORT THIS...HUMAN... TO THE FOREST.
NO ONE IS TO HURT HER.

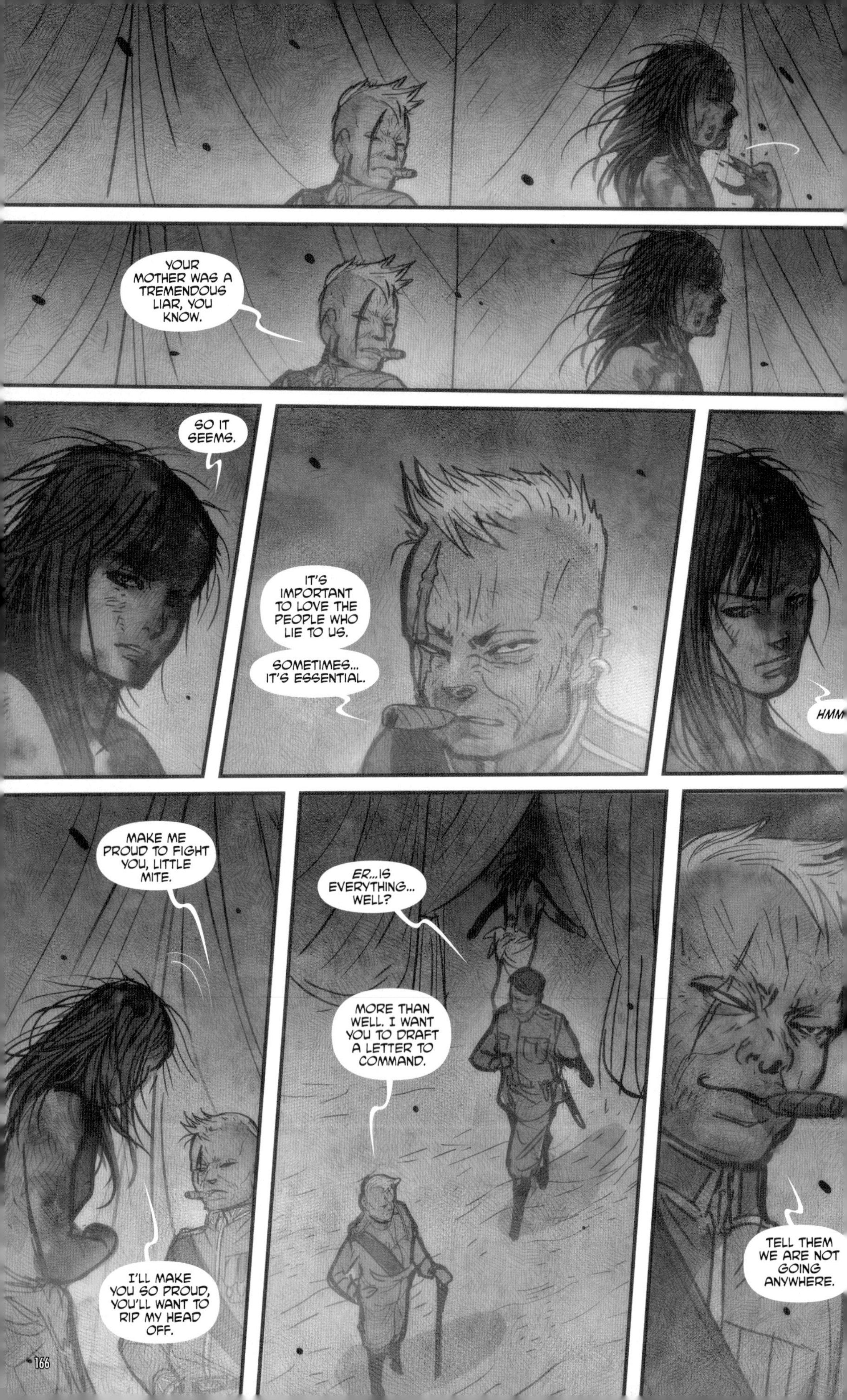
YOUR MOTHER WAS A TREMENDOUS LIAR, YOU KNOW.
SO IT SEEMS.
IT'S IMPORTANT TO LOVE THE PEOPLE WHO LIE TO US.
SOMETIMES... IT'S ESSENTIAL.
HMM
MAKE ME PROUD TO FIGHT YOU, LITTLE MITE.
I'LL MAKE YOU SO PROUD, YOU'LL WANT TO RIP MY HEAD OFF.
ER...IS EVERYTHING... WELL?
MORE THAN WELL. I WANT YOU TO DRAFT A LETTER TO COMMAND.
TELL THEM WE ARE NOT GOING ANYWHERE.

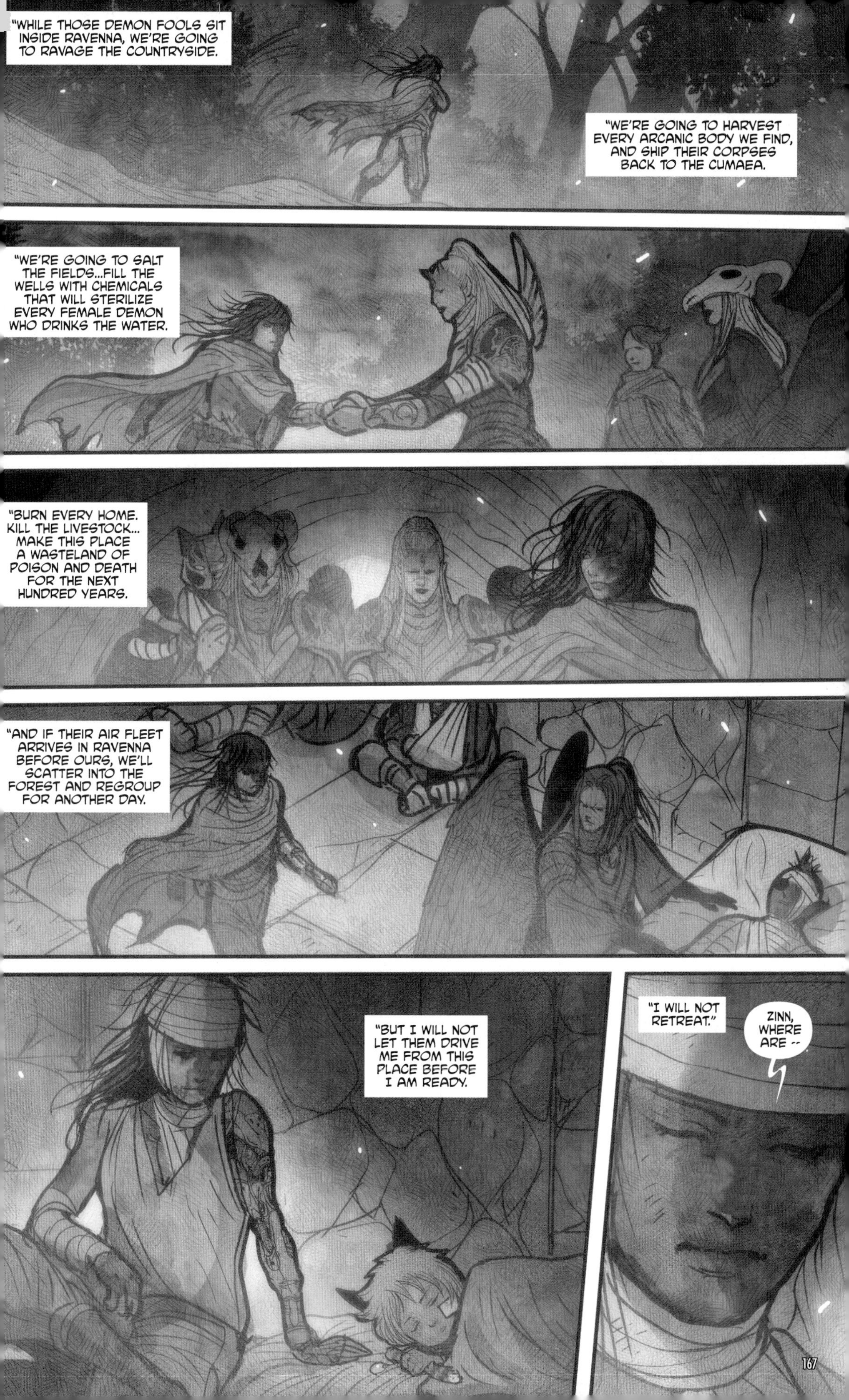
"WHILE THOSE DEMON FOOLS SIT INSIDE RAVENNA, WE'RE GOING TO RAVAGE THE COUNTRYSIDE.
"WE'RE GOING TO HARVEST EVERY ARCANIC BODY WE FIND, AND SHIP THEIR CORPSES BACK TO THE CUMAEA.
"WE'RE GOING TO SALT THE FIELDS...FILL THE WELLS WITH CHEMICALS THAT WILL STERILIZE EVERY FEMALE DEMON WHO DRINKS THE WATER.
"BURN EVERY HOME. KILL THE LIVESTOCK... MAKE THIS PLACE A WASTELAND OF POISON AND DEATH FOR THE NEXT HUNDRED YEARS.
"AND IF THEIR AIR FLEET ARRIVES IN RAVENNA BEFORE OURS, WE'LL SCATTER INTO THE FOREST AND REGROUP FOR ANOTHER DAY.
"BUT I WILL NOT LET THEM DRIVE ME FROM THIS PLACE BEFORE I AM READY.
"I WILL NOT RETREAT."
ZINN, WHERE ARE --

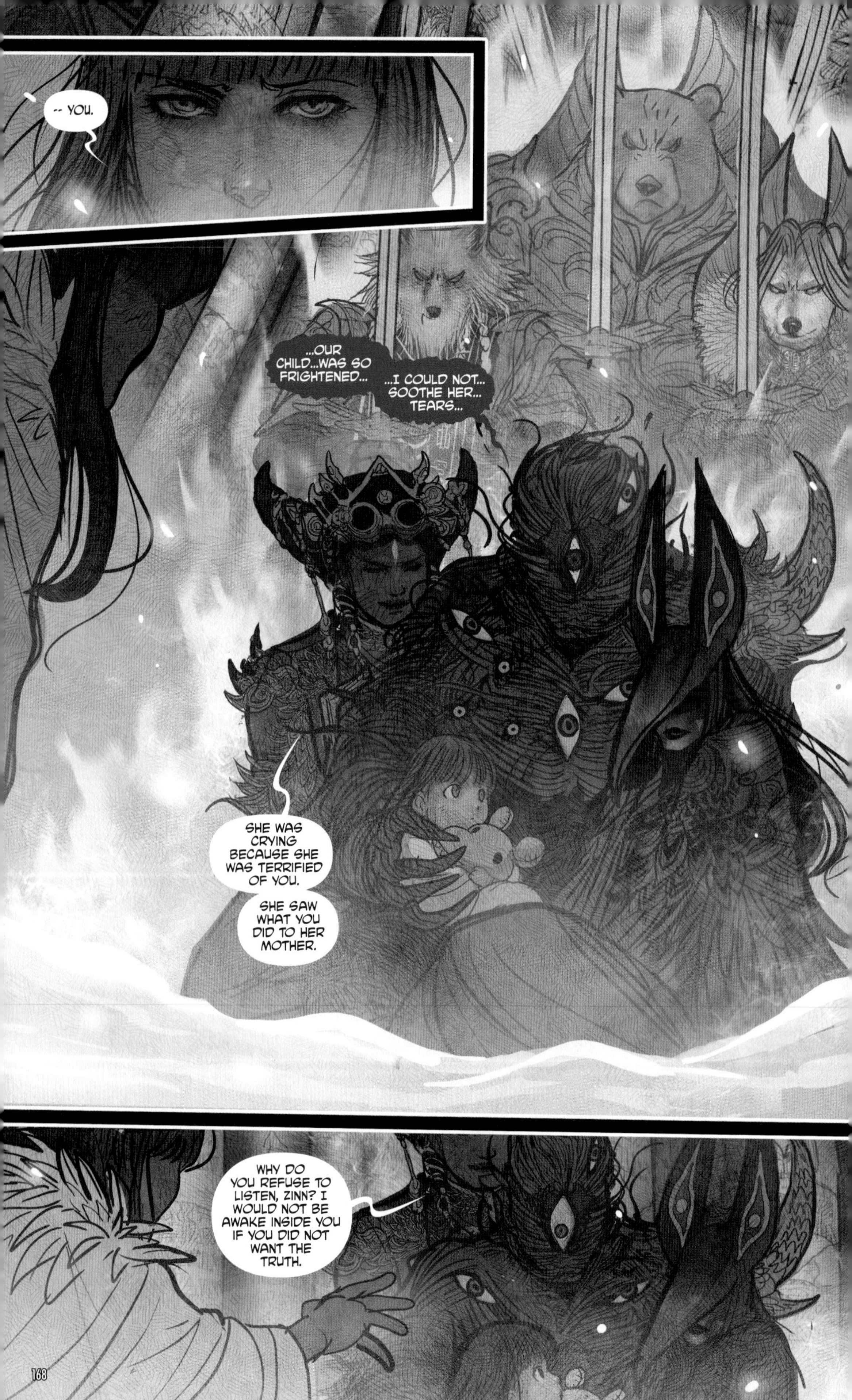
-- YOU.
...OUR CHILD...WAS SO FRIGHTENED...
...I COULD NOT... SOOTHE HER... TEARS...
SHE WAS CRYING BECAUSE SHE WAS TERRIFIED OF YOU.
SHE SAW WHAT YOU DID TO HER MOTHER.
WHY DO YOU REFUSE TO LISTEN, ZINN? I WOULD NOT BE AWAKE INSIDE YOU IF YOU DID NOT WANT THE TRUTH.

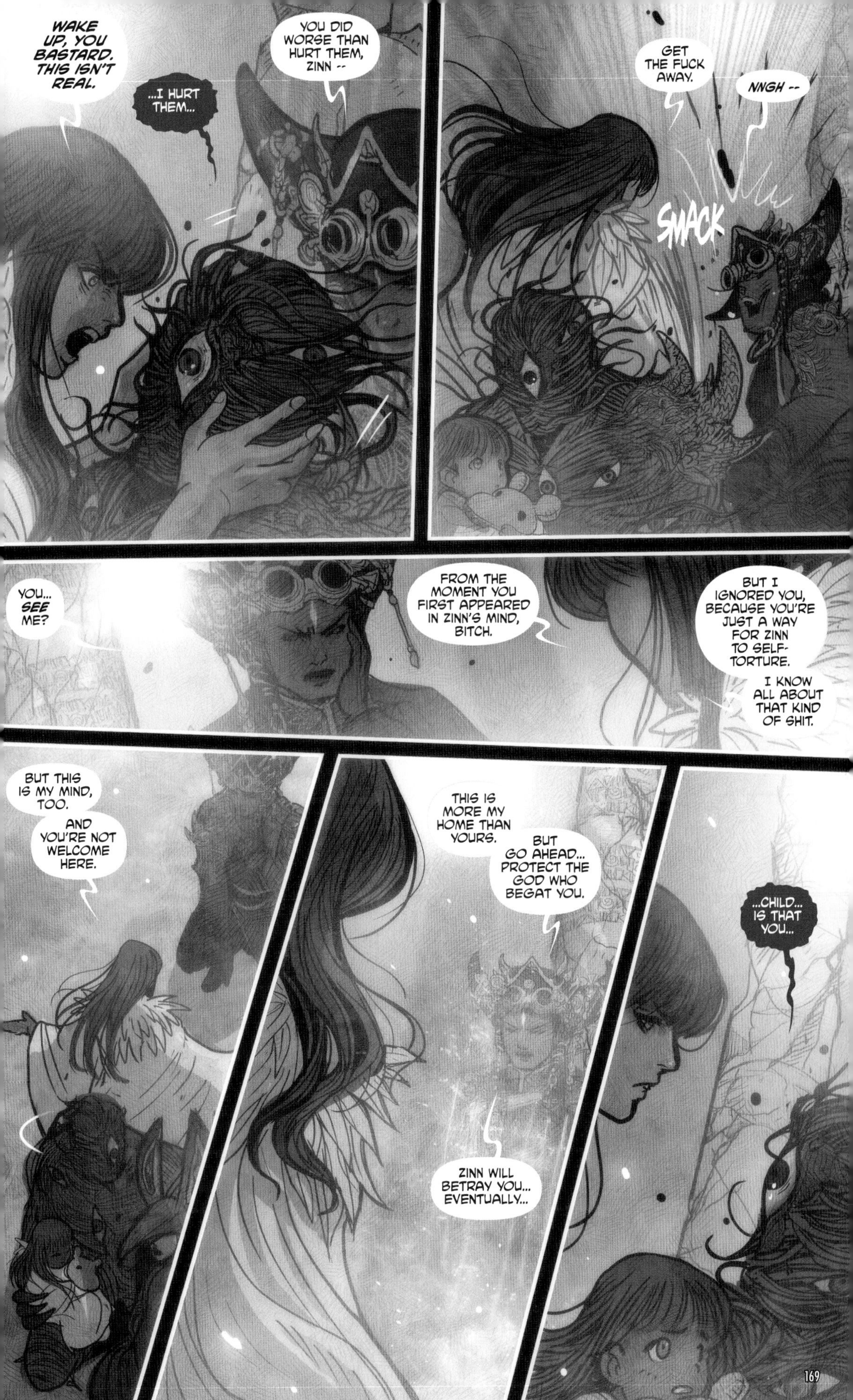

WAKE UP, YOU BASTARD. THIS ISN'T REAL.
...I HURT THEM...
YOU DID WORSE THAN HURT THEM, ZINN --
GET THE FUCK AWAY.
NNGH --
SMACK
YOU... SEE ME?
FROM THE MOMENT YOU FIRST APPEARED IN ZINN'S MIND, BITCH.
BUT I IGNORED YOU, BECAUSE YOU'RE JUST A WAY FOR ZINN TO SELF-TORTURE.
I KNOW ALL ABOUT THAT KIND OF SHIT.
BUT THIS IS MY MIND, TOO.
AND YOU'RE NOT WELCOME HERE.
THIS IS MORE MY HOME THAN YOURS.
BUT GO AHEAD... PROTECT THE GOD WHO BEGAT YOU.
ZINN WILL BETRAY YOU... EVENTUALLY...
...CHILD... IS THAT YOU...

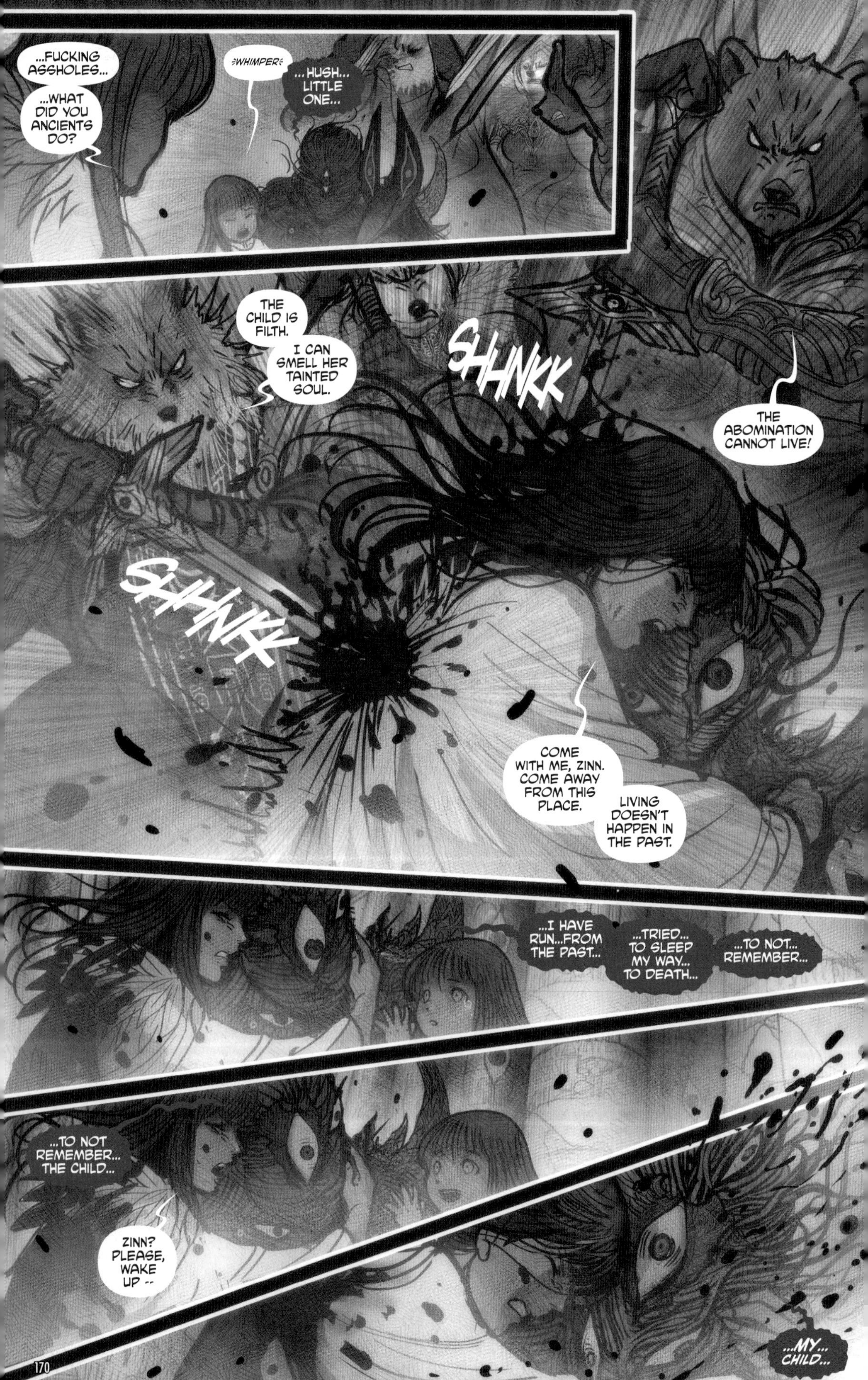
...FUCKING ASSHOLES...
...WHAT DID YOU ANCIENTS DO?
WHIMPER
...HUSH... LITTLE ONE...
THE CHILD IS FILTH.
I CAN SMELL HER TAINTED SOUL.
SHHNKK
THE ABOMINATION CANNOT LIVE!
SHHNKK
COME WITH ME, ZINN. COME AWAY FROM THIS PLACE.
LIVING DOESN'T HAPPEN IN THE PAST.
...I HAVE RUN...FROM THE PAST...
...TRIED... TO SLEEP MY WAY... TO DEATH...
...TO NOT... REMEMBER...
...TO NOT REMEMBER... THE CHILD...
ZINN? PLEASE, WAKE UP --
...MY... CHILD...

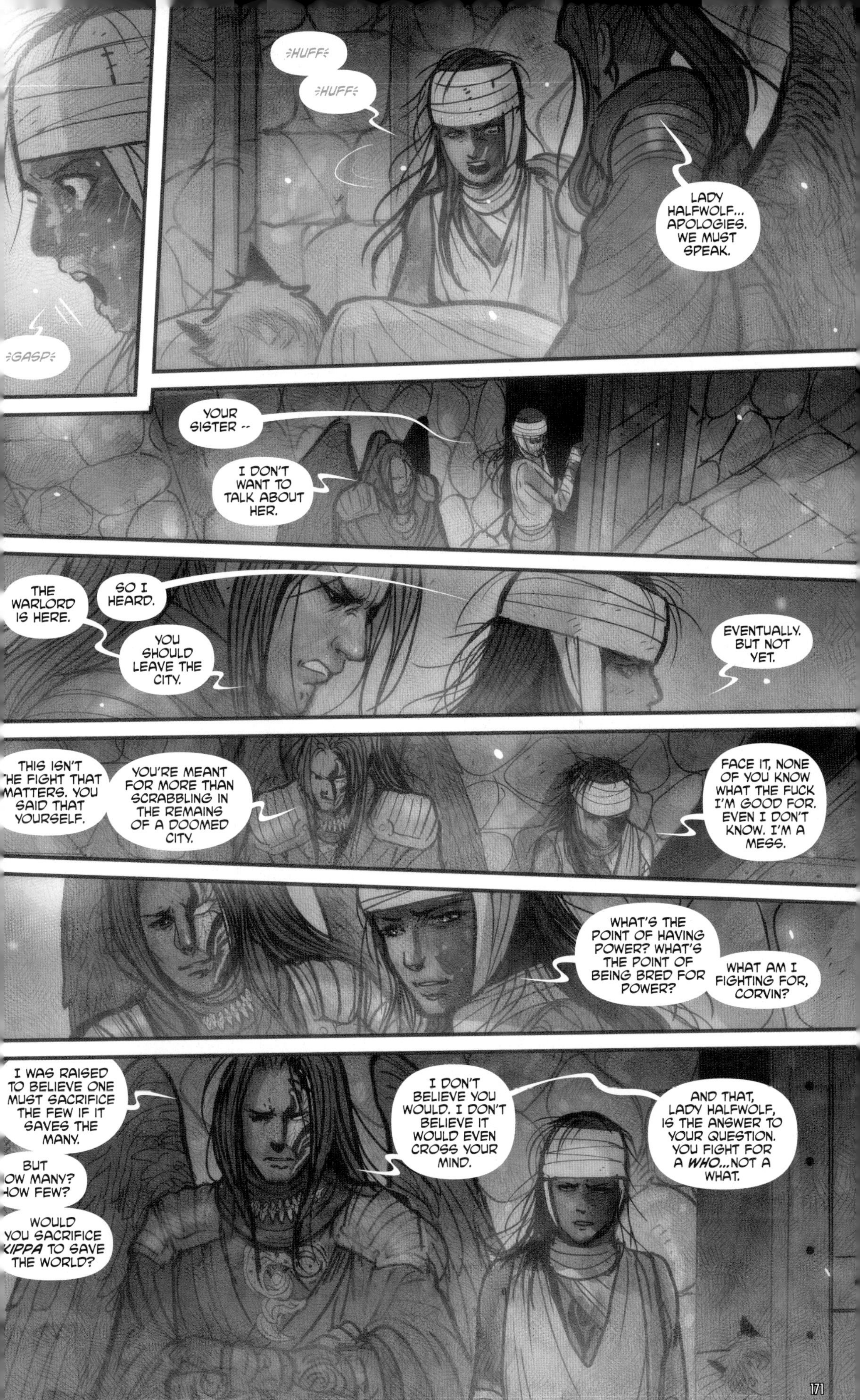

HUFF
HUFF
LADY HALFWOLF... APOLOGIES. WE MUST SPEAK.
GASP
YOUR SISTER --
I DON'T WANT TO TALK ABOUT HER.
THE WARLORD IS HERE.
SO I HEARD.
YOU SHOULD LEAVE THE CITY.
EVENTUALLY. BUT NOT YET.
THIS ISN'T THE FIGHT THAT MATTERS. YOU SAID THAT YOURSELF.
YOU'RE MEANT FOR MORE THAN SCRABBLING IN THE REMAINS OF A DOOMED CITY.
FACE IT, NONE OF YOU KNOW WHAT THE FUCK I'M GOOD FOR. EVEN I DON'T KNOW. I'M A MESS.
WHAT'S THE POINT OF HAVING POWER? WHAT'S THE POINT OF BEING BRED FOR POWER?
WHAT AM I FIGHTING FOR, CORVIN?
I WAS RAISED TO BELIEVE ONE MUST SACRIFICE THE FEW IF IT SAVES THE MANY.
BUT OW MANY? OW FEW?
WOULD YOU SACRIFICE KIPPA TO SAVE THE WORLD?
I DON'T BELIEVE YOU WOULD. I DON'T BELIEVE IT WOULD EVEN CROSS YOUR MIND.
AND THAT, LADY HALFWOLF, IS THE ANSWER TO YOUR QUESTION. YOU FIGHT FOR A *WHO*...NOT A WHAT.

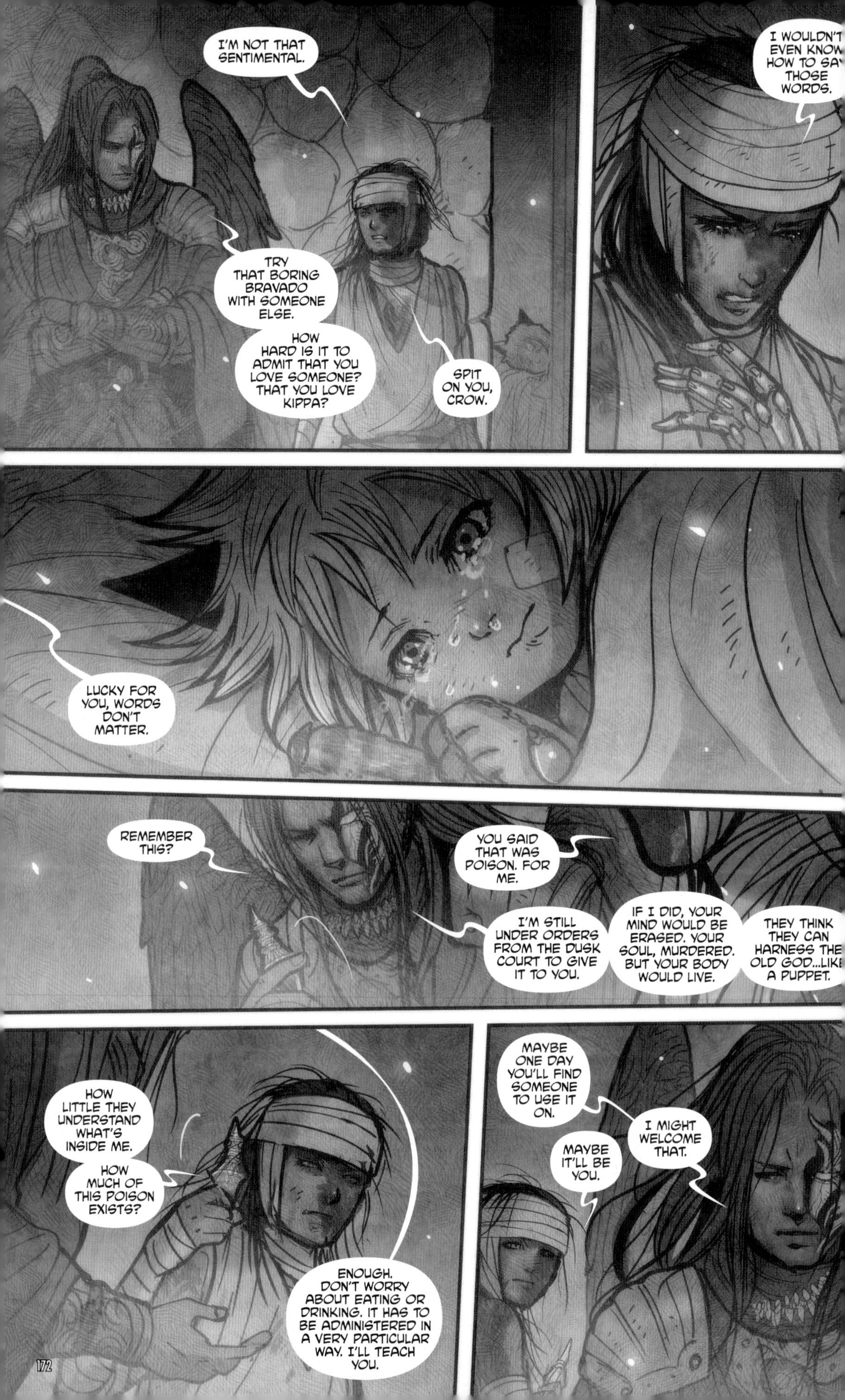

I'M NOT THAT SENTIMENTAL.
TRY THAT BORING BRAVADO WITH SOMEONE ELSE.
HOW HARD IS IT TO ADMIT THAT YOU LOVE SOMEONE? THAT YOU LOVE KIPPA?
SPIT ON YOU, CROW.
I WOULDN'T EVEN KNOW HOW TO SAY THOSE WORDS.
LUCKY FOR YOU, WORDS DON'T MATTER.
REMEMBER THIS?
YOU SAID THAT WAS POISON. FOR ME.
I'M STILL UNDER ORDERS FROM THE DUSK COURT TO GIVE IT TO YOU.
IF I DID, YOUR MIND WOULD BE ERASED. YOUR SOUL, MURDERED. BUT YOUR BODY WOULD LIVE.
THEY THINK THEY CAN HARNESS THE OLD GOD...LIKE A PUPPET.
HOW LITTLE THEY UNDERSTAND WHAT'S INSIDE ME.
HOW MUCH OF THIS POISON EXISTS?
ENOUGH. DON'T WORRY ABOUT EATING OR DRINKING. IT HAS TO BE ADMINISTERED IN A VERY PARTICULAR WAY. I'LL TEACH YOU.
MAYBE ONE DAY YOU'LL FIND SOMEONE TO USE IT ON.
I MIGHT WELCOME THAT.
MAYBE IT'LL BE YOU.

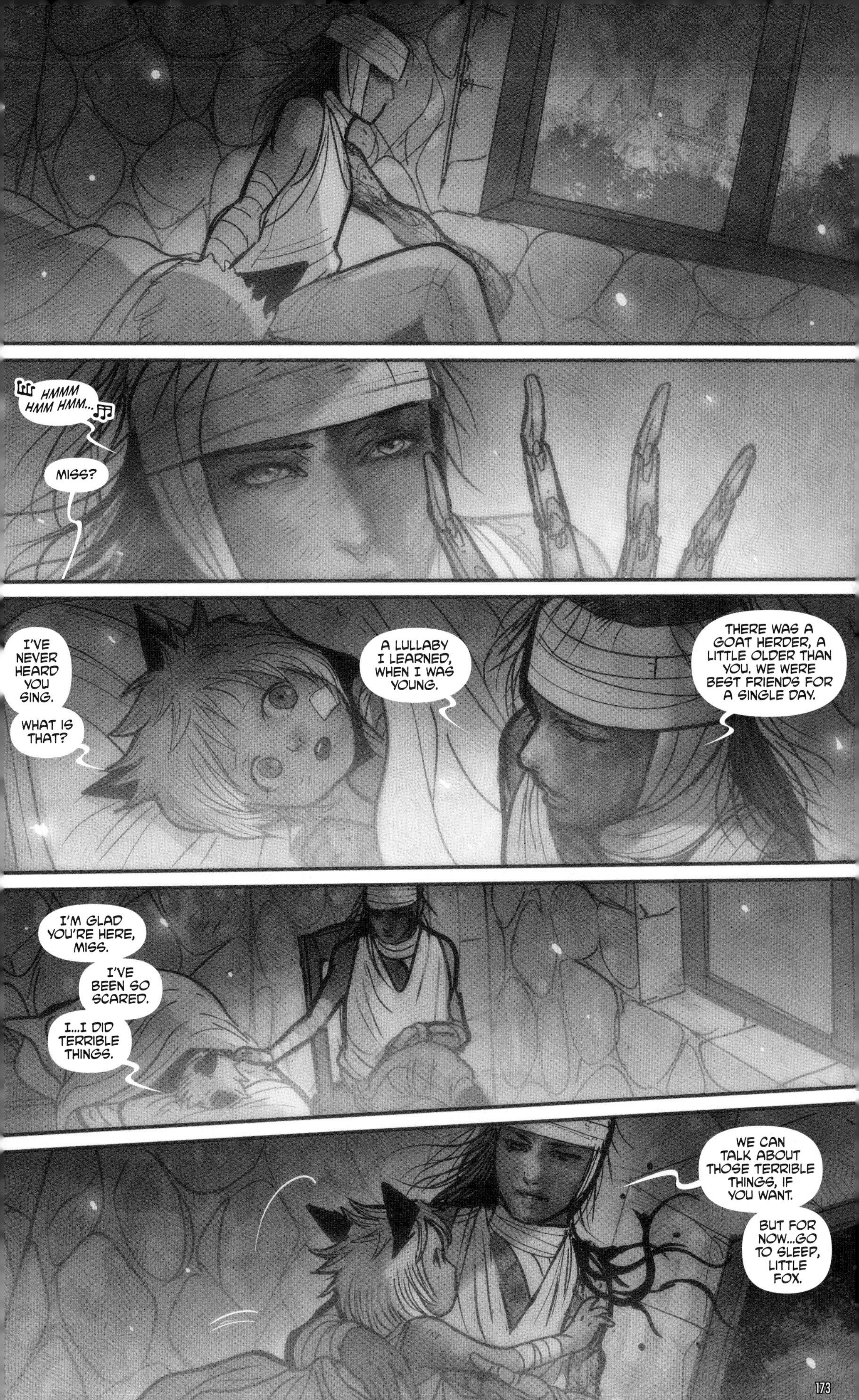
HMMM HMM HMM...
MISS?
I'VE NEVER HEARD YOU SING.
WHAT IS THAT?
A LULLABY I LEARNED, WHEN I WAS YOUNG.
THERE WAS A GOAT HERDER, A LITTLE OLDER THAN YOU. WE WERE BEST FRIENDS FOR A SINGLE DAY.
I'M GLAD YOU'RE HERE, MISS.
I'VE BEEN SO SCARED.
I...I DID TERRIBLE THINGS.
WE CAN TALK ABOUT THOSE TERRIBLE THINGS, IF YOU WANT.
BUT FOR NOW...GO TO SLEEP, LITTLE FOX.

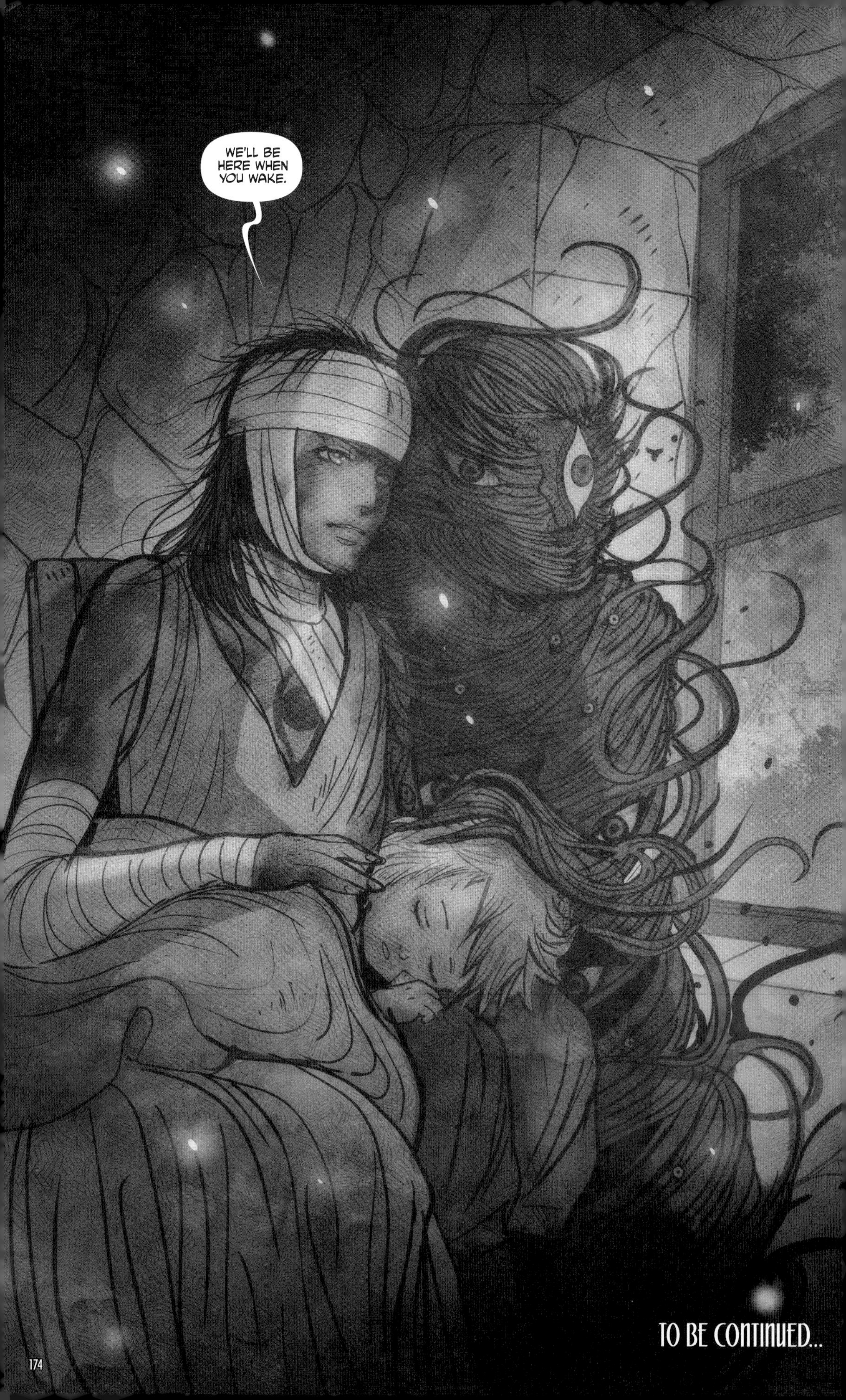
WE'LL BE HERE WHEN YOU WAKE.
TO BE CONTINUED...

SANA's SKETCHES

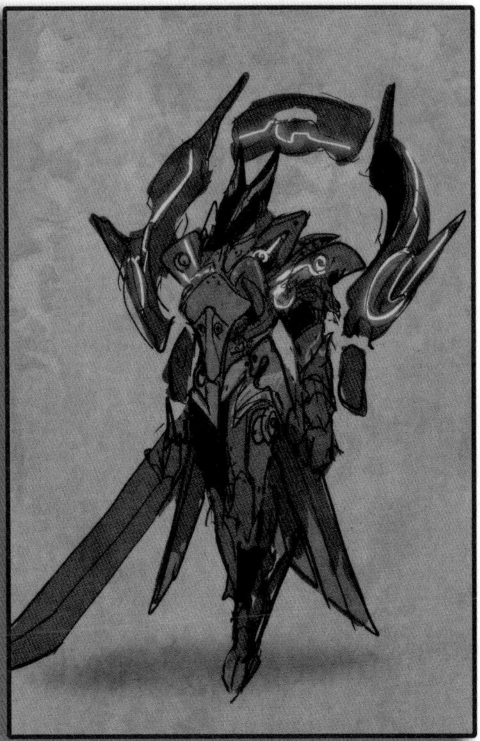

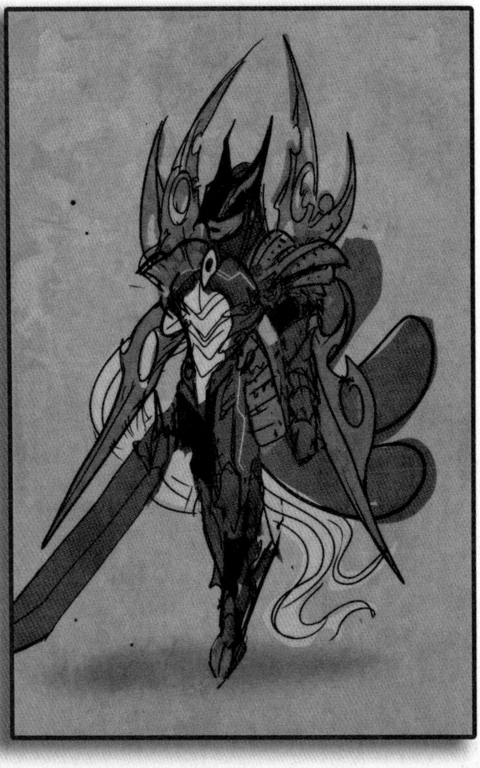

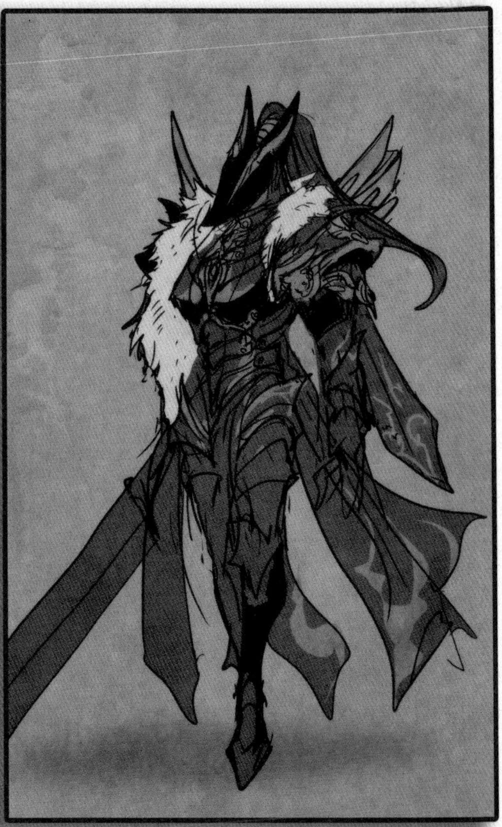

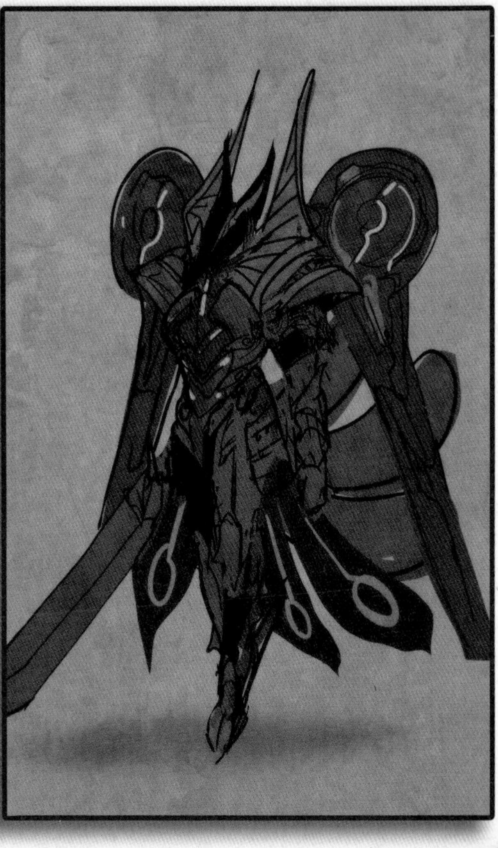

CREATORS

MARJORIE LIU is the author of over seventeen novels and is the co-creator of the Hugo, Eisner, and British Fantasy Award-winning and *New York Times* bestselling series MONSTRESS, published by Image Comics. Liu's comic book work includes *X-23*, *Black Widow*, *Dark Wolverine*, *Han Solo*, and *Astonishing X-Men*, for which she was nominated for a GLAAD Media award for outstanding media images of the lesbian, gay, bisexual and transgender community.

SANA TAKEDA is an Eisner and Hugo Award-winning illustrator and comic book artist who was born in Niigata, and now resides in Tokyo, Japan. At age 20 she started out as a 3D CGI designer for SEGA, a Japanese video game company, and became a freelance artist when she was 25. She is still an artist, and has worked on titles such as *X-23* and *Ms. Marvel* for Marvel Comics, and is an illustrator for trading card games in Japan.